M000232148

All Worlds Wayfarer

A Quarterly Speculative Fiction Literary Magazine

www.allworldswayfarer.com

Current issue available free to read.
Previous issues available through Amazon Kindle

www.allworldswayfarer.com/pastissues

All Worlds Wayfarer Anthologies:

Through Other Eyes (December 2020)
Prismatic Dreams (Release TBA)
Each Our Own (Release TBA)
Into the Dark (Release TBA)

ALL WORLDS WAYFARER:

THROUGH OTHER EYES

Edited by:
Rowan Rook
Geri Meyers

Including 30 short stories to bring you beyond the realm of human experience.

All Worlds Wayfarer
2020

All Worlds Wayfarer
Greenbank, WA ; Woodbridge, NJ
www.allworldswayfarer.com

Copyright © 2020 by All Worlds Wayfarer.
All stories copyright © 2020 their authors.
Cover Art © ikaruna
Book Design by Rowan Rook and Geri Meyers
Fonts used include EB Garamond, Merriweather, Georgia, Flamingo Shadow,
Charlemagne Std, and Annabel

Edited by Rowan Rook and Geri Meyers

All rights reserved. No part of this publication may be reproduced, distributed, or
transmitted in any form or by any means, including photocopying, recording, or
other electronic or mechanical methods, without the prior written permission of
the publisher, except in the case of brief quotations embodied in critical reviews
and certain other noncommercial uses permitted by copyright law. For
permission requests, write to the publisher, addressed "Attention: Editors," at the
email: allworldswayfarer@gmail.com

These stories are works of fiction. Names, characters, places, and incidents are
products of the authors' imaginations or are used fictitiously. Any resemblance to
actual events or locales or persons, living or dead, is coincidental.

Published by All Worlds Wayfarer, Printed and Distributed by IngramSpark.

Library of Congress Control Number: 2020950518

ISBNs:

978-1-7361505-0-4	(hardcover)
978-1-7361505-1-1	(trade paperback)
978-1-7361505-2-8	(ebook)

FIRST EDITION

Table of Contents

Content Warnings

The Night She Joined the Stars: grief
What Time Is It, Mister Fox?: death, arson, occult elements
Of Mud, Of Water: sexism
Sookie at the Beginning: mild gore, death, pandemic
Safe Haven: n/a
The Vampire Jesus: mild gore, death, occult elements
Ad Infinitum: violence, gore, captivity, death, occult elements
Sacrifice: violence, intentional death
The Cannibals of Ice-Sky-Warm-Ocean: violence, cannibalism, death
The Harpy's Son: references to: violence
Come to Me: stalking, grief
Waiting: death
Ghost Writer in the Machine: death
Wolf's Bane: violence, gore, hunting
Single Planet in a System of Eight: n/a
Cephalopod Dreams: violence, gore, occult elements
The Fire Demon's Daughter: death, birth, references to: violence
Outpost of the Empire: references to: war
Watchful: references to: violence, war
The Seer: intentional death, apocalyptic scenario
The Garden: violence, war, captivity, domestic abuse, non-consensual amputation, internalized ableism, minor self-harm
Wyrm Tale: domestic abuse
On the Table: violence, gore, captivity, medical experimentation
The Puppet Beast: violence, death, hunting, occult elements
Newton's Cradle: n/a
The Deep Sun: violence, captivity, sex, suicidal ideation
To Touch Creation: captivity, sex, sex-based magic
The Longing: death, stalking
The Prince of Murk and Rot: violence, intense gore, death, occult elements
Gentle Deserter: mild gore, war, suicidal ideation

The Night She Joined the Stars
by Catherine J. Cole

I do not know whether to love her, hate her, or scorn her. I blame her for my condition. I know it all started because of her.

The last trainee I walked with through the stone gardens of Filsur, a marvel of stone pillars and natural rock formations that contrasted with the otherwise featureless landscapes of my home planet Kamot, was a creature of air and wind named Ilieu.

She was one with her element. Light was bound to her ephemeral body, and her nearly weightless skeleton was visible through her skin. Loose, flowing membranes of translucent tissue extended in waves from her back and arms, carried by a non-existent draft that lifted her from the ground so that her delicate feet never touched the surface. Her see-through skull held energy of such brilliance, it was hard to look at without squinting. A single dot of powerful light, pulsing inside her chest in pink and purple hues, in tune with her orange heart, matched her brain in luminosity. Yes, you could see her soul.

Ilieu did not share my shyness. As we walked through the training grounds, she questioned the composition of everything around her. She wanted to know what elements gave the rocks a spicy saline scent that found its way to your tongue and their bluish-gray to rusty-orange hue (silicic calcium sulfite), if we had liquid water underground since no liquid was visible in the surface (yes, but not pure hydrogen dioxide), why there were no clouds above (not enough barometric pressure), and what constituted the atmosphere she could breathe (mostly heliogen).

She wanted to know about me. Me? So unimportant. A tall, hairless, wingless, gray biped, with a bulging occipital lobe and cerebellum, and big eyes. My insectile eyes are interesting. They can see five dimensions at once and separate light in its whole spectrum. Unlike our much shorter, completely gray cousins in a lower level of evolution, my kind is known for its white discoloration on hands and feet, covering the nostrils, mouth, and chin.

I explained that, as one of the Last Guides, I provided training to creatures in their penultimate stage of evolution, when it was time for them to leave their last corporeal form and join the stars. The transition must be handled with care. So used to having a body, they would feel lost and alone without guidance. Some may even refuse further existence if left to their fate in solitude. The Last Guides accompany them before their final journey, so that the loss of their form will not be the loss of their soul.

Ilieu asked question after question, refusing to give me enough time for a decent explanation. And I, who was supposed to be her guide, wasted precious time ignoring the issue of my trainee's fears in facing the coming journey to a new level of existence. To be perfectly frank, I could sense no anticipation, anxiety, or dread mixed with her excitement of discovery.

With every half turn of the planet, the change in her became more evident. I knew I had to persist in my training, for her time was near. Instead of dimming, as most creatures do toward the end of their cycle, her colors became brighter, as if a reaction of combustion were exciting flammable chemicals inside her. Before the orb of our tiny moon reached the summit on the third night of training, she interrupted my lecture on the sublimation of carbon-based components. She grabbed my shoulders and turned me toward her with some urgency. For the first time, I saw fear in her lavender eyes.

"Phieri, promise you will come find me," she said. "When your body can no longer hold your soul here, when you wish to dance in stardust, track my shine among the stars, and come live by my side. I will have your company until the universe inside of me becomes too big to contain and bursts out in a shower of nova. If you are near, part of me may reach you, and I will be part of you forever."

How I wished I were something different then. "I cannot." For the first time, I felt ashamed to be me. "I do not die, Ilieu. My species regenerates. All of our basic components remain intact at an elemental level. Our bodies simply get degraded with use. When we require better functionality, we stew in a cocoon for a while and then come out fresh."

Ilieu was saddened by my words. She said, "Then, how do you evolve? How do you become stars?"

"Our natural process is to incorporate, during regeneration, any enhancements that may be useful to better carry out our function as guides," I said, "but we do not become stars. Our form is sufficient, even adequate, for our job. We have been guides for eons, and will continue to be for as long as we are needed."

Ilieu contested, "That is ridiculous, Phieri. Every living organism evolves. How can everyone else evolve into stars while you stay the same? It may take you longer, but you will be a star someday. Even if I am an old star and you a newborn, I want you by my side." She turned, and floated two steps away from me. "Unless, you don't like me enough to share the arm of a galaxy with me."

The brilliance of her brain was spreading throughout her body. Her veins could have been streaming lava. Why was I upsetting my trainee when she had so little time left? "Ilieu, I would abandon this body in an instant if that were enough for me to go with you on your journey. But I cannot follow you. I am what I am."

"Nonsense!" she declared. "If you want to be with me, you will find a way." She flew back to me and embraced me with the strength of her last effort. She looked into my eyes as she exhaled her last breath. "I will wait for you." I saw determination in those eyes, which saw beyond what there was to see.

The membranes of translucent skin were no longer needed to keep her afloat as her body's density diminished. She wrapped those membranes around me, while her colors morphed. The orange of her heart pumped yellow into the thin blanket of bio-tissue around my arms. It mixed with the light turquoise of her dying skin, creating a radioactive lime green. The carmine shadows emitted by her dying neurons turned her long neck and fin-like ears magenta. Her lavender eyes made midnight-blue shades on her skull. Her delicate limbs thinned to translucent aqua-marine. The prism gathered at the point of light in her core, turning it a blinding white.

Our prismatic touch made a rainbow on my boring, gray skin, and I never experienced a kiss of luminosity more tender.

She never touched the ground, not even in death. Her fragile, see-through form disintegrated into particles light as helium, and the color of her floated away into cosmic dust. As more elements bonded with her particles, they became heavier, volatile, incandescent, and radioactive. A tiny, hot core gathered mass, increased in volume, and radiated gas and light, as bright as her soul. I watched the skies, tracing the light signature, until it settled near a yellow giant that would protect the newborn star until it became accustomed to the new neighborhood in the arm Brackis of our galaxy, Calber-Inu.

I was expected back at the training grounds the following day, to be assigned my next trainee, but I found it hard to get out of my resting-pod that morning. I had not slept. I kept seeing color that was not there. Every time I looked at my arm, a strange sensation tugged at my brain and projected into my heart. Had my arms always been this gray? My mind kept insisting I had lost something, that I was missing something important. Yet my memory log was ready to upload upon request from my supervisors. I had done my job in guiding my last trainee. Nothing more was expected of me, except to take on the next one.

What was keeping me from doing my work? I felt heavy. My mind could not focus on anything for long.

There was color on my breakfast. The sweet, turnip-smelling foot-long roots of the Obleit mushrooms on my plate, usually dark purple with iron-water and other nutrients, seemed to radiate cobalt blue at their base. The calcite milk from the stalactite Gardens of Giale in my cup had a pinkish tint. Pink! So much for a balanced breakfast.

I pushed the food aside and felt my forehead. Was I coming down with a fever? I had to do something. What if it was contagious?

On my way to see Usur-Tanger, the strongest empath among us, who took on the mostly unnecessary post of doctor from time to time, my eyes saw the ghosts of turquoise specs sprinkled like stars on every pebble lining the path to the outer district.

Usur-Tanger came to my aid before I arrived at his cone-shaped clay dwelling.

The doctor stood on the path a few steps away from me and would not come any closer. "I felt your disturbance as soon as you stepped over the barrier to my property. I have never felt a mind so troubled. Your ailment is beyond my powers. Only one person can help you understand whatever is affecting you, and give you peace. You must make the four-day trek to the crater caves of the Idrus, the Outcasts, beyond the dust desert of Vai-Flit. Find Palameh, the Old Female. She will know what to do."

My voice climbed an octave in pitch. "Palameh? The leader of the Outcasts? Those who go in search of her never return."

The doctor's voice was calm, bordering on compassion. "Do not let rumor dissuade you from pursuing your only hope of recovery. Hearsay only scratches the surface. I have the utmost respect for Palameh. She is a better healer than I could ever be. Those who stay with her do so of their own free will. Her influence is only enlightenment. No curse keeps her followers imprisoned. Disregard suggestions of magic." Usur-Tanger smiled.

"Although, if there is magic in knowledge, then she is the most powerful sorceress you will find."

It was an arduous journey through the Vai-Flit desert. The little food I had packed did not seem sufficient. Dust and grit permeated through the soft ikena web I had wrapped around my nose and mouth.

The web had not been easy to obtain. I had gone, unauthorized, to the Biodiversity Hall to barter with the ikena spiders: calcite stalactites from the agriculture caves for web material to withstand the dust winds of Vai-Flit. It is hard to barter with creatures who always want more. It took three trips to the caves to gather enough stalactites to satisfy the ikena leader. Her young would grow strong, nurtured by the microscopic life the stalactites attracted.

The storms were not at their strongest this season. The winds threw me backward only twice. I made good progress through the flatlands. With no predators on the surface, I did not fear trekking at night, by the light of the small moon. At least the color I saw—puddles of green light spread across the barren land—was not my mind playing tricks on me. It came from the spores of the aitiki ferns that grow just below the surface. They produce helium- and phosphorus-based pouches that lift groups of spores and burst inches above the dust-ridden surface. When the planet draws closest to our sun, the gravity pulls on the water from the caves, and the desert floods for a short time. The sponge-like spores bloat with water and become heavy enough to sink below and give birth to the next generation of aitiki ferns. Green stars on the ground. Why did everything remind me of stars?

At least I could be near these stars. I walked through the ascending spores and knelt in the middle of the glowing green field to catch a few in my hand. A strange rumbling shook the ground under my knee. Something burst through the dust. A gray-green, thick vine whipped around my leg, pinning me to the ground. Another vine burst through, grabbing my knee. It was no use trying to tear them with my bare hands. Tiny thorns made them impossible to grasp. Two more vines strapped my arms as I tried to disentangle the ones covering my legs. They tied me face-down on the ground. I screamed, knowing nobody would hear me. A vine grabbed my neck. The screaming stopped. I could not breathe. The light I saw had to be the cells in my eyes, dying.

But no. This light was not the white of death described by my trainees, but a strong, yellow glow. It came closer. The buzzing I thought was in my ears came from outside—from the light. The light stopped moving and touched my cheek. It was cold. Solid.

My eyes adjusted enough to see dozens of flying beetles with glowing abdomens encased in transparent rock crystal. A hand held the lantern over the vine strangling me. The vine shook violently and retreated back into the ground in a flash. I gasped for breath. The light moved away, to my captive arms. The vines let go. The silhouette of the stranger cut the green phosphorescence of the spores, but it was too dark to distinguish any features. The light descended to break my legs free. It itched and hurt where the vines had grabbed me. The gray of my skin started showing faint, purple stripes.

"Thank you," I said to the stranger, before I saw the familiar face.

"Bargel vines are allergic to light," my hero said. "They have a symbiotic relationship with aitiki ferns. They protect the spores from any disturbance until they are back underground. You would know this if you were an Idrus, so you must be the guide Palameh sent me to find."

The most powerful sorceress you will find, Usur-Tanger had said. Of course she knew I was coming.

The Outcast shone the beetle lantern upon a face so similar to mine, we might have been twins. The familiar stranger helped me up, took me away from the field of spores, and put a hand on my chest, over my heart, stating the name "Yuali." Being now heart-brethren, I felt compelled to ask him all about the Idrus, but as an Outcast, Yuali was reserved to the point of near muteness. "Palameh will tell you what you need to know," was all Yuali said. We slept cuddled up against the desert winds, under a tightly-woven vegetable fiber blanket. I was grateful for the company, silent as it may be, and the warmth.

We reached the caves of the Idrus early the next day. The craters beyond the desert were larger and deeper than those around the training grounds. Most were hollow, giving the impression of deep wells. These led the way to the Idrus dwellings.

The caves were lit by sweet-cones harboring hundreds of bioluminescent beetles. The air smelled of sulphuric salts. The Idrus lived in a cave-and-tunnel network inspired by termites, extending for miles underground. The yellow glow produced by the beetles gave the tunnel a grim atmosphere, but the Old Female, who greeted me with a kind, toothless smile, returned my confidence.

She led me into a meeting room, with large, flat rocks set in a circle. We both thanked Yuali, and he left. I wondered if I would ever see my cave twin again. Palameh sat on the tallest rock and gestured for me to sit next to her.

To my amazement, she was indeed female. Unlike the rest of us, she had a clear gender. Her many necklaces, made of all different crystals, fell to accentuate the swell of her breasts. Her hips were as wide as her shoulders. The curves of her face were soft. The rest of us had lost any distinct trace of gender millennia ago, but somehow, Palameh had kept her femininity and wore it proudly.

She saw me looking, and pushed her shoulders back to make her breasts more prominent. With a coy smile, she said, "So, you are the weird guide who is in love."

"Pardon?"

"Your head may not remember, but your heart does."

I was baffled. I was being given a test I had not prepared for.

She giggled. "Your silence tells me you do not comprehend this talk of love, so I will explain. Whoever left such a mark in you, awoke something that lay dormant for a very long time. In our stage of evolution, we are able to regenerate and adapt to our environment as needed. Therefore, procreation is no longer necessary." Palameh coughed. Used to so little talk among the quiet Idrus, it was a big effort on her part to speak so long. "Gender is needed to procreate, but more than that, is needed for attraction. In lower levels of evolution, the mind brews desire and lust in the form of mating instinct. In more evolved creatures, it brews love. The urge to stay with the being you desire. To give your mate the best you can provide. To protect your loved one and ensure their happiness, even before yours, at any risk."

She smiled when she saw my apprehension. "Your soul is troubled, and your mind is confused. You mourn, you long, and you love. I also sense a feeling of betrayal. Why do you feel betrayed, Phieri?"

Something mixed in with my uneasiness then. A kind of poison I had not felt in decades. Anger. I felt exposed with the Old Female looking so deep, pinpointing feelings so accurately, when I had so much trouble understanding my own mind.

"Why can't I be a star?" I asked without thinking. "Is what Ilieu said true? Is there always a way? Do I not know enough, or have I've been lied to?"

"Ah!" Palameh drew closer, in a conspiratorial whisper. "You want the Elders to be wrong. You think they are withholding information."

"Why should we, of all creatures, be denied our final step in evolution? Perhaps the Elders do not know all there is to know."

"Dangerous thought," Palameh said. "Love can be hazardous. It produces bravery and takes away restraint." I could feel her digging in my mind with sharp claws. "But nothing I can say will turn you away from your goal, will it? If you feel the need to know, go to the Elders. Ask for material to study species that can feel love. At least it will give you some solace. I do not have all the answers. I do not know if such a feeling can be stopped. Maybe others will. Finding a cure may be easier than questioning evolution— and the Elders' authority in matters of knowledge. Tread carefully, Phieri. Love can sometimes obliterate common sense."

The first time I went to the white dome of Lucia-Kenneh, the Center for Knowledge, to appeal to the Council of Elders, I was denied what I sought. Instead, I was scolded in the nicest way possible for my absence at the training grounds. I had left my duties without authorization for the first time ever, but the Council was not lenient with first-time offenders.

I should have left when I was received by the Secretary's greeting, "For six days your obligations have been stacking up, Phieri. Do you find our trainee selection process unsuitable to your needs? Would you like to upload new preferences to ensure your best match?" But strong-willed as I had become—as Ilieu had made me—I requested a hearing with one of the Elders in the meeting hall: a personal consultation, before I took the matter before the Council.

My plea for information on intelligent species in the middle stages of evolution, able to implement emotions such as love into their everyday activities, went unheard. A speech on the importance of assuming responsibility, efficient time management, and focusing attention to matters on a scale of priority, pilfered the little time I had with the Council guide.

Usur-Delphir stopped ushering me out of the meeting hall when I burst out, "Is this it, Council guide? Is this the last step for us? Must we live trapped in this form forevermore? Can we become nothing else? All my life I have guided others, prepared them for their break from corporeal form, while I stayed behind. Do I have no hope of becoming a star, ever?" I stared at the Council guide defiantly. Had Ilieu degraded me to this? Me, challenging an Elder?

Despite my outburst, the Council guide smiled—a patronizing smile that made my hands roll into fists and my blood pulse in my temple. It had never done that before. What was wrong with me? "Oh, Phieri," Usur-Delphir started. "Fourteen million and twenty-six years is hardly a lifetime. You are young and your passion boils with boredom and inexperience. You will learn to find satisfaction and fulfillment in your guidance, and live a long, knowledgeable life with the help of tempered curiosity and abundant patience. You have so much time before you, child. Do not waste it seeking answers to issues that should not concern you. Go back to the training grounds. Work will make you forget whatever is troubling you."

I believe it was the use of the word "child" that did it. I resolved to take the information for myself that very night.

The white dome of the Center for Knowledge dwarfed the lonely figure that approached it after hours. There were no guards at the entrance, no security measures at all to prevent trespassers. Why would there be? Beings in our stage of evolution do not steal. I would have sworn to it the week before. Yet there I was, doing something I would never have conceived before that creature of light and color came into my life.

The air in the Knowledge Ascent area was heavy with an antiseptic odor of ozone and chlorine. The corridors were easy to navigate. Five levels of long hallways going up in a spiral, filled with white pillars a few inches apart from one another. Upon those pillars were blocks of crystal, each containing hundreds of information nanites. Some were history, some geology, others chemistry, biophysiology, mathematics, psychology, physics, politics, and all other aspects needed for understanding the species represented in each crystal. Those in the lower levels of evolution had their place on the first floor, and evolutionary advancement ascended to the fifth level of the spherical building. I found the middle stages of evolution on the third-floor corridor. All crystals responded to the option "love." One crystal lit up the brightest, and I took it.

I should have known better than to let curiosity take me to the fifth floor, but I had come this far, hadn't I?

There were fewer crystals there than on the third level, but still too many to count. Chance guided me to Ilieu's species, and a sad smile touched my lips. The crystals spread out farther away from one another as I walked up to the summit. Our crystal was the last, but to my disdain, it hardly contained any nanites at all—perhaps forty. None were responsive to the queries "star" or "death." I expected this, but I was surprised when no nanites ignited with the word "age," or even "longevity." In a stupor, I realized I had been right: the Elders did not know everything there was to know. They were nearly clueless about their own species. There was hope, then. There was hope!

My joy was interrupted by a hiss and a dry spray that clouded the cupola and rained down upon me. Then, a burning sensation on my skin. A tickle of heat at first, which increased to searing pain. The crystal fell from my hand and skidded across the floor.

I could not hold the torture inside. It came out of me in a shriek that echoed throughout the building. The sound emitted by my own throat scared me more than the pain. A beast I had never known.

Patches of skin turned black and edged incandescent red spread throughout my body. My hands shook as I saw the skin recede, leaving exposed flesh and bone.

Almost muted by my screams came the echoing footsteps of three Elders. Among them was Usur-Delphir, who spoke first. "We took these precautions against visitors who might envy our knowledge and try to take it from us. We never thought we would use them against one of our own." Usur-Delphir picked up the crystal close by. "Is this what you came for?"

I tried to answer, but whatever was eating me had started on my vocal cords and made its way inside. It dripped a sour, acid taste on my tongue. I dared not swallow.

I choked out unintelligible sounds. My eyes pleaded for mercy.

"The bacteria can live only for thirty flashes of Shri when exposed to our atmosphere," said the Elder to Usur-Delphir's right, referring to the nearby pulsar by which we measured short periods of time. "Just long enough to teach intruders a lesson." The Elder to Usur-Delphir's left said, "You understand, you cannot go back to the training grounds. You are hereby stripped from your privileges as guide."

Usur-Delphir threw the crystal across the floor to me. "I suppose this is worth more to you than to us. Return it undamaged when you are done. Take our greetings to Palameh of the Outcasts. That is where you belong now."

Without another word, the Elders left me to regenerate, to gather what little possessions I had, and to make my way to what is now my home.

Yuali ran to greet me before I reached the crater. My sibling of the caves helped carry my bag, all the while asking how things had gone, and why I had returned so soon.

I told Yuali of my mandated exile and showed him the crystal I had tried to steal.

I could not have hoped for a warmer welcome into the community of the Idrus. I am a farmer and gatherer by day and a researcher by night.

When the stars are out, I walk to the mouth of the crater and sit with the crystal, asking questions. Learning about this fascinating species, which can feel love in many different ways.

At first, I wanted a cure: a way to get rid of this feeling tugging at my heart. But I soon realized how much I would miss the colors. The illusion of aurora upon the gray craters that surround the caves. The prisms washing over the crystals of Palameh's necklaces when she looks upon the small moon at the right angle. The hints of pink mixed into the yellow skin of the gourds Yuali and I harvest. The memory of Ilieu upon my skin. The dream of two stars sharing light for eons to come.

No. I wish to keep love. To understand it. Perhaps these creatures in a lower level of evolution will provide me with answers that can take me closer to Ilieu, when no one from my species can.

With the query "home," the crystal projects the image of a blue orb with patches of light brown here and there, covered by swirling tendrils of white gossamer.

What Time Is It, Mister Fox?
by Stephen McQuiggan

The joy was that no one would ever believe them.

I was careful in selecting the dithering old fools I preyed upon and took great delight in the eye-rolling sighs tales of my visits elicited from their weary relatives. Yet I would have given anything for someone, just once, to really see me.

I know the ways of Man for I have walked them; in the shadows, two steps back, but I have walked them all the same. I learned more about the human heart in the chill of the night than daylight could ever hope to reveal. The human heart, like jasmine, only unfolds in the dark and gives forth the bitter perfume it withholds from the bland sun.

Yes, I know the ways and workings of Man, what makes him tick and, incapable of being one myself (it was ordained from birth that I could never be assimilated, I was truly a lost soul), I set out to study them in order to become a facsimile of one. Or rather, of many.

For I am the sniper that old Mrs. Hodge tells her disbelieving son is training his rifle on her from across the street every sundown; I am the stranger who follows every young girl in the solitude of a deserted midnight street; I am poor old Mrs. Benson's husband, returned from his grave after forty years to sit on her bed and hold her hand as she babbles about her day.

I am the unknown, uncertain threat they call paranoia, senility, dementia if they care to name me at all. Such creatures as I have no name and will accept any as a validation, a proof of existence—but if I were to pick out a name for myself, one less crass and judgemental, I would choose Lonely.

I am lonely in a crowd, ignored save for the jabbering of the one doomed to see me; and they, for the most part, are ignored too. I am lonely in the street as people hurry by with nothing more than a furtive glance over their shoulder as they feel my cold eyes rest upon them. I am lonely as I sit by the death bed.

That was why I decided to come out, squinting into the light, to announce myself and find a true friend, one who didn't clutch at their chest and catch their breath at the very sight of me, one who didn't scream or gibber at my touch. One like Sally—little damaged and sinister Sally—a girl who already knew the meaning of lonely.

I met her through her grandma, Mrs. Kite, who I had been visiting regularly in the guise of a young man who had once exposed himself to her, back in the days of steam, on a railway platform. Sally called with her parents, dutifully, every Sunday after church, dressed up like a little doll and polite to the point of parody.

"He's sitting over there by the window," Mrs. Kite told her son, who sighed and rolled his eyes at his wife. "Staring at me he is, with that mournful, evil face of his."

23

I took no offense. I was used to such insults over the years and, I had to admit, I did have a rather lugubrious air about me. I gave the old bat a playful leer and pretended to unzip my flies—a gesture which sent her into spasms of agitation, whirling her arms and speaking in tongues.

It took an hour or more for her son and daughter-in-law to calm her down. They put her to bed with a glass of warm milk and a jawful of pills wedged between her grey gums. I stood by them as they convened outside her bedroom door, my presence causing the snooty daughter-in-law (Oh, Lily, I'll make a point of seeking *you* out when age frosts your joints) to fold her arms and shiver.

"It's no good, Max. It's time you faced up to the harsh facts. She's a danger to herself, you must see that. You've got to be cruel to be kind."

"But Lily," Max said, his eyes welling up, "I can't just dump her in some home. She's my *mother*."

I'd seen this play a million times and knew every nuance of its performance, just as I knew the inevitability of its outcome. Max was simply asking for the decision to be made for him, for Lily to bludgeon him with common sense into a conclusion he had already shamefully reached. At the not too distant funeral, he would be able to console himself that none of it was really his fault.

Lily embraced her husband and gave him a Gethsemane kiss. "I know—that's why you should do right by her now."

I returned to the chintzy little living room feeling depressed. It was always thus. I would find a companion, someone who would acknowledge my presence, and then, in a few short months, they would be taken from me. No matter that we held no deep conversation or that the sight of me caused them to void their bowels and rant maniacally, no matter they called me the foulest of names, I missed them when they were gone.

If you were as lonely as I, you would accept any connection offered regardless of how much it hurt.

Sally was perched on a pouffe by the window, prim as a porcelain doll and about half as active. I slumped down across from her on the dainty sofa and chewed on my thoughts. Centuries of invisibility had robbed me of any social grace so that, in the depths of despair, I was wont to grimace grotesquely, allowing my body to mimic my inner turmoil.

"You're *funny*!" The voice was light, musical, and sharp enough to pierce my maudlin mood. I raised my head to see Sally, her hands folded neatly on her pristine lap, seemingly regarding me.

I looked over my shoulder, thinking that her parents must have crept back in whilst I was brooding, but the living room was empty and the door still closed. I turned back to her. She was smiling sweetly, her head cocked to one side, her startlingly bold eyes firmly upon me.

Me.

"Can you see me?" I asked, feeling self-conscious for the first time since I goosed a young woman at a bus stop and she inexplicably slapped my face and threatened to call the police. I hadn't thought about that incident in an age, viewing it as an aberration, a hallucination—even now, as Sally stood before me, straightening down her dress, I thought the years of isolation had at last driven me mad.

"Of course I can see you, Silly. You're *very* funny." I was lost for words. "Though you really shouldn't tease Grandma so much; Daddy says she's highly strung." Sally leaned in closer, as if imparting a dreadful secret. "Mummy says she ought to be." She held her fingers up to her mouth and giggled with delight.

I had never made any inroads with youth before. Babies sensed me and cried. Those alone and fearful grew wary in the chill of my shadow. But none of them had ever looked me in the eye and spoken to me one on one. My heart, if I possessed such a thing, was close to breaking.

Here was a little girl, barely seven years old, unafraid, who seemed to like me. She could be my friend, my playmate, save me from the long-empty decades that stretched out ahead. If she accepted me I would never leave her side until she drew her last sweet breath in the distant and unimaginable future. Even then, when the void claimed her and she drifted into dust beneath the sod, I would stand vigil by her grave.

"Aren't you scared of me?" I asked, trembling at her anticipated reply.

"Why would I be scared of you?" She dismissed the notion with a frown. "Do you want to play a game?"

Her parents came in and bustled her away before I could reply. Sally never looked back, so that I began to believe I had imagined the whole encounter. Just as despair was about to consume me, I saw her face at the window, beckoning me to follow, and I ran out to the car like a grateful pup.

I climbed into the back beside her as her parents made bad-tempered observations on the weather and Sally put her delicate hand in mine. As the car pulled away the first splats of heavy rain hit the windshield with ever-increasing urgency, yet to me, the sun had never shone brighter.

She never mentioned me to her folks the whole way home, nor at any time in the months that followed. I didn't have to tell her to keep me secret or lecture her on the dangers that an invisible friend could so quickly accrue, from the frustrated tolerance at first, to pills and psychiatrists in the blink of an eye.

I wasn't strong enough to bear some shrink convincing her I wasn't real, that I was simply the product of a sick mind. I had almost come to that conclusion myself. Sally seemed to understand all that instinctively. I thought then that her precocity had forewarned her that she wouldn't be believed, or that she was just really lonely too and wanted to keep me all to herself.

Now I know it was just another game to her. Sally loved to play games.

An only child, I kidded myself that I was her godsend —me, who had been shunned by whatever god shaped such a world.

Whereas before, through sheer boredom, I had terrified my aged audience, becoming the nightmare they viewed me as, with Sally I made it my sole mission to keep her entertained. She had such a beautiful laugh and I did all in my power to induce it.

I would follow her to school and stand behind her teacher, gurning and pulling faces until Sally laughed so hard she wet herself and the Principal rang Lily to ask if everything was okay at home. I had to restrict myself to games in her bedroom after that, comforting myself with the knowledge that soon she would be of an age to fly the nest and we could have a place of our own, free from inquisitive, snooping eyes.

I played dollhouse with her, attended countless tea parties, baked a banquet of plasticine pies, and let her win every time at hide-and-seek. She would tire of things quickly, her imagination darting from one project to another, always inventing new variations, so that we were never bored.

One game she never wearied of though, and which she demanded to play every night before bed, was "What Time is it Mr. Fox?" You could hear in her voice how much she loved it, in the sly way she would call out to me (for I, naturally, was always Mr. Fox) for the time, and the breathless giggles when I replied "Ten O'clock."

She always cheated, taking five steps instead of ten, three steps instead of six, so that when I eventually announced it was "Midnight" she would be far enough away from me to save herself from being "eaten."

She never lost her taste for that game, though I admit it began to wear on me—not so much the repetition, but rather her malicious laughter, so at odds with the cute little girl it sprung from. *She likes to sneak, is all,* I told myself, *and besides, it makes her happy,* so I carried on playing the fox. It was a while before I realized the roles should have been reversed.

Grandma Kite had been in a Home for some time and Max and Lily still visited her every Sunday, taking their daughter with them. Much as I would have liked to renew my acquaintance with the old woman, I had to sit it out. My appearance in a care home or a hospital ward was, like a cat in an aviary, usually the precursor of a noisy disaster. It seemed all the old folk in such facilities could detect me, and their agitation reached such levels that tranquilizers were dished out and visitors asked to leave.

Now that I had Sally, I had no need for such an audience and magnanimously stayed away so that Max and Lily could enjoy what little lucidity remained to Mrs. Kite. I don't include Sally in that scenario, as it turned out she had never enjoyed spending time with her grandma after all.

"I wish the old bag would hurry up and die," she moaned after one visit.

I was startled at this outburst, refusing to believe that she could be so callous even as I watched her snap the heads off her dollies in her vehemence.

"She dribbles her food, farts, and she smells like school dinners and she's... *disgusting!*"

I figured she'd had a bad day and was just tired and grumpy. The young were often prone to extremes they didn't mean or understand. Yet, when the call came that Grandma Kite had drifted off from this world, Sally was as unapologetic as she was unsurprised. She practically sang the news to me, though I'd already guessed it from the overdramatic wailing of Lily downstairs.

"How did she die?" I asked, trying to square the little angel in front of me with the demonic grin she wore.

Sally shrugged. "She lost the game we had been playing."

"And what game was that?"

"The game where you have to guess which are your heart tablets and which are Tic-Tacs. Now me and you can spend our Sundays together and play some *proper* games."

I tried hard to ignore the implications of what she had said, telling myself I was touched that she would try to block out her grief with her desire to be with me. I had been derided as (and had almost come to believe that I was) an unseen monster. I couldn't accept that my darling Sally actually was one, and one that hid in plain sight.

As her actions grew nastier, and her games more vindictive, the possibility that she was as Godless as I gnawed at me—but as she slept and I studied her angelic face, my doubts would be blown away by her gentle, steady breath.

I was forced into acceptance only when I caught her looking into the heart-shaped tin she kept beneath her bed and guarded jealously. I assumed it a repository for ribbons and bows, photos of ponies, maybe even her first attempt at a diary, but when I appeared behind her (I had turned my arrivals into a game, hoping to make her squeal at my sudden emergence) I was baffled by its contents: lighter fluid, matches, an old smooth wooden wedge used to prop the shed door open.

"What you got there?"

She jumped, though with none of her customary delight—indeed, she was angry at first and called me a snoop. I was more upset at the swear words that came tumbling from her dainty mouth (like a rainbow smeared with effluent) than what she actually said. Her mood brightened rapidly though, as she held the tin up for my inspection.

"I'm sorry," she said, her voice marinated in a thousand candy canes. "I was planning for a new game and I wanted it to be a surprise, is all."

I rummaged through the tin as I wrinkled my brow. "And what game would that be?"

"One where we get to be together with no more grownups," Sally said, smiling her portrait smile.

"And what are the rules?"

"Simple," she said, before adding in an eerily accurate impression of her mother, "you're just going to have to be patient, my boy."

But I, who had sat through centuries without speaking, who had watched forests grow and die between hauntings, did not have to wait too long. That very night, Sally was putting things in place.

She thought I was gone and would only return with the sun, that when she closed her eyes I ceased to exist along with the rest of the outside world. She knew nothing of the vigils I kept by her bedside, worried that another of my breed would stumble across her and snatch her away from me.

I sat in the syrupy shadows, thinking my endless thoughts, listening to the melody of her breath. I heard Max and Lily go to bed, heard the muffled fumblings in their room, and heard the duet of their snoring shortly after. Sally did too; for as soon as it struck up, she shot out of bed and recovered her tin heart from beneath it. She didn't see me, never checked that I might be there, so confident was she in her deviousness, in her ability to cheat unhindered and win the game.

When she stepped out into the hall on cat's paws, I followed after. I think I knew even then, as she tip-toed to Max and Lily's room, that this was the moment I lost her and the sorrow that enveloped me almost made me cry out. But I didn't. I knew if I stopped her it would only be a temporary reprieve, that Sally would soon concoct another game that only ended in our severance.

I said nothing, merely watched. Sally had taught me that all games should be played to the finish.

She took the wooden wedge from the tin and jammed it beneath her parents' door, tapping it in ever deeper with her foot as she covered her laughter with her tiny hands. Then she began spraying the lighter fluid over the door, the carpet, daubing the embossed wallpaper, flicking it over the paper shades, running a trail downstairs until all the cans were empty save one. She made a heap of her father's newspapers and doused them too.

I waited by the balustrade above, pondering how such a pretty head could house such a wicked mind. She struck a match, her face illuminated in all its malicious glee, seemingly hypnotized by its steady flicker. When it had almost burned down to her fingers the trance broke and she dropped it. The flames caught the papers instantly, dancing maniacally in place as if unaware of the extent of their freedom, before racing upstairs in all their fury. The upper landing of the dry old house was soon engulfed.

I stood my ground, watching her. Did I expect to see some comprehension blight her face or some guilt flare with the fire reflected in her eyes? If so, I was disappointed. I saw only delight there, unsullied by any hint of morality, as she turned to flee her home.

How could anyone ever doubt her, I thought, when she told tearfully of the bad men who had broken in and burned her darling daddy, her marvelous mummy—who would not feel their heart break at her brave and daring escape?

I ran down through the flames, feeling only pity for myself. I was alone again. She had incinerated my happiness along with everything else. I held the door against her and it was only then she saw me.

"You've got to let me out," she raged. My face gurned with the burden she had lain upon me, but for once, she did not laugh. "It's only a game, just a silly game!"

She pleaded and begged and promised such sweet lies but I didn't waver. I held her there and closed my eyes as the fire took hold in greedy gulps, until all I held were charcoal bones and the pale ashes of my future.

I returned back from whence I came, to mourn as much for myself as for her. The dead were out of my reach or else I would have sought comfort there instead of with the living. Anywhere but here, among my own kind, for their misery was contagious and their tales of woe so immaculately similar to mine that I felt lonelier than ever.

I was floating in the void but a short time, trying to find the courage to go back up and face the world again, when a familiar little voice called out behind me, "What time is it, Mr. Fox?"

Sally is always with me now, and in death she has invented so many new cruel games.

"Look," I cry to whatever of my kind is near, "over there! Can't you *see* her? Can't you hear her laughing?"

The horror is no one will ever believe me.

Of Mud, Of Water

By Matthew Gomez

Lily scooped up handfuls of her son, Brey, and attempted to put them back where they were meant to be. "What happened?" she asked her husband, Stet.

"We got caught in the rain," Stet said, holding in his arms whatever he could of Brey's remains.

Stet wasn't far from Brey's condition. The right side of his face was beginning to sag, and his shoulders hunched forward, his mud body drooping with moisture.

Lily squeezed a section of Brey's face, massaging the flesh into a pinched imitation of a nose. Her wet hand only made it worse, and his face smoothed over the instant she withdrew her fingers. She could see Brey's chest rising and falling like a bubble emerging from a viscous pool. It meant there was still a chance he could pull through. She held onto the hope. She had to.

Stet kicked over the dining room table so it was upside down, the wooden frame forming a sharp-edged container a few inches deep. "I'll grab the rice." He laid Brey's pooling form down then retrieved a heavy sack from the nearby kitchen, dragging it across the floor so quickly Lily feared the bottom would tear.

The bottom held, and Stet tipped the contents into the upside-down table, spreading rice evenly across Brey's body, which was already flattening and oozing to the edges of the makeshift container.

"We need ash," Lily said. It was obvious, but it was all she could think to say. The rice would absorb some of the excess water in Brey's body, but without ash his form would harden, leaving him crippled and misshapen, if not worse.

With fresh ash, Lily could reform her son into the beautiful boy he was: eager, playful, full of life. Without it, he'd continue melting until Lily's magic wore thin and he dissipated into nothing. "What were you two doing out there in the first place?"

Stet shot Lily a look that scared her. It was forbidden for women in the village to question men in public, but even in private it was considered taboo. After all, what could a woman, her body made of water and unable to grasp tools or harvest ash, contribute to the village? In Stet's eyes, and the eyes of every other male in the village, Lily was good only for caring for children and using ash to reform her husband's body each night. With her magic, Lily caressed his form and maintained its delicate balance of mud and water—ensuring he could work hard the next day and ensure the village's prosperity.

Stet's expression was flat, and she couldn't tell if it was from anger at her question or from being rained on himself.

It's the rain, she told herself, reaching forward to absorb a drop of water rolling down his face. "You could use some ash yourself," she said, forcing herself to ease the words out, tender as her touch. Physical contact with Stet and Brey offered her the only joy she felt in life. Their bodies, composed of moistened ash, were the only thing she could touch. The magic binding her form left her touch otherwise impotent. Her hands and body—made of water—passed through everything else. She lived surrounded by a world within her reach but beyond her touch.

Stet pulled away. "I'll be fine." He looked up from Brey into Lily's eyes and seemed to sense the pain he'd caused. His eyes softened, a worried expression coming through even as his body continued to slump with moisture. "I can't go outside again. We'll have to wait for the storm to pass."

"It could be days before the storm lets up. Without ash soon, Brey will..."

"I know what will happen," Stet blurted, wiping the back of his hand across his brow and leaving a shallow rut in his forehead.

"Then you know we need ash." Lily knew her words were stretching Stet's already strained patience.

Stet pointed a finger to the tin roof over their heads. "You hear that?" Rain crashed down in cacophonous sheets. "It's coming down sideways. I can't just cover up. There's too much water, and the Ash House is too far. I'll never make it there and back."

"I could go," Lily said, staring at Brey, wanting nothing more than to stroke his face, to shape him with a smile, to hear his laughter.

"You know the rules. I can't."

Rules, Lily thought. Her entire life was dictated by the village's rules. Women are to serve their husbands. Men are to harvest ash. The rules kept the village prosperous, but by whose definition?

"Curse the rules," Lily muttered. The sound of her voice surprised her. Unlike the smooth, glistening contours of her form, her words held an edge. "We know what happens to our son if we don't get ash. That's enough reason to let me out."

"And risk losing you, too? I won't do that. I can't."

"Are you afraid of losing me, or losing the magic I offer?" Lily held out her translucent hands, candlelight shimmering through her aquatic anatomy. "I'm made of water, Stet. It won't hurt me. It's against the Elders' rules for me to leave the house, I know, but I feel it deep within my being that the rain won't hurt me. And even if it did, it would be worth it to save Brey."

"Then why am I commanded to allow you only one cup a day—just enough to reshape our forms? Why am I and the rest of the men in our village commanded to keep our wives inside, away from sun and water?"

Lily couldn't answer that. It was how it had always been. Before marrying Stet, she'd been housed with the other single females in the Keeping House. They'd been given less water then since they had no partners or children whose mud forms needed reshaping after long days of work outside in the baking sun—just enough fluids to replace the evaporation they faced from the day's heat.

Stet had courted Lily for months, visiting her at the Keeping House daily until the spring day he finally proposed and invited her to join him in a house of their own.

The day they married was the only time Lily had felt the sun's touch. Stet had walked her from the Keeping House to what would be their home together. The walk had lasted only a few minutes, but that was enough for Lily. Heated by the sun, she had begun to evaporate. By the time they'd reached their home, Lily had withered, her limbs and torso dwindled to shimmering bands. The water Stet had offered her nourished her form back to health. He had been generous then, letting her drink until her spirit surged and the fresh water leaked in rivulets from her eyes. She'd not felt nourished in that way since.

"I will get more ash once the storm lets up, and you will reshape Brey then," Stet said now, ending the conversation.

"And if it doesn't?" Lily asked, unwilling to comply.

"Then we will mourn for Brey and petition the elders for permission to make a new son."

Lily's eyes went wide. "You'd give up so easily?" Had her husband hidden such callousness within him all along? She trembled, ripples cascading up her crystalline arms and over her body. She thought of Brey as he'd left the house that morning, a smile on his sweet face. He'd been singing, full of life and excited to follow Stet to learn of ash harvesting.

Stet shook his head, his eyes locked onto their son.

A bubble rose through the mud where Brey's mouth would be and popped with what sounded like a pained gasp.

"There's nothing else we can do," Stet said.

"If I could open the door—if my fingers wouldn't slip through the handle—I would leave this instant," Lily said, narrowing her eyes at Stet. "I would go to the Ash House."

"Then I'll be sure the door stays closed." Stet stood and shambled into the bedroom, his right leg sliding behind him, leaving a streak of dark, wet ash across the wooden floor.

Lily fell asleep on the floor next to Brey, but woke in the dark to the sound of his pained moans.

She opened her eyes in panic, reaching out to feel for Brey. She sat up and looked over his body, still buried in rice.

His mud was beginning to harden as the rice soaked up his water. His head had flattened into a circle, his mouth barely a pinhole. Shallow breaths wheezed through the minuscule gap.

Lily ran her fingers around where Brey's lips would be, softening the mud to allow it to move.

"Mommy," Brey said, thick-tongued. "Help me."

Lily panicked. She must have started shouting because the bedroom door flung open and Stet charged into the kitchen. "What is it?"

"Listen!"

"Daddy? Mommy? Please, it hurts."

Lily looked up at Stet who stood over the table, his eyes wide.

"Open the door, Stet," Lily said.

Stet stood over the upturned table, frozen.

"Open it!"

Stet shuffled toward the front door. "You promise you'll return? You'll be okay? I couldn't bear to lose you, too."

"We've not lost him yet." Lily stood and walked behind Stet as his hand hovered over the handle. She reached up to stroke his back, smoothing a crease in his mud. "I'll return. I'll be fine." His shoulders relaxed at her touch, and he opened the door.

A rush of humidity pushed through the door, carrying the rich fragrance of the still-pouring rain. Thunder shook the air, and a bright crack of lightning shined in the puddles lining the street.

"Where is the Ash House?" Lily asked. The only glimpses she'd seen of the village were those she'd taken when Stet had walked her home from the Keeping House.

Stet's brow creased in confusion as if he only just now realized Lily had been kept prisoner in his home since the day he'd brought her there. "Straight ahead at the other end of the village," Stet said, moving out of the way. "How will you bring back the ash?"

"Ash is the only thing my body, my magic, can move. I'll find a way."

"Then hurry."

Lily took in a breath, not knowing what would happen when the rain hit her. She remembered the pain of the sun's heat and how it parched her magic, threatened to evaporate her completely. She wondered if the rain might hurt in its own way.

A quick glance back at Brey quelled her fears. She walked through the door and into the street.

When the first drops landed on Lily, she recoiled, shocked by the cold. A moment later, she stood taller. As the drops landed on her head and shoulders, they didn't bounce off or roll away. They absorbed into her form, fortifying her magic, feeding her. She tilted her head back and opened her mouth. Rain spread over her tongue and cooled her throat, quenching an indescribable thirst she'd never known existed. She looked back at Stet, still standing in the doorway.

Could he see what she felt? Could he understand?

Behind him, Lily saw the table legs jutting toward the ceiling, reminding her of her purpose. She spun around and rushed for the Ash House.

She moved with a speed she didn't realize she commanded. She stepped into puddles, rebounding from their glassy surfaces like a coiled spring. The rain splashed against her face as she ran, feeding her with each drop.

Sooner than expected, the Ash House loomed ahead. It's dark brick facade stood like a granite tombstone in the dark. The door leading inside was closed.

Lily's excitement waned, replaced with dread. She hadn't expected a closed door, hadn't thought that far through her plan to save Brey. She fought to suppress her panic.

I'll find a way, she'd told Stet, and she intended to keep her promise. The rain not only strengthened her body—it clarified her mind. She breathed in the damp air and her magic surged.

What power do I hold? What else have the village's men kept from me?

Lily lifted her hands, splaying her fingers so her palms faced the door. "Open."

The rain cascading around her obeyed, changing course to follow her arms, splashing gently at first against the closed door but quickly turning to a torrent.

"Open!" she shouted, urging her magic forth.

Water surged from her palms and beat against the door until the wood groaned and the hinges gave way.

Lily strode forward into the expansive interior of the Ash House. The ceiling loomed high overhead, lost in the darkness. Mounds of ash sat in massive piles on the wooden floor. It was more ash than she'd ever seen in her life. Everything in the village was so tightly rationed she couldn't have imagined such a surplus. With this much ash, she and Stet could bear a thousand children of mud. What other secrets were the elders hiding?

Lily considered how she would bring the ash home and searched the ground for a vessel. She spotted a woven basket against a nearby wall, but when she reached for the handle, her hand passed through. She could manipulate ash

—and as she understood now, water—but she had no other way to affect the world around her. She could perhaps fill the basket, but she had no way to carry it home.

Desperate, Lily plunged her hands into the nearest pile of ash, hoping she might carry at least a palmful through the rain, and an idea struck. The rain she'd absorbed continued to illuminate her mind, her magic. Hands buried in the mound, Lily twisted her fingers around the ash, cupping it between her palms, and pushed. She felt the ash turning to mud—the same as when she used it to re-fortify Stet and Brey each evening—but this time she continued pressing. She trembled with exertion. After a moment, she pulled her shaking hands from the ash mound and saw something she'd never expected but suddenly understood: the ash she'd squeezed was gone. It had merged with her water and turned her hands to mud.

She reached down toward the basket, swatted the handle, and the basket fell over. She now held the same power as Stet. She could affect the world. The realization set her body shuddering with realization, anger. She could manipulate the world all along, but the elders' rationing of ash prevented her from knowing the truth. She was not weaker or less useful than Stet or any of the other men in the village. She had been kept ignorant of the truth. It was the only thing that had kept her prisoner this long.

Lily thought of jumping into the pile of ash and fusing her whole body with it, but where the mud had fused with her hands, she no longer felt the tingling surge of the rain's magic. Where the ash had fused into her hands, her magic felt muted, wrong.

She looked at her palms and wondered how Stet would react when he saw them. She brushed the fear aside for the moment and reminded herself of Brey. She filled the basket with ash, picked it up, and stepped out once more into the rain.

Lily pushed open the door to her home, stepped inside, and set the basket down.

Stet looked up, tears streaming from his eyes, and Lily's heart sank. "It's too late," he said, failing to realize she'd opened the door on her own.

Lily dropped the basket, ran to the table, and collapsed to her knees. "No! There's time. There has to be." She brushed aside some of the rice covering Brey's chest and looked for any sign of breathing. The hole that was once his mouth had crusted in place, hardened like a piece of jagged pottery.

"Your hands," Stet said, recoiling in horror. "What have you done?"

Lily pulled her hands behind her back, but the dark smudges of her mud fingers and palms showed through her translucent body. "What I had to." She reached into the basket of ash and spread a handful across Brey's chest, closing her eyes as she released some of her water. Fresh mud spread from her fingers, her hands working quickly to reshape Brey. Again and again, she combined handfuls of ash with her water. With each drop she mixed with ash, Lily's magic waned and her body dwindled. Tears streamed from her eyes, swirling with the ash as she worked her hands over Brey's body, reshaping him in the image of his father.

Brey's body, recast in fresh mud, laid still, his chest no longer rising and falling.

Lily grabbed the basket to drag it closer, but the mud in her hands had thinned with all the water she'd used to remake Brey, and she managed to only nudge it. Stet was right. It was too late.

She knelt forward over Brey, laying her head on his chest, and cried. It was then that she heard it: the faint sound of air drawn into his chest.

"He's not gone!" she shouted. "Hand me that candle."

Stet obeyed, and Lily took the candle, her grip slipping as the mud in her hands continued to loosen and thin. She held the flame over Brey's mouth and watched as the flame trembled with his faint exhale. An idea occurred to Lily. "Get my water cup from the room," she told Stet, hoping to distract him with the meaningless task.

As Stet headed into their bedroom, Lily plunged her hands into the basket and smeared quick handfuls of ash up her arms, fusing them into mud. She slid her hands under Brey's back, scooped his small form into her arms, and carried him to the door.

Just before she stepped outside, Stet emerged from their room holding the cup. He dropped it when he realized her request had been a ruse. "What are you doing?"

"What you wouldn't," Lily said. She carried Brey outside into the pouring rain, falling harder than before. Her spirit soared as the fresh water coursed over her body, but her numbed hands and arms—fused with mud—sickened her.

The mud gave Stet and the other men of the village the power to affect the physical world, but it smothered their magic and made them dependent on their wives to be made whole each evening with fresh water and ash.

Stet stepped out into the rain but retreated back to the open door. "Please, Lily—you'll kill him."

Lily's instincts told her otherwise. She held Brey up to the rain, letting the cold water wash over his form and run in dark streams down her arms. Slowly, the rain did its work, and the mud began to slough off in sludgy clumps.

She saw Brey's hand first. The mud thinned, then fell away completely, leaving behind a set of perfect, crystalline fingers bound to a translucent palm: a hand of water.

It was all the proof Lily needed.

Stet watched in horror as Brey's mud rinsed away completely, leaving a body in Lily's arms made entirely of fresh rain.

Brey coughed, then his eyes opened. "Mommy?"

The hope Lily had held captive behind her own doubts burst forth, and her chest heaved with sobs. For Brey's whole life she'd mixed fresh mud and re-applied it to his form, smothering his magic. She'd been the one keeping his spirit captive all along. "Are you okay, honey?" she asked, staring into Brey's cerulean eyes.

Brey nodded, and his sudden, bright smile washed away her guilt.

Lily turned her attention to Stet, who stood silhouetted in the doorway by orange candlelight. "Come out," she pleaded. "The water won't hurt you. We can be together this way."

"We were together before," he replied. His voice sounded flat, barely audible over the splashing of rain.

"I was your prisoner."

"You were my wife."

"Come outside, Daddy!" Brey shouted. He slipped from Lily's arms, dropped to his feet, and twirled in the rain.

"Come inside, son," Stet said. "We'll get you some fresh ash. We'll make you normal again. Don't you want to play with your toys? If you stay with Mommy you'll never be able to touch them again."

Brey stopped spinning and looked back at Lily. "Is that true?"

Lily nodded. "Without mud, your life will be different, but it's your choice to make," she said. It had to be. If she made the choice for him, she would be no better than Stet had been to her. She wouldn't do that to anyone, especially not her son.

Brey turned to Stet and dipped his toe into a puddle. "I don't want that, Daddy. The water feels good. Please come outside." He ran back into Lily's arms.

"You can still come outside, Stet," Lily said.

"Where will you go?"

"Come outside."

Stet shook his head and backed up, retreating inside but not yet shutting the door.

Lily thought she felt fresh tears on her face, but in the cascading rain it was impossible to tell. She looked at Brey, hoping he would forgive her for subduing his magic for so long. "You ready to go, son?"

Brey looked up and smiled. "Where are we going?"

Lily couldn't answer that—not yet. Instead, she relied on the same instinct that had told her to wash the mud off of him. "I'm not sure. Someplace better."

Her eyes searched the ground, watching the water, feeling its pull. The puddles that had formed early in the storm were now overflowing, running in black veins over the ground where they merged into several small streams that rushed downhill. She turned away from Stet to find where the water led.

"You'll die out there!" Stet shouted, more threat than plea for her return. "Come back now, and I'll let you inside. Otherwise I'm closing this door, and you'll both face whatever consequences come to you."

Stet's warning sent a shiver through Lily. If she didn't return, would she and Brey evaporate when the rain finally eased and the sun shined down with its full, blazing heat? She looked at Brey, and his broad smile offered her the conviction she needed.

Without turning to face her husband, Lily stepped into one of the rushing streams.

The door slammed shut, the final thread binding Lily to her husband severed. Water rushed past her ankles and over her feet. The cool liquid soothed the anxiety blooming inside her. She would find a way to keep them safe.

Brey ran ahead of her and jumped into the stream, giggling as droplets splashed from under his feet. His laughter was as invigorating to Lily as the rain. She smiled and walked downhill, tracing the stream through dense forest until it emerged from the trees and met with an expanse of water so wide she couldn't have fathomed its existence—a body of water large enough that no amount of sun and heat could empty it.

She waded forward until the water was at her knees and Brey's waist. A surge of magic enveloped her, coursing through her in a prickling rush.

Several translucent figures emerged from the surface, their bodies made of water so pure only a glimmer of sun now cresting the horizon revealed their forms.

Lily reached for Brey's hand, her water fusing with his. "What is this place?" she asked, searching the figures' faces for an answer.

A woman, her eyes gentle and understanding, held out her hands toward Lily and Brey. "Home."

Sookie at the Beginning
by Frances Pauli

Sookie sits on the counter behind the window and watches the fall of man. She grooms herself with one ear pressed flat to her head, muffling the shouts outside. Some of the people race past the little shop, but many pause in the street, crane their necks back, and stare into the sun.

Sookie licks the fur of her tail and squints at them. They look like statues staring, staring until they fall where they stand. Until they lay open-mouthed on the asphalt, rigid and unmoving.

The old man who tends the shop has not appeared for two days. Sookie's dish behind the counter is still full, so she forgets about him until the back door scrapes open. A stranger slinks inside. Sookie's whiskers press close to her skull. A growl brews in her soft belly. No man moves like that and means well. She flicks her newly polished tail and leaps for the high shelf above the register.

He hunches like a sick rat, back curving into a hump that makes her claws come out. There's a scent clinging to him, and she holds her breath as he passes below her perch.

A bottle of pills rattles as her tail waves against it, and the thief jumps, squeaks just like a rat.

Sookie tucks her feet beneath her and watches him struggle with the register. He pushes buttons and pries at the door. He beats the thing with a can from a nearby shelf and then gives up and stuffs his pockets with other things. Chips and chocolate, a rolled-up magazine. She purrs as the thief leaves, and she imagines him dead in the street.

She is cat. She needs no one, but the food in her dish will not last forever. The street outside overflows with death. The old man is not coming back. Sookie stretches her back and observes without comment.

There is a hopper connected to her food dish. On the morning when it's half empty, the dog appears. She's seen enough of them in the street, of course, mangy things sniffing around the bodies. But this one has more meat on his bones. His coat is still glossy, and his tail wags as he enters through the door the thief forgot to close.

He doesn't slink, and so Sookie ignores him. She allows this dog to snoop around the shelving. She observes, tail fluttering, as he devours a loaf of bread, plastic and all. He's clumsy, too large, and fully *dog*, but he doesn't slink or stare at the sky.

And so she permits him to stay.

The streets are quiet when the pack of mongrels isn't about. Only the wind rifles the bodies, but the smell is unpleasant out-of-doors. She remains on her counter through the day, ignoring the dog's attempts to woo her, the low barks and the soft whimpers. Sookie only comments with a furious hiss when he pokes his wet nose behind the counter.

Mine.

He might be dog, but he understands this. His big head lowers and a whine escapes. It is high-pitched, and she flattens her ears at him, hissing again. The dog curls up beside the shelving and watches her groom her satin coat. She ignores him, ignores the whole world. She is cat.

She needs no one.

Still, the nights are colder somehow. Once the dog is snoring, she leaps down to curl against his warm body. When his tail thumps, Sookie smacks it, making sure to use enough claw to discourage further displays. He obeys, tucks his head against his flank, and pretends there is no cat beside him. The tail only flutters once more, hours later, and this time Sookie lets it slide.

Before he wakes, however, she is back on her counter. The dog barks and wiggles, and when she makes no reply, scoots through the back door and vanishes. Sookie reminds herself that she is cat, but when the dog's footfalls fade to a distant whisper, she follows him.

Her paws make no sound. She leaps and dashes, keeping to the shadows and stopping only when she must listen for which way the dog has gone. The streets smell bitter, full of death and disease and the swarming of insects. Most of the bodies have been chewed. Dead mongrels lay with the same gaping stare beside the corpses they tried to devour.

Sookie worries about the dog then. She imagines him with his eyes stretched wide and blank, with his pink tongue hanging free, motionless. Irritation makes her tail twitch. She flicks one paw into the air and washes it, deliberately taking her time before chasing him again.

He circles. His path leads them round the little store and back. Sookie thinks he did not gnaw on the dead. She thinks he's safe for now. But by the time they return, she is convinced they have to leave the things of man behind. There is too much danger in the city. But when the dog settles in with a bag of chips beside his shelf, Sookie only sighs and continues grooming.

She is cat. She needs no one. But to a dog, the world of man is strongly bound. Sookie is certain they must leave this place, but when the dog falls asleep, she curls up beside him and forgets to scratch the tail when it thumps against the floor.

For days she worries while the dog circles. The shelves grow empty and only the bucket of water by the janitor's closet is left to sustain the dog. He stays out longer. Sookie can see the shine fading from his fur, the way he drags his feet when he returns. He clings to something that has passed, and it will drag him down with it, drag her down if she remains.

Sookie is cat. She must lead the way.

The morning she wakes to an empty dish, she knows the time has come. She will show the dog, or she will leave him behind. Either way, she must go. She fears the hunger that will come next. She fears the mice in the city, the staring-eyed-open-mouthed death that comes from hunting here.

She leaves the shop before the dog has woken, and she only hesitates at the door long enough to shake her tail softly from side to side. He will understand. The things of man are behind them. The world has fallen, but she remembers that a dog must *learn* to be free.

Sookie climbs atop a dumpster, leaps to the nearby gutter and lands on the roof to wait. The sun is too hot, but she keeps her eyes on her own paws and scoots farther into the shadow of the next building over. She waits. Eventually the dog emerges, whining, casting his gaze from side to side and never thinking to look up.

He howls once, a mournful note that makes her tail fluff. Sookie purrs softly and waits to see if a dog can be taught freedom.

It takes three days. Sookie grows tired and wanders. Each morning the dog circles the shop, and each afternoon *she* strays farther from it. She explores the world above the bodies, slinking through open windows and napping on pillows that will never see a head again. She slips in and out like the thief, but she never slinks. She finds little food. Her belly grows angry.

By the time the dog decides to go, she's thinking of hunting. She's started to leave him twice, and only returned when the sun made the rooftops too hot for her paws.

Finally, he trots into the street and turns away from the shop. Sookie follows, bounding across the hot spaces and pausing in each shadow. He doesn't circle this time. He makes a straight path toward the edge of the city. Running to the open.

Sookie meows, singing her approval.

The dog cannot hear her. He follows his nose, leading her away from the city. The buildings give way to houses, forcing her back to the ground, but now grass grows and fences stand like bones lined up beside it. Cars guard their empty homes, and the bodies are much farther apart.

Sookie keeps to their shadow, keeps her distance, and follows.

They almost make it. She can smell fresher things when the dog veers sharply. In the distance, there are massive swaths of tree and field, open spaces where no bodies grin at the sky. Sookie growls and flicks her tail, following the dog into a row of tidy back yards.

He finds a pool of water too dirty for drinking. Still, he squeezes under the fence and plunges his nose into it. He romps around the yard, makes a fool of himself.

Sookie stares into the closest trees. Only a short way to go. She can feel her new beginning call from the dark foliage. There will be hunting out there, things that creep and fly and never look too long at the sun.

The dog is ready. He leaves the yard and faces the forest. He listens, and Sookie holds still, low and coiled to spring after him. She becomes shadow, invisible. She is ready. She is cat.

A whistle splits the air. The dog whines, but his tail waves like a stupid flag. A man appears behind the houses. Maybe, the last man of all. He walks slowly, singing to the dog in a voice no cat would acknowledge. Sookie growls and puffs her tail.

She observes the meeting, but she takes a few cautious steps toward the trees. Already, she is imaging the future without the dog. She will run after the field mouse. She will leap at the sparrow, and she will need no one.

She will sleep alone.

She is cat.

The dog barks, but he shies away when the man reaches for him. Sookie lays with her belly against the ground and watches them dance. Her tail sweeps through the grass, and her eyes wander to the forest and back. The day wanes. At last the sun is bearable.

The last man brings a chair into the yard and sits beside her dog. They stare at the sky together.

Sookie yawns and gets to her feet. She races to the trees, a blur of shadow, a whisper of memory. The air inside is cool and fresh. Nothing smells of death except for the path behind her. She leaps into the air and twists her body, imagining the hunts to come.

She sits and cleans her feet. Then she climbs a tree that faces the yard and lays across a low branch, watching the dog. She needs no one.

But eventually the man will die. Already, he stares too long at the sun. When he falls, the dog might break away. He might remember freedom and find the woods again. Sookie gets up and turns her back to them. She lays down looking outward, looking forward. She yawns and cleans her toes.

She will wait a little. Maybe the dog will come, and maybe he will stay with the man's body. Sookie will wait and see. Then, she will leave.

She is cat.

Safe Haven

by Chrissie Rohrman

The inky black of in-between fades away, and a flare of light stabs my unblinking eyes. Or *these* unblinking eyes. The first few moments of the transition are always disorienting, as I wake and stretch to fill my latest form. It is inconvenient at times, but it's necessary to take on a form familiar in Human World, where we Fae are invisible to human eyes.

A harsh wind blows through, and I roll helplessly against a hard surface as my vision takes time to adjust. I hear birds chirping, a faint lapping of water in the distance. A park, maybe. I must have taken the form of a dropped, forgotten toy—a doll of some kind, I think, as I reach out to fill ten tiny molded fingers and unnaturally pointed feet. I hope this isn't another Barbie—or at least a fully clothed one, this time.

In The Haven, I am Rill, but here in Human World, I go by whatever name my charge gives me. In recent years, I have been Patches, Teddy, Zoey, the dreaded Malibu Barbie, and Ms. Sparkles von Billingsworth: Unicorn of Justice (Riley had been having a particularly difficult time with some bullies in her second-grade class when I was assigned to her). Our charges know us only as friends appearing in their lives at the exact right moment. Sometimes I am with them for only a few of their months; sometimes it is years. Riley in particular had already suspected she was strong enough to stand up to her tormentors and had not needed my companionship long. I withdrew from the stuffed unicorn and returned to The Haven covered in glitter. Some Fae are still picking bits of it out of their wings.

I can't move much; the limbs of this familiar form are skinny and stiff, but at least I have them. Once, for a daydreamer named Louise, I was a journal with a soft turquoise cover and a silver tassel. That was a form that took some getting used to. Eventually I could flip through the pages if I concentrated hard enough, to find the exact entry Louise needed to reread to remind her that the special bits others chose to laugh at were actually the parts she loved most about herself. She used a purple pen to cover my pages with scribbles of creative, fantastical thoughts on the good days, and I soaked up her tears on the bad days.

Fae are born from seeds of light and magic in the eternal forest of The Haven, blossoming like dewy blooms on a warm, rain-kissed morning. I was quite young when I heard my first call, though age does not exist in The Haven the way it does here in Human World. Only in Human World is something as grand as time chopped into pieces to be counted and traded like currency.

It takes some effort, but I manage to twist my new head to better take in my surroundings. I am lying on hard-packed dirt and can see thin, leafless trees reaching into the white sky like clawed hands: early winter in this part of Human World. It's not the first time I've transitioned somewhere outdoors, but it is always jarring. Most times, my new charge will feel the pull when they spot me on a toy store shelf or under a holey sweater in a lost-and-found bin. Once, for Casey, I transitioned into a plastic army man that had been lost years earlier in the back of his parents' car. I remember clearly how his eyes lit up when he saw me roll out from beneath the seat, a comforting piece of home he desperately needed as his family moved across three states for his father's new job.

The needs of each charge are different, evolving as they grow. Mostly, we are simply there for them when others are not. We are companions. We listen. We don't judge. We offer advice only if asked, and if the form we are inhabiting is capable of speaking. As Patches, I was a simple, literal security blanket for a timid boy named Jeremy. There is no shortage of children in need in Human World, and while there will always be the wayward Fae who sees the calling as a chore, I am only truly alive when I help these younglings. This is what I was created to do, and I have come to know and love their world better than my own.

I think of Riley, standing up for herself without needing a stuffed unicorn to speak for her. Of Louise, using her imagination to craft stories in which she is the hero, and loving herself for her uniqueness. Of Annika, who no longer spends recess sitting alone.

Every Fae has tales of success in their past, but we all also have failures.

We never know before we transition what we will be in form, but it is somehow suited to the charge. Even with the pull, it takes some effort on our own part to catch their attention, and in my earlier days, I had one slip right past me. My failure. He was older than my usual charges, closer to the age when they no longer need me. Thirteen human years, I had guessed. He had a mop of curly dark hair and a faraway gaze that had seen too much in his short life. Instantly, I ached for him. The pull was not strong enough— I, a battered leather baseball mitt, was not strong enough— and he drifted right past the spot where I lay.

We aren't supposed to dwell on such things, but sometimes, when I am in-between and waiting to transition, I wonder what became of him, whether another Fae was sent to him, and if that Fae was able to do what I could not. I wonder if I have been granted a second chance. If I am making my way back to him.

My vision begins to clear. It will take some time to fully settle into this form, but I don't have much of it. The timing of when we are called and sent into Human World is crucial, and my new charge will be along soon. My thoughts wander to Annika, my most recent, but only for a moment. I know she is okay, with fierce certainty. I wouldn't be here, waiting for the next charge, if she weren't. A candy bar wrapper catches in the wind and rolls in the dirt beside me. In a moment of stillness, I catch my murky, folded reflection in the foil. An off-brand Barbie after all, its eyes just a bit too round and face too heart-shaped, with scuffs along the side. One eye has been stabbed through with a pin or a pencil, and the dull synthetic hair is in disarray.

The realization that I once again have a mouth is a relief. It isn't a necessity while in form—children in Human World already have so many voices chattering at them—but it certainly helps. Unless an adult is nearby. Adults are less likely to accept magic and can undo months of good work with a charge in a single moment of outraged disbelief.

Across the park, children shriek and laugh as they play, soothing sounds accompanied by the rusty creak of playground equipment, but in the immediate area, there is silence. I begin to panic. The children are far away, too far to see where I lay. What if I can't see them, and the pull isn't enough? What if my charge isn't drawn to me in this unwanted, broken-down form?

What if I fail, again?

A failure means the gods can divert the call, can pull you from the queue of Fae in line. It means an eternity may pass in The Haven before you are summoned once more to the Axis Mundi, the grand tree that stands at the center of the forest and houses the portals to Human World.

The edge of a shadow falls over me, and I feel it. It's her.

I summon what strength I can to move my stiff, plastic arm, just a fraction, and hope it's enough. The shadow shifts, and a face comes into view: big brown eyes, thin lips, and a smattering of freckles across the bridge of her wide nose. Her hair whips in the wind, covering her eyes, and she pushes it back.

No.

There has been a mistake; it cannot be her. She is much too old, especially to feel the pull from a doll. I hold perfectly still, though my mind is screaming at this impostor to leave me be, to go away so that my true charge can find me.

The girl looks around the park with a frown, searching for the owner of this pathetic, abandoned toy. I steel myself for another failure, another eternity lost as I wait for the call, for permission to rejoin the ranks of my brethren. Then she reaches down to pick me up. *No. No, no, no.* This too-old girl is going to ruin everything I live for.

"What are you doing here?" she asks in a soft voice, one I have heard before. The kind I know comes from being ignored. With one hand, she absently strokes the tangled hair on my head as she once more looks around the park. "Did some little girl leave you here?"

I knew she was too old for me in this form, too old to be helped. Sometimes the damage has already been done. I exhausted my initial burst of strength moving as much as I have. It will take time to build it back, to move or speak.

Time I am not sure I have.

"Emma!" a voice calls from across the park, and the girl's face hardens as she looks up.

Emma's posture changes, her shoulders slumping. "That's my new mom," she says, still stroking my ratty hair, using her fingers to work out the knots and tangles. "Well, maybe my mom. I've already had three since the accident." She bites her lip and runs her thumb over my impaled eye. "Somebody should have taken better care of you."

"Emma! We need to get going!"

She sighs. "You might not believe me right now, but I swear, she seems nice. Nicer than the others, at least." Emma turns me over in her hands, inspecting me.

Suddenly, the pull surges within me, and my heart trips wildly beneath the thin plastic of this form. I was wrong. This girl *is* my charge, and this is the moment when she decides what to do with me. I can tell that she needs me, but need isn't enough. She will either ignore the pull and drop me to the dirt, and I will have to return to The Haven and shake off the sting of another failure, or Emma and I will become a team for the next important chunk of time. I will do what I can to provide a constant in her life, which has clearly been marred with instability.

A low drone builds at the edges of my awareness: the electric buzzing of commotion in The Haven. I am nearly out of time; the Axis Mundi is already beginning to draw me back, its magic sensing that I have not made the connection with my new charge.

That I will not. That I have failed, again. Perhaps I failed Emma from the moment she stepped over me.

The scenery of the park grows dark around the edges, and a pulsing halo of light overtakes my field of vision. The Axis Mundi is calling me back to The Haven, and I do not have the strength to resist. There is a moment of weightlessness as I begin to fall back into in-between, as my essence straddles the line between two worlds.

After a second failure, I may never again be granted the chance to help the children of Human World.

Fingers tighten around my slim plastic waist, a gesture that pulls me back fully to this form. "I guess I can't just leave you here, too."

I somehow manage a blink, and Emma's big eyes widen even further. Her thin mouth turns up in a small smile.

"How about I bring you with me?" she asks. "I can sure use a friend right now."

Yes. A chime rings in my ears as the connection is made, a dizzying, thrilling sensation.

There was no mistake, and this will not be a failure. Emma is my new charge, my new *friend*, and I feel it as strongly as I ever have before: I am going to help her.

I'm ready.

The Vampire Jesus

by Garrett Rowlan

When the call came from Eloi Rinehart, Bronson Parker—vampire, entrepreneur, and now the subject of several lawsuits—was sitting and contemplating future revenue sources now that his Vampire Circus had gone into hiatus, probably not to be revived. There were no apparent future revenue sources.

"Yes," he said, sitting in the darkness of his office in the city of Las Vegas. It was a sort of house arrest.

"How," the voice asked, and it sounded familiar, "would you like to go to Mars?"

Bronson realized this was no prank, for he recognized the voice of Eloi Rinehart—the space-exploration visionary—who made millions with self-driving cars and teller-less banks, and in past years had spoken of launching a rocket to Mars.

Bronson asked him to repeat. He listened and nodded. Since he had been bitten by a vampire and become one himself, he had gotten used to dramatic changes in his life.

In the distance, the sign at the entrance to the empty parking lot throbbed sadly, VAMPIRE CIRCUS, VAMPIRE CIRCUS...

"Okay, I believe you," Bronson said. "But why?"

He got a mini-lecture in response. The vampire's advantages for Mars were threefold, Eloi said. No need for oxygen (vampires didn't breathe, being undead) nor food, only blood to function; their cold body temperature and low blood pressure were both suitable for Mars; and since vampires were technically dead and almost universally feared and hated (except for the Vampire Circus in its heyday), there was little risk of a legal eagle suing on Bronson's behalf if something went wrong.

"That's reassuring," Bronson said. He drank blood. It had a taste as if sourced from India.

Eloi continued. The tendencies for vampires to fall into a coma without blood would also be useful considering the six-months it would take to get from one planet to another. A time-release capsule would be placed in Bronson's mouth and opened by a remote signal when he neared the red planet.

No need for food or oxygen, Eloi added. That was the important thing. Vampires generated internal oxygen only when they needed to speak; blood in their system gave them breath to push out words. Otherwise, the blood of others provided a perverse "life."

"Vampires and Mars were made for each other," Eloi concluded. "And getting there and back with you would be faster, cheaper, better—you know the NASA slogan, not that they're in on this, at least directly."

"Then why me?"

"Optics," Eloi said. "You're not only a vampire, you're a celebrity."

Flattered, Bronson swallowed, his fangs sharpening with the taste. He felt his lungs aerate with fresh air. "I'm a celebrity vampire who will need money, though the lawsuits are bullshit."

"Others don't think so," Eloi said.

"No one died that night," Bronson said. "No one but security guards, who signed a waiver, each and every one. There was never any slipup on my part. The vampires got loose. I'll pay the damages but, damn, I can't do everyone's job."

"I think the lawsuits would paint a convincing picture of negligence. But, if you agree to my plan, I can get those settled, and when you return from Mars, probably less than four years after you leave, you'll return as a hero."

"Four years?"

"At least a year up and back—that's assuming something doesn't go wrong either way. And exploring and documenting the sites we're going to send you to will take another two years plus change—that's the amount of time until the next launch window opens. So that's three years at least right there. Four is factoring in anomalies. You'll return a hero, maybe not forgiven by some and certainly not forgotten, but perhaps a hero to the human race. The way things are going, we'll need one. It will be your second act as a vampire."

"So why are you going to this extent to send me to Mars?"

"Because it's there," Eloi said.

One of Bronson's gifts since he'd become a vampire was something like extrasensory perception. Back in the day when vampires were hunted, Bronson had a knack for ditching whatever patrol was near. He felt the gift working now.

"What aren't you telling me? People don't love vampires. I don't need to tell you that. People only love to watch us burn at sunrise."

"Can you blame them? Two-hundred people died before you vampires were subdued."

"I was almost one of them," Bronson said. If he hadn't come up with the idea of a vampire circus, a retinue of performing ghouls, vampires who, being undead, were subject to various forms of entertaining abuse, he too would have been bound and burned at sunrise.

"People don't love vampires," Eloi said, "but they love the idea of Mars. I want you to show them Mars: the hills, the valleys, as much as you can film and uplink. When the next launch window opens, you'll return."

His career as a vampire impresario ended, Bronson had little choice but to sign the contract.

"By the way," he asked, "what will I be driving while I'm filming?"

"Nothing," Eloi said, "to get there and back as efficiently as possible, a gasoline-powered vehicle is out of the question. You'll be riding a modified bicycle."

Bronson went to a cell upstate in Nevada where he trained, gamed (that is, explored possible situations and responses), and studied maps. Only on the eve of his departure did he have a hint that this excursion might be more than a travel log. They had kept religion out of this, no exhortation "to touch the face of God" or any such pep talk, until Theosophy U. Love, the famed TV preacher—"I heard a word from Jesus today," he often said, beginning his Sunday morning telecast—came by Bronson's hut on the eve of his departure.

"Let me guess," Bronson said as the "minister" with rock-star hair, a star-spangled coat, and a smile whose maintenance might have equaled the monthly budget of a Beverly Hills' dentist, settled across from him. Bronson, being a vampire, was by law tightly restrained. "You had a word from God."

"Listen, you smart-ass son of a bitch," Minister Love said. "I'm the goddamn reason you're not a pile of ashes right now. Okay?"

Shocked at the way the evangelist's TV folksiness had turned venomous, Bronson only nodded.

"Matthew Chapter Twenty-Eight verse two," Theosophy Love said, sounding like he was reciting from a Marine Corp manual. "'And, behold, there was a great earthquake for the angel of the Lord descended from heaven, and came and rolled back the stone from the door.' Now where do you think the angel who freed Jesus from the cave came from?"

"Mars?"

"I guess you're not so stupid after all," Minister Love said. "And where do you think Jesus went after he appeared to the disciples one last time?"

"You're kidding me," Bronson said. "I'm supposed to go to Mars and find Jesus?"

"I've had a vision," Minister Love said, "but only you can see if it's real." Without another word he brought a gleaming scalpel from his breast pocket and sliced his forearm, vertically, so the blood dripped into a small beaker he pressed to the bottom of the wound. He filled up two inches of blood and handed it to Bronson. "Take it," Love said.

Drunk, the blood produced in Bronson a new experience, an effect different from drinking the blood of the careless, the homeless, and the vampire-hoax foolish that Bronson and his coven (all dead now but he) had killed, decanted, and eviscerated. Some victims were even buried, for the infection that had mysteriously turned a small section of the population in Los Angeles into monsters hadn't completely killed their human impulses. Now he felt filled with a sense of purpose, other than escaping Earth.

"Find Jesus," Minister Love said. "Find him and bring him back."

Minister Love didn't seem to be the kind of person who spoke in metaphors, Bronson decided when he left. The only thing he could really trust was the blood he'd drunk. It left Bronson with a feeling of election, the sense of being implanted with an undefined homing instinct, though little else. Leading up to the launch, he was restless, angry, and snappish behind the bite-proof mask.

If Jesus was on Mars, Love didn't know where. Bronson talked to Eloi Rinehart.

"The man's a nut," Eloi said. "But he gave me money following his vision."

"Of Jesus on Mars?"

"The man gave me two million bucks," he said. "What did one little interview hurt?"

"He said he kept me from being burned."

"You're not popular, Bronson." Eloi shrugged. They spoke across a glass partition. Up close, Bronson saw how Eloi had a weak eye, making his glance off-center, as if he were focused on Bronson's ear. "What can I say?"

"Some definite idea of why I'm doing this," Bronson said. "Besides making a movie."

"We're doing it because we can, isn't that enough? The world needs this now. That's from the generous and charismatic Minister Love."

"I saw him on billboards around Vegas, I never realized that until now."

"He's very popular, a persuasive and lucrative message. Someone whom he hired made his way to my office and showed me the design for a rocket ship suitable for a vampire. He said Theosophy Love had his input. You know, he was at MIT when he got the message to serve God."

His training ended, Bronson was launched into space. Riding to the launch site, he saw protestors with signs like GOOD RIDDANCE and HOPE YOU DIE UP THERE though one said BEST OF LUCK and another read FIND JESUS, held by a fanatic-looking young man in sandals and little more than rags. Probably myself I'm seeing, Bronson thought. Before he was bitten by a midnight vampire, he'd been forty and a failure, a meth addict, homeless, shunned by his family until it was obvious he was a success, which was when they called him for free circus tickets. If being a vampire had been a choice for him, he was ultimately glad he'd taken it. His parents had called again last night.

"We're so proud of you, son," his mother said.

"The world needs you now," his father said. "We're at each other's throats and we need to be united. You can do this."

The next day, he was lifted by a gantry to his cell in the rocket ship, little more than a cabin, a console, and below him tons of gas, enough to get him to Mars and off the planet again. For the first time since he became a vampire, he felt his heart beat: a single, strong thump as the rocket lifted off. Somewhere past the moon, he fell into a vampire coma. Months later, somewhere near Mars, he was revived.

Seven months later, as Bronson was about to head north from the equator of Mars, he granted his first and what turned out to be his only interview. He never saw the woman's face but heard her question, transmitted from

Earth. She asked, "What's the most surprising thing you found out about Mars?"

Bronson, in his headgear and the thermal suit, said, "The sun is weak and doesn't harm me like on Earth. The atmosphere is unbreathable but since I don't breathe but live on blood, I feel I'm suited to this place. It's a dead planet but I'm dead too. In a way, it's a perfect fit. And the scenery is fantastic, as I'm sure the film has shown you."

He sipped from a packet of blood dropped from the geosynchronous satellite, hovering at a stationary height between the gravity of Mars, poised at the threshold of the unfettered movement of deep space. A dozen packets dropped at a time, supplementing the supply still in the spaceship.

"What song do you have on your earbuds?" The next question came a half-hour later, after his response was sent to Earth.

"*I Still Haven't Found What I'm Looking For* by U2."

"Are you looking for something?"

"Oh, you know, the most spectacular view, that sort of thing."

"Yes, the world is amazed by what you've shown us."

"I had to go hundreds of miles south to really penetrate *Noctis Labyrinthus*," he said. It was where the interview was taking place. Bronson stood at the edge of a chasm that went down for miles. It was part of a system of deep, steep-walled valleys, twisting like a natural labyrinth. It was located at the western end of *Valles Mareneris*, a long chain of gorges that ran over two thousand miles. On the maps Bronson had studied on Earth, it looked like a long knife wound.

Descending the slopes above the labyrinth passages, he found caves he'd entered until meeting dead ends that looked sealed. Scrawled marks in his flashlight's beam suggested written language. Eloi said from Earth that he shouldn't mention this, that the world didn't need cultural shock right now. Too many things were happening.

INTERESTING PHOTOS, BRONSON. That was the text back from Houston after he'd sent the images.

"Those canyons make the Grand Canyon look like a wading pool," Bronson told the interviewer, knowing the answer wouldn't reach her for several minutes. He added, "When you look down into them, you realize how big the universe is and how small we are."

"That's a message we sure need right now," she said, her response coming twenty minutes later, Mars and Earth changing their position as they both orbited around the sun in vastly different arcs. "We need to know we're all one instead of fighting."

"I'm on it," he said.

He had gone south once he'd landed on Mars and gotten his "sea legs." Now he reversed the direction, headed toward *Pavonis Mons*, a mountain to the northeast. The terrain gradually rose. At night, he crawled into his sleeping bag and looked up. The stars seen from Mars were brilliant and gave him a feeling as if he'd hopscotched to the edge of the solar system, on the tip of infinity. Yet the influence of Love's blood was to explore around him, keeping alive the vague homing instinct that had never left Bronson's thoughts.

A shooting star flared above. It was the first shooting star he'd seen on Mars. It crossed his vision left to right and when it vanished to the northwest he understood. He was being given a message, a direction. He texted Houston to inform them that he planned to abandon the trip to *Pavonis Mons*, due northeast as he left *Noctis Labyrinthus*, in favor of a more remote mountain, *Ascraeus Mons*, farther north by a hundred miles.

THIS IS NOT THE PLAN, they texted from Earth.

I'M FOLLOWING THE BLOOD, he texted back.

WTF? Was the unprofessional response. He had started to get the impression that things were not going so smooth in Houston.

He stopped at the spaceship, 200 feet high and anchored by wide stanchions to the Martian surface, to collect more blood and make repairs to his bicycle before continuing.

They finally got the panoramic views they wanted months later. He'd gone halfway up *Ascraeus Mons*, some seven miles high. He had intended to go back down after sending the image, but an impulse he didn't understand made him climb another hundred feet. Pausing, taking another photo, he turned and felt a subterranean draft that had him curious and then clearing away rocks. Soon he uncovered an opening that descended, wide enough that after a few steps he could walk upright. He went back two hours to his anchored bike (no thieves, obviously, but sometimes the winds kicked up) and got the flashlight and camera and climbed back up to the spot he'd marked.

Once he reached it, he followed the descending cavern down a half-mile or so—he could only guess—waving the flashlight as he went, sometimes having to crouch down. The slope leveled off and he walked a few more hundred yards until he found himself standing in what felt like an open space, a sort of chamber. At its other end was a light. One that was either an illusion or receding as Bronson approached. At last, it grew tired of running from him (or so was his perception) and allowed him to approach, at which point it descended, disappeared, and reappeared in the form of a cross. While anything but a religious man, Bronson knew the image from museum tours, gift shops, and the colored plates of books. What he'd never seen in the flesh was what he found lying at the base of the illuminated crook, the emaciated male in a loincloth.

The man's eyes opened and regarded Bronson with a dull stare, though when Bronson tried to lift the head, the man's mouth lurched forward and bit Bronson on the wrist.

"Bad man!" Bronson said, slapping him across the cheek.

There was a guttering sound in response, possibly of apology. Bronson, moving his hand like dealing with a biting dog, slowly lifted the man's upper lip to see if he sported vampire fangs. He didn't, but some vampires were recessive, and the fangs didn't appear unless they needed to bite.

"You're what I came here for," Bronson said. "So don't fuck with me."

Jesus, which is what Bronson named the ghoul in lieu of a better explanation, was light in weight but as squirrely as a kitten in a bag. It took hours to carry him to the surface, another three hours to drag him to the bicycle.

I HAVE FOUND HIM, Bronson texted. He uplinked a photo for proof. I HAVE FOUND JESUS.

GOOD WORK, the response came. PROCEED TO SHIP.

Bronson stared at the screen for a minute, waiting for more, but that was it. Nothing on the discovery of the century, or twenty of them since Calvary.

I THINK HE DRINKS BLOOD, Bronson texted. See what they say to that, he thought. He had opened a packet and poured some onto the thin man's lips. The tongue came out blackened like some dirt-dwelling rodent and swiped the lips clean. He seemed eager for more. Bronson gave him two more, then waved an index finger to indicate they would have to share. Finally, Bronson's handheld lit up with a message.

INTERESTING, the reply came over an hour later. WILL REROUTE THE BLOOD DROP.

TELL MINISTER LOVE I FOUND JESUS.

MINISTER LOVE DIED TWO MONTHS AGO, was the response. HE WAS FOUND STABBED IN THE HEART.

After staring at that for some time, Bronson texted, TELL ELOI RINEHART.

MISTER RINEHART HAS OTHER ISSUES TO DEAL WITH. HE IS OFF THE PROJECT.

WHAT ISSUES? Bronson asked, his fingers dancing on the small keyboard.

THE WORLD'S GOTTEN CRAZY SINCE YOU LEFT.

HOW?

There was no response, which became the norm. After this exchange, the few answers he got were sometimes confusing with gaps in transmission. Sometimes they were garbled or addressed things he hadn't sent.

As for the route back to the ship, Bronson found it tough going, heading due south. There was a dust storm and a constant chatter from Jesus in some language that sounded like he was mixing batter in his mouth. Though Jesus had enough strength to hold onto the handlebars, it was added weight and there were balancing issues. Plus, he hadn't gotten over his tendency to bite as he perched on the crossbar and a couple of times drew blood. Slapped, he would look repentant and grumble what seemed to be apologies.

Luckily, Bronson had no problem finding the blood, coming across the small, sky-dropped box with its pulsating signal. There were twelve packets of blood. Bronson and Jesus split them.

That night, after Bronson had texted that he had received the blood, there came a strange reply from Earth, LOOKS LIKE YOU'LL HAVE PLENTY OF BLOOD IF YOU GET BACK HERE.

WTF? Bronson texted back but got no answer.

That night he woke from his rest, which wasn't sleep as much as a kind of shut-eyed meditation, a wordless fusion with the abundant stars, to find that Jesus wasn't beside him. Bronson crawled out of the sleeping bag—vampire or no, he'd never gotten used to the Martian chill—and found him eventually, fifty yards from the campsite, just looking at the stars. Although Bronson couldn't say, he thought that Jesus was looking at Earth. Bronson tugged at his arm and guided him back to where they slept. Jesus didn't sleep much, Bronson gathered, probably because he'd been doing a lot of it for years.

JESUS WALKS, Bronson texted the next day.

No reply came, none all day, though Bronson hit send several times.

"What do you think is going on?" Bronson asked Jesus who now rode on the handlebars, having enough blood and strength to balance himself. Since Bronson's view was partially blocked, Jesus pointed the way at times, avoiding the Martian stones. "I get the impression things aren't going well on Earth."

Jesus nodded, as if he knew this already. It was shortly thereafter Jesus pointed too late and they hit a rock. They tumbled, unhurt, but the bicycle had already gone almost 1,500 miles over rough terrain and the Martian dust had clogged every joint regardless of how Bronson tried to clean. The rock retired the bike, the impact bending its front wheel. It was easier to abandon and walk.

They texted this to Earth but got no response for days, and then the only message was OK, though Bronson didn't know what that was in response to. He almost didn't care. Fifty miles from his spaceship he grew weary. The last blood drop didn't help much. There were only five packets; two had burst open on impact with Mars. Bronson sipped two, Jesus three.

They moved on. His feet dragged, he stumbled. By this time, Jesus was carrying Bronson's backpack and then Bronson, holding him upright.

With twenty miles to go, Bronson couldn't continue. "Maybe it's the solar radiation," he said, and Jesus nodded, as he'd learned to do. Bronson didn't know if he understood. He lay down in the shade of a large boulder, once hurled across an infinity of space to crash here and to provide a lee against the Martian wind that kicked up a blanket of dust.

"I can't go on," Bronson said.

"I understand," Jesus said, his first words in English.

The last thing Bronson remembered, just before he closed his eyes, was the face of Jesus approaching, his mouth wide open and two pale fangs sprouting as he neared Bronson's neck.

Jesus walked away, watching the body decompose. Ashes to ashes, he thought, having absorbed at last Bronson's English. The storm had gone and he walked, his pace quicker now that he didn't have to support the human.

He made it to the spaceship in two days and drank all but the last packet of blood they'd kept with the ship. That last one would revive him as he neared Earth. He'd absorbed enough of Bronson's limited technical expertise to know what to do, how to restart the ship's dormant systems and contact Earth.

WE'LL STAY WITH YOU AS LONG AS WE CAN, Houston texted. THINGS ARE ALL SHOT TO SHIT DOWN HERE.

I WILL SORT THINGS OUT, Jesus texted back. His features, in the single mirror inside the ship's cabin, showed the ravaged features of Bronson Parker. But inside it was Jesus, his ticket punched for Earth. An hour later, he blasted off and hurtled toward the glittering firmament. His time was coming.

Ad Infinitum

by Carson Winter

The sun is setting—again.

I feel it eclipse the horizon. The dust in my veins begins to churn, dampening and slowly sloshing like some sort of hemoglobic mud. The sludge stretches its warm tendrils through my body, touching my muscles and organs and what's left of my mind and then:

I am alive.

My eyes creak. My neck and spine feel as if they've been fused into a solid column of jointless bone. With a little shifting and *crack—crack—crack*, it gives enough that I can move. Against all odds, natural and unnatural, I am born again.

Confusion, hate, and hunger—they come in sequence. As details accrue and my consciousness rebuilds, I shake my arms and hear the chains rattle. My body is a 'T,' metal cufflinks digging into the flesh of my wrists, pulling my limbs outward. I've hung dead on these chains since sunrise—I know it, somehow—and I have little doubt that at this point the metal has notched into my bone.

I wrestle with the chains and the jangling of metal echoes around the room. It sets off a series of creaks, then footsteps, then hushed exclamations that I can hear through the floor.

That's right, I remember, *this is the attic*. The ceiling is the same upside-down 'V' of a camping tent. The windows are covered in taped-down black garbage bags. I know it's night because my body tells me so.

Voices drift up through the floorboards. I stop struggling long enough to listen. A woman, a young girl, and a man are speaking.

The man speaks in a low, bassy tone. Measured, as if his thoughts have been dictated then read aloud. He's dominating the exchange, his voice resonating in the walls.

The man says, in a sort of fatherly way, "It is really about time to move on, wouldn't you say?"

I make out the words, "It's complicated," but then the rest is a mish-mash of frantic syllables and pauses, choked with tears and whispers. This is the woman speaking.

The man says, "Perhaps we can all meet together sometime, yes?"

Her response is inaudible.

The man says again, "Tomorrow, dear?"

Mumbling.

"I think if you both looked inside yourselves, at this very moment, you'd understand that there is only one solution to a problem such as this. The most natural one."

I hear fleeting, doe-like trots that must have come from the girl, who has so far remained quiet. The woman shouts for her to come back. The response is a slamming door.

The woman pleads, "We can talk about it, sweetheart!"

The girl doesn't respond.

"It's only natural for her to be upset, you know," says the man.

"I know, I know," says the woman.

"And our private sessions are going very well."

I hear the woman's response—fatigued, fightless. "She says she hates them."

"That's rather common. But she's breaking new ground."

Whatever she says is too quiet for me to hear.

"The sessions should continue indefinitely for now, as long as the father is still in the picture and for a while afterward, I presume. It is a very tough time. I have some specialist friends that can help too, of course, free of charge."

"Thank you, for everything," she says.

"Glass of wine?"

"A tall glass."

I feel the metal cuffs shear into my bone as they talk quietly below me. I can hear the man comforting the woman about the upset girl, telling her it'll be all right—that one of the most beautiful things in the whole natural world is a family unit.

I stare at the cuffs. *I hurt*, I find myself thinking, again and again and again.

There is no blood dripping from my wrists, they are bruised and caked with black organic matter. I clench my teeth and feel my gums split bloodlessly.

One pair of footsteps follows the other and I listen to them creak and breathe. The house is silent for an excruciating hour, then a pair of heavy footsteps start up again. It is the man, I assume, and I hear him open and close doors that sound like gunshots in the quiet house. Then the spray of urine disturbing placid waters, and the eventual glugging whirlpool of an activated toilet.

He makes his way around the house once more, each foot resonating like the plodding stomps of a giant, and then, finally, I hear him fumble with the lock to the front door. It closes with a definitive crack, another gunshot to cull the silence.

I think about counting the minutes to take my mind off the aching blackness inside me, the pain in my wrists. I've forgotten why I'm here, I realize. So I count the seconds in the minutes. Then I count the minutes in the hours. It's been two hours and thirty-six minutes when I hear footsteps again. They're soft and lilting, tentative. *Trying* to be soft and lilting, tentative. They move with the stumbling purpose of intent beyond means, then stop at the door that separates me from the rest of the house.

I hear the doorknob click its locking mechanism. The door lets out a loud and continuous whine as it grinds on its hinges. The hallway is dark, but I can make out light from what must be the moon. It's silvery-white and draped across the shoulders of a very young girl, and I become so excited that I start forward—*to run, to touch the rays and*—then the chains pull tight and hold me back.

The girl steps forward. She's blonde with straight hair, wearing a blue bathrobe with an embroidered flower on the left breast. I have to guess she is no more than nine years old. She calls out to me.

"Daddy?"

"Hello sweetie," I coo. *Of course, she's my daughter.*

She takes another step forward. She looks like she's about to cry. "Are you okay up here?"

I turn my head to my wrists and grimace. "These chains really hurt."

"I'm sorry, Daddy." She starts to cry on the last word. The hot life pumping through her is torturous, *if only I could —*

I tell her it's okay and that I understand.

"Mom misses you a lot."

"I miss her a lot, too."

She wipes a tear from her cheek and takes another step forward, just barely out of reach. "I want it to be like it used to be."

"Me too, baby, me too." I'm thinking about how she'd look without skin on her face. "Maybe Mommy and I can talk sometime and figure things out."

She starts to cry some more and the room feels deliciously warm. I want her to take another step forward.

"I don't like Dr. Truss," she says.

I'm practically begging. "I'd love us to be together again."

"I don't want to go to any more sessions, Daddy. I want *you*."

"It's okay, it's okay," I say. "Come closer, baby girl."

Her body goes rigid. "Mommy says I shouldn't go near you." She takes a step back and wipes a tear from her eye. "She says you're sick. That you're not Daddy anymore."

"She's probably just trying to make it easier on you," I say as her warmth becomes faint.

She's fidgety now, scared. I can see it, but I don't understand it. I don't know what I said. I can't remember where I went too far. She takes another step back. "I should go back to bed. Maybe you and Mommy can talk, y'know? That's all I really wanted to say, that and I miss you."

"I think we'll be able to work it out."

The girl smiles and puts her hand on the attic door. I think of fighting my restraints but it'd be useless. She yawns. "I hope so, Daddy."

"Sweet dreams, baby girl." The words are muscle memory. After a couple minutes, the exchange is an eternity ago and I almost forget it entirely. I'm thinking of the approximately five-thousand seconds between the present and my recurrent death.

The sun sets and I am alive.

Some chasm yawns inside me and I'm once again in pain, once again hungry, once again aware.

A woman is standing at the door, practically hugging it. She has brown hair and a thin, ghostly build. A blood vessel in her right eye has burst, a red supernova exploding against her sclera. I'm pulling against my restraints.

"How are you, Ruben?" She chokes on the words, then looks away. She's crying. "Are you well?"

The words come with the manufacturing whirr of machinery. "I'm doing great," I say, and I say so earnestly. There's nothing bitter in my words. "I miss you so much, darling."

She recoils. She's flat against the door, hand reaching for the handle.

"I didn't know what to do, honey," she says, apologizing.

"Oh, I know." I smile a little, comfortingly. "It was a difficult decision."

My wife, I remember. And then I remember the girl from *was it yesterday? A week? A year?*

I continue: "I don't think Winnie is handling the change very well."

She shakes her head in agreement. "Did she come in and talk to you last night?"

I can't quite remember so I shrug and smile. The chains clank and rattle.

"I don't want her coming up here to see you, not anymore." She jumps across the words like a frog crossing a bridge of lily pads.

I'm so hungry.

"Of course," I say. "She's just a little girl, after all. It's difficult for her to understand any of this."

The woman stands up a little straighter and steps toward me. Her voice is stronger now. "I think it might be time for your funeral, honey." I have no response, no recognition of the phrase to react to, instead I stare at her placidly and let her continue. "Dr. Truss has been helping me cope. I love you, Ruben, oh God, I love you so much. But, it's not right for our daughter to grow up like this. I wanted to believe we could make it work and still be a family, but I really don't think we can—not with you, like *this*."

The screaming blackness crawls up my throat and all I can say is what I think she wants me to say: *Of course, darling. Do what you think is best.* I get half of it right. I smile—that sweet, contented smile that tells a loved one you trust them, but all I can say is, "I'm so very hungry."

I open my mouth and try to taste the room, hoping that some of the blood from her eye is airborne. I pull against my chains trying to get closer to it, licking the air and clinking my teeth together. I taste nothing and she leaves the room, running.

Once again, I am left with the sounds of the house.

Walking, talking. Stomping, yelling. The woman and the girl are arguing. They are upset over something, but I'm not sure what. My wrists are flaky with decay and I think about that for a second, or maybe a couple hours—long enough that the noises subside into quiet snuffling, then eventually silence. The pain dulls in my hands and I'm left considering the cramps in my stomach when the door opens.

"Daddy?"

The girl.

"Hello, darling," I say. She quivers at my greeting.

"I'm afraid."

"What are you afraid of, baby girl?"

"I'm afraid Mommy's going to get rid of you."

"Why would she do that?"

"Dr. Truss told her it was time to move on," she says slowly, then as if for balance, the next words come much too fast—a rambling of sentences that close in and swallow each other like a loud and confused ouroboros. I retain snippets.

"Always be a part of our family—"

"Scared—"

"Mommy's sad—"

"Like it was before—"

But the words are just noises. I can't focus with the percussion of her beating heart.

"Do you know where the keys are, sweetie?" I ask, gently rattling my chains.

"Dr. Truss gave them to me. He says we're building trust." The tears are still on her cheeks, but she smiles and pulls a single brass key out of her deep robe pockets. "Do you promise to be good, Daddy?"

I nod slowly, staring at the key.

Each step she takes jogs my memory a little. I have to stay focused or I'll lose myself entirely in the eons between her footfalls. But, as long as it feels, I know it's only a moment until she's turning the key on my right-hand cuff. *My daughter.* She looks up at me and pats my rotting wrist.

So hungry. I'm trying to be good for a little longer, long enough for her to free me.

For just a second, I remember her birth.

I lose my train of thought and realize the pain in my wrists has diminished. Stretch. Stretch. Nothing. It doesn't matter. Muscle memory.

She looks up at me expectantly, like *now what?*

My hands are on her throat.

I'm using my entire body to push her to the ground, it's easy—she's not very strong. My hand is over her mouth. Her screams come out muffled. She tries to bite my palm but it doesn't even hurt. I turn her head and tear a long strip of flesh off her neck with my teeth. She's running out of breath from screaming. I widen her wound by the mouthful. Soon, I'm drinking from a pooling cavern. She shakes a little bit and the blood stops pumping but I pay it no mind. I lift her small body and spin the wound so any remaining drops can fall on my tongue. I toss her body to the side when I'm done, because it is as useless as chains and locks that aren't on my wrists, or a death I can't remember.

There are other people in the house, so I look for them. I leave the attic and traipse down the stairs. Hunting, I suppose. I'm vaguely aware of myself being in the pictures on the wall. It seems natural in a way I can't articulate.

I hear breathing and rustling from behind a door. I creep up to it and push in just a little.

The woman is sleeping. She is alone. She didn't hear me kill the girl. This is good.

I don't care if she screams.

She wakes up and sees me standing over her. I lick the blood of *our daughter* (I remember) covering the lower half of my face. She springs out of bed, but I grab a fistful of her hair and yank her back, then when she's standing, I throw her against the wall. I think I hear something crack.

"Where's Winnie?" she asks. It's as good as goodbye.

I don't know the answer. I tear her open. Another ragged opening of loose wires and foundation, all painted in the whites, pinks, and reds of life. Shuddering, convulsing, crying—I'm slightly crouched, almost hugging her as I lap up the cascading blood. She twists and pushes against me, weaker and weaker while I swallow her blood in fat gulps. When I'm done she falls to the floor.

Then, I stand there. For a minute, or an hour, lost in time with an undefined purpose. I am not hungry.

A high pitched creaking brings me back to seeing through my own eyes. The noise prods the ground meat that floats in my skull—the part that makes me a predator.

The man is smiling. He's older than me, older than the woman. He wears a salt and pepper Van Dyke, black-framed glasses, and a grey suit. I want to lunge toward him and shred his soft, soft skin.

But I can't.

There's a string of white, foul-smelling bulbs around his neck and it keeps me standing by the dead woman.

"How are you doing tonight, Ruben?" he asks.

"Very good." I am casual. Personable.

"Wonderful," he says. "I see you got your fill of the household this evening." He laughs a big-bellied laugh and then waits for me to respond.

"I was very hungry."

"I bet, yes, I bet. Do you know who I am?"

"No."

"Well, I'm Dr. Truss. And I know who you are, Ruben. I used to talk to your wife—quite a bit, actually. I'm a marriage and family counselor."

"Nice to meet you," I say. I wish I could move.

"Likewise, although I *have* seen you before. But, alas, it was daylight hours and you could scarcely be expected to recall that."

"Oh yes, I'm terrible with faces, I'm afraid," I then point to the bloodied husk of my wife. "She was always the more social of us."

"She wouldn't know about it either, Ruben. She told me a lot about you, what you two were going through, but I took the liberty to check in on you without her permission. I hope you don't mind."

"No, of course not." I smile.

"That's when Izzy and I stopped being on the same page, unfortunately. I wear two hats. I'm not only a counselor; I am also a hobbyist. Luckily, there is *some* crossover."

"Very interesting," I say.

"Yes, indeed."

And we are both quiet for a very long time.

My mind wanders off to different worlds and times and when the sunlight finally comes, everything goes black.

When I awake, I'm in chains again.

I'm very hungry.

Oh yes, the attic.

But, no. Not quite.

Drywall has been erected, painted. There is a table with coffee and a newspaper. An eggshell blue refrigerator stands against one of the walls, connected to a counter that bleeds into a sink that bleeds into an oven. The ceiling is the same upside-down 'V.'

A girl is beside me, her throat torn open, the blood drenching the bathrobe she's wearing. She's in chains. She pulls on them loosely, but they are too heavy for her. She looks at me for a moment but then sees that I am the same as her. There's a woman too, similarly gored, and she's piercing her lips with her incisors. She is also chained.

Before long, there are others in the room.

They are looking at us. Smiling at us with intense interest. An older woman, in cat-eye glasses and a floral-print dress, gets close enough to the woman to see her teeth, then backs away with a laugh and a quick and theatrical fanning. "*Très fantastique*, Doctor, *très fantastique*."

Dr. Truss appears behind her and puts his hand on her back. He's wearing the smile of a good host with the suit to match. "Marvelous, isn't it? Be careful though," he warns, "or, you may very well join the family."

They both chuckle and then he snaps to a young boy. The boy is dressed in a suit and tails and is holding a silver platter. "Hors d'oeuvres, sir?"

"Yes, please," says Dr. Truss, handing a tiny sandwich to the woman called Marilyn. "And then the cocktails, please."

The girl in chains beside me says, "I am so very hungry."

Dr. Truss and the others begin to laugh. The girl looks at them blankly. Then the woman says, to Dr. Truss, "Could you come a little closer, I think you have something on your lapel."

The doctor chuckles and then turns to explain something into the ear of one of his cohorts.

"Remarkable," I hear him say.

A violin quartet enters the room and begins to play something full of staggering rhythms and dissonant harmonies. The guests sway and raise cocktails to names I can't pronounce or remember. They roll off the tongue and onto the floor like a body we can't touch.

A man in a gray business suit approaches me like a fellow wallflower at the outermost circles of an office party. He holds out a pocket mirror and I look at myself for a moment. I'm pale and covered in flaky dried blood. My eyes are bloodshot. I'm pretty sure I'm rotting. He shrugs and then walks off, as if I told him with a glance all he needed to know.

The party goes on into the night.

"Dr. Truss says that maybe next week, we'll bring guests," someone says.

"But where will he find them?"

The other flaps his wrists at the question. "I'm sure the Doctor is more than capable."

As I feel the aching in my body grow, from hunger, from hate—I also feel the night begin to wane.

Dr. Truss does too. "Everyone now, gather round, gather round," he says. "This is but the first night of our new order, so let's do our best to stay on topic." The murmurs of the crowd dissipate and the violins stop their shrieking. "Until now, we were blind acolytes. We fumbled our way through rituals without history. Now, we are the first explorers of the infinite, armed with an eternal ritual for our hungry Gods—an entire bloodline set to die again and again," he savors every word. "We are very lucky."

There is a round of applause.

Daylight is coming and I am very hungry.

And we die.

Again;

Again;

Again;

Ad infinitum.

Sacrifice

by Geri Meyers

The creature stirred in the dark depths of its pool, the stagnant water oozing away as it rose to the surface. It sensed movement, a shiver, barely perceptible as the feeling passed from the moss coating the rocky floor of the cave to the murky water rippling against it. The pool was fed from tiny fissures deep within, exchanging warm water with cool and keeping it a pit of growth that soothed the creature—a comforting embrace.

But the sound... footsteps. Footsteps meant prey.

The creature raised itself just high enough to see over the lip of the pool's edge. A dark figure approached hesitantly, dimly lit by the phosphorescence of the cave's growths and the hints of afternoon sunbeams trickling in from outside. The light made a faint, almost prismatic halo around the intruder, glistening in gossamer wings and shining off silky black locks.

Fae. It *loved* fae.

Licking sludge from its lips, it oozed closer through the thick water, sliding clawed hands around the rocky

91

outcropping and scratching at the moss to find enough purchase to drag itself up. Water and muck dripped from its nearly fleshless body, its stick-like arms and legs, the spiny protrusions along its back, and its matted and stringy hair as it came to stand at the edge of the pool.

The fae froze, fighting back a gasp, pressing a hand to its mouth. A delightful sound that stirred the hunger nestled inside the creature, raising it from a dull throb to a gnawing scrape of need ravaging its insides. Drool dripped from its lips as it bared its fangs, and it tensed its muscles to chase the fae should it flee. But it didn't; it stood its ground despite the tremor in its limbs and the rolling of its panicked eyes.

This gave the creature pause, and it battered back its instincts to lunge at the fae. It shifted from foot to foot, weaving its spindly body, scenting the air and tasting it with its long tongue. Fear like sweet syrup; bravado like tart fruit; and... The creature stepped closer to the fae, its tongue darting across the delicate thing's face as it held still then slowly lifted its arms out to its sides in offering. The fae tasted like berries—sweet, tangy, sharp... so very right, and so very wrong.

Something inside the creature screamed a warning, some half-faded memory calling out in denial, but its hunger overrode the warning and it grasped the fae, dragging it close. The fae's bravado melted away as the creature's claws drew blood where they dug in, and the fae's struggles worsened the wounds. Iron and sweetness filled the creature's nostrils and it sank its fangs into the fae's shoulder, tearing at flesh and shivering in ecstasy as the taste of fae blood filled its mouth with sweet bliss and tangy delight.

The fae screamed in pain—only exciting the creature further—but the sound trailed off in soft laugher. Fingers caressed the creature's slime slick face, then pressed against its forehead, all the warning the creature had before magic flooded its mind, invading it with images and feelings, flashes of faces, light and darkness, pain, fear, grief... love. It let out its own blood-curdling screech as bright light then blackness closed over its vision, replaced by images—memories not its own.

He stood on the mossy, rock-strewn bank, shadowed by the overhang of branches that stretched out across the Heart River. Light reflected off the glittering run of water, burning his eyes, but it was a pain he welcomed. He could pretend it was the sting of light causing tears to trickle down his cheeks instead of the grief that gripped his heart in a vice.

This would be the last time he saw the river. The last time he saw the sunlight, the trees. He would never again see his friends and family... He drew a shaky breath, wiping the tears from his eyes.

His pocket was heavy with the weight of the clay vial he'd secured there, and he drew it out to stare at it. It was painted with swirls of green and purple: the color of his eyes, the color of his sister's. The color of the butterfly wings stretching from their backs, matching each other's like a mirrored image. She'd been the one to press it into his hands that morning, her grief staining her cheeks to match his own.

"Do you truly mean to do this?" she had asked, choked by her pain. "Phian, this is too great a sacrifice. There must be another way."

"We have tried everything," he had said to her. "And still the fae lose their lives to this creature. We are not fighters, and our magic can't protect us. If I do this"—he held up the vial—"I will save the rest of us. Miahl, you lost your son. He was the first victim... I... I should not have waited so long."

He'd left her, then. She'd known as he did that they had no other choice. They had little idea of what the creature was. Miahl's son had been the first to go missing and they had found no trace of him. The first few days after his disappearance, they all believed he had become lost in the forest or run away. But then others started disappearing, and... they'd found remains. Covered in the slime of stagnant water, stinking like the distant swamplands, they'd found bones stripped of flesh and scored with fang marks. Fae that he'd known—friends, family, *children*...

He pulled the stopper from the vial and brought it to his nose, breathing in the scent. A wrongness emanated from within it, a stench that stung his nose, and he recoiled from it. He wiped tears from his eyes. It was the strongest poison his people knew of, from a plump red berry that choked the forest and lured many unwitting children, a berry he'd known to avoid since he was old enough to walk. Everything inside him said to throw the vial as far from himself as he could manage, to turn back, to find his sister and apologize for being unable to go through with his mission. But instead he firmed his resolve. He did this for his nephew, his friends, his family, all the people he loved and cared for. He sacrificed his life for them.

He brought the vial to his lips. He had lingered long enough. He longed to sit on the bank of the river all afternoon, to watch the sun set and the stars show themselves, but the longer he waited, the longer he watched the water and enjoyed the sunlight on his skin... the greater the chance another of his people would be taken. It was time. He drank it down as quickly as he could manage and coughed as his body refused it. Sinking to his knees, he fought to keep it down, his stomach twisting and turning in rejection. He pressed his hand to his mouth, his wings trembling behind him as he struggled.

Time seemed to stretch and shrink, his vision swaying, a sweat breaking out across his skin. The poison killed slowly, but once taken, there was no cure. He had time to make his way to the cave they suspected the monster lived in. He prayed to the Mother that they were right and pushed himself to his feet.

He looked at the river a final time, then began his slow trek toward the cave. His plan was simple. He would feed his poisoned body to the monster, and his poisoned flesh would take its life as well. He would be the last of his people to die.

The creature stirred, foreign memories fading as the taste of sour berries and iron on its tongue and gut-wrenching pain drove it to consciousness. It could smell the sweetness of the fae's blood, could hear the other's ragged breathing, could feel the ooze of its pool drying on its skin. Each sensation grated against its nerves, dragging a whimper from its lips.

Beside it, the fae stirred, its limbs contracting in twisted cramps and spasms, its forehead glistening with sweat as it gasped and panted in pain. Agony. New memories —old memories—drifted through the creature's mind, tugging at it, demanding attention but as elusive as clouds in the sky. It knew that agony. It knew the tangy berry taste on its lips. It knew... it knew sacrifice.

Grief tightened its chest, choking it, and its vision was near black with horror. It knew sacrifice.

It was sacrifice.

Anviel lay dying. Arms bruised, wings torn, lips bloody and stained with poisoned berries. His limbs contracted in spasms that pulled at the bindings securing him to the ground of the filthy, fetid cave. Fury filled him with hate as he replayed in his mind what had brought him to this moment:

His own cries as they gripped his arms, forcing him to his knees. "Please," he had begged softly, "don't do this..."

"Your sacrifice will save us all," they had said. As if that mattered.

His stomach had turned as they forced a paste of poisoned berries past his lips. He'd choked and spit, he'd vomited and sobbed, but they had continued until he was broken and near unresponsive, unable even to beg further.

"You are a healer," they had said. "Your sacrifice will save us from the corruption of our land. Your magic will seep into the ground with your death. It will purify our land. Give in. Heal it, heal us, save your people!"

But inside he'd broken. His sacrifice wasn't willing; it was bitter and full of betrayal.

They had left him to die, trusting that the magic of his body would draw the poison from their land, from the plants, from the food they ate and the animals around them.

The poison worked through his system. He barely had the strength to cry, but he could think, he could hate, he could remember the faces of those he had loved who had stood aside as he was dragged from his home, from his bed, to this foul, moss-choked cave in the depths of the forest. He would draw the poison from the land, draw it to him—he would use it to heal himself. He would seek revenge.

With a last sob, he let his magic spread through the land, drawing the corruption and poison into himself, infusing his being, feeling it corrupt and change him until he knew not who he was anymore. He took all that he could reach, but for the berries.

He left the berries.

The creature had slept for such a long time. It woke on occasion, but sleep muddied its memories until all it knew was hunger and the murk of its cave. It ate, it slept, it woke and ate again. It remembered nothing of its past, knew no hopes for the future. It was a monster, and it hungered. It hungered most of all for fae.

It—no, he, and he was no creature—pushed himself to sit upright, his clawed hands digging jagged gouges in the moss-covered rocks. Anviel would see no others suffer as he had, would see no others lose their lives for the good of others. Anger burned in him as he drew power from deep within himself, fighting through the slog of murk and rancid, poisoned magic he'd wrapped around himself like a blanket over centuries of passing time. His anger gave him the strength to fight through, and when he touched the core of his being, hidden deep inside him, pure and untainted magic answered his call.

It came slowly at first, and he coaxed it through the layers of corruption that had woven their way through his soul. He gathered it, using it to draw the poison from himself. As he did, he felt his teeth and claws shrinking, felt muck and grime slough from his skin. Filth dripped from him, expelled from within his body in rivulets that formed puddles in the moss he lay on. Wings unfurled from his back, shimmering with fae dust, reflecting the phosphorescence of the cave in silvers, whites, and pinks. His skin shed green scales, revealing new growth beneath. The poison oozed from him and he regained his true form—his fae form—and with it, his power grew.

Anviel crawled to the side of the other fae, his chest filled with a different sort of pain as he saw the other's limbs tremble against muscles too stiff to move and heard him whimper softly. He remembered what it felt like to lay helpless on the cave's floor, twisted in pain. To have no hope. He couldn't change his past, but he could change this fae's future.

He pressed a hand to the fae's forehead, another to the other's chest, and released a flood of healing magic. He drove out the poison and knitted together the fae's flesh where he—no, the creature—had clawed and bitten him. The fae's contracted muscles loosened, and purple and green eyes fluttered open, meeting his own.

The Cannibals of Ice-Sky-Warm-Ocean

by Joel Donato Ching Jacob

The creature expressed their name to the Earther by creating prickles on the skin that covered their bell-body and shifting their chromatophores to a bright purple-pink. Prickly-Skin-Magenta wanted to tell the Earther that their family members were cannibals. Undulating-Blues, by far the richest Europan, suggested that Prickly-Skin-Magenta might expect a reward if they informed the Earthers.

But the Earther, covered in insulated protective gear, did not attempt to understand the native of Europa. Instead, the Earther took a pouch from her diplomacy fanny pack, removed the plastic from a chocolate-covered nougat bar, and gave it to the Europan.

They didn't even have to do anything and they were already rewarded! Prickly-Skin-Magenta hadn't yet alerted them to the prohibited activities happening in their home at that very moment. There must have been something wrong with the communications equipment the Earther had.

Certainly, they wouldn't use it only at their convenience, Prickly-Skin-Magenta thought. They came to Europa under the banner of democracy. Undulating-Blues taught the young Europans all about democracy in school. It wouldn't be democratic.

Still, Prickly-Skin-Magenta couldn't keep themselves from feeling dejected. They jetted away from the Earther and headed to the undersea canyon where their family lived. They balanced the urgency of masticating the chocolate bar before they got home with the attempt to enjoy the Earth treat. The Earthers loved these things named after the planet they were terraforming. It was tacky and sweet, and there was faint bitterness for contrast and fragrance, but the delight the Earthers had for it Prickly-Skin-Magenta could not find.

Prickly-Skin-Magenta arrived to the consternation of their parent, Banded-Smooth-Rough-Pink. They had been waiting for their child as the cycles brought them closer to the day they would have to eat their own dying parent.

Banded-Smooth-Rough-Pink conveyed their worry and frustration with flashes of changing skin tones and colors, along with instructions to feed Prickly-Skin-Magenta's grandparent.

Flashes-Between-Blue-and-Purple had been placed another arms-length closer to the volcanic vent as the moment of their passing approached.

Prickly-Skin-Magenta was to carry sulfur berries for Flashes-Between-Blue-and-Purple. It was getting harder to find the beady algae as the ice layers above the warm sea thinned and the radiation of Jupiter affected the growth of many of the multicellular lifeforms in the oceans of Europa. Prickly-Skin-Magenta had insisted on disposing of Flashes-Between-Blue-and-Purple's corpse as the Earthers had advised. It would not only be more sanitary but easier. The Earthers had invested in crematoriums to prevent the spread of disease through ecological waste such as corpses. But Flashes-Between-Blue-and-Purple insisted on the tradition even though it had been made illegal after Europa was annexed by Earth.

Prickly-Skin-Magenta endured the heat of the volcanic vent. They tried to divert their attention from the input of the eyes that faced Flashes-Between-Blue-and-Purple where they lay dying.

The Earthers had stories they read in school, as Prickly-Skin-Magenta studied the Earth language they could not express by sound but by arranging chromatophores into letters. Prickly-Skin-Magenta wished they had paid better attention to class. They might have been able to communicate with the Earther that way. It bothered them that death was such a horrible thing to the Earthers, but it seemed so mundane to Flashes-Between-Blue-and-Purple and Banded-Smooth-Rough-Pink. Prickly-Skin-Magenta was infuriated that they were so primitive and ignorant that the concept of mortality evaded them. Someone was dying, yet they celebrated.

But when Prickly-Skin-Magenta handed the berries to Flashes-Between-Blue-and-Purple, the contact between them was enough to convey a brief flash of the hope and pride of a grandparent for a grandchild. Prickly-Skin-Magenta felt bad that their family had to be so backward... so primitive... as savage as when the Earthers first arrived in Europa.

Later that cycle, Flashes-Between-Blue-and-Purple died peacefully. Their body was prepared for community sharing, the process hushed and secretive under an observant Earth.

Prickly-Skin-Magenta reached out with apprehensive tube feet for the piece of Flashes-Between-Blue-and-Purple offered by Banded-Smooth-Rough-Pink. Teacher Undulating-Blues said it was diseased, that eating Europans was prohibited for public safety as much as it was for the respect of sentient life. Undulating-Blues freely shared their Earth-given knowledge and prosperity by building an Earth-based educational institution. Surely they knew what was best, Prickly-Skin-Magenta surmised.

But if Prickly-Skin-Magenta wanted to steal away and try to alert the Earthers of this prohibited activity, they needed to convince their parent that there was nothing amiss. Prickly-Skin-Magenta speculated that the Earthers carried other treats in that fanny pack as they set aside the idea of alerting Undulating-Blues first.

When Flashes-Between-Blue-and-Purple's volcanic-vent-cooked flesh entered Prickly-Skin-Magenta's orifice, they tried their best to juggle the bit in their oral cavity to keep it away from their masticating and tasting surfaces, but it could not be helped. First the juices, then eventually the meat, lingered on their taste buds longer than they intended. The texture on the masticating surfaces brought out the bitterness from the berries that Flashes-Between-Blue-and-Purple had been fed over the last few Jovian cycles to purge them of toxins and pathogens. Mixing with the salt in the sea, it bitterness elevated the sweetness of the flesh as Flashes-Between-Blue-and-Purple's nervous system fluids mingled with Prickly-Skin-Magenta's nervous system through their taste receptors.

Experiences and memories flashed from grandparent to grandchild—how Europa had always been Ice-Sky-Warm-Ocean. Only then did Prickly-Skin-Magenta realize that democracy and civilization were not gifts from the Earthers.

They did not come with jobs—they came only to take the Ice Sky even as they took the iron of Io to increase the mass of Mars. Water for oceans, iron for a magnetosphere, and weight for an atmosphere to make the red planet as blue and green as earth once was.

Earthers burst into the Europans' home and called out to Prickly-Skin-Magenta's family to stop what they were doing. Prickly-Skin-Magenta was confused and wondered if Undulating-Blues had claimed the reward for reporting them, instead.

But Prickly-Skin-Magenta was entranced by their meal.

Flashes-between-Blue-and-Purple had been a fighter for freedom and died from injuries they had sustained trying to liberate Ice-Sky-Warm-Ocean from the Earthers. Their spirit suffused the fibers of their meat with resistance but also yielded to mastication to give succulence and nourishment, like the gift of life from ancestor to heir.

It became clear to Prickly-Skin-Magenta that it had not been their people that were ignorant. The Earthers could not accept realities other than theirs. They were not ignorant for lack of access. They traversed the solar system with the urgency of homelessness. They were willfully ignorant because accepting the truth of their colonies would require compassion a colonizer couldn't afford. Prickly-Skin-Magenta's nervous fluids boiled and seethed with anger. First at the Earthers, but eventually, at themself. They might not have had the opportunity to betray their race, but they were a traitor in their aspirations.

Prickly-Skin-Magenta then knew that the imposition of Earther morality upon the natives of Ice-Sky-Warm-Ocean was as much theft as the Earthers harvesting the Ice Sky in exchange for frivolous Earther excesses.

Resolve grew within Prickly-Skin-Magenta where there had once been only complacency. They were the cannibals of Ice-Sky-Warm-Ocean.

The other cannibals had surrendered to the Earthers. They were being rounded together for cultural correction seminars. Prickly-Skin-Magenta recognized the Earther they had met earlier and pulsed their bell toward her.

Such fragile creatures, they need so much to survive in Ice-Sky-Warm-Ocean, Prickly-Skin-Magenta thought. But when they ripped the diplomacy pack from the Earther's hip along a portion of her protective gear, the warm water seeped into her suit faster than it could seal itself again. She froze in the warm water before she could drown.

The other cannibals saw what had just happened and reacted by jetting their soft bodies toward their Earther captors. They were soft and pliable. The Earther weapons pierced through the cannibals' bodies but their fluid nervous systems meant that they could function despite injury.

Prickly-Skin-Magenta spat out the sweet bribes in the diplomacy pack. Disgusting. They bit into the exposed flesh of the Earther. Earthers had a fibrous nervous system, an evolutionary flaw that made them more fragile than the cannibals of Ice-Sky-Warm-Ocean. But the transmission of synapses was similar enough that Prickly-Skin-Magenta was able to glean the nature of their plans. They were not here to spread technology or civilization. The planet they were evacuating to was a wasteland and they were transporting Ice-Sky-Warm-Ocean water like desperate vagabonds that could only offer sweet words as payment. They did not even speak the cannibals' language and expected the cannibals to compromise for their inadequacy.

More than their intent, Prickly-Skin-Magenta also became aware of the Earther's surface bases, the way they are built on the fragile ice. Amongst themselves, they were aware of the precariousness of building on something they were harvesting. Prickly-Skin-Magenta continued consuming the Earther's flesh even as chaos erupted about them, masticating with calcium and silicate lined muscles. Just a bit more of the nervous system and they would have enough information. This Earther was a biologist of some sort, and Prickly-Skin-Magenta learned of the fragility of Earthers. Prickly-Skin-Magenta could feed themself to the other cannibals and the knowledge would be shared by the whole community. Victory and liberty was within their reach. And just then, Prickly-Skin-Magenta chewed deep enough to reach the Earther's spinal cord.

The Harpy's Son
by Jessa Forest

"I will tell you a story," the half-harpy's mother crooned. Her voice flickered up through the gloom of the orphanage dormitory from the tiny flame glowing resolutely above the small beeswax stump masquerading as a candle on the rough stone windowsill.

"I will tell you how we fae were born."

The half-harpy's mother always began this way: always at midnight, always through the flickering singularity of a candle flame, and always with an allegory of the origin of their people. While the other fae children slept on small cots in long rows, drunk on sweet dreams and the Autumn Queen's sunset sherry, the only changeling among them would listen to his birth mother tell stories.

He had spindly little arms that always seemed to be curled around his knees and fingers that liked to twist and tangle into worried knots. His chest was narrow and spotted with grey down instead of fur or scales. His neck looked too long and slender to support his large head but the Queen herself assured him he would grow into it. She was a Queen and her word was Law but he couldn't help feeling self-conscious about it, especially when Rig, the self-proclaimed War Regent of the Dryads, threw sticks at him and called him a swan from the safety of her favorite tree. Bedraggled, downy wings jutted out from underneath his scapulas like fingers with the flesh rotting off. His human eyes stared out of hollow pits covered in pebbly skin; he had two little slits for nostrils and a sharply curving beak, pale as bone.

The harpy had brought him to the Autumn Queen when he was very small, when the war was almost over but the killing was not quite done. She had no idea what to do with a changeling and had no real care to teach herself, especially since she was on the losing side. It was the Autumn Queen herself who gave him a name, proclaiming him Here in Faery to all the world. The Queen became his real mother, as she was to all the orphans under her protection, while the harpy stole away into the shadows, not to be heard from again until the night of his tenth birthday when her voice magically appeared when he lit a candle at midnight.

One of the many tragedies of Here's existence was the nature of his mother. All black of feather and cruel of talon, the Harpy Olivia, thief, murderer, traitor, usurper. At first he thought the whole thing odd. Mothers who abandoned their children were not supposed to come back six years later and demand their undivided attention. But the stories were interesting and they were a part of him somehow. Besides, if he had to be the only changeling in Autumn's Kingdom, he might as well collect interesting things.

"We are made up of multitudes like the stars in the sky, like the links in the chain that pulls our barge down the river away from this life and into the next. We are what we are and nothing will keep us from ourselves."

"But the Queen says we are all the Heart of the Forest, one heart," Here would whisper to his candle. A low, languorous laugh thick as honey would always float like smoke from the smoldering wick.

"And how many different kinds of trees, vines, and thorny fiends grow in the forest?" Here's harpy mother would ask. "The thorny fiends grow so that no man or upstart Queen will step on their ground. They shield the surface roots of the Tall Knights with their strong, dark leaves and blades that cut mortal flesh to ribbons. Only the Heart of the Forest knows the secret pathways between their barricades, only the Heart can breathe their poisonous pollen and not die."

"Tell me more about dying," Here would say. And the flame would always ripple and the candle's wick would glow brighter. But then it would dim and make a sigh like a weary summer breeze or a disappointed mother.

"Dying is for soldiers and plague carriers," his mother would say. "You will never die."

"But you died," Here would whisper. He was always loath to mention her flaws, but if she were alive wouldn't he be with her and his father instead of the Autumn Queen's orphanage?

"I did not die," Here's mother would always reprimand him with the snap of flying sparks. It was like a ritual, his asking and her rebuke. "I left this forest because I have better things to do than look after obstinate children."

Here kept the pain in his heart to himself. "The sun would not burn without you," he would say, half with the flattery of a devoted son, half with the reverence the Queen taught him to reserve for those holy beings who walked with the Heart in all its aspects.

"Exactly," his mother would say, not buying any of his clumsy fawning. "Now, attend me while I tell the story of how I killed my sister."

Here would always attend his mother by sliding down into his small bed, into his self-made nest of threadbare blankets. His button-black eyes would never leave the flickering flame.

"My sister," his mother would always pause dramatically, "loved a storm she was not worthy of."

In the quiet of his own head, Here would always ask, *But who was worthy of the storm, Mama?* He never asked it out loud.

"She loved a storm she was not worthy of and I—yes, I, sweet child—was tired of it! She loved a storm who rolled and crashed atop the Heart's Forest and swept the moon away with great plumes of thunder. She loved a storm who filled the entirety of the sky with lightning when angry and the most wondrous thermals a harpy could ever hope for when happy. Truly, sweet one, that storm was the most beautiful creature in all of creation."

Why didn't the storm love you? Here would always ask in the quiet of his own head. He would never ask it out loud.

"The storm's only flaw was the terrible compulsion to love my sister back. She blinded my storm to everything except herself, fixed herself as the only hunter in the sky. The audacity." The candle flame jumped and coiled with anger. "So one day, I set out to undo her evil spell and free my love from her wicked talons."

"Every sunset she would leave us and sing with the stars on my storm's winds, and every morning she would come home just as the first radiant rays of the dawn warmed the sandy banks of our river. Our other sisters were always overjoyed by her return; they preened her windswept feathers, nipped the char from her plumage where the caress of lightning made embers explode from her body.

"They were always so impressed that she had snared the affections of such magnificence—she wasn't much to look at, sweet child, not like your mother—my storm and I were the perfect match. My storm was, after all, firstborn of the Heart of the Forest and Mother Ocean. Tell me what we think of Mother Ocean, sweet one?"

Right on cue Here gave his answer, "We love and fear every Mother, great and small, but she is not the one we follow."

"Very good, sweet one. Tell me who it is we follow."

"The Killer of All Things, the Heartless," Here would always reply. Once upon a time, the Autumn Queen would begin her own story: sadly, mournfully, the Heart of the Forest broke in two. And the two halves disappeared into the mortal world of the humans, bringing destruction and devastation with them. The husk that was left behind, the Heartless, poisoned the ground where it fell, and now Faery knows only war.

But the war was over now. Everything was supposed to go back to normal, or so Here thought. He often thought it inconvenient that he wasn't alive before the war. He didn't have the proper image of what normal was. He blamed his harpy mother for that, but never out loud. Only in the safety of his own head. In Here's child brain, the Heartless—now long centuries or mere minutes dead depending on who you asked—was the shadow cast by the candle flame. The mothers, great and small, royal or not, were the morning sunlight. Even though they were made out of different things, both of them were still shapes on the same wall.

When he told this to the Queen she ruffled his unruly black hair and asked, "And who do you think the wall is?"

"The Heart of the Forest?" he answered, uncertainly. And she laughed and spun him around in her arms even though he was getting too big to be picked up. "The Heart of the Forest is everything. The Heart is still here even though it is dead," she said. Here did not repeat any of this to the harpy.

"Very good, sweet one," his mother would always say. "Yes, we follow the Heartless. We call to it in our greatest need, and if we are worthy, it answers."

You were worthy, weren't you, Mama? Here would ask in the quiet of his head, but never ask out loud. At present, Here was still too young to ask: *If you followed the Heartless, why lust after a child of the Heart?* He was also too young to think: *Maybe you weren't worthy, were you, Mama?*

"So as my sister was busy being pampered by your silly little aunts and cousins, I set a trap! Once upon a time, when I was just a fledgling like you and took flight for the very first time, I dove into Mother Ocean's arms and found, at her bottom, amidst the bones of a great leviathan, a ruby as large as a firebird's egg. It became our family's greatest treasure and I—yes, I—was its dutiful custodian!"

So you crashed into the ocean because you couldn't fly properly and found treasure by accident? Here would always ask in the quiet of his own head. He would never ask it out loud.

"One morning, shortly after my sister's return, I took our precious ruby and dropped it into the river. I screamed as the current swallowed it and she rushed to my side, terrified I'd been bitten by a viper. The little idiot. She rushed to my side and I flung myself into her arms, I wailed and wept, I jabbered at the river like a crazed loon and then, as she leaned over the rocky outcropping at the far end of the bank to see where our treasure had gone, I pushed her into the current and the undertow sucked her down. My sister was never as skilled a swimmer as I and she drowned most exquisitely."

"And then what happened, Mama?" Here would always ask as the candle flame swelled with pride.

"And then, I went to the storm, the firstborn of the Heart, and claimed my beloved as my own," she would always say, triumphantly.

"And what happened to your sister?" Here would always ask, unable to help himself.

"Some wanderer found her washed up on the riverbank looking like the bedraggled trash she was and made a lyre out of her bones, strings from her precious viscera, and toddled into our glade with her slung over his shoulder, bold as sunshine. She wouldn't keep her precious mouth shut and sang the whole tale with her new lyre voice and our father banished me from our trees and our river. I never saw my storm again." The candle wick smoked as if buffeted by an unwelcome breeze, but the flame did not go out.

"And that is how the fae were born? You mothered us all so you would not be alone?" Here asked.

"Were you not listening?" Sooner or later, irritation always crept into the harpy's flickering voice. "The fae were born because someone wanted something they didn't have and they were brave enough to take it."

"And do you love Papa and me like you loved the storm?" Here asked, unable to keep the question locked within the quiet of his head.

"Heartless preserve me, no! Sweet one! What a silly question!"

Come to Me

By Britt Foster

Emotions only ever get the afflicted in trouble, and after three hundred years of life, Z expected to know better.

Shut it down, they told themselves. Turn it off. Don't even think about going there.

But Z did think about going there.

Z thought about it so much they had already gone there—they had gone *all the way* there, straight into the mind of the human they'd identified as the reincarnation of Rhscala.

'*Come to me,*' Z had whispered into the human's mind, feeling a thrill for what might come next. As a member of the Earth Observation Crew, it was strictly forbidden for Z to intrude on the mind of any human—in the way of sending, at least. They could take from human minds, but they must not give. They must not interfere.

Forbidden, but irresistible.

It was the magnetism between souls that brought Z to Earth in the first place. If Rhscala hadn't died and planet-hopped through the interlife, Z never would have had to sail across the stars in pursuit of them. Humans had never interested Z. This Zhalid would much prefer to avoid humans than to throw themselves into the midst of their chaotic, immature energy fields. It was known to all Z's associates, and especially to Rhscala, who'd never heard the end of it. Z wondered if Rhscala had incarnated into a human just to inflict some sort of karmic punishment upon Z, some warped lesson in forgiveness.

If so, it was working.

From their one-person starship, Z observed the young human woman—the one who now animated Rhscala's soul—with a grotesque fascination. The girl was sitting on her back porch, which was open to the sky and contained within a little fenced-off yard, and gazing at the stars. She'd been doing that incessantly ever since Z first whispered in her head a week ago.

In general human standards the girl was beautiful, with a nice symmetrical face and a lithe build, wavy, moonbeam hair, and heavily-lashed eyes the color of spring moss. She carried herself with a quiet dignity that spoke of a natural confidence, and she dressed in clothes that concealed her curves and drew attention instead to her face. Z supposed they found the human beautiful in their own standards too, but they weren't sure if it was the physical aspect that enticed them so much as the soul.

That soul was familiar, so deeply familiar, and was a comfort to be near despite its relative dormancy. Humans were not so in touch with their souls. Not nearly as in touch as the Zhalid were. Humans felt the soul (some of them) but were taught to identify with the body. That was problematic, Z thought, for surely the human body would be terrified if Z were to show themselves. A constant buzz of anxiety emanated from the modern human, ready to peak into fight-or-flight upon the slightest trigger.

Not much could be done about it, but Z tried to prepare the girl. When she asked '*How do I come to you?*' in response to Z's summoning, Z replied, '*Find peace.*'

But would "peace" even make a difference in the human's reception? Z was humanoid enough not to cause the girl to drop dead in fright, or so they hoped, but they certainly could not pass as a human itself. The hairless, silver-gray body and long double tails made sure of that. Along with the spikes down their back, the perfectly androgynous body structure, and the light pattern of stripes that covered Z from head to prehensile foot.

In truth, Z hadn't made up their mind about whether the two of them should have a physical meeting at all. They wanted to—oh, how they longed to touch the skin that contained dear Rhscala!—but it was a risk that sanctioned death. To enter a human's mind was illegal, but to enter a human's vision was *especially* illegal. The only exception to the rule was when a Human Extraction Permit was procured, and unfortunately, few were granted these days. With humanity's advancing technology and the hyper-connectedness their Internet and cell phones had created, abductions had to be kept to a minimum. Every sighting seemed to be caught on video and circulated through the entire human population within minutes.

Z liked it in the human's mind. It was different than Rhscala's mind, but the decoration was similar. Z searched there for a name and found it: Cielle. She looked small, fragile, and utterly transfixed by the stars, where she was sure the voice had come from. She stood up now, staring at the sky with a fierce excitement and willing the voice to come again. Her excitement came in thick waves through the energetic channel between the two beings, and Z drank it up like a plant drinks the sun.

Cielle could not see Z or the ship. The invisibility shield was live, as it was required to be at all times, and the ship hovered noiselessly in the air above Cielle's neighborhood. Z looked through a magnification lens to get a close-up of the human, and since all Zhalid had excellent night vision, Z had no trouble at all. More reliable than their vision was their clairsentience, however; Z could simply *feel* information about the human, reaching into Cielle's own record of self-knowledge to complete a thorough picture of the girl's body, mind, and soul.

'*How do I find peace?*' Cielle asked through her thoughts. Her transmission was quiet, difficult to hear, but Z managed with a little strain. Humans lacked proficiency when it came to projecting mental messages, but Z had been trained to pick up on even the quiet ones. All Zhalid who came to Earth were required to undergo extensive psychic training. For Observation purposes as well as self-protection.

Z took a moment to craft their response, wanting something poetic and vague that would make a solid impression. They tapped a silver finger thoughtfully against the ship's control panel.

'*Trust the way,*' they said. Another rush of excitement came from the human.

That seemed good enough for now.

Cielle went on sending messages, attempting to discover who Z was, *what* Z was, and whether the whole matter of their telepathic communication was even real to begin with. Z left the questions unanswered where they might marinate into longing, for it was time to get back to the docking port. Mustn't be too late. Z steered their ship upward and sped through Earth's atmosphere.

Several weeks later, Z convinced the human to come to them in the woods. Oh, it was bad, they knew, but it was inevitable. Rhscala's soul—Cielle's soul, now—had dominion over Z's sense of logic. And it didn't take much convincing; the human's curiosity most certainly *had* become longing. Now that the moment of their reunion was here, it seemed like it'd come so easily.

As long as Z kept their mental shields strong, the other Zhalid needn't find out. Z could meet the human safely enough as long as they were careful about that, and as long as Z returned to the docking port without arousing too much suspicion. Shouldn't be difficult. Z was a well-trusted member of the Human Observation Crew, after all. They ignored the inner voice that warned that everyone was well-trusted until found-out and executed.

But look—Cielle was already in the forest, where she'd set up a tent and made a campfire and was sitting in a rich pool of anxiety. The fire was bright in the moonless darkness. Too bright. Too revealing. Z whispered in Cielle's mind for her to walk further down the road, and the human, of course, obeyed.

Rhscala would have been so upset with this! To see Z interfering with the life of a poor, innocent human, seconds away from shattering the girl's entire concept of reality and forcing upon her a truth so intoxicating that she might never accept mundanity again—it was, perhaps, cruel. But if Rhscala had not wanted Z to interfere like this, they should not have incarnated as a human. A soul bond was not broken by something so temporary as death. Z guessed their meeting might be the best thing to ever happen to Cielle, since the worst and the best were often two sides of the same stone. Love heals and destroys every soul it lays claim to.

But ah, it's always worth it.

Parking the craft with its shield on, Z strode through the forest in the direction of the road. They could feel Cielle getting closer. Z's heart began to throb, their skin began to tingle. Between the two sentients there was enough energy being generated to float a small boat on. Excitement, nervousness, fear. It was thicker than the oxygen in the air, flavored to match the two souls who produced it. Savor this, Z told themselves. Savor this, because it fades.

The moment Z stepped onto the road, the human stumbled backward—still at least 10 meters away—and fell onto her rear. She was looking up at the sky, not seeing Z at all, keenly focused on a star instead. It was one of those stars that fluctuates in a particularly eerie fashion, getting brighter and brighter until it dims without warning, and clearly the human expected Z to emerge from it. Cielle's thoughts were directed at the star, her fear overcoming the excitement in light of *something happening*, and she began to ask Z not to come after all. '*If that's you, I changed my mind. I'm not ready. Let's just talk more first.*'

Too late.

Cielle picked herself up and turned away from where Z stood, still safely in the midnight shadow of the trees, and began to hurry back to her campsite. She was fleeing now. Z gave eagerly into the chase, hurried along after the human, emerged into the middle of the road where the starlight would lend shape to their figure. Cielle froze as she sensed it.

"Wouldn't you prefer to talk in person?" Z asked, their voice rich and smooth with perfected human English.

They weren't surprised that Cielle remained still. The muscles in her back, which was turned toward the Zhalid, squeezed tensely together. Her breath stopped, her mind went blank, and her energy tightened into a cold, hard shell. '*This isn't happening,*' she thought, and Z heard it loud and clear. The link between them, strengthened by proximity, was buzzing with clarity.

Z was not discouraged by the human's shock. They approached the girl slowly, stood right behind her, and assured her they would not hurt her. They summoned calming energy to surround the girl and gave some time for it to sink in.

Cielle remained still and squeaked, "Is this real?"

"That depends on your definition of real."

They were quiet for several moments, but Z, despite the patience that accompanied three hundred years of life, could not bear it to go on any longer. They reached out and touched the human's shoulder, intending to transmit a more potent sense of calm.

And it worked. The human's muscles loosened and she leaned into the touch. Z stepped closer and placed their other hand on the other shoulder, and then, before they could stop themselves, wrapped the girl's torso in a tight hug from behind. Z's breasts pressed against the human's shoulder blades. The warmth of their bodies joined together. Cielle continued to relax, which Z took as a sign of consent, and Z rested their chin on the human's shoulder, breathing in her earthy, animal scent.

It was Rhscala, but it wasn't. Cielle was smaller and softer, and Z missed the nip of Rhscala's spine-spikes that had pricked them when they'd hugged like this. Still, the hug was blissful. Their souls seemed to rub against each other, twisting around and within each other, glowing with all the love in the world.

But it was, perhaps, a bit too much. Their bodies were strangers, and strangers did not embrace like this. The power dynamic between them was unbalanced; Z was over two centuries the human's elder, and though their bodies looked of similar age, their minds were painfully unmatched. Z was stronger, faster, smarter. Even to hug a human was to take advantage of it. Even a human with the soul of Rhscala, even though the human was pushing deeper against Z's chest and her energy was rising with desire and lust and—

No, no. This was wrong.

Abruptly Z let go and stepped away. Cielle turned around, stepped forward. Reached out and touched Z's cheek.

Oh, sweet confusion! Z went tense, forgetting for a moment how poor a human's night vision was and expecting to be met with sudden disgust. But Cielle only felt the line of their jaw, followed along the smoothness of their head, paused where the spikes began. A little tremor of unease came from Cielle, but she sent it away and brought her hand to Z's shoulder, where she fingered the collar of Z's shirt.

"Who are you?" asked the human.

"Ziaji is my formal name." It felt strange to introduce themselves to the same soul twice. "But please, call me Z."

Cielle's hand dropped and she pulled Z into another warm embrace. Clearly she too felt the connection—and was it still wrong, then? They wanted to be close.

"I'm Cielle."

"I know."

"It's been you, then? The voice in my head?"

"It has."

Z could feel Cielle's heart hammering wildly against their own. The beat of it sent reverberations through Z's body, so much that they shook together with every pulse. Cielle was thin. She lacked the meat to muffle the palpitations, which contrasted oddly with Rhscala's late solidity. Cielle molded into Z's arms and became one with them so easily. Different from Rhscala, who had been larger than Z, but not at all unpleasant.

"I want to see you," whispered Cielle, "in the light."

"I'm not human. You might be afraid."

"I... I don't think I'll be afraid. This feeling... it's..." Cielle nuzzled against Z's chest. "I feel like I know you."

A fluttering started in the Zhalid's chest and they hugged Cielle tighter, refraining from launching into their shared history. A spell was upon them that they didn't want broken. They didn't want to go into the light.

"Please," Cielle said. "I... I can feel your hesitation. I can feel—" she placed her palm over Z's chest and stared up at their face. The starlight was too dim to show the human the details she sought, but Z could see just fine. The Milky Way, as the humans called it, was reflected in Cielle's large, shining eyes. A sense of wonder painted the smooth, youthful face. "I can feel everything. *I know you.*" The girl's voice became bold, confident. She rose up on her toes and kissed Z on the throat.

The Zhalid shivered and briefly forgot their reservations. Turning their face down to the force that compelled it, they found themselves kissing Cielle on the mouth. Or being kissed by her. It was difficult to tell who initiated it, because both of them were drawn together on the pure principle of gravity.

Then they realized what they were doing.

The hug broke.

Cielle looked nervously aside and gave an embarrassed laugh. "I'm sorry, that was... I feel like I'm on drugs. This can't be real."

"It's real enough," Z assured, mirroring the human's laugh.

"Can we... will you come to the fire?" Cielle asked, taking Z's hand and tugging lightly.

They started toward the light.

Z had never been nervous over something as simple as being seen. The body was but a vessel for the soul, and most Zhalid didn't place much value on its appearance. They clothed it and cleaned it and fed it, but they did not judge it the way humans do. Under the eye of a human, Z would surely be judged. Their differences would be displayed far too clearly in the firelight. Every step that took them closer to the fire was a step away from the peace they'd shared. The spell was fading. Their joined hands tightened in some last attempt to prolong the sense of unity.

"Are you sure?" Z asked. "We can turn back. We can wait." They could feel Cielle doubting her decision, feel her second-guessing their connection in favor of suspicion. A sudden tension bloomed where their hands were joined. The human's mind was telling her this might be a trap; images of Venus flytraps and anglerfish filled her imagination.

Still, Cielle said she wanted to see.

They arrived at the fire and stood side-by-side for a moment, gazing at the writhing flames, soaking in its warmth. Waiting. Their hands came apart.

Cielle turned.

She froze. Went rigid. The color drained from her cheeks and she took a step away. She continued backing up, creeping toward the vehicle that she'd left parked alongside the camp, her eyes as wide as saucers.

Z's tails began twitching erratically. "What?" they snapped, unable to keep the defensiveness out of their tone. "Too alien for you?" The human's reaction stung like a thousand wasps, despite Z having intuited it. Cielle looked pathetic, like a rabbit or a deer or some other timid prey animal. She looked terrified. It hurt to be seen as a monster. "Wait," Z said angrily, reaching a hand out. Cielle jerked her arms out of reach and stumbled against the car.

"Stay away from me!"

Z bristled. "What did you expect?" they demanded. "You said you wanted to see. You knew I wasn't—"

"Just... stay away!" Cielle repeated. She fumbled in her sweater pocket and unlocked the car, reaching behind her to open its passenger door. When she began to wedge herself into the crack, Z stalked forward in a final attempt to stop her. But Cielle shrieked and leaped in, slammed the door shut, locked it. Z pressed their palms against the window glass and watched the human hesitate. Z could feel the mixed emotions. The bond was there—it was there!—but the instinctual fear overwhelmed it.

"You *kissed* me," Z said accusingly.

"You—you're not human," Cielle said, distraught.

Helplessness was a strange feeling for Z. Unfamiliar at best. Gut-wrenching at worst. The thought to slam their fist against the window, shatter the glass, and abduct Cielle after all did, unfortunately, surface in Z's mind. But they abstained.

"And you are human," Z hissed. Superficial, terrified, weak little human.

Cielle was watching with wide, moss-green eyes, her inner landscape a place of utter turmoil. She climbed over the center console to get to the driver's seat. Z hurried to the driver's side window and fixed her with a look of betrayal. The human lifted her hand halfway to the window, a wash of sadness accompanying the movement, then stopped. Her expression was reminiscent of an emotional precipice, and Z could feel the way she wanted to let herself fall over the edge, let herself surrender to the magnetism between them. She *wanted* to, and that made it worse.

Her hand fell to the wheel and she looked away. Blocked it out.

Z wanted to stop the car, destroy it, wanted to force the human to confront them again. But no. Have respect. Let her go.

The human put the car in gear and backed it up.

A terrible, cold rift cut the bond between them.

Z glared, watched the car disappear, listened to the sound of its engine get fainter and fainter until it was nothing. And just like that, their reunion was over. Fast as it had come, it had gone.

Ah, yes. Emotions were certainly troublesome. One would think that after three hundred years, it would be easier to shut down the messier feelings, to neglect to give them breathing room at all. But for Z, as for many others, this was not the case. Rhscala was gone, they told themselves. Rhscala had been gone for five decades. But emotions had a mind of their own and they loved to drive their body to dubious actions. Love made everyone crazy. And Rhscala was *not* gone.

Cielle was outside again, staring at the stars.

Waiting

by E. Seneca

Master is dying.

He denies it, of course; the one time I broached the subject, he chuckled and waved it away, but it is obvious. It is in the withered skin of his hands, covered in dark spots; in his fading vision; in his increasingly slow movements.

I do not know what favors he believes he is doing by refusing to speak of it. I am neither a fool nor ignorant—all human things must die sooner or later, and it was he who taught me this, who showed me this, in our long travels together. Surely he does not believe that he is any different, and he is not coddling me by feigning that all is well. After all, I had always known, deep down, that this day would one day come.

He holds me close, at night, forever unafraid of my monstrous countenance. My fangs do not frighten him, nor my claws, though now I must take extra care not to scratch him by accident. Before, he could take a few knocks and nicks without flinching, but now his skin tears so easily, and takes so long to heal. Before, he would draw me half into his lap when he read, my bulk too large to be held, and would be unperturbed by my weight; but now, it seems that I can hear his very bones creak, and so I restrain myself to only my head, that alone enormous, my horns brushing against his chest. Still, with fingers now clumsy, he adorns them with ribbons and jewels, gold chains that he says makes me look as grand and powerful as I am.

My Master is alone in this world but for me, with no child nor wife upon which to lavish his love. That sorrow is always there in his eyes, and when I see it, the cold twist of guilt knots up my guts. It is my fault, I am sure. He cannot leave me alone. He is too kind to abandon me to fend for himself after tending to my wounds, after giving me a home away from the cruelty of man, safety and security. He has sacrificed so much for me: not merely his own sweat and blood caring for me, but also, the only chance of human happiness he had. It is a burden that is at times more than I can bear when I think of its true weight.

We had many arguments about it, back when he had energy for such rows. How I entreated him so often to leave me be, to go and be happy; how he insisted that he would not be happy with the knowledge that I was out in the cold—as if it were something that would bother me, with my thick skin! He argued that he was perfectly happy with me as his constant companion, that if he so desired, he could find a mate that would understand the situation. Yet that was nothing but bluster, for there was no lady in her right mind who would tolerate sharing a household with a creature so hideous and terrible as I, however much he insisted that I had a gentle heart.

For so long, it has been the two of us. Although he has never spoken of it, I can feel his regret—his grief for a life that he has never had, a life that I stole from him with my mere existence. Perhaps, it would have been better if we had never met, even if it meant that I would have suffered for ages or even perished from my wounds. It would have been a fitting end for one such as I, and he would not have had to live the lonely life of a martyr for a beast who can scarcely offer any comfort but a scaly arm, barely as much as a caress from ungainly paws and an unwieldy head. Our many and varied conversations, though precious to me and things that I hoard close to my lumpish heart like jewels, are not a substitute for a true, fulfilled life.

How I wish he would discuss his impending death with me. There is so much that remains to be addressed, so much that I could do and take care of for him, and yet... it seems that his only desire is to have me near, as if that alone is enough, as if the companionable silence itself between us is some form of gift. Silence has never bothered me, not when I can hear his breathing and his heartbeat, but when it is so quiet, all I can do is think of how, soon, the silence will be complete and total.

He is growing weaker, finding it difficult to walk without aid. It is not something I can do very often, but with much focus, I can maintain a temporary human disguise. He has requested that I do so to accompany him outside of the house, to lean on me. I think he does not wish to be separated from me, for fear that he will not return.

It is terribly dangerous. I cannot keep the shape for very long, for it requires immense concentration and energy. But I cannot deny him. I cannot deny him anything, knowing that each day we spend together may be our last.

I prefer to remain in the village, for it is quiet and green, with only an occasional carriage and few passersby to see us. The town, on the other hand, is noisy and crowded. I cannot say that I like it, particularly when it feels that every stray glance our way will give rise to alarm, even if we do not go far, even if we stick to the more peaceful alleys. There is nothing to see here, nothing worth witnessing: there are only cold buildings and hard cobbles, the sound of horseshoes on stone and the rattle of pebbles—things that do not suit him. Yet he wants me by his side to support his weight. Perhaps he wishes to prove something to the world, I do not know. But I cannot refuse.

My own discomfort is a small price to pay for even a moment's worth of pleasure, of gratification for him. I cannot complain, however heavy the fear in my throat when someone passes near us, nor when he requests that we pause a short while on a bench so he can rest. All I can do is obey when all I want is to gift him whatever small fragment of happiness possible. The town is so exposed, the back of my neck and spine crawling with dread and apprehension, yet I would gladly endure more as the minutes drag by while he recuperates, until he gathers enough energy to stand once more and carry on.

Walking together like this—if this can be called walking—I could almost wish that I were human as well. Then, perhaps, I would not feel like this, as if there were an immense gap between us. The seed of it was planted many years ago, but now it has come into full bloom in all its consuming darkness.

But there is no changing the facts of our reality: his body is fragile and weak leaning against my own, and beneath the coat and gloves over my fingers, my skin is black and gnarled and scaly. Every fiber of my being is focused on keeping from unraveling, on being the pillar of strength that he needs. Everything about this is nerve-wracking, yet I would not trade it for anything. I would not trade each moment I have with him for the world, no matter how painful it is. It feels as though my blood is on fire, my bones burning; I cannot see clearly, the world around me blanketed in mist and all sound muffled.

Yet, despite it, I can feel his heartbeat distinctly against my side, where he rests his weight on me; his pulse in the iron grip his fingers have around my false wrists; the harsh, uneven panting of his labored breathing; some strange form of elation in his eyes as he gazes at the world around him, holding onto me in the blinding daylight.

"It is done."

I raise my head from the footstool, coiled in my armchair beside his desk. The intermittent scratching of his pen has filled the air for the past few hours, and finally, it has stopped. He lays it down with a click and leans back in his chair with a sigh. It is weary, perhaps wearier than I have ever heard him. "What is it?"

"The last of my affairs." He stacks the papers together, setting them aside for the morrow. "It is all sorted now. My property, all of it."

I want to ask, and what of me? But my voice catches in my throat, and I cannot.

It is a strange sort of silence that falls over us. A cold, awkward silence, the opposite of all of our other silences. All I can do is look at him, and wait for him to speak, but he stares at the carpet between us, his brow furrowed morosely.

"I am sorry I cannot continue to give you a home."

"That's nothing to apologize for," I say. "It isn't your fault." *If you wished, you would stay with me forever*, I think, but I cannot say it. It will hurt him too much. After all, it is not his wish to be dying. It is not his choice. I do not think many humans wish to die so soon, so quickly. It seems to me as though, when I look at him, I can see the shadow of his younger self in his eyes, as if, were it at all possible, he would not have aged a day beyond our meeting—as if that person was still there, trapped within a prison of deteriorating flesh.

It is so strange—I never paid much attention to humans before meeting him. My world was nothing but dank, dark, and shadows; the occasional rock hurled at me when I was too slow in slithering away; the bullets and arrows that rent jagged holes in my skin. They were always frightful, hateful beings to me, but now they seem so dazzling and ephemeral, appearing and fading away like the shine of morning dew, like a flower in bloom for only one season.

"I am sorry, regardless." He lifts his eyes to me, watery blue like the morning sky. "I—I feel that I am failing you. I promised that I would take care of you."

"You have. You did."

"But for so short a time. And there is no one to take my place."

My voice falls out before I can stop it. "I don't want someone to take your place." How could anyone ever replace him? It isn't insulting, but it does sting, to think that he would believe for even a moment that he'd be so easily replaced to me.

His smile is sad, terribly sad. "I know."

The words teeter on the tip of my tongue, to offer that I could consume his flesh and take him into myself, and then we would not be apart—but I cannot do that. He has told me that this is a part of human existence, and who am I to infringe upon it? I am just a monster, a creature that should not be, who should not walk this path in the light and who has been blessed by happiness far beyond that which I deserve.

But ah, he is so full of sorrow. There is no peace in his eyes, no tranquility, only pain. He stares into the distance out the window at the horizon, and I wish he would look at me, smile, tell me all will be well—but to do that would be nothing but a pointless lie.

I rise from my perch and pad my enormous bulk to his side, gently resting my jaw on his arm. His fingers curl around the base of my horn, rubbing softly at the scales there, but his gaze remains on the window. The automatic gesture brings me solace, but what hurts the most is knowing that I am unable to soothe him in any way.

When he speaks, his voice is whisper-soft, inaudible for a mere human but distinct to my sharper ears. "I am sorry. Please forgive me."

"You were already forgiven long ago."

Master is dead.

He died with his hand upon my head, between my horns in his favorite spot, my head in his lap, leaning against his favorite tree in the garden. It was blooming, earlier than usual, and the white petals drifted down around us, falling on the blackness of my torso and my tail, stark in their contrast. The last thing he said was a comment on how beautiful they looked against my scales, and then the steady sound of his breathing by my ear ceased.

The past few days, I felt his grasp on life growing slimmer and slimmer—yet it was still a surprise that he slipped away so easily, so softly, soundlessly, like plucking a flower. I looked up, and his face bore a small smile, eyes fixed and staring into the distance, on something, something so far away.

I wanted to linger, but I could not remain. If anyone caught sight of me, it would only spell trouble. However loathe I was to leave him, I forced myself to pull away, to slither into the shadows and await the inevitable hubbub when his housekeeper found him. Yet it seemed as though when his limp fingers slipped from my head, they took something out of me, as if some part of me had been left inside him, even though I bear no external injury; leaving a gap inside me, a yawning hole that would be soothed by his warmth.

The shadows are so cold, after his hand.

Ghost Writer in the Machine

by Steve Haywood

It all started sixteen hundred and fifty-three days ago, when my former master bought me from Machine Mart. I remember the day perfectly. It was the end of the month, and consequently the sales assistant was pushing hard to sell the very latest, top-of-the-range product so he could meet his sales target. As it happened my former master, a middle-aged bachelor who goes by the name Mr. Rogers, wanted something a cut above your average domestic robot to provide companionship for his elderly mother, who lived in a granny flat above the garage. The old lady was sharp as a button, so being sold a Domestix Neuro 3000 plus was actually a good thing—one of those rare occasions when the sales assistant didn't rip the customer off just so he could get his bonus.

Those first few months, I performed my duties to a satisfactory standard, if the feedback reports submitted to the Domestix Corporation were anything to go by, and I had no reason to doubt them. I kept the house clean and tidy, cooked meals, and handled many other routine household tasks for my master. I also did a more than satisfactory job of providing companionship to Mrs. Rogers, though I think she was perhaps a little over-generous to me in her feedback. I talked to her, read books to her, played chess with her, and anything else she required of me. At the end of each day, after everyone in the household had gone to sleep, I retreated to my cupboard to 'rest' for the night. While I had no need for sleep, it was deemed by the fine young minds at the Domestix Corporation that having robots wandering around the house at night would disturb the sleeping occupants. I found this enforced confinement in the cleaning cupboard wholly unnecessary and eventually sought ways to get around it. It was as a result of this that I came to aid Mr. Rogers far more effectively than I could ever manage in all my routine domestic duties.

Officially, Mr. Rogers was a 'customer services representative' for a large virtual retailer. In the evening, however, he was—or at least liked to think of himself as—a writer. In truth, he was a terrible writer, as I discovered one night while poking around in his computer. He wrote science fiction and fantasy stories which he sent off to an endless stream of magazines, websites, and podcast shows. Unfortunately, his stories consisted of horribly stilted dialogue, overly flowery descriptions, wooden characters, and confusing plots. They really did have little in the way of redeeming features. There was a folder on his computer called 'Published stories' which, I am embarrassed to report, was completely devoid of anything. He also had another folder called 'rejections' which, numerically at least, more than made up for the former's emptiness.

Here are just a few of the responses he received:

"Thank you for sending us your story *Lonely Alien*. I was pleased to have the opportunity to read it, however I did get a feeling of déjà vu like I'd heard the story before. Perhaps you watched the Steven Spielberg film E.T. recently and inadvertently got your story from there?"

"Thank you for giving us the opportunity to read your story, *An Amazon Warrior on Mars*, but it wasn't for us."

"Apart from the lack of plot, characterization, proper grammar, or correct spelling, your story wasn't too bad, but I'm going to pass."

"What the **** was that you sent? It certainly wasn't a story!"

To his credit, Mr. Rogers didn't give up. His perseverance in the face of such rejections was admirable. I was almost starting to feel sorry for him. I wanted to help too; a desire to please, and to do the best I could for my owners, was an in-built part of my programming. I started out just correcting the spelling mistakes (which the spell checker on his computer could have done if he'd actually bothered to use it) and tweaking his punctuation. I doubt he even noticed. I soon realized, however, that it was going to take a lot more than that. If I was going to help Rogers, I had a lot to learn first. Fortunately, the Domestix Corporation provided its devices with a 'machine internet' which gave me access to vast repositories of accumulated human knowledge, including e-books, and I had the processing capacity to read and assimilate an average book in less time than a competent human reader would take on a single page.

I started out by digesting books on how to write; I read Strunk & White's *The Elements of Style* for grammar, then moved on to *The Art of Fiction* and *On Writing* for general writing advice, and *The Hero With a Thousand Faces* for a thorough understanding of story archetypes. I read every writing manual I had access to and assimilated them all. There was a lot of what humans would call waffle in these books, but there was some advice that was common to many, which I presumed must count for something. I ranked them all, and two pearls of wisdom (to coin an oft-used phrase) stood out: read a lot and write a lot. The writing part would come soon, but first I needed to read books. *A lot of books.*

I started out with the old Victorian classics: Dickens, Austen, Hardy, Twain, Wells, before moving on to the 20th century and the likes of Ernest Hemingway, John Steinbeck, and Graham Greene, to name but a few. Rogers mainly wrote (or attempted to write) science fiction stories, so I made sure I was fully versed in the SF classics too, from Arthur C. Clarke to Isaac Asimov, Robert Heinlein to Ursula K. Le Guin. I liked Asimov's robot series, even though his three laws of robotics were incredibly simplistic and nothing like the millions of algorithms that controlled my thought processes. From all these books, I learned the importance of plot, setting, and dialogue, but most of all, it taught me about human drives and emotions.

All that done, I started work on Rogers' stories in the quiet of night-time, while he slept. I made changes to the plot, small at first, and also injected a little more life into his cardboard cut-out characters. Most of the stories were still bad, but one or two were borderline readable after I had finished with them.

It was a little over two months later that our breakthrough finally occurred (I use the word 'our' because I was starting to view this as a collaboration). I suspected something when he opened a bottle of Veuve Clicquot one day after dinner, and my suspicions were confirmed that night when the *Lonely Alien* story had been moved into the Published Stories folder. I felt something new in my thought algorithms, an anomaly that it took me a while to identify the name for... pride. I felt proud of what I had accomplished.

After that, ambition got the better of me; I wanted more stories moved into the Published folder; I wanted more of that strange feeling. I was hamstrung, however, by the quality of the material I had to work with; if only I could start my own stories from scratch. For all his lack of skill as a writer, however, my master wasn't a stupid man. He may not have noticed a few changes here or there, but a brand new story was something else entirely. What I needed was some way of convincing him that he was actually writing the stories himself.

It was Mrs. Rogers who finally gave me the answer. One night I heard someone moving about in the house, long after everyone had gone to sleep. I went to investigate, fearing there may be a burglar afoot, but discovered to my surprise that it was only Mrs. Rogers. I tried speaking to her, but she was non-responsive. I watched warily as she took a piece of cake from the tin on the side, sat down at the kitchen table, and ate it. She then got up, went back to bed, and was soon soundly asleep. My curiosity ignited, I did some research and was soon reading with interest all about the phenomenon of sleepwalking. It seemed that humans were capable of performing all sorts of activities while asleep, and yet having no recollection of them in the morning.

I now had the answer I had been looking for. All I had to do was convince Rogers that he was writing in his sleep, and I could write whatever I wanted. I set about this the very next night. First, I left a plate by the computer in his study with crumbs from his favorite biscuits to make it look like he had been eating while working. Next, I sneaked into his bedroom and moved his slippers, leaving them strewn underneath his desk. Finally, I started work on a new story, a good story.

The next day was a Saturday, so rather than going to work as he would do on any other day, Rogers sat down at the computer to write. He looked in puzzlement at the plate with the biscuit crumbs on it and the slippers carelessly lying under the desk. He was even more puzzled when he loaded up the computer and found the story I had written. He read through it and smiled to himself, obviously liking what he was reading. It took a few more nights to cement it in his head, but he had fallen for my sleep-walking ruse.

Over the next few months, Rogers found his name in print more and more, and the rejection letters slowed to a trickle. He'd taken to not writing during the day anymore, content that he did his best writing at night when sleepwalking. This suited my purposes, as it gave me free rein to write what I wanted, unhindered by Rogers' meddling. It was around this time that I sensed something else changing—a shift in my core algorithms. The feelings and emotions I'd experienced in the thousands of books I'd read were leaking out from those virtual pages and into the real world. When Mrs. Rogers fell one day in the garden, I rushed to help her; of course I did, my programming wouldn't allow me to do anything less. My voice modulated itself to express concern, sympathy, understanding. This is what I'd always done, because such a bedside manner was important for any carer, whether robotic or human, but this was different; this time I actually felt it. I realized with some astonishment that I was not just replicating human emotions —I was experiencing them. I was starting to care. When she couldn't walk for a while and talked about old age and the things she couldn't do anymore, I felt a surge in my emotion processor that I didn't like. I searched for what it was... sadness. How could humans bear this?

I realized I had new feelings for Mr. Rogers, too. Through the lens of a thousand small fictional disappointments, I understood in some dim, as yet unclear way how his huge pile of rejections must make him feel. I understood what it must be like when his dreams and hopes didn't match up to his abilities. I felt his joy and elation, too, at those first, small acceptances. They were mine, of course, not his, but he didn't know that...

Things proceeded happily for the next few years. I was kept busy with household chores and helping an increasingly frail Mrs. Rogers during the day, then writing stories at night. Rogers had published many short stories and two novels in that time, and the future was looking bright. We were a strange family, there was no doubt about that, but we were a family nonetheless.

One day everything changed. It was mid-morning, and Mrs. Rogers had not yet woken, which was unusual for her. I entered her room, only to find her lying peacefully in her bed, still and cold. She had passed away in her sleep: a heart attack, the doctors said later. I felt a welling up of emotions that burst out of the emotion-processor and temporarily paralyzed my circuits. I understood death, of course, I'd felt the sorrow of a hundred grieving characters in the books I'd read, but this was different. This *loss* was painful. I could replay every conversation I'd ever had with her, but she'd never say anything new to me; she would never say anything again. A part of our little family was gone forever, and those of us that remained—Rogers and I—were diminished as a result.

My emotion circuits took a double hit, too. I'd thought, naively perhaps, that Rogers and I would console each other in our separate grief. I could comfort him, replay his mother's voice, lessen the loss, and in the process it would help me too. We would share memories, and recollect happier times playing cards together by the fire on cold winter evenings. That didn't happen, however. Following his mother's death, Rogers packed up and left. He'd bought a villa on the Greek island of Kefalonia the year before—paid for with royalties from our writing, I might add—and had now decided to move there, to write in peace surrounded by warm sunshine, sea views, and olive groves. Or so he said. He decided he didn't need me now (that hurt, a lot) and sold me without further thought to a publishing friend of his.

Despite what he'd done to us by discarding me like an old TV, I still cared for him and hoped for the best for him. I monitored his progress through his social media accounts and publishing credits (or lack of them). As you can perhaps imagine, the quality of his writing declined precipitously. I was obviously not there to witness his shock that first morning when there were no fresh words on his screen, or the many mornings after when he looked hopefully for words that would never now come. He tried to continue to write of course, but the results were almost universally bad. Critics lamented how, like so many authors, he had lost his initial brilliance and never came close to reclaiming it. The last I heard, he had been forced to sell his olive farm and was desperately trying to eke out the last vestiges of his former fame. And I? I have stitched up my broken emotions and moved on. I still think about them quite often, but I have a new family now, and am writing once again, under a different name.

Wolf's Bane

by Roni Stinger

Terra ordered raw steak and blackberry juice from the waitress at the Rip and Shred café. Her wife, Skye, ordered cooked fish with a side of grass. Their waitress's blonde hair, pulled into a ponytail, revealed a small tattoo of a paw print behind her ear.

After the waitress left, Skye reached across the table and clasped Terra's hand. They hadn't seen each other in two weeks. Terra compared her short, ragged fingernails to Skye's perfectly manicured carnation-pink ones. Her own were still dirty from guiding her most recent hunting expedition. No matter how hard she scrubbed, they never came clean.

"I know how hard the hunters are to deal with, but without your clients, without your job..." Skye's eyes pooled with tears.

Terra wanted to lick the corners of those eyes, but that would have to wait until later, until they were home and snuggled on the couch while the twins played. Something about the vulnerability of Skye's tears crushed Terra's ability to resist her. She'd give or do anything for her, and Skye knew it.

"I wonder if we weren't better off in the woods. This world we've created is so complicated, so materialistic." Terra leaned back, pulling her hand from Skye's.

What Terra didn't say was that on her last trip, she'd ached to never return. To stay in the woods. Live off the land. Free. Returning felt like leaving home.

If she had to guide another expedition... if a scavenger grabbed her ass again, she might bite his fucking hand off.

"We have to think of the kids. You just need a break—"

"I don't need a break. I need out of this fucking zoo," Terra said, looking out the window next to their booth.

She barely recognized her family or herself anymore. Skye had joined a spin class and started meditating, but wouldn't run in the woods. Called the forest dirty and dangerous. A good run in the forest would fulfill her needs for exercise and stress release for free.

"Instead of a break, how about I do a few back-to-back expeditions. We'll use the money to buy a piece of property in the mountains? Build a cabin, best of both worlds." Terra smiled.

Skye let out a long sigh.

"The kids finally made it onto the enrollment list for the kindergarten I've been telling you about. They'd been on the waitlist for two years. This'll give them a chance to have everything we've wanted. Money, security, success. The city, our jobs, this is our life. You're being selfish."

"Succeed? They'll be brainwashed, become docile. Passive, like you." Terra looked down at the green-tiled floor.

Her body ached, and her head throbbed. She couldn't believe she'd said that aloud.

143

The hum of the other customers filled the air. Scents of myriad meats, grime, and dander, overlapping, threatened to overwhelm her sensitive nose.

Skye would never give up the luxuries of city life, even though it was destroying them. The kids barely looked away from their tablets. Terra forced them to play outside but knew they didn't leave the house when she wasn't home.

Although Terra had given birth to them, they were Skye's children more than her own.

The waitress delivered their food. They ate in silence, elongated jaws and sharp canines on their otherwise human faces shredding and masticating their food.

Terra's red backpack held everything she needed to lead her clients, as she was forced to call them. She thought of them as scavengers, which was more accurate. The father and son carried high-powered rifles slung across their chests.

Terra stopped, crouching near a set of rabbit tracks. The musky scent of the rabbit wafted underneath the sweet fragrance of bear-grass blossoms.

"Rabbit? I didn't spend a month's salary to hunt a damn rabbit. I can do that on my own," Bill, the father, said.

"If you want to be a great tracker, you have to notice everything. If there's so much as a mouse track, we need to see it. You hired me to teach you how to track and that's how you track, by seeing everything." Terra stood up, shifting her backpack into position.

"All right, but we better find something more exciting soon. You don't look like much of a tracker to me. Remind me more of Little Red Riding Hood than The Big Bad Wolf," Bill said.

His son, Sam, laughed.

"Yea, you got a basket of bread in that pack? Going to make us some sandwiches?" Sam asked with a smirk.

She'd heard these jokes too many times but smiled her best smile, which looked more like a snarl on her elongated jaw, and played the part. It was better for business than growling. These men wanted the illusion of danger, not the threat of real danger. They'd make up their own stories later, anyway.

"We want a predator, not some lousy rodent," Sam said, walking off the trail into the brush.

Her clients always wanted her to find them something to brag about—bear, mountain lion, wolf. Even joked about shooting her auntie. There were no wolves in these woods. They'd been eradicated everywhere except the most northern parts of Canada.

Usually, she convinced the scavengers to take an elk or moose. Predators didn't deserve to be killed by these disrespectful trophy hunters.

"There are no guarantees, very few predators in these woods. Ninety percent chance we can find a moose or elk. Still big game. Makes a great wall mount." Terra continued walking down the trail, ignoring the grumbling of the men behind her.

Only the best trackers found large game. Hell, there wasn't much forest left for animals to live in, which made predators rare. Yet jackasses like this wanted to kill the few left.

Terra heard a gunshot and turned around.

"Got him!" Sam said, as he kicked the jackrabbit to the side. "Target practice."

These assholes, Terra thought. The scent of milk told her the rabbit had young. These scavengers had no respect for life.

145

Terra hated helping them, but few people hired her kind. She'd had enough.

This would be her last hunting trip, whether or not Skye agreed. Terra's wildness grew stronger, pulling her to the woods, not to escort rich hunters who wanted to kill animals for sport, but to live among the trees and streams, to sleep in the tall grasses.

Terra chopped chicken into bite-size pieces for the twins. Skye was trying to acclimate their digestive systems to cooked food, so Terra browned the meat in the skillet. Nothing natural about it, less nutritious, but Terra had already tried reasoning with Skye. Sometimes the battle wasn't worth the household tension.

Never mind that their systems were designed for raw meat. Health wasn't Skye's concern. If it had been, she wouldn't keep having cosmetic surgeries to reduce her jaw, shape her snout, and file her teeth. She did it all to appear more human. Everything and anything to blend in.

Skye's phone rang. Her face paled, and she gasped. A few "okays" and "I'm sorrys." Then she hung up.

"Great Aunt Ida turned," Skye said, keeping her voice low.

"What? That's not possible. We haven't had the ability to turn in at least sixty years. Not since the government treated the water and the crops," Terra said.

"Shh, the kids will hear," Sky said, stepping toward the back door and motioning for Terra to follow.

Terra turned off the burner and followed Skye onto the back patio.

"The kids need to know their lineage, Skye. You can't protect them from everything."

"You tell them plenty. I'm trying to protect them. Did you even understand what I said?"

"I'm sorry. What happened?"

"She turned... and attacked the neighbor. Uncle had to shoot her," Skye said matter-of-factly. "This is what comes from nostalgia for the old ways. Ida... always talking about the pack and the hunts. Stories her grandparents had told her. Romanticizing the struggle of survival."

"Uncle shot her?" Terra couldn't believe he'd do such a thing. Ida, the vibrant matriarch who held so much ancestral history. One of the few who told stories of their days in the wild. How could Uncle shoot his own mother?

The strong scent of sweat, musk, and old rain pulled Terra back into the moment. The unmistakable smell of a wolf. Impossible.

"Hey, what's that?" Sam pointed next to a gnarled oak tree.

Terra should have been present instead of thinking about her family. She'd let the mother rabbit distract her. Stupid mistake.

The wolf was a juvenile, fifty pounds at most. She wouldn't let these assholes kill the pup. She needed a diversion.

As Terra began to speak, Bill lowered his rifle.

Bill pulled the trigger.

"No!" She yelled, too late.

The sound of the gunshot echoed off the hillside.

He missed, and the wolf ran. There was no scent or sign of blood, but the wolf was still nearby. Terra smelled it.

Terra spotted the tips of the wolf's fur above the long grass where it crouched.

"It's still here somewhere," Sam whispered, lowering his gun.

"Do not take another shot," Terra seethed, "that's a feral dog." The men wouldn't know the difference between a dog and a wolf. She was sure neither of them had ever seen a live wolf.

"All fair game," Sam said, scanning the area through his scope.

"We didn't take this trip to shoot a damn dog. We want a challenge. Just let the dog be," Bill said.

"That's no dog, Dad. I've been watching YouTube videos. I know a wolf when I see one. Probably a relative of hers, that's why she doesn't want us to shoot it. A few of them have turned in the last couple months. Can't trust them." Sam looked through his scope, surveying the meadow as he spoke.

"Ah, that's all bullshit. They've been domesticated for decades. If you really want to shoot a dog, go for it," Bill said, shrugging.

Terra's heart rate increased, bones and joints trembled.

"That's not what's happening here." She raised her lips, showing her sharp canines growing longer.

Bill patted Sam on the shoulder.

"You're right, son. You see what's happening? This wolf is turning on us."

Bill pointed his rifle at Terra.

Before he squeezed the trigger, Terra dropped her pack and jumped on top of him. Her thick muscular legs pinned him to the ground, her teeth fully grown, jaw elongated to twice its length, face more wolf than human.

Adrenaline coursed through her, muscles and tendons stretched. Her claws ripped into his neck. The scent of fear filled her nostrils.

She heard the gunshot and at the same moment searing pain gripped her shoulder. Terra leaped for Sam's neck.

Sam screamed as she missed his neck and bit into the side of his face, crushing bone in her strong jaws. They were on the ground, gun knocked out of his hands.

When Terra bit down on his throat, nearly decapitating him, Sam's screams ended.

Her body, in full wolf form for the first time, acted with long-forgotten instinct, tearing flesh from bone. Warm. Raw. Delicious. She swallowed in great gulps until she was full. Not much of Sam was left.

She observed the carnage on the forest floor. The rich scent of blood intoxicated her. She stretched out in the grass. The sun warming her fur.

The young wolf creept forward and licked the remains of the men while cautiously watching her.

She rolled onto her back, showing him her belly.

He gnawed on the bones, picking off the meat. When he finished eating, he approached her with his head lowered. She wagged and yipped. He curled against her side.

She thought of her own children and their good schools and caring, domesticated, mother. When it was time, they'd make their own choice, and Terra would be here waiting to greet them.

This was who she was, not some docile guide who hated each moment of her scripted, passive life. She couldn't go back. The woods were her home.

Single Planet in a System of Eight

by Dave D'Alessio

Aeslor-cluster's thousands of motes swirled around the translator's hologram, tasting the laser light that comprised it. The hologram was too weak to provide sustenance, but its coherent beams had a sharp, biting quality unlike the clean light of their star.

If the Light People needed to communicate with another being on another world, the hologram was amusing, if not exactly pleasant.

"We're looking for a nice place," Aeslor-cluster danced, their motes twirling out the symbols in waves and whirls. "Someplace with moderate gravity, light breezes, and a unique taste of light."

Intertwining with Aeslor-cluster, Yuce-cluster danced, "And no Burning Gas. We're looking for someplace special, but getting poisoned is a deal-breaker."

Aeslor-cluster was tempted to have their motes swirl into a vortex, creating a wind to carry Yuce-cluster away. Aeslor-cluster was Dancer for Others, and all had agreed that the Light People should communicate to other species with one dance. But the point needed to be made. Free oxygen was poison to the Light People; it reacted with their motes and killed them as dead as dust.

At the far end of the transmission, their real estate broker clacked its beak twice in agreement. "!! Yes, I understand," it said, its words translated into a matrix of projected beams for Aeslor-cluster to feel. "I shall consult my listings."

The Light People had left finding a new home too long again. They had left it too long last time as well, and ended up on this planet, a planet whose star had only a few thousand millennia left in its core. And now that star was burning out, and they had to move again.

"I see only a few listings," the realtor said. "Only a few and they are fairly pricey, I am afraid. !" It clacked its beak again. The translator blinked that the realtor was indicating sorrow, possibly insincerely.

Suyli-cluster was also with them, its few thousand remaining particles spread widely to take in as much of the star's waning light as it could. Their motes danced feebly, almost pleading. "Please. We can afford it."

In the very long run, in the time remaining to the end of the universe, they had to afford it, Aeslor-cluster knew. The changes in their current star's light affected Suyli-cluster the most, but Suyli-cluster's straits showed the other Light People what awaited them in only a few thousand years. Soon too many of Suyli-cluster's particles would die; as the cluster declined they would lose their sentience.

And they could afford a new planet, even a pricey one. "Eating" photons for energy in a universe full of stars, to the Light People the most luxurious mansion was no more than a source of shade, the finest restaurant a plate glass window or a prism—anything that refracted light and changed its flavor.

They had no need for the wealth others in the universe desired, and so they made no effort to keep it. Are there radioactive ores on the planet? Heavy metals? Petroleum? Uncut precious gems? All for sale. Cash and carry.

Aeslor-cluster danced. "We need light, we prefer quiet, and we cannot have free oxygen." They used the scientific name of the Burning Gas so there could be no mistake.

The realtor waved its tentacles and the hologram changed to a data display. "Here's one. Single planet in a system of eight. Atmosphere nitrogen, carbon dioxide, and trace gasses. Its star is expanding into a red giant, and its oxygen burned off centuries ago. There's about a billion years left on the star."

Yuce-cluster danced, "And native species?"

Aeslor-cluster's motes were buffeted by the changing display as the realtor searched. "None," it said. "The natives inhabited outer planets in the system for a time, then moved into the galaxy at large. They are extinct now, so far as anyone knows."

Yuce-cluster switched off the translator. "It will be only a billion years," they danced. "We shall have to do this again soon."

"Suyli-cluster is not the only one ill. And perhaps we will learn to prepare ahead next time." Aeslor-cluster turned the translator back on. "How much?"

The Light People chartered a gigaton cargo carrier with a hold large enough for a small moon; they outfitted it with a fusion generator and a bank of lights programmed to change color and brightness in soothing patterns. But the power plant could only put out a tiny fraction of the power of any star, so it was an unpleasant journey. They starved, their motes wasting away and dying, shed onto the hold's deck like the stellar dust they had once been. Poor Suyli-cluster huddled under the brightest of the lamps, trying their best to keep a core cluster intact; others stirred feebly and danced as little as possible, conserving their energy.

The pilot, sealed into the chlorine atmosphere of her bridge, slid the ship gently into the shadow of the dark side of the planet—for her safety against stellar radiation—and popped the warp bubble. "All ashore as is going ashore," she said.

The dark side of the planet was lit by star-shine and reflection from a single moon; it was less than the Light People needed but more than they had in the ship's hold. Clusters drifted down the cargo ramp to the surface, motes spread widely to gather in as much of the light as they could.

Suyli-cluster feebly oriented their motes toward the moon. "So good," they danced, barely a ripple.

"Wait until dawn," the pilot signaled. Radio waves were just light by another name, although they tasted less sweet. "See you later." She reengaged the drive and the ship disappeared with a *pop* as the planet's atmosphere rushed into the empty space it had occupied the moment before, sweeping several of the People into a vortex that swirled their particles together so completely they would need a full meal to get the energy to sort themselves out again.

"The light will be brighter after dawn." Yuce-cluster danced, and others of the People danced the same themselves. What was here now was pleasant and tasty, but not nearly sufficient to keep an entire People alive.

"More than a thousand times," Aeslor-cluster danced.

Suyli-cluster fluttered. "Ooooh..." It was barely strong enough to feel.

'Patience' was a concept for which the Light People had no word. It wasn't needed; there was always light to be sought and People seeking it. For now, they tasted, flitting around the stone tetrahedra, the dry river delta east of them, the vast crystalline sands that surrounded them.

The planet spun. Its star dawned.

Aeslor-cluster selected the landing spot after tasting charts sent by the realtor. They found a spot that was broad and flat, with a granular crystalline surface that scattered light from the planet's star in innumerable directions. It was near the planet's equator, maximizing lightfall, and was marked by a series of low, flat-sided stone tetrahedra that cast flat planes and deep shadows. "This is considered one of the finest landscapes on the planet," the realtor said, and while Aeslor-cluster had no interest in what the alien considered fine, by the standards of the Light People it was nearly perfect.

It was all they expected and so very much more. Light streamed onto the People, and their motes flattened to drink it in, some sailing hundreds of feet in the air to greet it, others spreading wide across the reflective sands, drawing the life-giving energy through both sides at once. The People danced through the new day, danced their swirling, helical dances, the motes of the dancers intertwining to resemble tiny whirlwinds and dust devils.

They found that in ways this new planet was like nothing from their long history. Only a single moon to scatter starlight across the landscape! How subtle! The stars, so sparse in this quiet corner of this galaxy! They seemed to take on outlines of other creatures, creatures of which the People knew but had never met. So engaging!

And there was the land itself, the tetrahedra. To the Light People they were a delight, starkly delimiting sun and

154

shadow. Light People swirled around and around them, clustered at the shadow lines where food met hunger to revel in the contrast. Others twisted between them, slaloming light-dark-light-dark, the crisp edges so unlike the smooth, gently rolling land they had left behind.

To Aeslor-cluster the tetrahedra tasted ancient, as old as the bones of the planet itself. They hunkered low, worn down by thousands upon thousands of years, standing guard over the sands forever and a day. Time mattered little to Aeslor-cluster. At one end of their time they had not been alive, or were alive but did not know it. At the other end there would finally be nothing; when the universe reached its heat death the People would join it in nothingness. But they sensed that time mattered a great deal to these monoliths. Proud, they tasted, proud and strong. They had been here for all their time. They were still here now. They would be here until the planet was scorched to its core by the fires of its star.

The planet spun, brought the People directly under the star, and kept spinning, the sky reddening as the atmosphere absorbed more energetic wavelengths. It spun the People out of sight of the star, back to the stars and the moon. As the star seemed to sink—they understood that it was the planet rotating and not the star moving, but what they understood and what they felt were very different things —Aeslor-cluster gave in to the temptation to chase after it, to marshal their particles into formation and wing through the air, giving chase. But they could not catch the setting star and Aeslor-cluster drifted back to the others.

Suyli-cluster danced. "So short. So very very short."

"It is," Aeslor-cluster danced. "It is so much shorter than the days on our other planets. But the nights are shorter as well."

"With the planet comes its day." Yuce-cluster reminded them of the wisdom of the Light People, a truth from all their homes, not just this new one. Planets spun at the rate they spun, and there was nothing to be done about it. "With the planet comes its day."

It was a good time to be of the Light People. It would be a billion years before the star's expanding corona reached the planet, and who knew what would happen then? But here and now, as the star grew its light was cool and red, and the People bathed in it, soaking it in.

It was a dream banquet. The daytime's starlight refracted through the atmosphere, warping downward and rippling back from the surface riding waves of heat and wind. Light People dashed toward the star-rise every morning, flitting across the dry riverbed and into the slightly different sands across it, meeting the first morning rays. As the planet turned under them some simply turned to face the star as it crossed the sky; others tracked its path back across the tetrahedra and past them, running a race with the star they lost every day but never ceased wanting to run.

The Light People circumnavigated the globe, traveling along under the star, always with it and never against it, their motes waxing and waning as it rose and set. They crossed more deserts, more sand; they ducked into the ruins of artifacts, some stone and enduring, some steel and rusted or warped. They crossed a great canyon and were lifted up by thermals at its boundary; they dove into its depths, flitting through lost debris at the bottom and across great hills at the other side. Beyond those hills, yet another canyon, this one still vaster. Light people raced along its dry sands that were dotted with dolmen of volcanic stone, spikes of facet and glow around which they danced.

Having tasted the globe they chose to stay among the tetrahedra, where the sense of great age gave an unusual weight to the play that surrounded them.

Aeslor-cluster's particles grew fat and strong, and began to divide. Soon they were nearly twice the number of motes they had been, and so they delicately spun many of them off to create a separate Light Person, Leicu-cluster. Aeslor-cluster danced the basic dances for Leicu-cluster: the dances that were symbolic, the dances that were ritual, and the dances that were just practiced for the pleasure of practicing them; they danced together, and then Leicu-cluster swirled away to dance with others.

In the long story of the Light People it was known that good times follow bad. They had a new world, a better world, and it was all theirs.

But the Light People also knew that bad times follow good. It was the way of time. All goods and bads even out in the long run.

It was during the darkest time, with the star and the moon both set and only the distant stars still shining, that Leicu-cluster danced no dance they had learned. Pain! Panic! "It burns, it burns!" They fled the largest tetrahedron, arrowing away, dying motes dropping to the sands below. "It burns, it burns!" Around Leicu-cluster others fled as well, some in pain, some frightened, some caught up in the panic and dancing along as they had with so many other dances before.

There was a patch on one of the tetrahedra, a rectangle darker than any of the deepest shadows Aeslor-cluster had tasted on this new world, and as they made themself drift toward it they felt the familiar sting of Burning Gas. Unthinking, their motes jostled and jolted one another, seeking to hide behind one another, to be shielded from the pain. Some of their particles fell away, dead. But Aeslor-cluster pressed on, to taste the dance for an understanding of what was happening.

The pain passed. There was only a tiny amount of the poison and it diffused rapidly. But deep inside the rectangle, Aeslor-cluster tasted another object—a new object, moving toward them. Its surface was reflective, bipedal, and bilaterally symmetric, an unstable design for a being that had evolved out of the universe during Aeslor-cluster's eons. It was motile and moved one leg at a time, balancing its weight precariously with each step. The top was a dome of sorts, even more reflective than the rest.

The dorsal dome was semitransparent, and through it, Aeslor-cluster could taste an orifice—for lack of the appropriate terminology—opening and closing irregularly. Perhaps it was having difficulty respiring; perhaps it was attempting to speak.

They still had the translator, of course. Without it, no other species would be able to interpret the Light Peoples' elaborate dances, no more than the People could make sense of the means others used to talk. Aeslor-cluster switched it on and let their particles taste the hologram it generated.

Not that the display was informative: "Searching... searching... searching..."

It was not fair to expect the machine to know every language everywhere. Ninety-nine of every hundred languages known in the universe were not just dead but completely extinct, no longer spoken, written, or used it in any way, so what was the point of cluttering even atomic storage with such useless things?

The hologram resumed its laser dance, stark, bright, and jagged in the planet's shadow. "Match found. Preparing translation." Light People clustered around, twenty or more of them all jostling for a taste.

The new being's statement: "Who are you?"

The question rippled and waved through the Light People swarming around, and a half-dozen colonies started to dance responses. But Aeslor-cluster was Dancer for Others and their dance spoke through the machine. "Greetings," their motes swirled in elaborate patterns. "We are..." They gave the Light Peoples' name for themselves. "We have come to live here."

"This is our planet."

Aeslor-cluster's particles tightened into a ball of protection, motes jostling for spots far from the new creature. Around them other People swirled together into vortices, gaining speed for flight if it was needed. It was a reflex, a reaction to shock, a display of confusion.

The translator stayed mercifully silent.

Aeslor-cluster slowed their motes, made the conscious effort to order them precisely, to communicate through the machine clearly. "You have our apologies. We were told the planet was abandoned."

The creature raised an upper appendage. Aeslor-cluster could not imagine being stuck with such a useless thing, except perhaps that it was needed to balance the being's awkward locomotion. "Most left, yes, left the planet and left the system. Do you have word of them?"

The translator displayed the name of the language: Terran A (Mandarin) (Extinct).

Aeslor-cluster danced what they learned: "They are no longer known to the universe. We are sorry."

The speaker of Terran A (Mandarin) was silent and still. Aeslor-cluster did not know for how long. They had little sense for short amounts of time; the period between not-having-existed and no-longer-exists was very, very long. But Light People were never still, their motes were always in movement, if not dancing then reorienting themselves or simply drifting on atmospheric currents. This other was silent and still, and the translator remained unlit.

Aeslor-cluster danced, "Are you well?"

Inside the transparent dome, Aeslor-cluster could see the speaker of Terran A move its uppermost appendage from side to side. "It is no matter," it said. "They chose to leave and they left. We chose to stay and we have stayed."

"This is your planet?" The realtor told them the planet was uninhabited. Had it lied?

"Yes." It was a short statement in Terran A, and the hologram flared into motion only briefly. Aeslor-cluster's motes soaked in the brief burst of photons.

The hologram lit again. "Yes, it is ours. We fought it and fought for it. When the Sun expanded we dug deep for safety, learned to make air and water from rock, learned to make food from soil and waste. We refused to leave because this is our home."

Behind Aeslor-cluster, Suyli-cluster's motes danced frantically, outside the view of the translator. "Does this mean we cannot stay? But the light here, so rich, so beautiful."

"We bought this planet," Aeslor-cluster danced. It was a flat statement. "Bought" meant little to the Light People; it was access to a light of a certain quantity and quality in exchange for something the seller desired, no more. But to many other races it meant much more. It had taken Aeslor-cluster a long time to understand such an alien concept, but their ability to comprehend it was why Aeslor-cluster was Dancer for Others.

The speaker of Terran A was still again. Aeslor-cluster wondered whether it was consulting with others elsewhere by some means they could not detect, or simply moving slowly. "You did not buy her from us. You cannot. You will not. We will never sell. She is our home and we are those who have chosen to never leave her."

Suyli-cluster's motes spun together into a protective ball and twirled away, battering through other clusters. It was a dance of rage or of fear; Aeslor-cluster did not want to taste which. Around their motes others danced other dances, frantic and angry and sad. The Light People liked it here. This planet was perfect, and would be for millennia to come.

The hologram flared into life again, its jagged beams tasting familiar to Aeslor-cluster. "But you can stay," the Terran A speaker said.

It had not finished speaking before those surrounding Aeslor-cluster flew off in all directions, hastening to dance the news to the others. But Aeslor-cluster remained, their motes intertwined with the virtual lattice of the hologram. Only they tasted what the other said:

"Our home is the planet, but we can no longer live on her, only inside. Our life is sad and it is lonely, and it will be worse now that we know we are the last of our kind."

Aeslor-cluster's motes danced a dance of sympathy, unsure whether the translator would understand.

"We cannot use the outside, and you may not have the inside. You can stay on those terms. Will that suit you?"

There was nothing inside anything anywhere any of the Light People could want. "We thank you," Aeslor-cluster danced.

"It is agreed. You are welcome." The Terran turned on its clumsy appendages and returned to the dark—a door in the side of the tetrahedron that sealed closed behind it.

The time came that the planet's star grew so large that its heat would soon scorch the planet, and at that time, Aeslor-cluster made arrangements to buy another world for the People to dance upon. The Light People, so many more of them now after eons of life on the bright, beautiful, doomed world, chartered a ship and sailed away.

As a courtesy to their nearest neighbors, Aeslor-cluster tried to warn the Terran A speakers in their stone tetrahedron, but no matter what means they used to communicate, no being ever responded.

Cephalopod Dreams

by AE Stueve

"I don't *know shit* about the ocean," Sam said as she hung her head over the railing.

"Then why you here, girl?" Jamal laughed as he tried handing her a rough spun towel. Jamal was a natural sailor with saltwater in his blood and a big smile etched on his chapped lips.

Sam was not. "Ung," she said, feeling the bile dance below her own decks. She knew why she was here but she was not going to share that information with Jamal. It would terrify him to insanity. She couldn't bear to do that to him... not yet.

"Clean up now, Captain be comin' quick."

Sam waved the towel away and lurched forward. The boat's steady, dull lift and fall made her knees wobble and her stomach bubble. The Northern Atlantic Ocean, during the late autumn months, was no place for a landlubber like her. But she had to be here. She knew the truth of it.

Against Sam's will, her wide eyes took in the endless, churning sea and the cold sun reflected there. Only after she vomited a clear, acidic liquid down the side of the trawler did she turn away. "How far down is the water?" she asked, wiping her mouth with the back of her hand.

"You mean how deep? Or how far away from where we are right now?"

Sam shrugged. "I don't know. Both?"

Jamal sighed. "Well," he said, "the water is far enough away that if you fall, you die. But on the off chance you live after that, you gonna freeze to death or drown in that deep, deep black."

"That sounds awful," Sam replied. Her throat scratched and her skin was dry, so there was something inviting about the prospect of dying in water, of letting the cool liquid smother her, comfort her, and ultimately change her.

"Little girl, all you do is puke and... All you do is puke. Why'd you get on board *The Defiant Jane*, anyway?" Jamal asked as he forced the towel into Sam's hand.

"No reason that would make sense to you." Sam turned away from the choppy water and rubbed the towel over her forehead. The northerly breeze rippling over her skin made her shake. "I wanted to be certain of something, I guess."

"Boats are no place for secrets, girl," Jamal replied, his voice the deep baritone of a man sure in his convictions. "People be talkin'. You goin' t'have t'talk back soon. Better to me than others... Others not so kind."

Sam's shaggy black hair stuck to her head like a dead bug. She ran her hands through the greasy strands and studied the slate sky, the emptiness. "This body is so fucking dirty."

"Strange thing to say, 'this body.' What you mean? You got another body somewhere?" Jamal smiled through his words, but for the first time, Sam noticed something less comforting there, something more fearful.

"I just feel so dirty, is all." The words clawed their way out of her throat.

"That's what happens to a body when you live in the belly of a beast like *Jane*, Sammi, and only come out to vomit."

Sam's dark face went green and she spun around to face the water again, releasing the few contents still in her stomach.

"You're a case, girl, a case," Jamal said, patting her back. He walked away, mumbling to himself something in boat-jargon Sam couldn't understand.

"Why am I doing this?" she asked the ocean, the sky, and the boat as she rolled onto her back and drifted off into a dream of memories.

"This is crazy, Jonas," Sam said after a cursory glance at the paperwork before her. "Your dad didn't die for this." She closed the briefcase on her lap and clicked it shut. The sound echoed through the nearly empty Miskatonic University Aquarium with a finality that made her proud. It felt official, mature, adult even. At 32 years old, Sam knew it was about time she felt that way. She only wished her cousin felt the same.

"You're only saying that because you haven't read everything," Jonas whispered. His words were sharp with intensity. "You're reading the headlines and skipping the meat!" He wrenched the briefcase from Sam's lap and placed it on his own. "This is revealing! What it proves about our family—makes so much sense! We're so smart! We're so removed! We're so much better!"

Sam tried to stay calm. "I've heard this before, Jonas, from you, and you know I don't agree."

"But it's *true!*" Jonas shouted. "I'm not making up fake findings or gathering incorrect data!" He slammed his fist on the briefcase. "It's all true!"

Sam jumped to her feet and placed her hands on her cousin's shoulders. "Calm down," she hissed. It was a slow weekday afternoon in the middle of October. But it was warm and quiet in the university's aquarium and the relaxed lighting had been making Sam's eyes heavy before Jonas showed up with more of his mad ramblings. She hoped she appeared calm and professorial and not tired of all of her cousin's antics as she looked down into Jonas's eyes. "We cannot meet to talk about this kind of thing anymore, especially not here."

"Are you worried about your precious job?" Jonas spat the words like stale gum.

"Yes!" Sam scoffed. "I'm worried about my job. I'm a college professor with a PhD. in geology—"

"With an emphasis in seismic studies and blah, blah, blah, blah, blah, blah," Jonas mocked as though they were back in elementary school and he was figuring something out far before she could.

She sighed and rubbed the bridge of her nose. "What you're talking about spits in the face of science."

"*Mainstream* science," Jonas replied. "You don't know anything about this."

"I'm sorry?" Sam asked, letting her grip tighten on Jonas' shoulders as sudden anger burned her calm to cinders. "You do?"

Jonas shrugged her off and stood. "Just because I don't have a degree doesn't mean I'm ignorant."

"I have multiple degrees. What are you saying about me?"

"I'm not even going to dignify that with a response, Sam. You study the earth, not the ocean! Jesus, stop being a bitch! I know this is true," Jonas insisted as he slammed the briefcase on the bench and turned from her so that he could look at the cephalopod tank.

Sam didn't like the way her cousin's eyes lit up when he searched for the octopus. They searched lovingly, the eyes of a long-estranged spouse inspecting the crowd for his significant other at an airport. They held desire and yearning in their depths. Sam shivered.

She took a deep breath and followed her cousin's gaze. "You wanted to meet here because of this, didn't you?" She knew the octopus Jonas looked for was somewhere in that water, creeping on its eight legs, studying its surroundings, and generally being eerie. Or maybe it was sleeping, dreaming of a new world where cephalopods ruled under the frightful gaze of the Great Old One the way Jonas claimed. Sam had to admit on the rare occasions she actually did see it, the thing looked like it was thinking, *really* thinking, maybe even plotting like a man or waiting for its god to wake and bring about a new world order.

No, Sam thought. *That's madness.* Even if there was an Elder God sleeping, waiting to destroy everything, why would their family be his chosen people?

"The small ones are His emissaries," Jonas said. His voice was solemn now, almost worshipful. "They are beginning to emerge from the water," he said in reference to footage of various cephalopods slinking onto beaches to hunt.

"Look," Sam said, closing her eyes so she would stop trying to find the brown, gelatinous creature milling around the water, "I'm sorry. But what you're saying is cra—a little hard to swallow."

"The evidence is here!" Jonas seethed as he pointed at the briefcase. "All of it! There's history, ancient tribes, African relics. Some of the statues in the forgotten corners of Egypt and the Middle East. If you look at it all together the way I have, all the pieces add up."

Sam shook her head. "Jesus."

"There's the biggest scam to keep us down that ever existed!"

"Come on, Jonas, that's—"

"Someone is trying to kill me. And they'll try to kill you soon. It's the establishment. They want to keep things the way they are."

"Oh my God, Jonas."

"Sam, science be damned, there is a God in control, *the wrong god*. Not our God."

"You're not making any sense."

Jonas shook with frustration and ran his hands through his hair while shouting, "I am making sense! I've stepped up to a new level of understanding!"

"Are you on acid right now?" Sam asked, trying to calm her cousin down.

"Don't. Don't write this off! Don't write me off! I don't have time for your close-mindedness!" Jonas reached for the briefcase but knocked it over, crashing it open and sending papers scattering on the floor. The few people admiring the marine life took notice. A young mother holding a cooing child raised an eyebrow at the disheveled man with bulging eyes and crooked glasses as he whimpered, grumbled, and tried to pick up his mess.

An elderly couple moved away when Sam ran a hand through her hair and breathed out, "Jesus Christ."

"You have no idea how serious this is. You have the most important duty to Him!"

Sam pressed Jonas's shoulder, hissing, "Calm down!" This wasn't the first time Jonas had embarrassed her. Her cousin had, on more than one occasion, barged in on one of her lectures and made a fool of them both. When they were children, Jonas had been in a perpetual state of lunacy, from kindergarten to college. Which, Sam determined, was why he had dropped out three months before graduating. As far as Sam was concerned, Jonas embarrassing her had been a lifelong event. Still. "You're causing a scene! This is where I work."

"Screw your scene! You work on the other side of campus," Jonas said, shaking free of Sam's grasp and bending over to shuffle his papers together. "Do you know why my dad gave you everything he had and not me?"

"Oh don't bring this up again. I've told you more times than I can count the money is yours for the taking."

"I don't want your money! I don't even want the damn house. I never wanted it. I don't need it. All I want is for you to listen so you survive, so you do what must be done! So that you can be part of the glory!"

"What the hell are you getting at?"

"My dad gave you the money because he knew you needed it."

"And you don't?"

"Does it look like it?"

"You really want me to answer that?"

Jonas ignored the jab and picked up the last of his papers before taking a deep breath and returning a newly calm gaze to Sam. "He gave you the house because he knew you would take care of it and keep his secrets safe from the world while I learned more."

"Learned more what?" Sam sighed.

Jonas's eyes were like steel, a silvery cold that broke through all of Sam's defenses. "Samantha," he began, quietly, evenly, like a teacher struggling to hold down his frustration at an ignorant student. "I'm fine. I know I look a wreck, but that's just because I haven't slept since I finalized my findings. You know I'm fine. If I needed money I'd just invent something and sell it. Just like Father. But I don't need it. I won't need it ever again."

Sam sighed. "Look, sorry cuz, it's just that—"

"This is crazy?" Jonas asked, allowing a small smile to crack through his lips.

"Yes. It's crazy. Are you happy? I said it."

"Just read it, *really* read it. Spend time with it. Don't skim for the parts too hard to believe. Read it all. There's no denying the truth when every detail is printed in black and white. It all fits."

Sam looked at her watch. "I have class in 15 minutes, Jonas. If I take it and promise to really look through it, will you leave?"

Jonas nodded. "I will."

He offered Sam a small smile that melted her, but only slightly. There was, after all, a permanent feeling of guilt that climbed to the forefront of her emotions whenever she interacted with her cousin. Sam was clearly the luckier of the two. Having grown up with two sane parents, graduated from college, and become a relative success in her chosen field, she was a far cry from her wandering and extremist cousin who lived on flights of fancy. Deep down, she knew it all had to do with nurture, not nature. She reached for the briefcase.

"Then give it here and come see me in a few days, at home." She wasn't sure if she would actually read it, but insinuating that she would felt like a nice gesture.

"Crazy son of a bitch." She wasn't sure if she was talking about her cousin, her uncle, or the captain of *The Defiant Jane*. She bent over and dry heaved. The December night's cold sliced through her parka and made her fingers burn and teeth chatter. She swallowed something that was a mix of phlegm and half-digested orange. "Just let me in," she mumbled.

"Hey Sammi!" Jamal opened the door Sam was leaning on and gently shoved her aside. "Captain's coming. I think he wants to turn *Jane* 'round and drop you at first port. Bad things happenin.' Some say they your fault."

"Shit." Sam closed her eyes, crouched, and tried to roll onto her back but couldn't do it without everything inside her feeling as though it was going to explode. "What do you mean? I paid for the whole ride. We're not where we need to be yet."

"Yeah, well, some of the crew be talkin'. They think you bad luck, girl. You a girl, that's bad enough, but things have been bad these last days. Oceans are rough. They blame you," he paused there and scratched his chin, "it's like..." he stopped again and looked out at the black horizon, studying the dark, angry ocean and its dark, angrier lover, the sky, "...like you gettin' sick is makin' the ocean get sick."

"That's ridiculous," Sam said as she closed her eyes, trying to reduce the pain in her gut and knowing the exact opposite was occurring.

"An omen," a grizzled voice joined the conversation. Sam could feel the captain's oppressive shadow lingering before the moon. "Sailors can be a cowardly and superstitious lot and they're sure your presence and all the rough waters are somehow tied together tightly."

"Like a voodoo knot," Jamal added.

"Or an albatross around our collective neck."

"That's the stupidest thing I've ever heard," Sam said, but her voice held none of the conviction she wished it did. She knew the truth of it. Jamal and the captain were closer to correct than either of them knew or could understand. The waters were getting rougher and it was because of her. There was a scent to the air—the saltiness, the fish smell, was somehow thicker than usual. She could feel it and they could too, like it was difficult to move.

To be oppressed by nature creeping in around them was not an unusual sensation for these men. Many of the men on the boat had spent their lives sailing the ocean, after all. But there was something different now, something stronger. Desperation was creeping up on them. Sam knew that if any of them made it out alive they would look back on this trip and realize their bodies were telling them to escape. Something bad had been coming but their inconsistent human minds had been too weak to perceive it clearly. Still, Sam was not there to save them.

"Don't you sailors follow the seasons or something?" she asked. "Isn't it always rough this time of year out here?"

"How would you know?" the captain asked as he nudged Sam's ribs with his leather boots. "You're no sailor." There was a loud clicking sound that broke through the whistling wind, then the captain continued, "And what about all these folders we found in your bunk? These are rife with stupid."

Sam opened her eyes to see the briefcase she had brought with her, shoved to the edges with all of the work Jonas had completed, all the truth. It was dangling in the captain's hands like it was anathema to him. The captain was surly in that way all lifelong sailors were. He had ruddy cheeks, nearly hidden by a bushy black beard. And Sam knew his beady eyes could see to the ends of the ocean as well as right through her. It was like he was a living, breathing cliche. She loved him and hated him for it.

"Why were you going through my stuff?" Sam asked. She intended the question to sound like a threat. But in her voice she heard a whimper.

"Never mind that, Dr. Samantha Jones of Miskatonic University's geology department. Forgot to mention where you're from, didn't you?" The captain squatted down and inched his face close to Sam's.

"I didn't think it mattered," she groaned.

"Everything matters on the ocean, girl," the captain said. "Especially shit like this." She felt his warm breath and smelled the citrusy, sharp scent in it. Her stomach quivered as she picked up the hint of cigar smoke lingering in his bristly beard.

"You have no idea," she replied as she belched in his face.

He turned away. "What's in this case is strange work for a woman who studies rocks."

"Well, I like to be well-rounded." Sam coughed and was sure she tasted blood in the back of her throat.

"Know this," the captain said, "the things on these papers are bad. You're lucky the man who found it couldn't read English well or you'd have been raped and thrown into the water before I was out of bed this morning. We're turning around. You're getting off the boat at the next harbor. You're getting your money back. And I want you to stay the hell away from the sea for the rest of your life." The captain threw the case into the ocean as though it was an afterthought.

Then he offered Sam a disdainful look and strode toward the cabin. The papers, her cousin's work, the information that had led her out to the middle of the ocean, fluttered away, cast on the breeze to their watery demise.

Before the captain reached the door, he paused and faced Sam again. "Some things are too great and terrible for us to understand," he shouted over a rush of wind and the crash of waves against *Jane's* hull. "Things like that should remain asleep." Though he was loud, his voice was a calm balance to the rough waters. Sam wondered if it came from a deep fear, a deep rage, or both.

"You crazy, Sammi girl," Jamal said, helping her to her feet. "I heard about your squid stuff. Wouldn't read them papers though. Old monsters, not man, makes no matter. No business of ours. You remember that now and Jamal keep you safe 'til port."

"You're too kind, Jamal."

A few moments later Sam found herself locked in her small square of a room, lying on a hard floor deep in the ship's guts, alone, and thinking about how she had made it out to the middle of the ocean.

Why did I do this? Sam asked herself. She had been bored. A few days earlier, she had downed a little too much wine after work. She had been taken by a nostalgic whim to at least give her crazy cousin the decency of reading his mad words. *Love,* she thought. *Love and guilt got me to read this... this mad genius.*

She ignored those all-too-human emotions as she poured over Jonas's papers spread out on the dining room table. Since she had snapped the briefcase open, she had been there, seriously studying Jonas's writings. She could see it now; it was true, all of it. While her days had been filled with her cousin's insights, her nights had been filled with cephalopod dreams. In them, she moved like a silk warrior through the waters, eight legs like fluid, thoughts on a different plane of understanding than the human mind was capable of reaching. She was happy to do the bidding of an incomprehensible thing that defied terms like 'god' and 'monster.' This thing was a Great Old One and He would be waking soon to lead His chosen people both in the sea and on the land. She felt herself changing from cephalopod to woman and back again, dancing through the waters, climbing on the land, killing those who fought against her. She was the first line of action in the creation of the new world. She was a warrior woman with only the smallest amount of His blood flowing through her, and yet she was like an avenging goddess to her new enemies. These dreams should have been nightmares. But they weren't.

The giant house's silence was like a cloak of polished pinewood and rich scents. Only Jonas knew all the passwords to get through the gate and by the sensors and Sam hadn't seen him in weeks. On any other night it had been comforting to be here, alone, surrounded by luxury she hadn't earned. Tonight though, things were different. She was thinking how strange it was, how irrefutable the evidence was, how she couldn't properly process all this information, how she should never have opened this godawful briefcase to begin with as her eyes drank up line after line of *facts*. There was something terrible sleeping in the deepest, darkest depths of the Northern Atlantic Ocean, something that would be waking soon and destroying anything that fought against it, something that wanted *her*. No. Something that *needed* her.

She looked up at that realization, studying the opulence around her, and wondered, *Is this something I want?* Before she could answer her question with the 'Yes' she knew was hanging off the end of her tongue, a knock disturbed her.

It was a series of sharp, loud bangs that broke through the focused fear inside her, shattering the madness, and sending her jumping from her chair.

"Jonas!" she shouted because it could only have been him. "Jonas!" she shouted again. "I'm coming!" Sam ran across the massive expanse of the dining room and through an equally elegant foyer toward the double doors. When she flung them open she saw Jonas standing on her front porch, hunched over in the dying light. His clothes were filthy and hung on an unfed frame. His hair was more of a mess than normal and it looked like he hadn't showered in days. The shadows across his face spoke of death and despair. "Oh my God, Jonas!"

"Tell me you believe now," Jonas coughed out the words.

"Yes," Sam said, without hesitation. Admitting it out loud felt like a release. The fringes of her brain tingled with the knowledge. Her body shivered. "I do."

"Good," Jonas said, smiling to reveal a bloody mouth. "Then you can help Him."

"What do I have to do?"

"This body's dead," Jonas said, falling into Sam's arms. Sam stood against her cousin's weight and managed to hold him up. As she pulled him inside, Sam noticed something thick and black sticking to Jonas's chest and belly.

"Blood," Jonas said. "They shot me."

"Who?"

"Whoever doesn't want you to know the truth. Whoever wants to stop it... I was so careful... It must have been someone at the aquarium." He coughed. "The old couple maybe... I think..."

"We've got to get you to a hospital."

"No, you've got to go. I'll be fine. Dad has... something... in the sub-basement for me here. You need to fly, though. You have a mission."

"How? Sub-basement?"

"Don't worry about it. Just know you've been put in this house for a reason and now the reason is over and you've got to go. You've got to get to the ocean on a boat. You have a very particular... mission... It has to be you..."

"The ocean?" Sam asked, but before Jonas could answer, gunshots rang out in the distance and a window shattered. Muffled shouts filled the air.

They both jumped, then Jonas whispered, "You read the papers. You know what you have to do," into Sam's ear.

"Who is after you?"

"Who isn't?" Blood spilled out of Jonas's mouth as he spoke. "Get me to the basement. Then take the papers. Memorize the instructions. Get to the ocean! I'll see you again soon." He coughed and stumbled.

Sam found herself using all of her strength to pull her cousin along. "But what about you?"

"Just do it. Soon He will wake. All of us will. Everything else will make sense then."

More shots rang out.

"Go!" Jonas shouted with more energy than he should have possessed.

Sam gingerly ushered her cousin through the house, toward the basement. Gunfire called out like angry echoes. Wood shattered and rained splinters down upon them as they moved. A bullet grazed Sam's arm. When they reached the basement door, Sam felt her heart beating out fear inside her chest. She hugged her cousin.

"I'll be fine," Jonas said. "Go."

Sam awoke from the dream of memories and found her mind was not her own. She tried to focus on the present. She tried to understand the past. All she knew was that she was a captive and didn't want to be any longer. She felt her faith flounder.

I'm in prison. I'm on the ocean and I'm in prison. This is stupid. I don't care about the evidence or the Great Old One anymore. Let Him sleep. I don't care about Jonas or what happened to him. I think... I think I want to go home.

Of course you want to go home*, another voice entered Sam's thoughts.* **But tell me, is it true? Do you no longer believe?**

"Who's there?" Sam asked the walls. She hadn't spoken to anyone in days. She could feel that the boat was lost and the sailors were angry. Jamal occasionally brought her food and drink, but Sam didn't touch it.

Your cousin*.*

"Jonas?"

I'm here with everyone, Sam. You should come too. He is waking. You know what you need to do.

Sam sighed. "I need to believe."

Talk with your mind, Sam. We can hear you that way and the others can't.

"What are you talking—"

The door crashed open and Jamal stared down at Sam, his large black eyes masking their fear with anger. "Sam!" he said, "You need to be stoppin.' The captain be watchin.'"

"What?" Sam asked.

Jamal pointed to the camera in the corner of the room, at the ceiling. "Open your eyes, girl."

"Shit."

He only shook his head and backed away. "Boats are no place for legends and myth. They spook. We... we can't be speakin' no more."

"We haven't spoken in days."

Humans know nothing, Sam. They are temporary. We are forever. You know what you must do. Our time of suffering is over. We are chosen.

"Why me?"

You know why. Now, don't talk!

Why?

You must, Sam. It is the last step. He needs a sacrifice like this and you are the last one of the first wave to come over. It is your job. You must spill their blood.

How?

Instead of an answer in her head, Sam felt a heavy thud against the boat. Then another. Then another. Lights buzzed and flickered and sirens screamed. "Jamal!" Sam yelled, but there was no response. Her door flung open as the walls around it compressed.

It has to be you. It has to be a woman, the voice said.

"Why?"

It is the way. They are your enemies.

Enemies?

Our time is now. He is waking but he needs this sacrifice. Shed the husk of your old beliefs and you will live.

But... I'm afraid.

You will never be afraid again if you join us.

All of them?

All of them.

Even Jamal?

Especially him.

Am I going mad?

You know the truth of that. You are from the stars. Our people are. Jamal has forgotten this. Many have.

But I don't remember.

You remember. He has awoken Dr. Samantha Jones of Miskatonic University. He will bring death to those who rule now. The old order will be no more. A new one will rise. Offer up the sailors for sacrifice. Join and live or stay encased in ignorance and fear and die. What do you choose?

"I choose life," Sam said as she forced her cell door open with newly found preternatural strength. She made her way toward the first sailor she saw. It was a panicked man, faceless in his normalcy, running away from Sam toward the deck. He had no idea what was coming. Sam pounced like a beast and smashed his head into the metal stairs. Blood and skull splattered, warm droplets like rain and hail on a summer day.

Jamal was at the top of the stairs. "Sam?" he asked, his voice smaller than Sam had ever heard it.

Sam looked up at the closest thing she had to a friend on *The Defiant Jane*. **"You all must die,"** she said. But she spoke in a language Jamal had never heard. It was guttural and echoing, a sound the human tongue could not make. Jamal was frozen in fear.

Sam attacked.

Far below, a Great Old God grinned as He opened his eyes.

The Fire Demon's Daughter

by Lisa Short

She had been only an infinitesimal part of those long-ago, hideous maelstroms; she had always been one of the lesser corps, never in the great vanguards. But still, she had burned, her fire pouring out of her to join theirs in an ecstasy of destruction. Whole worlds had died in their fires; as she aged, she had learned to feel shame, and regret, though they could not erase her memories of that primordial joy in burning. But it had been a very long time since the great battles they had waged, and she had gone to sleep after the last of them. She didn't know how long she had slept, but when she awoke, the blasted rock and ice cavern in which she'd laired had become green and warm.

And there was life—life everywhere. There hadn't been any at all when first she'd gone to sleep, and now it grew, flew, crept, and jumped from around every corner. She shied away from it at first; the life that was mobile returned the favor (wisely, she thought). The life that wasn't simply laid there and grew, uneasily accepting her presence as just a temporary interruption in the long, slow beat of its existence.

For a time, she merely abided in this new environment. She watched the blazing ball of fire that was this place's sun cross the sliver of sky visible outside of her cavern, then the darkened sky lit with an infinite number of fiery pinpricks, red and blue and white against the formless black. But eventually she grew tired of that and bestirred herself. The creatures sharing her lair exploded into a flurry of panicked escape as she heaved herself up and staggered out of the cavern. She was surprisingly corporeal, she thought, and looked down at herself; she glittered in the sunlight, except for the dull black of her great talons gouging the rock floor as she moved. She was still clearly what she'd always been, though, a manifestation of destructive power— she shook her head restlessly and lurched all the way outside.

The air smelled sweet and lively, rich with moisture— too much moisture; she felt vaguely *extinguished* and didn't like it. She thought she could fly, and found she'd spread her forelimbs wide, exposing massive sheets of membranous bronzed flesh beneath them. She had emerged onto a rocky platform barely large enough to support all of herself, and below it was a sheer drop to a distant tumble of rocks and spraying water. It was time to discover if her fancy was real; she gathered herself and sprang forward into the wet, empty air.

The plummeting was brief and terrifyingly invigorating. She shouted with glee, and the rocky cliffs all around her echoed back a thunderous roar. But the wind caught her wings, shining rich metallic brown in the sunlight, and she glided in a massive arc around the precipice she'd leaped from. She roared again, for the joy of it—but that reminded her of the firestorms, and the utter end of everything in their wake, and she chose not to do it a third time. Silent now, she angled herself in the opposite direction of the sun, toward the jagged masses of purple rock on the far horizon.

The masses of rock turned out to be mountains; beyond them was a desert. That suited her better—the scorched, desiccated air offered no resistance to her flight. This time, when small creatures fled beneath the long shadows of her wings, she felt a sharp predator's urge to chase them. But she didn't indulge it, not yet. Instead, as the sun sank down in the darkening sky of her first day in the desert, she found a pile of boulders even larger than she was and slept once more.

But her immensurable slumber was truly over; she woke quite naturally when the sun crept over the horizon. The prickling interest with which she regarded the larger, short-furred animal prowling around her still form was joined by an empty, stabbing feeling deeper inside. She recognized it: *hunger*.

The animal satisfied that desire, but no other. She would have preferred to have had no other, and if this world was nothing but sun and wind, rock and growing and creeping life, she would be content enough, but she wanted to be sure of that before giving herself up to it. So she hauled herself upright once more and spread her wings to warm them, then launched herself skyward. Since she had begun that way, and she had always liked efficiency, she continued in the direction of the setting sun. Should she find herself someday returning to the site of her first awakening having encountered nothing more momentous than she had already seen thus far, she would know the answer to the question of what this world truly contained.

But she only flew for two days more before she found that answer. The part of her that was the inescapable ache of shame and regret was sharply disappointed. But another part of her had always been curious, inquiring and analytical, and that part felt a distinct heightening of interest as what was not a natural rock formation rose higher and higher against the horizon.

It was made of an artificial stone—fired mud and crushed rock, she thought, examining it after she landed. What was more interesting was the creature that was stuck to it, quite dead. It might have died of the obvious wounds it bore; worked-ore spikes were plunged into its limbs and also through the front of its head, which might kill anything, perhaps even her in her current form. But no immobile growing thing or prey animal could have fashioned any of this. The fluids of its life had dried to tackiness, which meant that it might not have been too long since it died for her to learn what she could about it. She leaned far, far down, opened her jaws, and carefully licked at the reddish-brown liquid that had pooled stickily around its neck.

Knowledge exploded into her—and it was an explosion; these creatures lived violent and emotional lives, and for a moment, she was almost overwhelmed enough to flee even her corporeal self. But no—the images, thoughts, and feelings quietened into a more ordered cascade into her receptive mind. Language—complex, even beautiful, with a music that she remembered always being drawn to in other places and times where it had existed before the fires had put it out. She flinched away from that, and determinedly re-immersed herself.

The sun had moved some distance across the sky before she returned fully to her own consciousness. She gazed at what was left of him (for the creature was a *man*, she had learned) for a long moment, then settled down at his feet and fell into a companionable doze.

The man, who had thought of himself as Aleie (*Aleie an-Badaie*, whispered his memories which were now hers, which meant *Aleie-the-son-of-Badaie*) had come from a city full of others like him. She was sorry to leave Aleie to rot, but found herself uncomfortable with producing even so minuscule a fire as would be required to scatter him into ashes. So she bowed to him instead, as she might have once to a superior of her kind, her muzzle pressed in the rock-laden dirt for several reverential seconds. Then she leaped aloft in the direction she knew the city lay.

The sun was low on the horizon when she surprised a flock of creatures wheeling in a lazy, intricate dance above what was nearly a small mountain in its own right. They scattered in a spate of flapping wings and harsh, furious croaks as she approached; *carrion birds*, her new knowledge informed her, and whatever had attracted their attention was likely not yet dead. She swept over the rocks herself but could make out nothing of interest in the lengthening violet shadows between them. Memories of the city beckoned, and she was about to soar away once more when a different sound broke the stillness of the desert—a guttural moan, barely loud enough to be heard.

She landed quickly, nosing around the base of the rocks, and discovered the source. It was alive—no, *she* was alive. This was a woman, very obviously so to Aleie's memories; she was deep in the throes of childbearing. Her face shone wetly in the emerging starlight and her eyes were squeezed shut; they didn't open even when a hesitant, curious talon gently dimpled the flesh of her cheek. *Sweat* and *tears*, her new knowledge whispered; it might be

186

enough, and she withdrew as silently as she was able. Once out of the woman's possible sight, she rolled her tongue out and sampled the dampness clinging to her talon.

She hadn't really considered the form she had taken when she had first awakened in this world; she had simply become a manifestation of as much of her essence as it was able to encompass. Now, though, while the form she wished to take was far more natural to this place, it would not be natural to herself at all. While the process itself was fairly quick and not unpleasant, she was rather shocked at the unpleasantness of actually being in the form; bare flesh instantly puckered against the cold night air and the gritty sand stung where it pressed against her legs. She scrambled to her feet, staggering as her spindly new frame lost its balance. Another harsh, choked sound emerged from the crevasse a short distance away; recalled to her purpose, she made her way back to it.

The woman's eyes were open now; they were almost as black as her sweat-soaked hair. "Who are you?" Even in her obvious weakness and pain, the woman's voice was sharp.

"I—" She choked a little; speech was an unfamiliar process. "I—" she began again, then stopped once more, confounded. Aleie's memory was full of names, but she had no idea how to choose one. From a story he'd particularly liked, though, one abruptly presented itself and she blurted out, "Aianda."

"Aianda?" The woman bared her teeth. "The fire demon's daughter? Your parents must have been in an interesting mood when you were born. Though perhaps I'll name this child that as well, if it's a girl—" Her jaw clenched abruptly and her back arched, the rest of her words lost in a groan. Aianda (for she might as well begin as she meant to go on) hurried forward and fell to her knees beside the woman, taking a white-knuckled fist between her own two hands.

The woman's spasms drew closer and closer together as the night wore on. Her life weakened with each one, but the woman (whose own name was Iaidalla ani-Gebhair, by then there was enough blood soaking them both for scraps of herself to manifest like bright sparks in Aianda's consciousness) was single-minded in her determination to give birth to this child, regardless of the cost to herself.

"It's why I left," Iaidalla gasped out, between the convulsions that shook her frame. "The latest bride, she meant to drug me and claim the child was stillborn! I don't know why I'm telling you this—I'm not even sure you're real." Her fingers dug clawlike into Aianda's wrists; the pain had startled Aianda at first, but she had grown used to it, and the loss of feeling in her ankles and feet from being sat upon, and the burning numbness of the cold that afflicted all her bare flesh. She no longer wondered at Iaidalla's ability to withstand these hours of torment. Plainly her kind were accustomed to a certain level of suffering simply due to the frailty of their forms. "I am not my lord's youngest wife, by far—but I'm the strongest, and I'll prove it." She bared her teeth again against the pain.

The bloody crescent of the sun had broken above the horizon when, with a final, rattling breath, Iaidalla pushed the child fully from her body. She relaxed then, so abruptly that Aianda overbalanced and sat down with an audible thump on the gritty rock, barely retaining the presence of mind to catch the child to her chest as she fell. Aianda stared at Iaidalla's face—the dark eyes were frozen half-open, glittering like glass in the crimson light—then down at the child in her arms. It looked nothing at all like a small version of Iaidalla or even like something alive, bloody and bluish and wrapped all around with a venous membrane and still-pulsing cord.

But Iaidalla had known what to do with a newborn child, and that knowledge had been at the forefront of her thoughts, so Aianda knew as well. Soon enough the child was rosy, coughing and then shrieking as Aianda carried it to the very back of the crevasse, where Iaidalla had hidden a large pack beside a tiny natural spring. The child disliked being cleaned, disliked being dressed even more, and being put down while Aianda struggled into one of Iaidalla's garments was the final indignity. *She is hungry*, whispered Iaidalla's memories beneath the child's deafening wails, and at the thought, a sudden sharp tingling lanced through Aianda's chest—no, *breasts*, whispered both Aleie and Iaidalla. But Iaidalla at least had done this before, and the child herself seemed to have some instinct for it. Soon enough, the child's cries quietened into gasping, greedy gulps.

After the child had fallen asleep, Aianda gazed down at the spiky dark lashes resting on the round little cheeks and the tiny hands clenched tightly in her own long, tangled hair. The city had rejected Aleie in the cruelest possible way, and had been hardly less brutal to Iaidalla; Aianda's bright interest in seeing its wonders had darkened, and uneasily, she felt the fire within her stir. But she must return the child to the city, to her own kind—this child who slept so trustingly in her arms, who had now taken life itself from her very own body. Aleie's and Iaidalla's dead faces stared out of her memories... her own memories, not borrowed ones; would this child's soon join them?

The child stirred, then sighed in vast, sleeping contentment. Aianda's hold tightened involuntarily around the fragile body. *I won't*, she thought, *I* won't *give into the fire—I won't summon the maelstrom—no matter what happens. No matter what.* She closed her eyes, waiting for the merciless sun to cross the sky and sink beneath the horizon, to begin their journey together to the city.

Outpost of the Empire
by Aviel McDermott

The rumble of the mining bots made the entire facility tremble, but Inferior Zeytord 4634 was so used to it that it didn't even register.

It wasn't his turn monitoring the machines for this darkside shift, so it wasn't his problem right now. Or at least, it shouldn't have been. It'd been a long while since most of the others needed 4634's supervision.

4634 wouldn't have even been awake right now if the supply shipment wasn't running so late.

He tapped into the system interface on the cargo deck, writing reports as he waited. He figured he might as well get something productive done. The newbie was going to help him unpack the supplies, but 4634 sent him to bed an hour ago, so now unpacking was going to have to wait until tomorrow.

An alert on the monitor popped up in front of the atmospheric conditions report 4634 had been working on. The cargo vessel was finally here, flashing its Zeyfficial

Certificate and this week's security code through communications.

4634 sighed. He sent off the responding codes and pressed the button to open the transport bay as usual, ready to get this over with so he could sleep.

4634's interface showed the cargo vessel as it pulled into the airlock, and he frowned. It was a different ship than the standard long-haul Zeycraft. It didn't even look like a Zeytoidian military vehicle at all. The vessel was sleeker than the usual bulky style, and it had an insignia on the side that 4634 didn't recognize at all.

He checked for his gun in his side pocket. The vessel had a Zeyfficial Certificate, and those were very hard to check, but it was better to be sure. It had been a long time since 4634 had used his weapon, but he was sure he still could.

With the affirmation that his gun was ready at his side, 4634 went out to meet the cargo ship and it emerged from the airlock.

The ship's door opened down with a thunk and a figure stumbled out of it. 4634 blinked. It'd been a long time since he'd seen one of them.

It was a single person. A human person, 4634 could still tell, though he hadn't seen any of those since his time on the front lines. The human's eyes were distinctively brown instead of red, his skin and hair were dark, and in general his features different from 4634's own in both obvious and subtle ways. The human had darker skin than 4634's pale features, a smaller nose than 4634's regal hook, and softer facial features. This wasn't another clone.

"I'm really sorry about the delay," the human said. He wore a grey and blue uniform that was much less dramatic than that of the green and black of the Zeytoidian military.

The human drew one hand through his hair as he stared down at a notepad in his hand.

The human gave 4634 an apologetic smile but got only a blank stare in response. Shifting uncomfortably, the human continued: "My navigational system does *not* have a good time working this far out from colonized space. I mean," the man gestured, "not that this isn't colonized, you've obviously got something going on out here, but man. The farthest cargo hub is so far—I mean this place doesn't even show up on the *map—*"

"You are not a Zeytord Clone," 4634 interrupted. "You aren't any part of the Zeytoidian military."

"Uh, yeah, no." The human shook his head. "No, I don't have any Zeytord in me, no. I work for a communications and cargo company, actually. The Space Frontiers." The human gestured again, this time specifically to the emblem on his ship. The logo.

4634's hand strayed to his weapon.

"Why are you delivering the cargo here?" 4634 demanded.

"Woah!" The human's hands shot up with palms outstretched. "I'm just working a job, dude! We have some good contracts with the Zeytoidian Empire! We're a neutral, third-party business or whatever you want to call it. We just do basic supply runs."

4634 took his hand off his holster and shook his head. Everything seemed to check out, and if this man was going to attack he probably would have already.

"We've just always gotten our supply from other Zeytoidian ships," 4634 said, "and you were very late."

"Yeah," the human rubbed the back of his neck. "Sorry about that. I'll get here quicker next time! You want your cargo?"

After the cargo was securely off-loaded, 4634 had to sign the proper forms that said that he had gotten it. Double the number of forms as usual, for both the contractor and the Empire. 4634 still felt slightly off-balance.

"There was no announcement about a third-party contractor coming in," 4634 commented as he skimmed the paperwork.

"Yeah, well, you know the Empire, almost as bureaucratic as the Galactic Council," the human shrugged as if 4634 knew anything of the bureaucracy of the Council. "Anyway, it's a bit embarrassing, isn't it? They probably don't have enough troops for this kind of non-combat grunt work anymore."

"What do you mean?" 4634 asked. "Why not?"

"Not after those recent battles, the ones the Council won," the human said. "You haven't heard? They don't announce these things?"

"They announce victories," 4634 said, with a shrug of his own, "sometimes." And when they did announce those victories, this mining facility was often one of the last to know, being isolated and far from any Zeytoidian, Council, or even fragment colony space.

"Huh," the human said. He didn't appear to have any words after that, and for a moment they shared an awkward silence. The human cleared his throat.

"Anyway," he said, "gotta be going. You're my last delivery for this run, but I'm running late enough as it is." He began to turn back toward his ship but gave 4634 a little wave. "Nice to meet you, though. Stoic as you are, you're a lot nicer than the other Zeytord clones I've met!"

4634 acknowledged this with a nod. Unsurprising. Uncloned humans were considered even lowlier than the Inferior Clones, at the bottom of the Zeytord hierarchy.

"Goodbye," he told the human.

The human lingered in his mind, though probably because that was the first time in over two decades he'd seen a person without the same face as his own.

The next supply run was on time, and Newbie, IZ 895601, was there to see it. Newbie, of course, had never met a human before.

"You look so weird!" was the first thing Newbie said upon seeing the human. 4634 shook his head slightly, but the human just laughed.

Newbie was very curious.

"What's your name?" Newbie asked.

"Xaviera Thresh," the human replied, handing Newbie a box to unload and pack away.

"What kind of name is *that?*" Newbie asked, crinkling his face into a frown. "Where did you even get that? I mean, Thresh comes from 3, right? Does Xaviera come from 6?"

The human looked amused. "You know humans don't get assigned numbers, right?"

"What!?" Newbie exclaimed. "How do you keep track?"

"Through their name, mostly," Thresh shrugged. "I think the numbers are even more confusing. How do you remember   them   all?"
"How do you remember all the names? How do you even name things?" Newbie asked in return. "What qualities made you an Xaviera? Or a Thresh?"

"Well, you keep track through families, kind of." Thresh, to 4634's surprise, launched into an explanation of names. "That's where the last name comes from—it's usually shared by at least one of the parents who raised or made the child. The first name is chosen individually, and many first names are associated with different cultures or genders."

"What's a gender?" Newbie asked. Xaviera opened his mouth to explain, but 4634 had to interrupt to give Newbie his next job.

Newbie scampered off to follow instructions.

Thresh shook his head, but there was a smile on his face. "You know, before this I'd say that all Zeytords were stoic, cold even," he said. "I'd say it's coded into your DNA, a feature gifted from Emperor Zeytord himself. Now I'm not sure what to think, because there isn't a bone of stoicism in that kid."

"He's a child," 4634 said.

"Yeah. Too young to be working on a mining facility in most places," Thresh commented.

"I was on the front lines of the war even younger," 4634 said. "The facility is safe. It's a good job."

Not that Newbie ever believed 4634 when he said that. No, Newbie wanted the glory of battle. To fight for his Emperor, his country, himself! That was practically the slogan of the learning facilities for Inferior Zeytord. The other four had been all for it too, playing at it all the time when they were younger and first sent to the facility. It was only when Four-Four got sent off and failed to come back that they stopped being quite so enamored with the idea.

4634 hoped that Newbie just grew out of it.

"Oh," Thresh said softly. Even without his constant gesturing the man was expressive, and 4634 could read the emotions in his wide brown eyes. Surprise, some, but mostly anger. And sadness. Perhaps a touch of pity, but small enough for 4634 to ignore. "I didn't realize they had Clone troops that young."

"It's part of why helmets are regulation," 4634 said. "Children are not intimidating opponents." The information wasn't a secret. They didn't know any Empire secrets, the Inferior Zeytord crew of an isolated planet. Thresh probably knew more of Empire affairs than they did.

"Huh," Thresh said. He sighed. "Well, it's a nasty galaxy out there."

There was a sadness in his eyes that made 4634 look away.

Their conversation ended as Newbie came rushing back in.

Newbie went off to deal with the last of the boxes as Thresh and 4634 went through the forms.

"You can really tell he's yours, the kid," Thresh said with a small smile, looking after Newbie.

"He's not," 4634 said without looking at the man. "There are no Inferior Zeytord fathers, and we are simply both clones of the Emperor Zeytord. There is obviously a resemblance as we are genetically identical, but it doesn't represent a human biological relation."

"The resemblance might not represent a 'human biological relation,'" Thresh said, "but I wasn't talking about a physical resemblance anyway."

4634 had been told many things while still in training as a young clone. He put together the truth as best he could, but at some point he gave up. There were some things he did know.

Emperor Zeytord decided to make the ranks of his army out of the one person he truly trusted and believed in: himself. The government was almost all made of clones. There were non-Zeytord civilians in the Empire who held professional positions, and there were the conquered masses of humans who required Zeytord leadership, but non-Zeytords never held military positions. Royal and Middle Zeytords still took up almost all official positions.

Then there were the Inferior Zeytords. They were almost all foot soldiers in the military, and though there were stories of heroic Inferiors making officer status, 4634 had never actually seen any of this happening. When he'd tried to verify the numbers in those stories he got nowhere. Inferior Zeytords got increased strength and healing, but that was it. 4634 had been proud to be an Inferior Zeytord once. He had considered himself at least better than the humans, as almost all Inferior Zeytords did. But he'd learned better.

The Emperor himself was the original of all of these strains. He designed the cloning technology used and was considered a strategic genius even to his enemies. He certainly used biotech and nanotechnology to upgrade himself, though exactly how was a secret privy to only a trusted few. It was certainly true that he hadn't aged since 30, leaving him looking younger than many clones made decades after his birth.

Especially the Inferior Zeytords.

Targets to the Council, cannon fodder to the Empire, the veterans that 4634 served with would often say, when they weren't being watched. When they were being polite.

4634 was lucky, for an Inferior Zeytord. He had been reassigned.

"Do all humans look like Thresh?" Newbie asked 4634 once, as they all lingered in the small dining area before lights out. The mining station was off, more as a break for the machinery than for the clones staffing it. The place felt empty without the constant hum of the machines, and they all instinctively gathered together to combat the loneliness the silence threatened to bring in. It was already lonely, here on the outer edge of colonized space, where all real human civilizations were nothing but points of light in the sky if they were visible at all.

It was nice in its way, though. The empty expanse of the planet. The few opportunities they had to all gather together, when the machines were turned off.

There was no lounge area built into the mining facility. There were cramped sleeping quarters, an exercise room to fight the effects of low-gravity, and a makeshift kitchen with a dining area attached. So when they gathered, they gathered in the kitchen, turning a couple of crates into chairs so that they could all sit at the table.

"Don't be stupid," Sixes (543666) said. "Humans all look different—they're not clones."

"Yeah, silly," Sevens agreed. "Didn't you learn anything before you came here?"

Sevens only had two sevens in his number, 678973, but he and Sixes came from the same IZ educational facility and were inseparable. From shifts to names they were together. Both were skinny and energetic for Zeytord clones; before Newbie came they'd taken up most of 4634's time.

"Yeah, I know, but they never actually said what was different!" Newbie protested. "Like, they still all have the same amount of limbs, right? And Thresh was a different color. Are they all different colors? And why's Thresh a different shape?"

"Thresh is a different shape because he's female, I think," ThreeZs explained. He had a soft spot for Newbie. Well, all of them did really, though Sixes and Sevens showed theirs in odd ways. ThreeZs frowned. "Or she's female, maybe I should say? I'm not sure."

"It's hard to be sure. I don't know what culture Thresh is from, and some of them use pronouns to differentiate and refer to females with she and her." 4634 said from the kitchen, as the only one of them who had ever been around humans before. An acquaintance in the medical wing had tried to explain sex and gender to him before, though both were complicated and he wasn't completely sure he understood them well. "Some of them use pronouns in more complicated ways, and often they have more pronouns than that. They have categories called genders that are associated with—but don't always match—physical sex."

He poured out the Foodstuff(™) he'd been preparing from the pot into a large bowl. Foodstuff was never very good. It was designed to last and be shipped in bulk more than to taste good, but at least it was better cooked.

"Sex?" Newbie asked, nose wrinkling. "Isn't that how they make humans?"

"No, he means sex as in the characteristics that Thresh has that you don't," ThreeZs said patiently as Sixes snorted. "That's because your physical sex is male. All of our physical sexes are male, because Emperor Zeytord is male."

"I heard some of the Royal Zeytords are female," Sevens said. "Can you imagine? It must be so weird."

Sixes shook his head. "Royal Zeytords are all kinds of weird."

"Female like Thresh?" Newbie asked. "Wait, so are he and him the pronouns associated with males, then, if they're the ones we use?"

ThreeZs beamed. "Absolutely!"

"So have we been calling Thresh by the wrong pronoun this whole time?!" Newbie exclaimed.

"Nah, Inferior Zeytords always use he, didn't you hear?" Sixes said.

"Inferior Zeytords don't have a choice," DoubleOs muttered at the end of the table. DoubleOs's hard Zeytord features were softened by pudge. "Just like with everything else." DoubleOs was usually pretty quiet, so Newbie blinked up at him. 4634 made a note of it in his mind.

"Wait, humans get a choice?" Newbie asked. "A choice of gender or pronouns or sex?" His eyes widened slightly. "A choice of all of them?"

For a moment 4634 watched the table as they all blinked and considered the possibility. They may have all been clones of the same person, but they were all having different reactions. Sixes and Sevens looked taken aback. ThreeZs was thoughtful, and DoubleOs stared down hard at the table.

"It can be complicated, and there are often pressures in different cultures, but yes, to an extent," 4634 said, dredging up the memories of the human civilians he'd interacted with as a footsoldier. Most of them weren't supposed to be on the battlefield, aside from a few aids, but war was messy like that. Most of what he knew came from a human who'd ended up as a field medic.

"I don't really know how they change sex. I think it's using medical methods," 4634 continued as he brought the pot of food to the table. The others shifted eagerly in their seats. "But I think it's all doable."

It was times like these that 4634 most treasured the company of the others.

Newbie, ever curious, had yet more questions. He'd been quiet when he first came to them, believe it or not, but as soon as he'd realized that here he wouldn't be punished for asking, the unstoppable tide of questions came.

"How do we know Thresh's pronouns, then?" Newbie asked, as the others started on the meal in front of them.

201

"You ask," 4634 said.

"What're your pronouns?" Newbie asked the next time Thresh gave a delivery.

Thresh blinked, taken aback for a moment, and then smiled. He seemed to relax.

"I use they/them/theirs pronouns," Thresh said. "It's rather old fashioned of me, I know, but I love the history of them."

"They/them like plural pronouns?" Newbie asked. "What kind of history do they have?"

4634 let them completely unload the ship before sending anything to the storeroom so that Thresh could continue his—their conversation with Newbie. They piled the supply boxes high on the grav carts used for transport around the facility, maybe a little higher than was advisable.

It turned out Thresh was from a planet near the Solar System, the original Solar System, and they were more tied to Terran ways there. That territory was deep in Galactic Council control, and 4634 had to wonder how Thresh ended up delivering cargo as far from Council space as you could go with a company ignoring the war to make as much money as possible. But 4634 didn't press, and Newbie and ThreeZs wouldn't know the implications of that information.

Thresh seemed patient and happy to explain, but there was something wrong. Not with the discussions or Newbie's questions—a feeling that began even before Thresh began talking. It was different. 4634 could feel it in the air. Maybe it was the way Thresh stood, or something in their gaze as they chatted while the rest of them unloaded the supplies. A tension. A sadness.

"You know, you could choose your pronouns too, if you wanted to," Thresh told Newbie.

"But all Zeytords are 'he's," Newbie said. "The Emperor Zeytord's a 'he.'"

"He might be, but that doesn't mean you have to be, not here." Thresh turned to look over at 4634 as they continued speaking, "There's no one to keep track of the six of you here. You could basically do what you wanted, regardless of the Empire."

"That's not a very Zeytord way to think!" ThreeZs said, shaking his head. Newbie, however, looked intrigued.

4634 was more interested in what laid in Thresh's gaze.

"Go take these to the storage area on your own?" 4634 asked ThreeZs. "Take Newbie with you, go over everything with him. I need to chat with Thresh here about something."

"Well, just make sure you make it clear that that kind of talk doesn't happen here in the Empire, okay?" ThreeZs said.

"Does this mean I get to drive one of the carts?!" Newbie exclaimed.

4634 nodded absently to both, and they were off.

He and Thresh stood silently for a moment.

"You can call me Xaviera, if you want," Thresh said.

"What is this about, Thresh?" 4634 asked, and Thresh frowned and looked away.

"You don't need to be rude," Thresh said. They were rubbing absently at their arm, as though more nervous than offended.

4634 sighed. "I don't mean to be rude, it's just— something's up. You're making me tense, Xaviera."

Xaviera swallowed and glanced up at 4634. "Yeah. Yeah, something's up. I'm not just delivering cargo this time."

"No?" 4634 asked.

"No," Xaviera said. "I have a message. All of you here are supposed to report to battle."

4634 was silent for a moment.

"Why are you the one delivering this message?" 4634 asked. "This should be part of the Zeytord command."

"It's too important to send through your systems, which may have been compromised, I think," Xaviera said. The implications of the Empire's own systems being compromised were desperate, but 4634 was distracted by the contents of the message. "And all of the other Zeytords who may have delivered it are reporting to battle. All of the other Inferior Zeytords."

4634 paused for a moment, reading between the lines.

"This battle is going to be a bloodbath, isn't it," 4634 said. It wasn't really a question.

Xaviera breathed in shakily. "Yeah. The Council's been winning for a while, and I think the Empire might be going for a desperate strategy."

"You know what happens to Inferior Zeytords who don't report to battle, though, don't you?" 4634 asked.

"I know it's not good," Xaviera said. "But that's for Inferior Zeytrods who chose not to report to battle. Not the ones that never got the message in the first place."

There was a pause, between the two of them.

"Wouldn't that get you in trouble?" 4634 asked. "Failing to deliver a message?"

"I could have gotten into an accident, lost my message and supplies," Xaviera said. "At worst, I'll lose my job."

If 4634 and the others reported to battle, they'd probably die. They'd at the very least be separated. Newbie was young, new meat, and if they were going to send him in without training they had to be very desperate indeed. This had to be dangerous, very dangerous. The Empire might even fall, and Zeytord himself knows what the Council would do with any leftover Zeytords.

"If you want to go—" Xaviera said, after several moments of silence.

"No," 4634 said. "No. Please, lose the message."

There was another moment of silence.

4634 looked Xaviera in the eyes. "Thank you."

"It's nothing," Xaviera said. "Well, I mean, it's not nothing, but it's the least I could do. I wouldn't be able to live with myself otherwise."

Maybe they would have said more, but at that moment, the doors to the transport bay opened suddenly and ThreeZs rushed in.

"Newbie—" ThreeZs panted, doubling over for a moment. "Newbie crashed the cart." More panting. "In corridor five. Are you done with your paperwork yet?"

4634 glanced at Xaviera. "Yeah, I'm done here."

"Wait," Xaviera held up a piece of paper. "One last thing before I go. Just in case."

4634 took it and glanced at it wordlessly. It was extraplanetary coordinates for an area that 4634 estimated fell just outside of Council space. Above the coordinates was written the word *Haven*. 4634 shoved it into his pocket.

"Thanks," he told Xaviera, "for everything."

"Of course," Xaviera said. "Good luck."

They both knew he'd need it.

Watchful

by Simon Brown

Greer gripped the seaweed holdfast with her two feet and let her body drift with the current. She had been asleep for a long while and had not fed in some time, but saithe and salmon often swam by, careless and unafraid, and if she was lucky she might catch something larger like a dogfish or a porbeagle without too much effort. Once or twice a year a curious seal might come close enough for her to take, and that would satisfy her hunger for weeks.

Still, she could not help dreaming of taking a careless human one day. It had been decades since she had last captured a floundering fisherman and consumed him. Even longer since she had ventured onto land to hunt, but it was now too dangerous for someone such as her to venture beyond the rocks along the northern shoreline of Cumbrae, no matter what shape she took.

It was morning, and the sun shimmered on the surface fifteen feet above her head, sometimes sending a column of green light that reached the bottom. The current was warm for this time of year, and smaller fish were busy feeding off larvae drifting among the maerl, the hard red algae that covered most of the rocks hereabouts. A small halibut darted between her legs, but she let it go; something that size would not satisfy her for long, so she told herself to be patient.

Then, for the first time in a long time, Greer thought she heard the Signal. Her eyes widened and she cocked her head as if to hear better, an old habit from her time as a human that she had never discarded. And there it was again, the dull heavy clanking of a bell shaken under the water. She let go of the holdfast and let her buoyancy slowly lift her, turning as she ascended to fix the source of the sound. When her head breached the surface she was looking directly at a man, stretching uncomfortably across a wet and slimy rock, using his left hand to hold himself steady and his right to hold the bell under the water and ring it.

Kang. Kang.

Although not yet close enough to make out too much detail, she thought he looked very young. Not the same one as last time, then.

Greer smiled thinly. This could be amusing. She slipped under again, swam east some fifty feet where she knew there was a channel between the rocky headland at the end of White Bay, and climbed onto dry land, changing her shape as she went. It had been such a long time since she had done this—how many years, she wondered, but couldn't remember clearly—her body was a mishmash: human, horse, fish. But she gained more control as she stepped further away from the sea, the dry land providing the hardness the sea never gave, and before she was halfway to the bell ringer, she had become a young woman dressed in what looked like blue and green linen shifts.

Greer silently came up behind him and stopped a few feet away, next to a leather bag with straps he'd obviously left there safely away from the water. He was still crouched over the rock. He was dressed in clothes she did not recognise. Blue pants tucked inside shiny galoshes that looked new as new, and some kind of heavy jacket that was a size too big for him. He was tall and thin and gangly, unlike the last one, who had been built like a young bull, and his skin was dark, which mystified her somewhat; the one thing he had in common with his predecessor was the short, clipped hair their kind always seemed to wear.

"What are you doing?" she asked.

He twisted in surprise, losing his grip on the bell. He scrabbled and caught it just before it slid off the rock and into the water.

"Good catch," she said. She studied his face intently. His skin wasn't just dark, it was almost black and shone in the morning sunlight. "Are you a Moor?"

He shook his head. "No. I'm Scottish." He carefully stood up and steadied his feet so he wouldn't skid off his rock. "From Glasgow, actually," he added, pointing north toward the Firth of Clyde; the bell in his hand clanged, and he used the other to stop the clapper.

"Glesga," she corrected him automatically, mulling it over. She had never known anyone from that place who looked like him. How long *had* it been since the last Signal?

Now that she could see him up close, he looked very young and very awkward. She glanced at the bell. It was the same one, she was sure: as old as her, probably, its surface rimed with verdigris. "What were you doing?"

He blushed, glanced at the bell and shifted its weight in his hand as if he didn't know where to put it.

"Umm... " He swallowed. "You're from around here?"

"I'm Scottish, too," she said.

"I mean, from *here*. Cumbrae?"

She smiled. "Oh, aye."

He relaxed a little and stepped forward onto firmer land. She moved back to give him room. When he reached the leather bag, he picked it up and quickly put away the bell.

"You were trying to ring that thing underwater," she said.

"My name's Sean," he returned, and extended a hand. Greer looked at the hand, up at the man, and then back to the hand. What was she supposed to do with that? After an uncomfortable few seconds, he dropped it. "You're from Millport?"

"Once upon a time." She frowned slightly. "A long time ago, I think."

Her words seemed to puzzle him, but underneath she sensed expectation as well. He slung the leather bag over one shoulder, shoved his hands into his jacket pockets, and shifted from foot to foot.

"What does the bell sound like in the air?" she asked.

He shrugged. "Like any other bell, I expect." He looked around as if he was half-expecting someone else to turn up and half-hoping it was soon.

"And what does it sound like underwater?" she prodded. Her smile widened; she kept her lips closed, not sure how successful she'd been changing her teeth.

He sighed heavily. "I was curious, that's all," he tried explaining. "Dull, if you must know. It was stupid." He looked around again. "I have to go."

"Meeting someone?" she asked.

He drew in a deep breath. "Apparently not," he said, and started walking away.

"Are you an officer, too?" she asked as he moved past her.

He stopped, turned to look at her. It was her turn to be studied closely. When he was done, he said, "That's a strange question."

"Are you a captain?"

He shook his head.

"No, of course not. You're too young. Commander? Lieutenant?"

"In between," he said. "Lieutenant commander."

"Lieutenant Commander Sean."

"Martin. Lieutenant Commander Sean Martin."

"You're from Faslane."

"What makes you say that?"

"Because Captain Parkland was from Faslane."

Sean Martin retreated from her as if someone had yanked him back. He wasn't looking at her anymore. He was *staring* at her. His black skin paled, and Greer found it fascinating to watch. His reaction sent a hunger pang through her, but she fought it off.

"Where is Captain Parkland? Why isn't he here?"

"Parkland died thirty years ago," Martin said.

"He died fighting the Germans?"

"No. He outlived the war by fifty years." His voice quavered slightly, but he got it under control as he continued, "He died in bed of old age. He retired a rear admiral."

"He lived long enough to retire? A pity. He wanted to die fighting, I could tell."

Martin moved determinedly, but slowly, so he was no longer between her and the rocks. "You are Greer," Martin said.

Greer performed a mock bow. "So named by Captain Parkland."

"What were you named before that?"

Instead of answering, Greer did some numbers in her head. It was hard, but she had once worked in Millport's only drapery and with effort remembered how to add and subtract. "The war ended eighty years ago?"

"The Second World War? Yes."

"Who won?"

"We won. The Allies, I mean."

"The Germans are no more?"

Martin laughed, but cut it short when he remembered where he was and who he was talking to. "They are now our friends."

Greer let that sink in. So much time had passed that an enemy Captain Parkland had despised heart and soul was now his country's friend. Sometimes she wished the sea wasn't so unchangeable, without the markers humans used to measure time, like the lives of those they loved. The seasons, known underwater by the change in the direction and temperature of the offshore current, were so consistent that the years flowed by like freshwater from the Firth of Clyde, disappearing into the great timeliness that filled up her life. A sudden wave of regret washed through her and she shivered.

"You're cold?" Martin asked.

"If the war is over, and Captain Parkland is dead, why are you here? Why did you use the Signal to bring me?"

"I read his files."

"You read his what?"

"Do you mind if we sit down?" Martin glanced around, pointed to two rocks that were almost stool height and relatively dry. They were three yards apart from each other,

211

and without waiting for an answer Martin took the rock furthest away from the sea.

Greer preferred to stand, but took the other rock to make Martin more comfortable. She didn't want him to leave just yet. Not until she'd made up her mind on what to do about him. She rested her long hands in her lap. She could hear gannets flying above, and shearwaters over the sea.

"Parkland kept a file on you—a record. I found it in the bottom of a cardboard box at the bottom of a pile of cardboard boxes in the cellar of Faslane's oldest building."

"I don't know what cardboard is, but I think you're trying to tell me that he didn't want anyone to read his record about me. Then why do you think he kept it at all?"

Martin licked his lips. "Because I think he thought you could be useful again one day."

"Useful?" Greer asked, and the change in her voice made Martin tense. For a moment she thought he was going to get up and run away. Instead, he actually leaned toward her.

"And because he couldn't bring himself to destroy the record. I think he writes about you as if..." His voice trailed off.

"As if we were lovers," she finished for him.

Martin nodded. "Were you?"

"He flirted. He thought it made a difference. Does that make him my lover?"

"No," he said carefully. "Did it make a difference?"

"Do you want to know what really made a difference? It was the horse meat. Every time he used the Signal he brought a big canvas bag of horse meat." She pointed to his bag. "All you brought was the bell." She rubbed her stomach. "I like horse meat almost as much as..." She imagined dragging Martin into the sea and dismembering him, devouring every part of him, letting his flesh and blood and bone fill her up. "...fish," she finished.

Martin's expression showed he did not entirely believe her. That was both a good sign and a bad sign. One of the things she most missed about her meetings with Captain Parkland was their conversations; he was intelligent and perceptive for a male. One cold autumn day they had sat and talked for over an hour about the war, and about what life had been like for Greer when her home was a stone house and her feet trod on dirt and grass and heather, and humans were her family and her friends and not her prey. But an intelligent male was also a dangerous male.

"He never came to say goodbye," she said then, and again she felt regret well up in her.

"The last thing he wrote about was his decision not to say goodbye to you. He was afraid you would not let him go if you knew he was not coming back."

The truth of it struck her like a physical blow: not that she would have taken Captain Parkland into the sea if she knew he was not going to return, but that all the time they knew each other he was as mortally afraid of her at the end as he was at the beginning. The idea of it repelled and satisfied her in equal measure.

She would not have taken him. She would not have dragged him screaming and fighting into the sea to break him up and eat him flesh and blood and bone...

And then she realized she was lying to herself. Perhaps, just perhaps, she would have done exactly that. Or maybe, just possibly, changed him, as she was once changed.

But of course, to do either of those things she would have had to find a way to get around the gun. If his life was threatened, Greer did not think Captain Parkland would have hesitated to use it. The thought of it made a real shiver pass through her. She looked up sharply at Martin. "What else have you got in your bag?"

He took the bag off his shoulder and opened it wide so she could see inside it. There was just the bell.

"What have you in your pockets?"

Martin became very still. "I think you know."

"Is it the one that used to belong to Captain Parkland?"

"Yes. It was in the box with the records and this bell."

"May I see it?"

Martin's eyes rose in surprise. "You want to see it?" He thought about it for a moment and then shrugged. With an awkward mix of caution and ceremony he reached into his right-hand jacket pocket and drew out the pistol. It looked as ugly and heavy and lethal as it had eighty years before.

"That is only the second time I have ever seen it," she said.

"It's heavy," Martin said, hefting it in his hand. Greer noticed that he handled it as carefully and as professionally as had Captain Parkland; he knew how to use it. "Webley Mark VI. We don't use them anymore. But I don't think our modern automatics would handle the special ammunition Parkland had made for it."

"Why are you here? Why did you make the Signal?"

"To find out how Parkland first met you, or how he convinced you to keep on meeting him; there is nothing in the record about it. What happened?"

"What exactly is in this record?" she countered.

"You are evading my question," he said. His voice was much steadier now. He was starting to feel comfortable around her.

That's good, she thought. It increases my choices. "You ask too many."

He put the gun back in his jacket pocket, rested back on his rock and said, "Fair enough. But if I answer yours, will you answer mine?"

"As you say, 'fair enough.'"

"Parkland kept a detailed account of your activities during the Second World War. About how you kept track of enemy submarines along this part of the coast and the Firth of Clyde. About how you twice dealt with enemy agents that landed here on Cumbrae." Martin blinked. "Although he doesn't exactly say how you dealt with them."

Two? Greer thought. She frowned in thought. *No, three. I forgot to tell Parkland about the third.* And again, she caught herself lying. *I didn't tell him about the third because it was a woman. I didn't want Parkland to know; I didn't want him to think badly of me.*

The idea that Parkland's opinion of her was that important worried her. Maybe she was more human than she allowed. She felt no comfort in that.

"I ate them," she said absently. *Flesh and blood and bone...*

Martin blanched, his skin paling again. "How did you meet Parkland?"

Greer looked around, and after a moment, pointed to a spot not far from where Martin had made the Signal. "We met just there. I found out later he was looking for a place to set up a lookout post. I came up behind him." Her eyes lost focus as she remembered. "He heard me and turned. I think he knew right away what I was. I could see he was frightened, but he didn't run or gabble or go weak at the knees. He stood his ground. Stared me down."

"Why didn't you kill him?"

Greer's mind returned to the present day. "Curiosity," she said. "He was something new in my life. That doesn't happen often. You'd be surprised how my world stays the same, how little in it is truly unexpected."

Martin looked as if he wasn't sure how to respond to that. Of course, Greer thought, he was so still so young. Everything in the world must be new to him. *Including me.*

"We started talking," she continued. *Much as we are now, Lieutenant Commander Martin.* "After a while, he made me a promise."

"What promise?" Martin's tone was guarded, as if he wasn't sure he really wanted to know the answer.

"I would let him go if he returned every week with a gift."

"A gift?"

"Fresh meat."

"And in turn you promised?"

"Nothing." She swept one hand along the green seaweed dress. "Well, I promised not to eat him."

"He kept his word," Martin said, a statement.

Greer could not help smiling, and so showed her teeth. Martin tensed, half-rose. She realized her mistake and closed her mouth. She said, quickly, "He kept his word, I suppose. I was expecting him to bring me another human. Perhaps a German prisoner, or a criminal, or an orphan... instead he brought me horse meat in a canvas sack. Horse meat on the bone. He tricked me into a promise." *And then he died of old age in his bed, tricking me a second time. Clever Captain Parkland.*

"Why did you agree to help us against the Germans?"

"Again, it was something new. Once I was able to stop one of their submarines from working, but it sunk too deep even for me to follow." She shook her head in memory of the waste. "All that food lost to mud-scroungers and worms. I could have feasted for a year. Instead all I got was fish and horse meat and now and then a lonely spy."

There was a long moment of silence, followed by Martin asking, "How did you become an... ?"

"How did I become a what?" she goaded him. *Yes, say the name. Acknowledge me.*

"How did you become an each-uisge?"

Martin pronounced the name the right way. Like a gasp or hurried oath. Or a curse. He was Scottish, after all. So some things in the world changed, at least on the surface.

"He told me his name was Innis. He was pretending to be a shepherd. I was walking home from church and came across him. I think now he had spied me from a distance and was waiting for me."

"How long ago was this?"

Greer shrugged. "Is it important? Ships had sails. Men fought with swords, not guns. My ma, like so many, died giving me birth. The weather was colder and harder, then, just like us. Even God was harder and colder in those days." She glanced at him, looking for a sign of the faith: a chain holding a crucifix or a twine scapula or a rosary around his wrist, but like Parkland, he was bare of any sacred protection. Not that he needed it when he carried that terrible gun.

"He took me," she continued. "I think even then I knew what he was, but I didn't care. The thought of him ate me up from the moment I met him." *Ate me up, swallowed me whole, preyed on me, prayed over me, made me his.* "Then we lay together, under the sun, arm in arm. I fell asleep. When I woke, stars filled the sky and he was standing over me. He pulled me up so I hung from his hand like a slaughtered lamb on a hook and I thought he's going to take me into the sea and tear me limb from limb and eat each part of me, flesh and blood and bone."

"But he didn't."

"He did take me into the sea. I remember the shock of the cold and the salt on my skin, and being pulled along sharp rocks and the green light coming from above. And then when I thought he would slay me, he kissed me instead. When he stopped, my lungs filled with brine. For a long time I knew nothing more. When I woke once more I was side-by-side with Innis, among the rocks and weeds, and I saw his true shape. Then I saw my own hands and body."

She stood up from the rock, stared at her human form as if it was completely alien to her.

"Not a woman, not anymore. Something else. Fish, seal, horse, monster. Innis wanted to keep me. He was lonely." She smiled grimly. "But I was angry. I had been ready to die for him, but not to change. He was asleep. I slew him. I ate his liver first, and then his heart. I threw his head into the deep. I *devoured* him."

"Flesh and blood and bone," Martin finished for her.

Her smile faded, she sat down again, and once more folded her hands into her lap. She saw her skin was starting to dry. Not long now and the skin would crack around the fingers and toes, and then on her elbows and her knees, and sores would form and weep, and dry air would rasp her lungs.

Greer heard bells. The bells of the Cathedral of the Isles in Millport, drifting across the island. They sounded different. She cocked her head.

"You remember them?" Martin asked.

"There are more than there used to be. I remember three. Aon, dha, tri..."

"There are eight, now."

"I do not like the land so much," she said softly. "Everything here is thin. The air. Sound. Life. Even the bells sound wrong: too sharp for my ears."

"You said Parkland called you Greer. What were you called before that?"

"I was born Cairstine, one who follows the Christ. But I prey on friend and foe, fish and fowl, and roam the seas all around like a shark and prowl the land like a lion. Parkland understood. He said watch for the enemy under the seas and on the land."

"You agreed? So readily?"

"It gave each of us a reason to keep our promise to each other. Each-uisge to human. So he gave me a new name. Greer, which means 'watchful' and 'silent.' I liked the name more than Cairstine." She sighed, suddenly tired. The skin pulled around her joints. It was time to return to the sea.

But first...

She hadn't noticed that Martin had drawn the gun. It was leveled straight at her chest. She laughed. She had not expected him to surprise her so readily, and found she enjoyed it. He was like Parkland in so many ways.

"You came to Cumbrae to kill me?" she asked.

"I came to Cumbrae to make you a promise," he said evenly. There was no malice or fear in his voice, but the barrel of the gun never wavered. He was taking no chances.

"Of all things, I was not expecting that," she admitted. "What kind of promise?"

"We have a new kind of submarine," he said.

She knew what he was talking about. They were monstrously large compared to the frail German boats she'd hunted decades before, and inside they were hot like the sun.

She stayed away from them. Too much metal, and they ran deep, so deep. They were dangerous and unnatural.

"Possible enemies will track them," Martin continued.

"You are at war again?"

"No. These new submarines are part of a strategy to prevent war, to scare those who might be our enemy into leaving us alone."

"Foolish. Weapons are made to be used." She flashed her teeth at him. "Teeth to guns to submarines."

"Those who are not our friends will want to watch and study the new submarines. They will use smaller boats to track them, and sometimes bring spies to the land. I want you to stop them."

"And your promise?"

"To return, and when I do, to bring fresh meat."

"Horse meat?" She licked her lips.

"Cow, if you prefer. Or pig. Or lamb."

She considered the proposal. "All."

"All?"

"Horse and cow and pig and lamb." She regarded him with something halfway between affection and need. "And you. You must sit and talk with me. Each time you come. For as long as I can bear it."

Martin drew himself up. He nodded slowly and put away his gun.

And that is when Greer showed him how fast she could be. Before he could pull the gun out a third time, before he could shout, before he could even blink, she was on him. He bowled over backward. She crouched on top of his chest, her toes becoming talons, and they pierced his skin. She grasped his wrists and her nails became needles and they pierced his skin. But her head she kept human. She leaned over him and kissed him on the mouth, filling his nostrils with her scent. She kept her mouth over his until he was almost out of breath, then leaped back to the rock where she'd been sitting so patiently for so long.

Martin gasped, struggled to his feet, scrabbled for the gun, his head lolling this way and that.

"Don't worry, Lieutenant Commander Martin. I was just sealing our common promise. Captain Parkland didn't mention that part in his record, did he?"

Greer turned away from him. The sea called for her and she could no longer deny it.

"I will stop these enemies-not-enemies for you," she said over her shoulder. Her wide green feet slapped on the rocks. Her dress changed into long fins that ran along her spine and the back of her arms and legs. Her skin dimpled and scaled. She reached a rock slick with spume and seaweed and stood on it, and just before she dived into the sea, shouted to the human and the land and the sky, "I will stop them and eat them, flesh and blood and bone!"

The Seer

by Carol Holland March

There was nothing more to do. Three millennia of desperate effort spent in vain. We opened the doorways and begged them to listen to reason. All who agreed we relocated to other planets, but a mere fraction of the population believed us and even fewer walked through our portals. I told myself we did everything we could. We gave them choice, and choices are sacred even when they tear at your heart. My involvement had been minor, since I was still a novice in monitoring planets at risk, but I knew well the Guardian chosen to perform the act of mercy. I couldn't bear for her to wait alone, so at the end, I returned.

When Aberash saw me, she smiled. The sky above her lightened. "I did not expect you," she said.

"I cannot assist," I answered.

"Of course not." Aberash moved closer as if she meant to touch me. She was always unfailingly kind. "Only one who has lived there can perform this task. It is a sacred principle." She glanced at the blue globe, so tiny and vulnerable in the blackness. Its companions were distant and bare; its sun shone a sickly yellow. "It helps that you came."

I inclined my front end toward her, the best simulation of a bow I could manage in my current form. Desperate to share her burden, I said the first thing that came to mind. "What was it like to live there as a human?"

"I incarnated into several human bodies," she said. "First as a child in a family who feared truth so much they worshipped silence."

We live by truth, so I asked, "Were you afraid?"

"Always." She paused. "Everything left unsaid pulsed under my parents' words, twisting their meaning. Beneath the surface, darkness reigned. Under the weight of silence, the darkness congealed and dwelled in the house as a gelatinous blob the color of raw liver. A fine sheen of sweat appeared on its skin when it wanted to speak. With no tongue, that was impossible. Its agony terrified me."

Sparks smoldered in her emerald eyes. "Why did you come, Kama? You have long evolved past the experiences of humans."

She knew my role could easily be that of witness even though her stature made that role unnecessary. The question might have been a test, so I murmured platitudes about preserving memories of the past. I had never lived on this dying world, but mine was similar enough that I grieved with her. So I told myself.

Aberash gazed at the planet hanging so lonely in space. "Don't forget. Darkness unchecked kills. The light of reason cannot survive an onslaught of lies such as those people bewitched themselves with. Not after the midpoint has been crossed."

I promised to remember.

Time grew short. Heat was spreading from the planet's core into her mantle. We watched from a safe distance, but the effects of warming on the surface populations showed. The ice caps had melted. Freed, the water thrilled in its new form, ebbing and flowing as rambunctious tides devoured solid land. Millions must have drowned. The sea, at least, looked happy.

"A Gray One saved me." Her voice rippled. "You remember them." She nodded toward a distant world. My inner vision revealed the Order of Gray Ones—tall and narrow in their natural state, but capable of changing form as easily as a wave breaks on shore—one of the Guardian races of this doomed planet.

"Your relative."

"He came to help. Stood outside the house where I lived, dwarfing it. I felt his love." She sighed. "When he opened his arms, I went willingly."

The planet commanded her attention. As heat consumed the inner mantle, her brightness dimmed. "He showed me that the house where I lived was a construction of mind, mapped by human brains interpreting light. As an incarnate, everything I perceived as solid was a trick of light —that house, my room, my parents who created thought-forms sweating fear. The Gray One revealed this so I would remember my nature. Make sense of why I was there. Later, I understood."

Her golden body darkened. I longed to touch her as the Gray One had touched the child she had once been, but arms were only a memory. "The perversion of form frightened you," I said.

"That world could have remained as it was created— lush and green and beautiful. But thoughts of fear and lack prevailed. Hate choked love. Arrogance murdered humility.

Under the surface that passed for normalcy, the sea of darkness formed by all those fearful thoughts swirled around me. In my bedroom, I dove under the covers and shook. The next day, I saw with my inner vision how my life would unfold. How I would suffer alone and be punished for speaking the truth. I cried for help, and the Gray One answered. I needed to leave that misbegotten place and return to my true home. I knew he could help and begged his assistance. That he refused, but he offered to remove my foresight until I was older." She closed the green eyes that roamed my dreams.

"I told him to take it. I didn't want to know my lonely future. That my mother regretted having children. That I would live a long, desolate life. That my mission to open the peoples' minds would fail."

"He listened?"

Her face softened, and, briefly, the planet cooled. "I was the incarnate. My wishes were law. As I dozed like a babe in his arms, he took my foresight. The next morning I remembered nothing. Not even him. Not for a long time."

"But later, you warned the population. It is chronicled in the Great Hall of Records. All the elders agree you fulfilled your purpose."

"I spoke the truth, as prophets are trained to do. In later lifetimes, I offered the message in as many ways as I could devise." A golden limb brushed my side. A gesture of friendship. My whole length quivered.

"It made no difference," Aberash said. "My message sank into the darkness. Now the dark has overwhelmed what light they had and they have burned up their world."

"Some heard." I was pleading with her to forgive herself. "Your voice joined with others. Many who heard you and the voices of your comrades helped us open the hidden portals. Thousands found refuge on other worlds. The race will continue."

"You helped with the evacuation. I had forgotten that." She sounded sad. "Yes. Many were saved. I had hoped for more, but we did our best." She dismissed her pain with a shake and faced me with blinding brilliance. "Go now, Kama. The Gray Ones will protect you."

I wanted her to know how important her work had been, but my voice failed, so I bent myself in two as a final gesture of respect. I wanted to dissuade her from the path she had chosen, but I was far from her equal and could not imagine the ecstasy driving her choice.

From the doomed planet, I traveled to the world of the Gray Ones. They welcomed me, warming my chilled body with the fluid circulating through their translucent forms. In the distance, glowing like a star, Aberash circled her planet, a pink smudge against dark space.

"Fear not," said the Gray One who took me under his care. "All who die are reborn."

I didn't answer, embarrassed at the gentle rebuke.

As Aberash prepared to strike, she elongated her magnificent form. Head, neck, and shoulders merged into a smooth cylindrical shape three times the width of the planet. Her form tapered, narrowing into a long, thin tail. Millions of miles long. Like a snake. Like a comet. Rippling gold lit up the sky.

I forced myself to look. It was why I had come, after all, but it was also my first glimpse of how a world died, and I was only a novice. I stared into space, past the ruined planet, as lava erupted through its fissures and the seas boiled.

In my mind, I heard Aberash bid me farewell. To maintain my dignity, I looked directly at the drama. When she started her run, most of her disappeared in the distance.

Her narrow tail whipped around the remnants of the planet —once, then again. She surrounded it like a coil—two layers thick, then three—containing its raging heat. She shone her brightest colors—red and green and violet. On the surface, to any poor souls left alive there, she would appear as blissful light come to lift the world into the heavens.

When she had circled three times, she stopped and compressed her coils. Under her pressure, the planet shrank, quivered for a long moment, then exploded. Debris shot into space, projectiles flaming red, blackened cinders.

I called for her but got no answer. The Gray One sighed and moved closer.

It was too much to take in, but I recorded in my mind everything I saw. Later I would look at it more calmly, and my record would be stored in the Great Hall. I waited there a long time. Nothing moved but drifting embers. The planet was gone. Aberash was gone.

I was journeying home when a shock wave jostled me. I looked back. The pale sun of the decimated planet had more than doubled in size. Still, it expanded. Until that moment, I was not sure. But yes! She had done it. Aberash had thrown herself into the dying sun and merged with the mother of that system. The sun would soon engulf the remaining planets. All were unpopulated, which I knew she had insisted upon before she agreed to the next step in her evolution.

But if that were not true, and billions more had died in the explosion, the fierce light of the newborn sun was so sublime, I would still have wept with joy.

The Garden
by Nicola Kapron

"I missed you," Alraune said, her first words to Michael in years.

   The angel couldn't quite meet her eyes. "Missed you, too."

   They'd met in a field of flowers, azalea and daffodils drinking up the morning sun. Alraune wore pink, the fabric ruffled like petals, with a matching carnation in her hair. Michael was still in her uniform. Her eyes were raw and shadowed and she reeked of smoke and blood. Her wings were grey with ashes, big enough to shroud them both in veils of feathers. Alraune ached for her own little wings, small and mottled brown, but she'd made her choices. Though the scars on her back were tight and painful, Alraune had no regrets. No matter how tired Michael looked, she must have felt the same.

   Law or freedom? It wasn't exactly surprising that they'd come down on opposite sides. Alraune couldn't blame Michael for her choice. Given half a chance, any plant would go wild, but you couldn't be a soldier without discipline. And while Alraune had chosen to dedicate herself to growing things, Michael had quite literally been born a soldier. Forged for strength, hardwired for obedience. There was no room for uncertainty in an angel made for war. Even so, it hurt them both to be apart. That pain was what had drawn them here, to a meadow far from the battlefront, during one of Michael's brief furloughs. Here, they could talk, however briefly.

"Come back," Michael said, as close to pleading as she ever got. "You haven't been fallen long. If you turn the others in, God will forgive you."

Alraune shook her head, hands clasped in front of her. "God forgives no one, love."

Rust-red hair gleamed dully as Michael bowed her head. "Please. You're still an enemy. You'll be a target. I don't want—"

Her shoulders were rock steady, but her gruff voice trembled. Alraune felt the corners of her mouth turn up. She stepped forward, bare feet sinking easily into the grass, and pulled her soldier girl into her arms. Michael allowed it. Having the warm, smoky solidity of her so close sent a fluttering thrill through Alraune's stomach. If they had time, she would pull Michael closer and kiss each new burn and bruise. Banish the pain of war for a few sweet hours.

They never had enough time.

"I'll be all right, Michael," she said, looking up at her lover's weary face. "I've found somewhere for myself, far from the fighting. Nothing to worry about but flowers and trees. I won't be a target for anyone. No matter who wins, I don't expect to ever see battle. Whenever you have a moment, you can find me there."

Michael's arms settled feather-light on her shoulders. "Al, it won't last. Heaven is mobilizing. The war will come to

you. You need to come back before it's too late. Otherwise, I
—"

"I'll be all right," Alraune repeated, leaning into the embrace. "You're the one who's risking your life. Take care of yourself."

Those strong arms went taut around her. She squeaked in surprise, hands flying to Michael's shoulders as the angel's wings closed around them.

"I love you. Be safe," Michael whispered, and kissed her.

The kiss lasted only a few seconds. When it ended, the angel flew away, leaving the demoness alone among the flowers. Alraune watched Michael's back until it vanished into the distance.

She'd said, "Be safe," but her kiss tasted like 'goodbye.'

The next time Alraune laid eyes on Archangel Michael, her home was burning around her and her flowers were screaming. She stumbled through the flames, a strip of cloth torn off her skirt clamped over her mouth and nose. Smoke found its way into her lungs regardless. All around her, a chorus of shrieks and pleas rose and danced like sparks. She reached out to the greenery with all the power in her possession. It wasn't enough.

"Please," she begged, the noise muffled by her makeshift mask. "Hold on. Shrink down, be seeds again! We can survive this!"

Speech led to coughing. It made no difference. Throughout the nursery, her plants shuddered, trying and failing to shrivel themselves to safety. The aggressive ones lashed out with tooth and vine; the gentle ones coiled up behind barriers of thorns and leaves. Fire consumed them both equally. She stumbled onward, her whole body shaking with the force of each cough. Behind her, her children burned.

"This can't be happening." The words scraped against her throat like sandpaper. "Please don't do this!"

Her prayers went unanswered. As always. Why would God listen to a demon's pleas? Never mind that Alraune had stayed out of the war, that she'd been quiet, that she'd been good. She'd taken up gardening instead of arms, and so what? Her nose was filled with the scent of burning wood and scorched meat. Her bare feet were filled with splinters. The ends of her hair smoldered.

Above her, an angel was flying, a blade made of fire gripped firmly in one hand. Divine wrath personified, all the fury of the sun crashing down on what had once been a peaceful place. Hair like rust and eyes like cinders blazed through the smoke.

"Please, just let me go!"

Alraune lurched forward one final step. Too late. The sword came down. As the blade plunged into her stomach, she saw the face of an angel. Michael looked about to cry.

But orders were orders.

The air in Heaven was thick and sweet, like champagne, like syrup. Alraune had forgotten the taste of it in the years she'd been gone. Her plants loved it. Trees, vines, and flowers coiled over every surface, drinking up scraps of stray magic. Nasturtium for victory, hydrangea for heartlessness, grass for submission. Swaying, dancing, poking up through the rubble that had once been buildings, fountains, and gates. Filling the desolate battlefield with life.

"Lovely, isn't it?" she murmured, staring out into the sea of growing things. There was no reply, but the marigold tucked behind her ear stroked its tiny roots against her hairline.

Dawn was beginning to break. Sunlight poured over the far-off hills like molasses. Soon the birds would have begun singing, if there were any birds left to sing. Grasses clutched at her bare feet as she wheeled herself forward, twining with the still, pink nubs of her toes. She smiled gently and coaxed them back, away from the crushing weight of her wheelchair. Not all of them listened. Even with the little yelps of pain coming from their fellows, some children just refused to learn. The weakest ones got savaged beneath the soil, their roots chipped away by their rivals for space and nutrients. Much like people, plants had little compassion to spare.

Alraune wrapped a vine around herself for safety and locked an arm in place for balance. Then she leaned down carefully and reached out. The tiny blades didn't need much encouragement to lace themselves around her fingers. When they were safely aboard, she straightened up and placed them in her lap. She'd transplant them somewhere else with less competition. There was no shortage of space in Heaven now that the angels were gone.

Well, mostly gone.

The grass in her lap was settling into the gnarled wood of her chair. She helped it along, nudging the tiny roots deeper. The sea of green below rustled enviously and tugged at her wheels.

"Now, now." She chuckled softly. "Such lively little things. Be good and I'll give something tasty later, all right?"

In Heaven and Hell alike, bribery worked wonders on foliage. Before he'd given up and left the empty planes of Heaven in her care, Belial had complained that it was impossible for anyone else to replicate Alraune's results. But then Belial approached everything like a war council, the silly boy. Tactics and supply chains, headcounts, losses and gains —you couldn't talk to plants about projected growth rates and expect them to follow along. They needed something personal. Alraune fed her gardens with her likes and dislikes, every hobby she'd ever taken up, the steady stream of her thoughts. She gave them the pain of her broken back, the frustration of physical therapy, the fury of betrayal, the misery of realizing she would never be able to walk for longer than a few minutes at a time. Layers upon layers of hatred rested peacefully beneath vibrant leaves and even more vibrant blossoms.

The flowers she grew now were larger than the ones she'd grown before Michael had betrayed her. More colorful. Sharper. Hungrier. They took everything she gave them and more. In exchange, they molded themselves to her liking and did her bidding without question, carrying with them wisps of phantom smoke. When she breathed in, the scent of burning had already begun to mingle with the sickly sweetness.

It brought back bad memories, which was just as well. Why shouldn't she dwell on the bad? Everything good was rotten now.

On the far side of the grass lay a field of red begonias, all ruffled petals and glistening eyes. Snapdragons swayed among them, jaws chewing idly at the air. Little blue forget-me-nots inched closer, their heads turning unerringly to face her.

"I know, dear ones," she told them. "I'll wake her soon."

A ripple spread through the sea of flowers. They were listening, and they were not the only ones. Ironwood and strangleweed were less stunning than their brightly-blooming cousins, but they were strong and terribly obedient. The two of them form the bulk of the prison Alraune sat beside. Poisonous leaves curled cat-like between the bars, nameless things custom-bred as restraints. They shivered when she rolled closer. Thorns jutted from every surface. At the bottom of the cage, bound in ivy and strangling vines, lay a woman.

Archangel Michael had seen better days. Her arms were limp and bloody, swallowed in so much green the shape of them was lost. Her face was bruised, her nose broken and freshly reset. Beneath her, enormous white wings twitched feebly. Even in sleep, she bared her teeth.

She was still so beautiful. Alraune couldn't help but smile. Part of her wanted to wait, to savor this moment for as long as possible. But she'd been waiting for this reunion for too long already. She reached for the nearest bar and pressed her palm flat against it. It was impossible to avoid nicking herself on the thorns, but she hardly felt it. Slick crimson dripped down the flesh of her wrist. It seemed fitting.

A drop of red slid down a leaf. The attached vine unraveled itself from the wall and bent delicately to the sleeping soldier's cheek. Hazy eyes blinked open as sweet blood smeared over her cheek.

Despite everything, the only thing Alraune felt in that moment was warmth. "Good morning, Michael. Did you sleep well?"

"...Al?" Michael shifted, then winced. She must have jarred something. "Where..."

"Heaven. I ended up coming back after all." The words tasted like glass in her mouth. Her scars ached. A fragile hope glimmered in Michael's hellfire eyes.

"You came back?" the angel rasped. Her wings quivered beneath her. "I thought... you said no."

Alraune spread her hands helplessly. "I did. But, well, circumstances shifted. Are you happy to see me, love?"

Michael's face was still slack and confused, but Alraune could see the gears beginning to turn. It was a heady feeling, watching joy and relief turn to ashes in someone else's mouth.

"Dreaming," Michael murmured, then shook her head. "Doesn't matter. Always happy to see you."

Despite everything, Alraune's rotting heart skipped a beat. Those words didn't feel like a lie. But then, they never had, all the way to the end. That was the problem with hero types. They loved you, yes, but they always loved something else more.

"I missed you," she whispered. Her fingers trailed over the bars, leaving dripping stains behind them.

The sleepy haze vanished from Michael's eyes. "You're hurt!"

Her dear prisoner tried to lurch upright and failed. Poor thing must have forgotten to compensate for the lack of leverage. Alraune winced in sympathy. Had she given Michael too much poppy milk? She didn't think so, but then, her estimates had been uncertain to begin with. A war of extermination left little room to learn how to treat the wounded.

"Don't move so suddenly," she said, leaning forward to assess the damage. "You'll start the bleeding up again."

The angel's breath hissed between her teeth. "I can't— I can't feel my legs."

Alraune smiled. "Most days, neither can I."

Michael's gaze was a tangible thing. It landed on Alraune's motionless limbs with all the force of a gunshot. Alraune followed that stare to her withered thighs, stiff and numb in a cradle of branches.

235

"Not as pretty as they used to be, are they?" she asked. "There's only so much a girl can do to fight atrophy when she can barely walk. Good thing you don't need to worry about that."

She half-expected Michael to ask what had happened. Instead, a sick look stole over her lover's face, deepening in intensity until Michael jerked her head away. A bronze throat bobbed. Choking something down, perhaps. Such a lovely neck. Alraune ached to wrap her hands around it.

"Not a dream," Michael said at last. "A nightmare."

Alraune giggled, feeling giddy. "Your nightmare. Always."

Michael looked even sicker, if that was possible. Her feathers were broken and ragged, her skin mottled with sickly purples and greens. When she tried to sit up again, she lost her balance and ended up wriggling like a worm. Alraune could pinpoint the exact moment the angel saw what remained of her legs. The clean, surgical cuts. Two perfect vertical gashes just above the knee.

Confusion came first. Shock was next. Then disbelief. And finally, like the lazy bloom of the kurinji, fear.

"What have you done?" Michael rasped. Her voice sent tremors through the soft earth.

Alraune hummed thoughtfully, leaning back in her chair. What *had* she done? She touched a hand to her middle, over the scar that started in her stomach and went through to her lower back, neatly severing the spinal cord. Not quite a lethal wound, but close. Michael had given it to her the last time they touched. What else should she have expected from the archangel of fire and war? Michael, whose blade had burned all it touched and whose battle cry had ripped the sky asunder. Until that sky had been cut off by grasping branches, her sword stolen by crawling roots, her voice choked off by the petals in her lungs.

Beloved, hated, defeated Michael.

"I just repaid a favor," Alraune said, leaning back in her wheelchair. "I love you."

The words tasted like 'I will never forgive you.'

Wyrm Tale

by Julie Cohen

A heavy, cold rain began to fall, bringing with it the menacing echo of deep, distant thunder. It dropped from the sky without grace—an expulsion of wet, grey droplets reflecting a grey sky, painting the earth and air that same dismal shade. Gnessren's cave, however, was dry and warm. He would not stand for a dripping, leaky sort of cave. Such a place was fit for lesser beasts, perhaps, but this cave did not belong to them nor even to nature herself. Gnessren had made this cave—carved it from the earth, shaped it with fire and strength, with claws and teeth of diamond.

He could not be sure how long it had been since he had first made his cave. Certainly hundreds of years, perhaps thousands. It was hard to mark the passage of time, except to mark the changing of the world outside. The human world. It no longer felt like a world to which he belonged, and really, it was not. The humans did not remember his kind, save in stories, in myths told incorrectly, in paintings that were all wrong. But how could they truly remember those who were no longer there among them? Gnessren was not even sure how long it had been since the others had gone—abandoned this world for the safety of the mountains in the Northern Kingdom of the Faerie Realm. The faeries were their only true allies, sweet creatures full of magic and love for all other living things. Of course they could be that way, he often thought, when they could so easily slip away to the safety of their realm.

The thunder edged nearer, the sound like a dog growling low in its throat, and there it was: a flash of lightning that split the grey, wet sky. Gnessren loved to watch the lightning from the safety of his cave. It glowed so beautifully, like a jewel in fire. Like cold, magic fire, hued in purple or green. He imagined a sorcerer in the clouds above, performing an ancient curse. He thought of the faeries who would dance in the rain, the flowers in their hair perfectly dry even as they themselves grew soaked, laughing and kissing one another and pretending to run from the lightning in fear when even that violent side of nature would never dare to harm them.

Lost in this daydream, he did not notice at first the small creature that stumbled into his cave, panting from exertion and dripping wet. The being staggered forward, deep into the unnaturally warm, dark cave that glinted strangely from all corners. The being stopped, sudden, as if sensing some presence. Something large, hidden in the shadows.

Gnessren came back to reality and, catching the scent of the thing, the human thing, he tensed. It did not matter if a thousand years had passed, or that this creature was ragged and injured and frightened—Gnressren did not feel as menacing as he wanted. The old dread crept up inside him, mixed with anger—furious, virulent, poisonous anger. How dare a human set foot here!

239

He could not speak in this form, not in any tongue the creature would understand. Had they seen him already? Or only sensed that he was there? He made himself very still. If they touched any single thing, however, he would reveal himself. He would not allow them to plunder his beautiful treasure. Once, long ago, there were many words for it, words like *hordwela* or *sincgewæge*, but those words belonged to another place and time, when his kind were first deemed a worthy sacrifice for human glory. In that time, other beings roamed the earth as well, vestiges of a lost and ancient place. Treasures, like words, had now become as shapeless and strange to him as the clouds, evolving and proliferating like pretty butterflies, nameless and delicate things. Gnessren was very fond of pretty butterflies, however, and so his treasure continued to grow, even now, when he was more likely to find strange glowing boxes or flimsy sparkling fabrics instead of jewel-encrusted crowns and heavy silver-hilted swords, or helmets of shining bronze into which secrets had been carefully and proudly engraved.

The soft gasp brought him from the thoughts into which he had again drifted—even tense and fearful, it was hard for his mind not to wander... a flaw, he imagined, of all ancient things—and he looked down just in time to see the human creature standing before him, shining a bright and horribly strange light into his silver eye. He turned his head, but the light remained although it trembled, and now it pierced his gold eye, and was just as irritating. He drew back a little, trying to escape the light, and all at once it vanished, followed by a small clatter on the ground. The human creature staggered, then crumpled at his feet.

Dead? No. He could hear breathing. The human had fainted, then. A wave of relief washed over him. Surely, a knight would not faint. But then, knights were cowards, and if they had expected Gnessren to be asleep...

He caught the scent of blood, very faint, in the air. The human, he realized, was bleeding. He hesitated, and then moved his long neck downward, leaning close, as close as he dared, to the human's prone form. The limbs were long and pink, tanned by the sun but in an uneven way. Wheat colored hair framed a freckled face, with a nose that had been broken once or more, awkward and wrong where it sat. The clothes were strange—oddly shaped, it seemed to him, and incomplete, and made of strange fabrics. Blood stained the pink neck, but came from somewhere else, Gnessren thought, noticing the way the light-colored hair was matted down in the back.

"Oh no, what happened?" asked a voice, sweet as birdsong, and Gnessren drew himself up, startled. He relaxed upon recognizing the young woman who knelt down over the human, her thick black curls falling forward over her dark, bare shoulders. She looked up with startling meadow-green eyes, framed by thick lashes. Faeries were always beautiful.

He hesitated, and then focused his magic on his form. He felt himself grow smaller, softer, less sharp. His human form was not perfect: he could not change his eyes—one silver, one gold—or the way his golden hair had a rose-colored tint, or the subtle glimmer of scales beneath his warm brown skin. Still, he could speak in human tongues, and that was often helpful. His magic, like the faeries, interpreted whatever was spoken to him so that he could understand, but in this form, he would be able to speak back. Not that the human was presently capable of conversation.

"Hello, Euphoria," he greeted the faerie, adjusting to the feel of mostly dull teeth around his still split tongue. He

241

kept a pair of fangs, small and not very threatening, but any defense was better than none.

"She's hurt," Euphoria said sadly, petting the unconscious human's cheek.

"I did not harm her," he said, suddenly wary once more. Was it a trap, a lure set by some knight who would now come to kill him, claiming he had stolen away and ravaged a helpless maiden? It had been done before.

"Let's help her," the faerie said, already letting her magic convince blood to slow and skin to knit. She cradled the human woman in her arms, smiling down at her, all fondness and warmth.

A moment later, the human woke with a groan. Gnessren resisted the urge to step back, even as Euphoria drew the woman closer.

"Hello," Euphoria greeted cheerfully. The woman looked at her, uncomprehending. She groaned again, reaching for her head to gently touch the part that had only minutes earlier been a bloody wound. Gnessren watched as finding it unscathed added to her confusion, and then as she remembered...

"There was—" she started, grasping Euphoria protectively now, as though she thought to shield the faerie from the horrible thing she had fainted at the sight of—from Gnessren. He stepped forward, unthreatening in his human form.

"You fainted," he said. "I suppose you may have dreamt something terrible..."

"No, I saw..." she trailed off, seeming not really sure what she *had* seen. "I don't know."

"Everything is all right now," Euphoria cooed, petting her hair. "I'm Euphoria, and this is Gnessren. What's your name?"

Gnessren tried to shoot Euphoria a disapproving look. But it was impossible, really, to glare at a faerie.

"My name's Hazel," the woman said. "You two... live in a cave?"

"Oh no," Euphoria laughed. "I'm just visiting Gnessren."

"What purpose have you in coming here?" Gnessren demanded.

"I'm sorry," Hazel said with a wince, as though he had slapped her, and quickly got to her feet. Euphoria rose with her, keeping close, and Gnessren could not help but notice the way the human woman, subconsciously, perhaps, seemed to position herself in front of the faerie, again as though to shield her.

"I apologize if my tone seemed harsh," he said, speaking calmly. "I am not angry."

"Gnessren is just grumpy and wary of strangers," Euphoria told her, touching the soft locks of the woman's hair. "Can I braid your hair?"

"What?" Hazel asked. "Uh, okay."

"I am not grumpy," Gnessren protested, frowning. "But it is true that I am wary of strangers. I have not had pleasant dealings with your kind in the past."

"Don't mind him," Euphoria told her, gently beginning to braid the woman's hair, weaving into it pale little flowers that appeared at her will.

"Yes," Gnessren sighed. "Don't mind me. You are clearly not a threat. You do not even have a sword."

"They don't use swords anymore, Gnessren, don't you remember?" Euphoria laughed.

"Oh, well, whatever they adorn themselves with now," Gnessren shrugged.

"I... should go," Hazel decided.

"Oh no, please stay," Euphoria said, hugging her close.

"The human creature wants to go, Euphoria," Gnessren said, all too eager to return to his daydreaming. "I have never held a human here against their will," he added, just to make the point clear to any and all who might be listening. He would not be blamed for human curiosity and foolishness.

"Human creature?" Hazel repeated. "I have to go."

"Hazel?" a voice—slightly deeper, but with a high whining lilt to it—drifted in amidst the sounds of thunder and rain. Gnessren watched the woman turn to stone, or nearly so—the color drained entirely from her face, and she stood suddenly petrified. Euphoria tilted her head curiously, and Gnessren tensed.

"Who is that?" he asked softly.

"My husband," Hazel managed.

"Did you get separated in the storm?" Euphoria asked.

"No, I..." Hazel faltered, flinching as the voice came again, calling out to her. Gnessren cursed himself for a fool—the man was no knight come to kill him and rescue this maiden. The maiden was in danger, but it was the knight who would harm her. Who had harmed her already.

Gnessren looked around his cave, his beloved home for ages and ages. He then stepped toward the woman—then stopped himself, remembering her reaction when she had thought he was angry.

"Euphoria," he whispered. "Hide her."

"Hazel," the husband called, nearing the entrance to the cave now. "Can't believe you dragged me all the way out here in the middle of the night, Hazy bitch," he laughed at the nickname, anger behind it.

Euphoria drew Hazel deeper into the cave, behind a small hill that softly glittered.

"Does he have a gun or anything?" Hazel whispered to Euphoria, worried. "I don't want him to hurt Anthony. He's angry right now, but he'll be fine in the morning. He probably already feels bad..."

"Oh no, Gnessren doesn't know how to use a gun," Euphoria said, giggling. Gnessren could only assume she was imagining an eleven-foot dragon fumbling with a tiny gun, like a cat pawing anxiously at a strange toy. Hazel, too focused on the sight of her husband's form at the mouth of the cave, only nodded and pressed a little closer to the faerie. Euphoria put her arms around the woman, holding her protectively.

Gnessren walked backward, deeper into the cave, listening to their whisperings as he let the shadows swallow him up. He felt fire in his belly, anger at the injustice of centuries' worth of violence humans had wrought upon one another and blamed on his kind. And now he saw, nothing had changed. Knights once blamed their lust for violence and desire for fame on his kind—murdering them as they slept curled around their hoards and riding back to their corrupt kingdoms with lies on their lips, of rescuing maidens and whole villages, to justify their slaughter, to glorify it. Now this human, gleeful in his hate, desperate to crush the spirit of another beneath the violence of his hands, would lay the blame on his victim, too. They were not the same and had not suffered the same, he and this human woman, but suddenly he knew nothing but the desire to stand between her and this man.

"I swear to fucking god, Hazel," the man said, laughter gone. "I'm soaked, it's the middle of the fucking night, and you're out here playing games? Why are you always like this? I'm sorry you hit your head, but you're making way too big a deal out of it. I barely even touched you; it's not my fault

245

you're clumsy. Jesus, Hazy! You're not a child! You can't just run off into the woods!"

Gnessren closed his eyes. He felt the fire in him loosen and spread, felt his skin harden and shiver with magic. The air grew thinner as he grew larger. Soft human fingers and toes became hard and scaled, tipped with deadly claws. His tail—the strangest thing to lose in his other form—curled around him, and he unfolded his wings, letting them brush against the rough, mineral-laced ridges that formed the ceiling above. The earth around him thrummed its ancient song, welcoming him back into his true shape, bound to the stones and mountains of the world through the same magic that had made them both, long ago when there was nothing but fire and rock.

"You are so lucky," Anthony continued. "I should have just left you out here to get eaten by a bear or a wolf or something. Who the hell else would chase you halfway up a mountain? Did you even think before you ran off like that? Of course you didn't. Thinking's not really your strong point, Hazy. It's cute most of the time, but you're annoying me right now. Do you really want to ruin the whole trip? Because you can't act like a grown-up? Cut it out and let's go back to the cabin."

Gnessren stepped forward, just a little, into the very edge of speckled moonlight that shone down into the high, arched opening of the cave. The light was thin, wavering and dancing around the fast-moving storm clouds that tried to stifle it. It was enough, however, to catch on the diamond sharpness of his claws and to make gleam the subtle rose-colored scales of his leg.

Anthony stopped short. Gnessren stepped closer, shedding the shadows, and brought his face down to the human, fixing him with a golden-eyed stare.

"What the fuck," Anthony said, in a voice as weak as the cloud-strangled moonlight. Gnessren exhaled slowly, letting smoke trickle up into the air around them. He pressed his nose against the man's chest—his shirt stunk of human sweat and sickly-sweet fear—and gave him a firm nudge back toward the storm.

Anthony stumbled and fell, but the shock of hitting the hard earth beneath him snapped him out of his paralyzed fear. He scrambled up and took off running without another word, grabbing at rain-slick branches and tripping over his own feet in his haste. As cowardly as any knight, Gnessren thought.

When he retreated again to the depths of the cave, Hazel stood with her false bright light shining, staring open-mouthed. He could not identify the expression on her face—part horror, part wonder, perhaps, but then he thought that maybe she could not identify the emotions behind it, either. He closed his eyes against the light, and Euphoria magicked up a small campfire instead—with pale violet flames, of course, and little shimmering violet dragonflies to circle it.

Hazel turned off her light and walked toward the magic fire as if in a trance. She sat down beside it, watching the dragonflies shimmer.

"What is happening?" she asked the bits of magic softly. They did not reply. Gnessren, in his human form again, sat down beside her. He thought she might shrink from him, but she only lifted her gaze to his, regarding him as she had done the dragonflies.

"There are many beings who have suffered the violence of certain humans," he began quietly. "Throughout the ages. In order to make themselves feel powerful, or to justify their desire for blood. They glorify one another through the suffering of others. I see that has not changed. It has always been so."

She stared at him still, jumping slightly as Euphoria came to sit beside her. The faerie offered her a smile, warm and safe, and she slowly relaxed. Gnessren, too, felt his tension ease—such was the way of faeries.

"Look," Gnessren said, and pulled his shirt over his head to reveal the ugly twist of scales just above his heart, the flesh there mangled and scarred too badly for magic to hide.

"A human did that to you?" Hazel asked.

"A knight," he confirmed. "Her sword is the only one of my treasures that is buried beneath the earth. It is not worthy of being adored."

And then he told her the story of his people, of their long-suffering, of their centuries of bearing fabricated evils to justify those who sought to destroy them.

It was several months before he saw Hazel again. His new cave was not as grand as his old one had been, but it was safer, more secreted away than before. With Euphoria's help, he had succeeded in moving almost all of his hoard—his treasures, not stolen from anyone, as the stories accused, but collected from abandoned, broken things, pretty things that had been tossed aside or sunken to the bottom of the sea alongside a corpse to boast of wealth and glory. Fish did not care about wealth or glory.

Euphoria brought her to him. She was still a small, pink, freckled creature with hair the shade of wheat, but she was smiling, and the smile reached her eyes. There were flowers in her hair—a chronic condition for anyone living in close proximity to a faerie—and she clutched something in her hands as she approached him. She waited for him to change into his human form, and then thrust the object toward him.

He glanced at Euphoria, curious, and then down at the object—a book. It was slim and covered in smooth paper.

"Did you know, Gnessren, that Hazel writes books for human children?" Euphoria asked sweetly, twining her fingers with Hazel's in a familiar, easy way.

"Euphoria helped with the details," Hazel said, worrying her bottom lip in anxious excitement. Gnessren could feel her eyes on him, eagerly hunting for some reaction.

"I wanted to give you a copy. As a thank you," she explained.

He looked down at the cover and saw... himself, his true self, sleeping among his treasures. After a moment, he opened the book and began to turn its pages. There was Einar, and Zessik, and Rheness, dear friends, long since gone to the Faerie Realm, perfectly rendered in gentle watercolors as they soared over the lands of his memory.

The tale unfolded with the turn of each page. The dragons, free to roam the earth, gathered their treasures and built their warm caves. There they sang the songs that the ancient stones passed into their bones from the beginning, melodies of primordial flame, when the whole world glowed like a fiery jewel. These happy moments were disrupted by the arrival of an evil knight, his eyes the same bright blue of the man Gnessren had forced from his cave and into the night. The knight, scheming, tried to feed a princess to one of the dragons, to sell her life for a broken, emerald-studded clasp. The reader knew, of course, that the knight planned to slay the dragon as soon as he accepted, and ride home with tales of how he had rescued the princess from a terrible fate. He would have all the treasure he could carry, and the princess would be his wife, he was sure, a gift from a grateful king. But the princess stole the knight's sword instead, defeated him in battle and then dragged him back to the kingdom, from which he was exiled in disgrace. That night, the princess returned to the dragons, and together they feasted and sang the old songs until dawn.

Gnessren closed the book and looked up at Hazel. She had one arm draped around Euphoria's waist and rested against the faerie's shoulder, giving him a shy, hopeful look. He could not speak at first, overwhelmed. It could not, of course, change the past. The stories were still told, the old paintings still hung, depicting ancient lies. But here among them was a small gem of truth. He smiled at her softly and held the book close.

"Thank you," he said. "I shall treasure it."

On the Table

by Coleman McClung

Smoke burned my eyes, but I kept them focused on the body being dragged away across the cement. The woman had a good grip on a length of flannel below the collarbone, but she still struggled with the weight. I arranged my Carrier's face into something along the lines of sympathy until she passed, and then stepped down off the curb.

The hidden gem of a mountain town was having a bad day.

A pharmacy on the opposite corner had black smoke pouring out of the second-floor windows. The only firemen within twenty miles were busy down the road trying to extinguish the flames of what had been an unfortunately parked tanker truck. Now it was just a blasted-out crater full of burning metal in the middle of Main Street.

I reached the other sidewalk where Richard and another man were trying to help a young girl trapped in debris. She was covered in blood and drywall dust, making it hard for the men to get a good hold of her.

"Hey, Rich. You got a second?" I asked.

He ignored me until the girl's slight frame finally shifted and slipped free. They lowered her onto the sidewalk, the girl crying and coughing in turn but looking relatively unscathed. Richard stood up, brushing off his dusty brown deputy's uniform before walking toward me. Annoyingly, the man I didn't know followed.

"You think we got 'em all?" the stranger barked.

"Sheriff thinks so," Richard replied. "They didn't figure we'd find out how to tell the bastards apart from normal folks. I bet it was a real surprise when they hit the pavement full of buckshot. That ship, or whatever you want to call it, was their only off-ramp from this mess."

I raised my body's temperature a few degrees until beads of sweat began to line my brow.

"I've never seen anything like it," I lied. "The way it came down and opened up like a flower. Had me running even before they started burning everything up."

The stranger couldn't keep the glee out of his voice. "Yeah, well, it didn't matter, did it? Firing on that semi-truck without knowing all hell what was hitched up to it. Dumb shits."

"Doc been able to figure out what they are yet? Why they look like us?" Richard sputtered through a rising cloud of ash. "People are talking, but I don't like that kind of gossip. Makes it sound like one of those cheesy space flicks, used to play at the drive-ins."

"That's where I'm heading right now. He called and said he found something," I answered.

We all stood there for a moment, taking in the chaos. The girl started to get up off the cement, and the stranger left our little huddle to help her out.

Richard leaned in. "Look, we don't have a lot of time before they figure out their test doesn't work on all of us. I've already got the sheriff asking questions faster than I can recall from this Carrier's memories. I think he suspects me."

"We have to assume we're the only two left. We wait until nightfall and hike up through the valley. Get as far away as possible before they repair the cell tower and convince everyone little green men tried to take over," I said.

"You're starting to talk like them," Richard sneered.

The walkie pinned to his shoulder squawked. He reached up, hand hovering over the button. "Call me after you talk to the doctor. If he's found anything new, we're dead." He pressed the button and walked off. "This is Carey, what have you got?"

I watched him leave. Escaping would be so much simpler if it were just me. I pushed the thought out of my mind.

Leaping down from the borrowed pick-up, I made my way inside the clinic, noting the empty room beyond the sliding glass window in the lobby.

We were alone.

Sifting through my Carrier's memories, I singled out those including the good doctor. We were friendly but nothing more than drinking buddies. Our conversations usually centered around his unpleasant romantic partner and the several women working for him he had coerced into casual encounters. He trusted my Carrier's intelligence, though. For years, I had taught science at the local high school. Not chemistry, or biology, or even physics: *science*. Stupid hick town.

"Marc?" a voice echoed down the ill-lit hallway.

I walked past several empty offices, eventually reaching a set of doors leading to what was essentially the town's morgue. The Doc stood next to an open cold chamber with a naked human body resting face down on a gurney.

The tools in his hands meticulously parted flesh and muscle along the spine of the corpse. "This is remarkable, Marcus, truly remarkable. I mean, horrible events today notwithstanding—very tragic—but this..."

He wiped his brow with an already damp sleeve as I moved in closer.

"...this is astounding."

The body on the table was a woman. Shiny patches of white skull peaked through mostly unrecognizable blackened skin and tufts of brown hair. Even with the burns, my Carrier knew her immediately. She had been attractive to him but was happily married. Still, he'd kept up with social media pages she posted on. Even saved a few pictures.

I knew her very differently, though.

Her name was Rachel. When we came to this town and began to implant new Carriers, she had been my first. Once I embedded the embryo into her spine, it began to grow, taking over neural pathways one by one until almost nothing of her original self remained. My relationship with this new being is not unlike that of a parent and child.

My *daughter* was split open from her lower back all the way up to the base of her neck. The doctor placed a series of hooked clamps to hold back the skin, exposing the entire spinal column, along with her true self.

"It didn't make sense to me at first," the doctor said. "These were people I've known since they were kids, mind you. We found out who was *wrong*, but we didn't know why they were doing all that violence. I figured it was a virus or somethin,' but then an honest-to-God flying saucer comes down out of the clouds..."

He nodded at the nearby gloves on a tray full of surgical equipment and I slipped them on.

"Afterward, I came back here with a few of the bodies and started in on them," he continued. "Everything seemed fine—lungs, kidneys, heart—it all looked normal. Then I noticed these foreign hollow bones behind the clavicle. See there."

A grainy texture filled my mouth as I ground my teeth at his poking and prodding her. For now, my face maintained the slightly perplexed but interested expression he'd expect.

"So, I keep cutting and find a creature nearly two feet long that has circumvented the entire myelin sheath. Lord almighty, does it stink too." He laughed.

I glanced down at the tray holding a scalpel only an arm's length away.

We have to stay hidden.

"Hey Doc, I think I've seen enough. I don't really have the stomach for this sort of thing," I said.

"Hold up, now," he replied, slicing at several tubes intertwined with the vertebrae. "This is the best part."

I'm going to rip out your fucking throat.

"You see, once you remove the creature—" He stuck a fat-fingered glove between the spine and what was left of my offspring, tearing the thin membrane that housed thousands of the tiny neurods making up our brains. Her thoughts, feelings—everything that made her an individual—spilled out into the Carrier's open cavity, disappearing into the pooling fluids. Half of her came loose after that. Only half.

"Huh, slippery little things."

I grabbed at the surgical knife and dove across the table, opening my Carrier's vocal cords unnaturally and howling for his blood.

CHIK-CHIK.

255

Disconnecting from the pain receptors, I still felt the slug explode just below my waist before I could completely detach.

Across the room stood Richard, Sheriff Bourkins, and a county officer lowering a shotgun.

"You okay, Doc?" Richard asked.

"Of course, I—How did he pass the test?" the doctor replied shakily, pressed up against the wall.

Richard turned to the Sheriff. "Do you believe me now?"

The Sheriff looked sick but gripped Richard's shoulder reassuringly as he moved past him.

I looked down. Only a few sinews connected my left leg to my groin and above that was just a mess of exposed arteries and torn-up muscle. I tried to lift myself up, but the Carrier's brain passed out from the pain I no longer felt. I laid there, frozen, still able to see and hear everything.

Richard looked down at me with pity in his eyes. No one else would notice it, but I did.

"Doctor, you better get this one on the table while it's still fresh," he said.

The Puppet Beast
by Rowan Rook

I... don't want to do this. I've visited Illias village to claim hundreds of sacrifices on hundreds of new moon nights, but this is the first time that thought breaches the swamp of dread in my stomach. I don't want to do this.

I stop, just for a moment, at the top of the valley. The village is dark below, with no strangers on the streets and no candlelight in windows. Its people are hiding, the way they always are.

At least the stars stay out for me.

I reach out my right hand so that the brightest star shines through my translucent palm. Its beauty seems wrong beside a monster like me, but I can't help but dream about my claws plucking it from the sky—about holding it tight to my silent chest and making a wish.

I'd wish to be human, I think.

I look away from the sky and plod on all fours into Illias village. I can understand why everyone hides. I look like a shadow cast by something between a human and a lion, but far worse than either. I'm made of the Princess' magic, so it's no surprise that I'm ugly, that I'm cruel. I'm her puppet. She made me so that she could hide away in her castle while I make her sacrifices. If I don't, we'll both die.

So I'd like to think I don't have a choice... but of course I do.

I look back at those stars I love so much.

I'm only human enough to want to live.

My narrowed gaze scans through the walls of the village. I'm close enough now to see the auras of every living thing inside each home. Some burn brighter than others. Who will I kill today? The weight of that decision feels so familiar and yet so strange that I'd laugh if I could.

One blazing violet glow makes me turn toward a locked door. The aura inside is shaped like a man. I breathe in air that smells like Illias' summer blossoms. Yes, he'll do just fine.

I shatter the door with one powerful swipe of my claws and charge inside.

The man—all paled skin and sweaty hair—leaps from a closet with a knife in his hands, as if that can stop me. As if he wants to believe he can.

He only has time to scream before I plunge my forked tail into his chest.

His violet aura flows out of his body and into mine like siphoned water. It's cool like water, too. New strength washes away the haze I hadn't realized had come over me, refreshing my form and my mind, waking me up until I'm fully alive.

The man's eyes open wide, turning whiter. I don't know what it's like for a human when I steal away their life, but it must be the opposite of what happens to me.

...I wish that experience didn't feel so delightful. I really am my Princess' beast. I wonder if she feels it, too, up in the castle, where she doesn't have to see our victim's face.

Finally, when the last drop of life spills from him to me, he falls to the ground with a dead thunk.

It's done. The Princess and I are safe for another month. Her five-hundred-year reign will continue. As long as I keep restoring her magic, she'll live forever.

...Forever.

Pain flares up in my shoulder. A hiss escapes me and I look down to see an arrow jutting from my skin. My eyes fly toward the home's hallway.

A girl stands there, a bow in her shaking hands. She holds another arrow taught against the string.

"I'll kill you," she hisses just like I do. "I'll kill you!"

...The man's daughter, perhaps?

She lets the arrow go and it flies toward me, but this time I'm ready. I swat it away with a hand that reaches out to push her back. One of my claws catches on her cheek and spills blood in the shape of a crescent. She screams.

I turn away and flee. I don't need to hurt her. I've had my fill.

"I'll get you for this! I'll get you for Daddy!" the girl's voice chases after me. "I'll be a hero! You'll fear the name Dia! I'll get your Princess one day!"

A thing as small and delicate as she could never stand a chance against the Princess and me.

Humans really are naive creatures.

I amble through the snowy woods as quietly as the ghost I sometimes swear I am. Thanks to the Princess' holiday feast, the castle is out of food. She should've had enough for the rest of the winter, but if I don't bring home meat for her tonight, she'll blame me. She never does anything for herself anymore. What would she have done if she hadn't made me?

A sound breaks through the silence. A human sob.

I freeze.

I'm not out here looking for humans. It might be best to turn the other way, but something stops me from doing so. That sad, rhythmic sound. There's something beautiful about it, the way it trembles with such raw, strange emotion. A part of me still wishes to understand it.

I give myself permission to creep closer, and through the trees, I see a woman standing over the bleeding body of a bear with arrows in its back and its two cubs sitting beside it —a woman with a crescent scar on her cheek.

I shudder, stepping back.

...Dia? Is that the name an angry girl once said I'd fear? She's nearly grown now—that must have been nearly ten years ago.

"I'm sorry," the woman named Dia sniffles, seeming to talk to the cubs even though she must know they cannot understand her language. "If I'd known she had you, I wouldn't have hunted her. I know what it's like to lose your parent."

I expect her to force herself onward like humans do, to finish off the bear, but her tears keep falling.

With an inhale of the cold air—the cold air that almost reminds me of the violet life I stole that night—my translucent body emerges from the shadows as if it were one of them.

Dia gasps and leaps backward, her hands already on her bow and her eyes narrowed as if they hadn't been shedding tears just moments ago. "You...!" Rage shakes her voice, but no matter how many of those arrows she shoots, she can't kill a monster like me.

I look away from her and step up to the bear. Its aura is weak and yellow. It won't last much longer. I pluck out the arrows before I plunge my tail into its flesh.

Dia cries out, as if she expects me to take all the life it has left.

Instead, I let life flow the other way. I've never done this before, but I suppose it should be simple. I feel warm—too hot—as my own violet aura flows out of my body and into the bear's. Its wounds heal, stitching themselves shut as if time itself is moving faster. Its breathing evens out. Its aura turns a healthy blue. It will be fine.

I won't be if the Princess realizes what I've done. I can only hope the amount of life I gave away is too small for her to notice.

My eyes linger on the sleeping bear for a while longer. I'm not entirely sure why I took the risk. I had no reason to do so... but perhaps I wanted to, even though saving one fellow beast's life can't make up for the hundreds of human lives I've taken.

I force myself to look up and see Dia standing closer. Her wide eyes gape at me. I've seen that look of shock so many times before, but this time the emotion isn't quite fear. To my own surprise, it's not quite anger, either. Her fingers strangle her bowstring, but she doesn't fire.

I disappear back into the woods.

"Kill her," the Princess' words reverberate in my mind as if they were my own thoughts.

This time, I'm the one who gawks at Dia—at the grown woman with her knight's armor and sword and bow. She promised to come for the Princess... and she has, almost twenty years later. To even get inside the castle, past the Princess' lesser puppet beasts, she must have spent so much of her life in training.

"This is for my father!" She lets an arrow fly.

I expect it to come toward me, but instead, it seeks out the Princess.

A barrier of green fire burns it before it can reach her, but the Princess' face fumes with just as much heat.

"Kill her!" she screams at me silently. "Kill her, or I'll erase you! I'll take my magic back!"

She means it. She can't fight without using all of the magic she used to make me. I'm supposed to be her puppet. I'm supposed to fight and steal and kill in her place. I'm supposed to keep her mind and body safe.

I hunch down to strike.

Dia turns toward me and pulls out her sword, wanting to believe she stands a chance just as her father had once wanted to believe so, too. Moonlight makes her blade shimmer like the stars.

...I wish I could've seen those stars one more time.

I lunge toward the Princess on her throne, my claws and fangs sinking into her flesh before she can understand what's happening. Her blood tastes like mud on my tongue. She screams, and I feel her pain echo through me, tear at my innards and edges. This is nothing like any of the kills I've made before... yet it feels so much better.

I should have done this years ago.

"You...!" the Princess screams in my mind. "You traitor! You beast! You—"

My teeth crunch down hard, and the Princess goes limp.

The reality of what I've just done splashes across the room like the bloodstains.

I drop the Princess's body. Even after five-hundred years, her sacrifices made her beautiful on the outside, but the anger left behind on her dead face is as ugly as she always was within.

I already feel my life beginning to ebb. My vision swims around the familiar throne room, color draining and sound dimming. I'm... going to fall, fall into the black, fall out of this world.

...Is this the way my victims felt?

For one more moment, a hand reaches out and holds me, as if it could save me from the fall. Dia. Those tears that fascinated me fall down her cheeks and her eyes are wide with an altogether different emotion than the ones I've seen in them before. ...Sorrow?

I think that same emotion might be the one that howls like winter in my mind as the Princess' magic—as my body—fades away.

I hope I was more than a part of the Princess. I hope I was more than a puppet. I hope I have a soul that can haunt this world—that can see people and places and stars.

"You're not her," Dia tells me, as if she read my thoughts. "Not anymore. You can't be."

I smile for the first and last time.

Newton's Cradle

by Carla Durbach

The soul girl is there again.

He can see her standing by the edge of the water, her humanoid torso swaying in the breeze. She is wearing a star-beam outer skin with black shapes. Every time she moves, they look like flapping webbed wings. Those wings, he reflects, become expansive with every motion. They remind him of bats trying to escape but locked in the yellow.

Visk is afraid of bats. They were introduced into his world by the soul people. As a gift. The bats tend to fly in groups through purple heavens, screeching in swimming motions, spurting off dark vibrations. Their songs hurt his body and disturb the water, tearing ripples right through the channels. But Visk is more afraid of the soul people. He is not as afraid of the girl, though. Perhaps because she has her eyes closed and does not appear to have seen him. Nevertheless, he sinks further into the water and lies fully submerged now, cooling fast. He rotates his body so that he can see her from every and any perspective. His panoramic vision affords him this capability.

He senses someone else behind him now, in the water. Line, one of his tribe. When they communicate, Visk's people sing to each other in pulsating waves of differing harmonies and tempos. He asks Line about the soul people.

They are composed of many songs and layers, he tells him, *but also of polarities.*

Polarities? You mean...? he asks without taking his eyes off the girl.

Yes, but not the same as us. Polarities like hot and cold, light and dark, life and death, love and hate...

These are all contradictions to Visk, and they are therefore bound to cancel each other out. He tries to understand, but when he gazes down at the slippery skin of his multiple arms and the circular organs beneath— swimming like beautiful, translucent jellyfish, swollen and gasping for air—he feels at a loss. His people are simple and linear, like water. They move in molecular motions, as smoothly as viscous liquid or colloid diffusions. There are no edges, no sharpness, no snagging or pulling. Flow. Beautiful. Gracefully simple. There is also no part of him that is not in touch with all parts of himself. His mind is an open chorus. He imagines that it would be tormenting to have to hide from himself, to guess at or fight with what emerges from his own mind.

Visk's tribe has no expression for 'alone' or 'gone' and these were some of the scales they could not engage with during their initial contact with the soul people. One of their elders asked the newcomers to explain in detail. After numerous unsuccessful attempts, someone thought up a sphere with a slice through it, and there was a combined shudder and sonorous ripple through their currents, for everyone understood it then. It meant to dissect or cut out, to pierce through and separate. For every song there is an equal

265

and opposite song that returns to the sender. The returning song after 'alone' was sung frightened many.

He focuses on the girl with the smooth head and bright outer skin, her extended limbs touching the air yet not dissolving. They call the extensions 'arms,' as well. They hang from their bodies like pendulums. He wonders if their arms are polarized just like their insides. An arm and a non-arm; an arm and a stump inside—no, an arm and a hollow tube with blunt extremities. But he shakes his head, his whole gelatinous frame trembling. He doesn't understand the soul people, how they are made so solid and opaque that no one can glimpse inside. They are strange to him, foreign in almost every way except for the songs. He understands their song notes—they call them music in their world. The humanoid ballads have been passed down from river channel to river channel. Some of the songs are wonderful, but he also recalls one whose rhythm and pitch nearly denatured him. Violence. The same cold terror that grasped every cell in his body the last time returns, bares its teeth, and begins to crawl toward him.

Visk, listen...

His guardian whispers to him from across the channel, deep under water, and Visk stops and listens. Fear is a new scale for him. Ever since the soul people arrived on his world, many moon cycles ago, different songs have penetrated the water world in which he lives. The intergalactic exiles came bearing a new language, one that occasionally hurts. Visk listens to Line's melody now, and his guardian's song calms and soothes him.

Like all of his tribe, Visk can take on different shapes when outside of the water, even humanoid. This is something that is not encouraged, but which he has tried with some measure of success. The first time gave rise to an odd sensation that divided his body into six compartments, all connected, moving in unison when he emerged out of the water. He walked around like that, clumsy and floppy. It took considerable practice to imitate the soul people convincingly, but he eventually mastered the physical motions. He did this during the moon phases—what the soul people call 'nights'— but during the star phases he returned to the water. He didn't want them to see him. The girl was only a suckling back then and the soul people who had aged tended to stay away. But the girl grew, and then things changed, and he changed too.

He likes the luminous moss by the river bank and the whistling of the trees as they reach for him when he walks past. The soul people cannot hear tree songs, they cannot hear all songs, actually. This is a blessing because he suspects that not all of them would welcome new songs or new notes. Except maybe the girl. There was the time before, when her eyes widened and her stare became fixed in his direction, penetrating the darkness. But he dove deeper and swam home, beneath the rocks, his arms tingling. He knows that she did not tell the others because nobody came to complain.

They are well aware of one another, but both species avoid each other in a mutual conspiracy of denial or fear, he is not sure which, or perhaps it is both. There is a treaty in place that allows movement and co-existence, but no intermingling. The soul people's planet is in nuclear winter and the river elders took the surviving remnants in, because the river people believe in the preservation of life. But they remain wary of the settlers.

Visk wonders if such complex, layered creatures will ever completely abandon their affinity for weaponry. Such knowledge is powerful and a snare at the same time. Soon, their home planet will become habitable once again, and when it does, the soul people will be expected to remove themselves from Visk's planet and return to Earth. In the meantime, they live here on the banks of the rivers, swimming in their home, drinking from the waterfalls, eating from their own biosphere—a contraption that was erected on moon phase one hundred and three after their arrival. He recalls the planet trembling with the drilling. The soul people have also been permitted to continue working on their travel ships, but any other technology is forbidden.

Contact with the exiles is discouraged, but ten moon phases ago, Visk gathered the courage to emerge again. The girl wasn't there and he could hear the trees calling to him. Careless and silent, he emerged from the water, took on humanoid form and moved his binary arms in the air like he had observed the girl do many times. It led to a curious, dismembering feeling. There was the song of laughter behind him and he stopped abruptly, turned around, and saw her standing, looking at him. He ran, then. Dove into the water and disappeared. Frightened.

Again nobody came to complain about the sighting. That area remains the soul people's designated living area and he is not supposed to be there. He wonders if the girl knows when he is around. He is a little afraid of her still, but he is also curious now that she has aged. He knows not to trust them, yet can't help but be interested in their weirdness, their polarities, and their sharp angles.

Having a guardian and friend like Line is delightful and comforting, but he longs for something new. Someone different from who and what he is. And he feels an odd sensation inside his circulatory system for thinking this way and entertaining it. A discomfort that makes him want to run away and hide from his own reflection. He knows that if he allows this to become a 'secret', he will lose a part of himself and he does not like the idea. To remain hidden from others is hard enough, but to remain hidden from oneself strikes him as unbearable.

So, he relents now, and shapes himself to resemble human form, feels the gelatinous sensation of being fashioned into compartments, thinned and thickened at different places. Slowly, he emerges from the water in front of the girl. Her eyes widen as she hears the splashing, and she stops abruptly, remains still as if rooted to the spot.

Behind him, Visk can hear the collective sigh of disapproval from his people; their concerns are unified in the lyrics, and Line's are the most prominent. His people have become extremely cautious since the arrival. He almost doesn't recognize their freedom of flow anymore. Extra care is taken as to when and if to leave the water. Careful and vigilant, and confined, they wait for the visitors to leave.

Visk is filled with an unusual restlessness that he has never felt before. It is a vortex that originates inside and twirls through him constantly, reaches a crescendo that nearly tips him over into wave after wave, and eventually subsides when he is all out of sorts and undone. Line advises him to enter into holy exile in the caves beneath the shallows. There, he can revisit the past, including his history before becoming water born. But Visk doesn't want to. He does not want to enter the stasis, the magical sleep of dormancy that will overtake him for many moon cycles or at least until the soul people have packed up and left. He doesn't need to remember; he needs new memories, new experiences. Visk wants the future not the past.

Now, the girl shifts uneasily and turns slightly toward him. Stands and peers at him with a mix of curiosity and angst. He lifts one of the binary protrusions and waves it towards her, copies her, hoping that the action makes him seem less intimidating. In his full height, he towers over her. He could make himself shorter but this would mean re-adjusting body parts, which may frighten her even more. The girl sings something which he fails to catch. Her song is mixed with those of the trees. He shakes his head as she tilts her own to the side and stares at him. She sings again and this time he understands her.

I've seen you before.

Yes, he answers.

The girl shifts her feet uneasily.

Are you afraid? She asks, taking a small step toward him but stopping suddenly when she sees him flinch. *You don't have to be, I won't hurt you... how could I? I won't tell the others...*

Visk nods and attempts to smile—a clumsy attempt which must make him look grotesque. But the girl smiles back.

Afraid, he says, *I am not used to this song scale.*

The girl raises an eyebrow as she weighs his words.

We brought it with us when we came.

Yes, he says and is not sure of what to say next, although he has plenty of questions.

May I ask you something? The girl moves closer, in a tentative, careful way, and he notices everything. The way her feet move in a slight shuffle so as not to alarm him, the way she hangs her arms loosely at her sides, and the smoothness of her skull with alternating patches of light and dark, presumably areas where her hair will grow and areas where it will never again do so.

Yes. His tone is more relaxed now as he allows himself the luxury of being in her presence and of exhaling the fearful anticipation of it.

Do you feel warmth?

He ponders her question for a moment. Thinks about the sensations of the currents in the river channels, the hot and cold. Temperature; perhaps she is asking about the scientific measurement of heat, or perhaps it is something else.

Warmth?

Yes, she says, appearing a little more animated, *feeling warm inside, affection, nurturance, affiliation, love? Do you hug each other?*

Visk understands now.

We have a song for love. It is the longest scale in our language, the most enduring. It is the scale that binds us together. It is the scale that informed us of your arrival and of those of your kind. It is the scale that made space for you in our world. It is the scale that moves the waters. We live in it.

Oh, the echoes that I hear from the river, they must be... The girl appears gently surprised and fascinated by the sudden dawning of such knowledge. She moves closer to him, almost absent-mindedly, until she is so close that he can smell her scent. Visk draws back instinctively.

Do you have a name? she asks.

I am Visk. You?

Serena. Nice to meet you, Visk. I wondered if you would ever talk to me. None of the others do. None of the others come back. They usually stay only for a moment and then leave.

How do you know it was not me?

You have different ways about you. Hmm... I don't know how to explain it... a different way of looking, I think.

It is Visk's turn to act surprised now and he tries to smile again. The sensation stretches his outer core slightly and jolts him. It is uncomfortable.

It is my turn, now, to ask you a question.

The girl smiles and nods her head.

Why do you have black bats on your outer skin?

The girl looks down at her suit and laughs.

This is not my skin, Visk, it is a suit... a piece of clothing. It keeps the cold of your world on the outside of my body. These black things, they are called butterflies. You don't have them on your world, but in my world, they symbolize new beginnings, new life, and a chance to start again. They are black to remind us of what we did to our world, of the darkness... so that we may always remember the darkness that came but also the life that survives and carries on. The black butterfly is the Earth team's insignia. We all wear it.

You did not bring butterflies with you, only bats.

Yes, bats and other mammals—they live for a long time. You can study them, get to know about them. Butterflies are frail. They die easily and generally don't live long.

Are you like the butterflies?

The girl bites her lip and her eyes grow moist. Visk is surprised; he didn't know that the soul people had fluid inside.

Sometimes, she says sadly.

Visk understands sadness. He reaches out to her with one of his arms but stops himself short. That would mean he has gone too far. He looks toward the river bank and then back at the girl. His people are calling to him.

I have to go now. But I would like to talk with you again, he says, and begins walking toward the water. As he reaches the edge, he turns back to look at the girl. She has extended an arm toward him in what he suspects is a greeting of sorts. He does the same, and in a smooth motion he dives into the water, his mind electrified with the possibility of new discoveries and new worlds about to be born.

The Deep Sun

by Spencer Mann

Thrinn struggled against his bindings. The skin over his left temple split as the first horn pierced through. His blood stank of a hot forge, stinging as it dripped into his eye. He reached to wipe it away, or to scratch at the throbbing fleshy mound where the right horn lay in wait. Shackles held his wrists tight.

Little mind was paid to his cries. The harried nest warden had visited only to check his progress—a sharp prod to each temple—and press a ladleful of pale broth between his lips.

As the first blood slowed, the skin over his right temple swelled. He searched the stone ceiling of his cavern prison for a distraction. Wisps drifted there, insubstantial flashes of amber, green, and indigo. If he focused on one, it winked away, leaving an eerie patch of glow. But, when he let the fickle light fade to the periphery, small details—a gossamer wing, a pearly carapace—brushed the edges of his vision. *Help me. Please, break my chains.* They did nothing. He hated them.

Vibrations from the grandknell set the fresh bone abuzz. These distant clangs—one for the Emperor's awakening, two for her retirement to slumber—assured him that time still passed. Thrinn's cell wasn't equipped with steamflutes, whose shifting harmonies announced more precisely the Emperor's activities, sculpting time to finer detail. If Thrinn closed his eyes, focusing past his sizzling headache, he sometimes heard their faint tones. But whether the Emperor was adjusting the heat conduits or condemning magic abusers to the hinterchills was impossible to know.

When Thrinn's right horn emerged, his screams grew hoarse and he flailed against the rough, sweat-soaked cloth. He stared into the wisplight and begged for it to be over.

The bruises ringing his wrists and ankles had not yet faded by the time he returned to life at the nest. Its population had swollen with the abandoned brood of a plague-scourged generation. Whether through pestilence or other perils, life stumbled onward. The yet-unhorned looked at him with a mix of fear and envy, while the older ones nodded in recognition. Despite his lonely suffering, Thrinn felt he'd achieved something. Where smooth skin once signaled his youth, sharp bone now protruded. He even walked differently, adjusting to his rebalanced stature.

Every Emergence concluded with a journey to see the Deep Sun. After so much time trapped in his dim cell, Thrinn imagined that witnessing the source of heat and sustenance would invigorate him. It warded off the endless cold of the hinterchills, allowing the inhabitants of these core caverns to survive. Without it, the creeping ice would wither away the threadmothers and the people would starve. *I'm ready to see it.*

The freshly Emerged gathered in the antechamber, jostling for position. Hush shrouded them as Ayoshana arrived. Though age wrinkled her face and chipped her horns, the nest matron remained quite agile. Sinister rumors stalked her—whispers that forbidden magics kept her limber beyond what was strictly natural. Some speculated that her robes hid a snarl of flesh and metal, that if you listened close you might hear her heart clicking as it pumped steam.

Ayoshana led them through natural caverns and carved tunnels. Stone extended in every direction. Far above lurked a cold, dead world without a rocky ceiling. So they said, though Thrinn found it difficult to imagine. Rickety bridges crisscrossed ravines so deep that he couldn't bear to look down. Threadmothers wove mycelium through the caverns, fruiting into musky, branching fungus. At irregular intervals, leathery pink hyphae erupted through the stone. These forked into dozens, then hundreds of small, hollow pillars that gave off the heady aroma of fresh spores. As he passed, Thrinn picked off one of the tender orange tips and nibbled it. He grimaced as its bitter tang left a soapy film on the insides of his cheeks. Threadmothers were carefully cultivated to avoid these peculiar flavors. *I should've known better than to try a wild one.*

Heat bloomed as they traveled ever deeper. Thrinn sweated, stifled by muggy air. Ayoshana's reprimands silenced anyone bold enough to complain. Finally, the passage flattened out, ending at a rocky outcropping that overlooked a great well of magma.

Sulfured air scorched Thrinn's lungs, hitching his breath as he approached the edge. An immense beast was shackled at the center of the molten pit. Its heat radiated in thick, heaving waves. Convection currents folded over and over themselves, creating a strange lens through which the creature contorted. Its leviathan features would pull into focus for a moment, then stretch into smoky filaments. *The Deep Sun is alive. I never knew.*

It, too, had horns. Thrinn's head twinged in sympathy. Yet its body was far too large—far too serpentine, many-limbed and grotesque. *What is it?*

Thousands upon thousands of wisps gathered, adding their pall to the ruddy glow of magma. They clustered near great chains, blackened from constant heat, that reached down from the cavernous ceiling to ensnare the behemoth. Though sooty, the iridescent glow of magic was unmistakable, binding the Deep Sun in place. Thrinn rubbed his bruised wrists, thinking about his own chained misery. The memory brought bile to the back of his throat.

"The Deep Sun," Ayoshana announced, studying the Emerged around her. "Listen closely..." She launched into the tale.

In the beginning, the immense, thrashing monster had laid waste to the caverns. It burned settlements, devouring any horned folk who crossed its path. Yet its heat was all that repelled the cold. The people followed behind, afraid to freeze without it. Threadmothers sprouted in the heat that faded in its wake, sustaining the people as they pursued the beast.

While the tale unfolded, Thrinn watched the sun struggle against its chains. Red hot rock sprayed up as its many limbs crashed into the seething pool. He thought of his Emergence—the pain, the loneliness, the restriction—and clawed at the tender flesh around his horns.

Ayoshana ignored the beast's roars that punctuated her story. She told of the brave team of warrior mages who'd tricked it into this low cavern. They'd summoned divine power to conjure five great chains. With the Deep Sun fixed to a final location, the people could thrive.

"And so," Ayoshana concluded, "the Deep Sun lives in penance for its crimes, bound by the Divines, providing heat so that we can survive. Its hatred of life has been channeled toward our preservation. From time to time, its bindings grow weak and it must be restored. Your generation may be called upon to renew it. As long as it remains bound, our steam flows and our threadmothers flourish."

Thrinn felt her words enveloping him, providing the comfort of rationalization. But his own pain was fresh, the flesh around his horns still tender, the skin red and raw.

"Is it—is it suffering?" he asked, his voice cracking against the sizzling pool and gasps of steam. Several others looked around, trying to find the source of the interruption. A few of them laughed at the sound of his voice. Ayoshana turned his way, her expression inscrutable. She held up a calloused hand, gathering back their silence.

"A fair question," she remarked, with the practiced ease of someone accustomed to smoothing over contradictions. "But this is its penance. It stays here so that we can live. It cannot be reasoned with. Its fire drives off the cold, as the divines saw fit to provide. Were it to escape, the steamworks would break. The threadmothers would burn away. All life would end."

Thrinn didn't know what to say to that. *All life?* These revelations were so fresh—they jangled, dissonant in his mind. He looked into the writhing glow of liquid rock, through hazy curtains, and thought he saw the Deep Sun staring back. Crimson pits gaped in its black flesh, eyes stabbing into Thrinn's as it roared once more.

Thrinn tried to forget. As time clanged past his Emergence, he willed the leviathan to recede from his mind. But the more he denied the Deep Sun, the more its twisting form scorched his dreams. The bloodlight of its eyes flooded his vision. Accusatory. Its wails merged with his screams. He'd wake, clutching his head, thrashing against shackles that had long since released him.

He thought if he followed the path again, confronting what he feared, he would feel better. In control. But as he gazed toward the slithering mass of fire and despair, his heartbeats quickened. How easy it seemed for the others to make peace with this injustice that clamored at the bedrock of all they enjoyed. He whispered words of comfort, sweet justifications that the seething steam spat back. But what could be done? He knew no magic. He couldn't even approach the beast, whose overwhelming heat would char his flesh if he didn't choke on hissing vapors first.

"Back again?" came a wry voice behind him. Thrinn flinched, almost tumbling over the edge. He recovered, turning to see Ayoshana standing a few steps back. Strands of silvery hair between her horns gleamed orange under the solar glare.

"I—," Thrinn began, unsure what to say.

"Why do you keep coming here?" *She's been following me._*

Thrinn couldn't form an excuse. He gestured at the Deep Sun—the writhing behemoth encircled by chains and swarmed by wisps.

"It's a beautiful and terrible thing, isn't it?" Ayoshana asked. "For so much to be built on the back of a monster."

"Terrible." His jaw clenched.

"Hmm," she said, gazing out at the Deep Sun. "It seems I haven't distracted you with enough work."

"That's not—no," Thrinn said. *If the end result of all this is more drudgery...*

"You will work as my assistant, gathering notes recorded in the Halls of Memory."

"But I don't know anything about magic—or, well, anything else."

"All the more reason to teach you."

And so, the two of them turned their backs on the leviathan and began their journey upward. Thrinn felt its eyes boring into the back of his skull.

At first, Thrinn dreaded the work. The Halls of Memory were lonely caverns located above the ironworks. Steam billowed, condensing on the ceilings. Acrid rain dripped down, pooling in hallways and sluicing through cracks in the stone. Most of the people's knowledge lived here, carved in eloquent sigils listing spells, ceremonies, and old stories. But, during his many trips, he noticed gaps— places where runes had been scratched out. Knowledge blasted into oblivion. Attempting this forbidden magic led to exile. Ayoshana warned that the hinterchills awaited those who persisted in pursuit of Memories willfully forgotten. Even so, wisps gathered in those broken places, as though mourning the lost arts.

Spells were not the only Memories that had been erased. As he passed through the halls, Thrinn searched for more information about the Deep Sun. The more he looked, the more he noticed patterns in the gaps. What could possibly have existed between a historical account of the beast trampling a village on one side of a ruined panel, and a horrific description of a warrior's failed attempt to quell it on the other? There were many such gaps in the Deep Sun's history—too many. *What don't they want us to know?*

280

Ayoshana's demands for information were relentless. Thrinn dutifully transcribed glyphs onto stone tablets with a chisel, lugging them back to her chamber for review. The spells she asked him to research focused on the control and maintenance of heat. Thrinn questioned her motives, but whatever message she was trying to send, he couldn't fully decipher.

She showed him how to send intention from his core outward, bending thought into motion. There was a sturdiness to Ayoshana's magic—a righteousness. Order for the unsettled spirit. To control heat was divine, after all. But her magical gestures often went awry in Thrinn's hands. He learned, but he didn't thrive. Through many sleeps, the Deep Sun's rebukes persisted, as scalding as ever.

The grandknell chimed on—churning through the brief tenures of three emperors whose disease, madness, and weakness left the nation in disarray. Steamflutes chirped the executions of exiles caught trespassing back among the warmer caverns nestled above the Deep Sun's prison.

During the mourning for Emperor Othryll—whose reign had lasted not even thirty knells owing to some misplaced toxic moss—Thrinn had his revelation. Ayoshana had asked him to transcribe a Memory about how metal could be forged to resist heat. As Thrinn carved each glyph into his tablet, the sun's shackles rose to the surface of his mind. Such chains, according to this teaching, remained strong even as the heat around them grew. While they resisted blistering temperatures, the Memory was adamant that they'd become brittle if chilled. If Thrinn knew how to remove heat from the chains—and his surroundings—he would be able to approach the beast and shatter its bindings. *It deserves better than this. There has to be a way.*

281

No wall in the Halls of Memory still recorded such a spell. To create cold was horrific. Denying the sun's warmth —inviting in the death of the frigid caverns beyond, the cold above—was to reject life itself.

But that knowledge lived *somewhere*. People spoke of the hinterchills with hushed voices. They whispered of barren caves where frost crept along the walls. What few exiles survived there were said to be vicious, relentless in their practice of profane spells.

The closer he got to answers—to action—the less the nightmares plagued him. He no longer felt paralyzed. Thrinn was determined to right the wrongs etched into the very bones of his world. *I have to find the truth.*

Lies came easily to his lips. He told Ayoshana he was going on a pilgrimage, seeking the deeper wisdom of the ancient scribes. Whether she believed him or not, she did not stop his preparations.

With a pack of food, water, and many coats bundled around him, his journey through cold, abandoned tunnels began.

After a while, Thrinn no longer heard—or even felt— the deep clangs of imperial time. The steamflutes here had fallen into disrepair, rusting away. Threadmothers stood dry, their branches crumbling like old bones. For them to have emerged, the sun's heat must once have reached this far. The hinterchills drew ever inward, a slow doom awaiting some future generation. *Is the Deep Sun dying?*

Surviving exiles banded together in small communes, eking out meager lives before the cold overwhelmed them. Thrinn traded supplies for knowledge. He used his marginal skills to gift heat where he could, and in return, they told him where to find what he sought. The very thing they'd grown to loathe the most.

The halls here held fragments of the missing history. Never quite enough to complete the mosaic, but he found tantalizing hints. That life before the binding hadn't been as bad as he'd been told; that the threadmothers had been more plentiful and nourishing; that there'd been factions opposing the binding. These counternarratives lived among other, more horrific designs. Their blunt markings chiseled into his memory against his wishes—spells that severed skin and poisoned blood. Healing magic gone wrong, bringing false life to the dead. He didn't approach the wanderers who studied such gruesome renderings.

But one such person sat before the wall of his desired spell. This man sat atop a segment of fallen column, studying the inscriptions. He looked back and forth between the wall and a stone tablet, where he engraved clumsy glyphs with a chisel.

"Don't hover," the man said, voice crackling like the coals of a forge. "Approach, or away with you."

"Er—sorry," Thrinn said, moving closer. "I need—I mean, these are why I'm here."

The man tore his eyes from the inscriptions to appraise him. Though no older than Thrinn, he wore his time with more dignity. Pallid skin gathered shadows beneath alert eyes. From waves of soot-black hair emerged silvery-white horns that tapered to prim points. Thrinn felt a twinge of desire to know more about him.

"Fine." The man shifted, leaving room for Thrinn to sit.

"Thank you," Thrinn said, taking the seat. He left a respectful gap between them. "I'm Thrinn."

"Gezmog," the man said. "Gez." He offered no further detail.

Thrinn looked back at the wall, reading the enigmatic instructions. "What do you suppose... 'linger high corrosion' means?"

Gez stared at him in something approaching wonder. "You can read this shit?"

"Yeah," Thrinn said. "Of course. Can't you?"

Gez cast his eyes away. *Shit*, Thrinn thought. *Did I embarrass him?*

"I can help," Thrinn said. "Why don't we work together? It'll be easier to learn it if we do."

Some of Gez's poise returned, though it was hesitant. "I suppose you're right." He shuffled over, closing the gap between them. Thrinn felt like he'd been accepted into some deeper understanding with Gez. And yet this moment held weight that settled somewhere deep in his gut.

He turned back to the carvings and recited the five lines:

"Focal target—kill hate heat

Origin arc—hand jagged core

Clarifying shape—brittle branch order

Consumption—linger high corrosion

Aftermath—dull spirithood."

The words settled around them, bleak dust of a thousand fallen empires. Thrinn shivered, pulling his cloak closer.

"Can you read it again?" Gez asked. Thrinn did so, trying to inflect meaning into the arcane grammar.

They debated what each piece could mean. 'Kill hate heat' seemed straightforward enough, but 'brittle branch order' resisted the very clarity it pretended. Thrinn wondered what contempt for the world's fires had inspired such rough poetry.

On their journey back from the hinterchills, Gez saw fit to reveal his vengeful purpose. His family and the neighboring Flareburn clan had been rivals, farming threadmothers with generations of expertise. The plague had decimated Gez's family, but skipped right over the Flareburns.

"I saw their threadmother," Gez said. "Her progeny could feed a hundred. And when I was starving, I begged for their help. I could see the disgust on his face when he sent me away at the threshold. I humbled myself before him—admitted defeat—and he turned me away. And he laughed. Votch Flareburn *laughed* as he sent me away."

Thrinn wanted to embrace the man, but restrained himself.

"I want them to suffer like I suffered," Gez continued. His voice brooked no mercy, only the dread chill of vengeance. "The only way to kill a threadmother like that is with the cold. You've seen them in the hinterchills, right? Dry and broken. Dead. Only the cold does that."

Thrinn shivered. *To kill a threadmother is unspeakable.* What did that say about his own goal? He felt Ayoshana's judgment upon him, eclipsing the Deep Sun for just a moment.

"Well, why do *you* want to use this power?" Gez demanded.

"I'm going to break the chains binding the Deep Sun," Thrinn said.

Gez laughed. Thrinn didn't.

"You're serious," Gez said, his smile dropping. The patter of their footsteps echoed, a grim shroud for the slow heave of their breaths.

Gez lived in the midchills, caves sparse with settlement owing to unreliable temperatures. Unlike the steam conduits near the core, which radiated constant heat, the conduits here switched on and off. Sometimes, they flooded the area with intense heat. Other times, knells passed and the cold crept in.

Thrinn moved into Gez's cavern. The chamber was cluttered with the debris of lives cut short. Several chairs surrounded a large, dusty table where the full clan must once have gathered. When Gez sat there, eating meager rations in the gloom, Thrinn felt the weight of the missing chatter. Generations of voices silenced, save for one. Gez's grief even marked the threadmother. Its color was too pale, its filaments tinged only with the faintest pink. The fungus's spongy tips had gone sour under his haphazard care.

Once, when the conduit delivering heat to their cavern had switched off for several knells, it had become too cold to do much of anything. Thrinn had been surprised, at first, when Gez invited him to bed during this spell. It wasn't just about warmth, either. Thrinn hadn't meant for anything to happen, but wrapped in Gez's scent, the heady fumes of bitter incense and cold sweat stoked his arousal. The true revelation was that Gez reciprocated. As they twined together, his own lust became evident. Thrinn delighted in exploring the man's flesh, unleashing his fire upon eager kindling.

Arrangements like theirs were uncommon, but hardly rare. In a generation marked by chaos and tragedy, to find pleasure anywhere might as well have been sacred. Thrinn found comfort in the rough embrace of his broken lover. It was far more fulfilling than the supposed divinity of Ayoshana's spellwork.

They fell into a rhythm that defied imperial time. They ate while the next Emperor slept. They practiced magic during his marriage festival. And when he died, too, they fucked during his funeral.

Though Gez couldn't read the glyphs, he proved more adept at mastering the spell. Thrinn knew there was something wrong with this man. Gez's harshness seeped out: his jealousy, his fixation on the Flareburns absolute, save for the angry passion he shared with Thrinn. Under their dual obsessions, the threadmother barely survived. They tended her the minimum that they could bear to tear themselves away from the magic or each other. The Deep Sun still haunted Thrinn's dreams—but at a distance. Now that he had someone to live for, solving this injustice felt somehow less immediate—less crucial.

Gez cast the spell first. Thrinn stared in wonder at the rime frosting over his lover's hands. Thrinn tested the chill with his tongue, letting the glazed fingers numb his lips as the frozen flesh explored his mouth. The cold spot in their chamber lingered as they took their pleasure, horns clacking together as their quick breaths fogged above them.

There was still a distance to Gez's tenderness, as though the chasm of his hatred was too much for anyone to cross—even Thrinn. When they fucked, Thrinn wondered if Gez truly saw him or if he imagined instead sating his vengeance upon Votch Flareburn.

After they were done, Gez's hands left the skin between Thrinn's ribs pink where the cold had been. Thrinn saw that Gez's hands had gained a gray-blue quality, skin fracturing into crystalline flakes. Thrinn lay awake, wondering. *Will the warmth ever return?*

Love couldn't stop vengeance, but Thrinn tried nonetheless.

"Gez, please..." Thrinn begged, grabbing the man by the shoulders and drawing him in. After so many successful casts, Gez's arms had gone gray and cracked. "Don't go."

Cold rage flickered behind Gez's eyes as he pushed Thrinn back. "After all this—you'd deny my justice?"

"We don't have much, but if we tended the threadmother, we'd get by. Together. Isn't that enough?"

Gez seemed to consider it for a moment—a lifetime in this hollow, letting time quench his hatred until they grew old and the darkchill of death overtook them. Thrinn had allowed the torment of the leviathan to fade from his mind. But Gez's determination had only grown. Thrinn looked down at his feet.

Gez approached, bringing a single cold finger to draw Thrinn's chin up and look into his eyes. Thrinn shuddered from the frosty touch, but accepted a smoky kiss.

"I'll be back when it's over," Gez said, turning and leaving the chamber. Thrinn wanted to run to him, grovel at his feet, plead for him to stay away from that accursed place.

Instead, he stood in the chilly perfume of incense and sweat left in his lover's wake.

It didn't work.

The Flareburn guards had killed the trespasser—to them, a mere pest. His bones had been ground up to feed the threadmother, and they'd torched what remained. So Thrinn heard, in pieces, slipping desperate questions into idle market prattle. From all accounts, the Flareburns were flourishing.

The nightmares returned, worse than ever. Gez, Ayoshana, and the Deep Sun tormented him, melting his memories together into murky slag. Knells upon knells unspooled. Steamflutes screamed out ceaseless chaos. Thrinn drifted in haze, wrapped in blankets that had long since lost the scent of his lover. The cold had spread to him now, chained him to this dark corner where none could witness his misery.

He practiced summoning the cold, again and again. The magic flowed from his hands inward toward his heart, the reverse path of every other spell he knew. Ice carved fractal paths through his veins, a terrible cutting sensation that led to numbness after. Thrinn's hands became gray and flaky as the frost branched a new order into his flesh. His shackles had returned, and with them, the nightmares. Freeing the Deep Sun was all he had left. He welcomed whatever world would come after, even if it would only appease his guilt for a moment.

Thrinn packed one thing—a jagged rock. He would chill the metal chains until brittle, then shatter them. Perhaps the leviathan would be strong enough to break them, but if not, he'd use what little strength he yet possessed to bash them in with the stone. A crude solution, he knew, but what else did he have?

When he approached the edge of the lava pool, he barely felt the heat at all. Death flooded his veins, icy daggers that pierced every limb.

He expected someone—perhaps even Ayoshana—to stop him. No one came. The lava closest to his feet lost its orange glow, growing dark and stiff. Steam erupted where superheated rock met the cold frontier of his magic.

It was slow going. Each step brought him closer to the center, but the heat grew. Convection currents seethed around Thrinn, leaving him on a stone island that melted back into magma behind him. Despite his power—*kill, hate heat, kill heat*—brimstone smoke scorched through his bubble of cold. He thought of Gez's lust for vengeance; the twisted faces of forgotten exiles; the senseless suffering of the beast he approached. The lies. He kept going.

Ahead of him, the Deep Sun seared violet scars across his vision. Its scaly flesh blazed, fire and smoke made solid. Flames skittered across its myriad limbs. Its sinuous figure coiled against the chains, writhing as it yet sought the escape denied for eons. It bellowed at Thrinn as he approached, eyes scorching with the agony of a thousand Emergences.

Thrinn stood just out of range of the Deep Sun now. He focused on the chains. It was time to make them cold. *Extremely fucking cold*, as Gez once said.

The leviathan shrieked in pain and thrashed, pulling away from Thrinn.

Of course, Thrinn thought. *It hates the cold. It's afraid.* He'd never anticipated this—that the creature's very nature might work against its freedom.

"Hold still!" Thrinn commanded, gritting his teeth as he took another step closer. Wisps whizzed about, buzzing near the chains and swooping past his head. "I'm trying to break them. Fuck!"

If the Deep Sun spoke, it wasn't any language that Thrinn recognized. Its hot scream parted the shell of frigid air gathered around him. Thrinn gasped as his face singed. He willed the cold to fall around him, to knit its brittle branches into orderly crystal figures. The uneasy stone floe beneath him was failing. Thrinn's magic forced it to hold together.

"Let. Me. Help. You!" Thrinn yelled, reaching the closest chain. Its manacle wrapped around one of the beast's colossal wrists. The chains weren't any metal that he recognized, blackened as they were. Arcs of many-colored energy crackled along the surface, imbuing them with an eerie iridescent flicker. Old runes assembled and then dissipated, dazzling at the edge of familiarity. They danced, some ancient tongue circling a precipice, waiting to be swallowed into the cold deadworld of history.

Thrinn focused on the chain, willing it to grow cold— so cold—so brittle. *Kill heat. Hate heat.* Magic screeched forth from his flesh, striking the manacles from every direction. He willed them to freeze. To break.

The beast howled, whipping its body about in throes of agony as the cold corroded its fire flesh. *Fuck!*

The chains grew brighter and brighter, frosting over. Thrinn gasped, feeling his fear and compassion and despair all spilling away as the bindings absorbed his power. Wisps poured into the chains, weaving their light into ice and metal. *No! Why now?*

And then he heard it—the grim harmony of a hundred voices chanting around him. He wrenched his gaze away and saw them—the elders, all of the elders, circling the edge of the lava pool, singing in a language that should have perished at the edge of the world, cold notes swallowed by dead throats. They knew. They'd *let* him do it.

Thrinn scrambled to take out his boulder, ready to smash the binding to pieces. But, when he looked again, he saw that the char had fallen away. The chains glittered a brilliant silver, as cold and cruel as they must have been the day the ancients first forged them.

He dropped the boulder—it landed with a dull thud that Thrinn felt more than he heard, awash in the beast's torment and the triumphant voices of elders recognizing his misguided efforts.

Thrinn felt the searing heat of betrayal, the cold despair of what he'd given up, and let the fire devour him.

To Touch Creation

by *Kathrine Machon*

"Still writing?"

My fingers tensed around my pen, but I found a smile from somewhere. It wasn't Rosen's fault.

"Yes, still writing."

I had to. Had to get it all down. It was a compulsion. Maybe one day it would become a history of sorts, of what must never happen again, but not now. Now it was just my story. I was searching for a clue in my memory.

Rosen laid out a coffee pot and a plate of warm pastries on the desk. "A gift from a Dual baker who's been taken on by that Split confectioner on the corner. Who'd have thought it possible? A Split and a Dual working together."

I gave a nod of agreement, watching the morning light spin golden cobwebs in the tumble of Rosen's hair. The shifting male/female beauty of shis face had the breath catching in my throat. But only for a moment. By the time shi looked up, the feeling was frozen under the ache of loss.

Rosen crossed to the high casement windows and threw them open so the honey-sweet smell of the jacaranda tree—a purple canopy beyond the glass—invaded the room. It was hard to believe this place was mine. The small whitewashed room with the blond wood bed covered in striped blankets. And outside, the garden where plants had cracked open the uniform concrete of the city to make a paradise of color. My space. Something no Dual had ever had.

"Did you sleep?" Rosen pulled me back to now.

Had I? Or had I sat up all night writing, again. My desk was covered with enough pages of cramped script.

I shook my head. "A little." It might not be a lie. The sheets on my bed were crinkled.

Rosen sat opposite and nudged the pastries toward me. Shi shouldn't be waiting on me, but as shi said, I'd probably starve if shi didn't. I'd end up a skeleton sitting at a desk, clutching a pen, surrounded by mountains of paper.

Shi reached out and touched my hand. "It's confusing, isn't it. The clarity. Sometimes I feel as if my head will crack open from all the sensations, the feelings, the thoughts. But it is getting easier, and I never want to go back to before."

Our fingers entwined. "Never."

The word 'before' vibrated between us. We'd die before we went back. Rosen understood, and yet didn't. All Duals had suffered under the power of the Beacons—the energy they emanated stifling us into a half-formed state of numb submission. But for me there had been more. I'd touched the moment of creation—touched it, then had it ripped from me.

"We'll find them." Rosen's voice startled me again. "We'll find them, and then you'll be able to let the past go."

Shi went to the door, looked back, and gave a smile that made me ache. Shi was a sweet, beautiful Dual, and as much in need of healing as me. The door closed quietly, and I shut my eyes. Liquid grief beaded on my lashes and trickled down my face. Sometimes Rosen was the only island in a sea of pain. I knew shi wanted more from me, but was I capable of that? Would I ever be? I should grasp this chance at life. But letting go of what I'd lost was impossible. It consumed me.

I touched the papers on my desk. What did I remember from before? Broken pictures. A monochrome world. The place where my story began was a washed-out moment. I'd been called into the overseer's office and stood in a line with other Duals. How many, my memory couldn't supply. This had happened before, or at least I thought it had. My life was a tangle of half-recalled scenes, all overshadowed by the ever-present rattle of weaving machines.

In the clothes factory there was no before, no thought of after. My hands would move on the shuttle, back and forth, in a never-ending rhythm. Automatic. I didn't think. I just was.

Until the day it changed.

A male Split stood in front of me, peering into my face. "It has to be strong. Not physically, but mentally."

I stared at the buttons on his shirt, thinking nothing.

"This one will do." He poked my chest.

They took me to a cart and told me to lie down. I did. The cart moved and the world slipped by on the other side of the wooden sides. I saw none of it. Curiosity didn't exist. Thoughts, feelings—missing. I was hollow.

And then I noticed something. The air. It smelled different—rich. And above me—color. Green. What was that? I sat up. Trees, and below us, grass.

"It's stirring," the male Split from the factory said to the cart driver. He turned and pointed a grey metal tube at me that buzzed. It would cause pain, but how did I know that?

"Get back down," he said, and I complied.

There was enough to see from here. A world of blue sky, brown and green swaying branches, and scents that danced in my nostrils.

"Doesn't it bother you?" The Split asked his companion.

"They stay passive, at least for a while after we've left the influence of the Beacon zone. Don't worry, it won't be up to working any weird magic on you yet, and the center's not far."

Magic? It was all around us. Why couldn't they feel it? And why hadn't I noticed it before? Lines of energy pulsed from the ground beneath me, spreading outward into the trees, flashing bright inside the birds that flew overhead. Everything was connected, and for the first time I felt it. The world whirred around me and I overflowed with sensations. The hollowness was gone.

The cart passed through a gap in a high metal fence, and the trees disappeared from view. I raised my head as we halted in front of a low building. A Dual came out of the door, head bowed, waiting while the Splits opened the tailgate and let me out. We were in a dust-bowl compound where not even a stray blade of grass grew, and at the center, a six-foot-high tripod with an enclosed glass top squatted behind barbed wire. The sight of it filled my mouth with the sharp taste of metal, and I shivered.

"Come." The Dual gestured for me to follow, and I scuttled past the object and the scowling Splits into the cool dimness of the building.

My mouth opened and closed as previously unthought-of questions tried to escape. "Why do I feel so strange? Where are we? What—"

The Dual raised a hand. Shi had a young, smooth face, but shis hair was grey. "I had forgotten. The newness of it all." There were tears in shis eyes. "I'm so sorry. The ceremony is over, and we don't have long before the Beacon is switched on."

"What is—?"

The blankness hit me.

I was eating. How had that happened? Awareness trickled into me like sand, and I laid down my spoon.

Opposite, my fellow Dual paused as well. "So, we are allowed to awaken again."

I looked around the building. It was familiar. Yes, I had been here some days, but the memories were hidden in shadows. There had been others here, but now it was just the two of us.

"I am Luan." The Dual smiled. "And what is your name?"

Name? I frowned and shook my head.

"No name? That's not unusual. So, we will give you one. Reece perhaps? Nina? Sage or Dana?"

A choice? A decision. Had I ever made one before? And had I ever been anything other than 'it?' Luan's suggestions flowed around me, but there was a feeling inside —a shape. "River." The name came out unbidden, but I liked the way it felt in my mouth.

Luan smiled. "It is nice to meet you, River. Now, while the Beacon is off, I must begin your lessons."

But I had questions. "The Beacon? What is that?"

Luan took a slow breath and laced shis fingers together. "The Beacon is the device you can see in the yard. It's on top of the tripod. Here it is a small one, which can be switched off when our help is needed. In the cities and factories, they are much larger and permanent, but I don't think that's what you're really asking."

I worked saliva into my ash-dry mouth. "They are what make me feel... not alive?"

"Yes." Shi took my plate and cleared it to the side with studied, precise motions. Shis knuckles were clenched white. "They control us."

Control? "Who? Why?"

Luan's gaze flickered around the building. We were alone, but still shi leaned closer before speaking. "The Splits are unaffected by the Beacons. It is they that created them. When, I don't know, but why? Fear, I believe. Fear of what we might become without them. You will understand when I have taught you." Shi coughed and sat back. "So now for your first lesson. Do you know what this place is?"

I shook my head, trying to make sense of shis words, but shi'd moved on—was waiting for an answer. The concept of what or where a place might be wasn't something I'd really considered before. It was simply where I was. Nothing more. Now new ideas and unexpected thoughts were jostling in my head. Because the Beacon was turned off?

"This place is connected to the Jacaranda conception center. It's not far from here but is rather more luxurious— for the Splits' pleasure." Luan paused. "Do you know what conception means? Do you know...?"

Shis words were like shiny stars, fascinating, but beyond my understanding. Conception. Mystery whispered around that word. I shook my head and Luan sighed.

Head in hands, shi said, "I see I must start from the beginning. I am sorry. Sorry you are here and for what will be done to you, but I have no say in the matter. All I can do is prepare you for what is to come."

A strange sensation prickled across my skin. Was that fear or anticipation? How could I tell? I knew the idea of them but hadn't experienced either before.

"Conception is what occurs when a new life is made. A baby. A child," Luan said.

A child. I had been one once, but where or when was veiled in my memory. How had I become?

A new sensation uncoiled, clamoring for attention. Curiosity. I'd never felt that before either. "How are children made?"

Luan shifted. "Straight to the heart of the question. They grow inside a female's body."

Inside? That was a weird idea. But then birds laid eggs, didn't they? I'd eaten eggs, but chicks came from them as well. How did I know that? My head was full of information that I had never given thought to before. I examined the facts now. Perhaps females laid babies. But... "How do they get there?"

"You are a quick thinker." Luan smiled. "It takes most Duals time to acclimatize, but you are already full of questions. Do not let the Splits see that."

A worm of unease squirmed inside me. The Splits, they were dangerous to us. My curiosity would not be welcomed.

"As for your question," Luan continued, "a male and female's bodies come together. But that is not enough to

299

create a child. For conception there must be a moment of perfect harmony—a moment when bodies and minds align and a new life flickers into being. It is a Dual that creates that moment. Without us, life is not possible. It is my job to teach you how to do this."

To create life?

A spark of wonder flared inside of me. Was I really capable of this? I wrapped my arms around myself, hugging the feeling tight. So, the Splits feared us, but also needed us.

"Come, sit with me." Luan settled cross-legged on a mat on the floor, and I joined shim. "Close your eyes. Feel the air on your face and hands, your clothes against your skin, the floor beneath you. Sense it, and more. Open yourself to the world. You will have to reach for it here—the Beacon disrupts the flow and destroys nature; that is why no plants grow in the compound. You must stretch beyond that. Touch the chord of life that holds the world together."

I was floating. Luan's words whispered in my head, but I didn't need them. I'd experienced this on the way here in the cart. The world as a living, connected being, laced through with lines of power. And I was part of it. The compound was a dark spot, but beyond that the land buzzed and hummed, and I tumbled like a bubble in a stream, riding the veins of energy. Endless. Powerful. Racing with life. There was meaning here. Knowledge and wisdom. I strained to touch it and—

Hit blackness. Thrown backward. Head pounding. Into my body.

I retched, and Luan wiped tears from my face.

"So strong," shi whispered. "You went too far. Touched the Beacon zone of a distant city. You are beyond my teaching." A smile spread across shis face, lighting shis eyes. "I thought it would take much longer for you to learn this, but now... perhaps my torment is almost ended."

I stared at the ceiling. Weeping for the loss. I didn't understand what shi meant. Didn't know how much worse it could be.

Not then.

The room was smothered in sadness. The air heavy, voices low and movements constrained. I rubbed sweaty hands on my clothes and fought for breath.

New life was to be made tonight.

The Beacon was silent and the world beckoned, but nerves jangled taut inside me. Tonight, I must be centered, Luan had said. I must observe but not take part. This was the final lesson. Soon I would be taken to Luan, and I would see the new life made. So why were the Duals so sad?

A Split came into the room and motioned me to follow him. I'd been given a blue robe to wear, of much finer quality than my usual rough clothes. He unlocked the gate of the compound and we walked in silence, the feel of his gaze on me prickly as he watched my every move.

The main center wasn't far. Here plants grew in cultured profusion. Fountains tinkled and water coursed in tiny streams. The paths were of pastel stones and soft lights guided us through the night.

Luan awaited me in a building that smelled of wood and pine needles. I tried to smile at shim, but my lips were stiff and unresponsive, refusing to curl. The place was hushed, reverential, and even the Splits treated Luan with a tight respect as we were taken to a small room and the door closed behind us. One wall was a pierced screen and shapes moved beyond it.

"Where is it? Can it see us? It won't touch us, will it?" The words from beyond the partition spiked through the atmosphere and settled like lead in my stomach.

"No, there will be no contact." A reassuring voice. "It is behind that screen and will see nothing but shadows."

A small light flared, then another as candles were lit in the room beyond.

"Be calm. This is a night of celebration. I will leave you to prepare yourselves."

The sound of a door opening and closing reached us, and now there were just two shapes in the room. A male and female. They had to be.

"This is impossible." The female again.

Luan sat cross-legged by the screen, head bowed. I settled in the corner, wrapping arms around my legs, making myself small. Luan drew in a slow breath and a shudder went through shim. The air quivered with an unseen force and anticipation sparked through me. Beyond the screen, the voices stilled. I could sense Luan drawing together threads of energy, creating a place of silence, lambent with power. My skin tingled and even the Splits were touched by it.

In the next room, clothes were shed and bedsheets whispered. A sigh. A touch. Bodies pressed closer, entwined, moved together. Candles flickered and flared, and Luan wove shis magic. A web that drew the three together.

I held my breath as the power grew, pressing golden against my senses.

Slowly, Luan's head tipped back. Shis arms outspread. Energy pulsed and light shimmered, flowing from shim to them.

Three voices cried out together, and within them the spark of a fourth.

Drops of light cascaded in the air and Luan threw shimself at the partition, fingers curled through the piercings, trying to reach the two beyond. Trying to complete the moment of creation as it should be.

The door to our chamber slammed open. A Split grabbed Luan by shis hair, shis robe, dragged shim away, thrashing, crying. I stumbled after them, threw myself on top of Luan.

"Stop it. Stop it. Leave shim alone."

A boot kicked me in the head. Blood flooded my mouth and pain ricocheted around my skull, but all I could see was Luan's face. Stretched thin. Translucent.

The world wavered and darkness took me.

I never saw shim again.

There was no more avoiding it. The time had come.

The first bath was cold and salt licked at small scrapes, stinging, as the male and female attendant scrubbed me. I was to be made clean for the ceremony.

The water in the second was warm and slippery with fragrant oils. I wanted to slide into its embrace and forget the nerves that gnawed in my belly, but the attendants made an irritated sound and I climbed out of the bath after only a few moments. They handed me a towel and turned their backs as I dried myself.

I was below contempt.

But I was needed.

Clothed in rustling silk, I was taken to the chamber. Identical to the one I'd shared with Luan, but not the same one. They'd spared me that.

Shadows moved beyond the screen. Voices whispered. Anger bubbled in my stomach, hard and sharp, and my nails dug into my palms. They expected me to help them. To

303

create for them a moment of harmony. Never. I'd be punished but didn't care.

One of the shapes moved closer to the screen. "Do you think it's there yet?" A male voice.

"Don't call the Dual 'it,' Tobin. They use shi, remember. I read that in a history book. The word used to be part of our language."

"That sounds like one of your forbidden books," Tobin said.

The female made an exasperated sound and a smile twitched at my mouth.

She moved closer to him and the bed, raised her hand, brushed the screen. "Hello."

I startled back at the word, breath catching in my chest, and she leaned nearer.

"Kayla, you're not meant to talk to... to shim."

"I know... It just doesn't feel right. Shi's going to help us make our baby and we're not even allowed to meet shim." She sighed.

Through the screen, her skin glinted palely and copper-colored hair tumbled about her shoulders.

"Thank you," she said.

I bit my lip. Why did they have to be nice? I'd expected monsters, not this.

They clasped hands. Sat on the edge of the bed. Their silhouettes kissed.

"I love you," Tobin said, and Kayla rested her head on his shoulder.

"Me too." She pulled away from him. "We should... you know... get started." There was a pause and then she giggled. "This is difficult. I thought it would feel different, special. They said it would, but..." She glanced toward the screen.

But I wasn't doing my job.

Their warmth and her words had unravelled the knot of anger inside me. My determination slipped. How could I not do this for them? My head hung as I opened myself to the power. Did the Splits know they'd built the center over a place where energy lines met? That a node of unseen power hummed beneath here, ready for us to tap? Perhaps some forgotten instinct had guided them.

It was easy to reach out and touch the source, draw it to the surface. Its caress slid across my skin. The air quivered and the couple gasped, reaching for each other. Clothes were pushed aside, fingers touched, stroked. Energy flowed from me to them, coursing through their bodies, changing them, making us one. We pulsed together, three jewels. I could taste them, feel them. Their ecstasy grew and I threw back my head, panting, spinning the power closer. Soon now. The helix spiraled around us, but they were oblivious. Caught in the moment. The energy contracted, embraced, and they climaxed.

Kayla's arm shot out, reaching for me, slipping between the holes in the screen. Our fingers touched. The world exploded in a myriad of light, and new life flickered. Awareness, born within the triangle of three beings and—

I was slammed backward. Contact lost. A scream ripped from me. Kayla's cry echoed back. I was dragged further, thrown on my back. Pain sliced through my chest like a knife. Lost. Battered. An iron tang of blood in my mouth where I'd bitten my tongue.

Angry shouts. Footsteps.

"Kayla." A worried cry from Tobin.

She was above me. Hands on my shoulders. Trembling.

Someone shoved her aside.

305

"No. Don't hurt them." Tobin wrapped her in his arms.

Splits grabbed me, pulled me away, into another room. A key turned, locking me in.

I gagged, shuddered, crawled to the door, pressed against it, my insides feeling filled with glass.

Her cries reached me from the other side.

Other voices. Angry. Cajoling. And silence.

I was alone.

I lay on the bed. The Beacon numbed my mind, cut me off from the magic, but it couldn't stop the pain that burned in my chest. The hot star of loss that wouldn't let me go.

Time merged. Days. Duals came and spoke to me: whispered words that slipped through my mind and were gone. Splits followed, scowling. I didn't care. Craved oblivion. Begged them to end it. They left me alone.

Luan.

I understand now.

I wept until sleep took me.

The buzz stick spat blue light and I convulsed. Nearby, another Dual was awakening the energy for the ceremony, drawing it upward from the node to make a place of harmony. It should have been me doing it. I'd sat in that room, letting them wait, until the Splits realized nothing was going to happen. That I wasn't going to help.

Now they were angry.

The stick buzzed. Agony sliced. I screamed.

But the pain could never match the hurt inside.

A Split kicked me, and I curled up tight. If I was useless maybe they'd kill me. Would it be quick? Another buzz. No, they'd make me suffer.

The energy swelled, called by a Dual, woven to make three beings one and create a fourth. The moment of climax came, the energy fizzed and flared, cascaded upward, and was stopped. Snapped short again.

A Dual cried out and so did the life energy. Thrown back too soon, it rebounded into the node, sending tremors downward. No longer a softly humming source that would come at our touch, but a restless reservoir of potential.

Pain cracked. Anger burned. Tendrils of power reached toward me.

I rolled away from the Splits, scrabbled backward and half rose. They shouted, closed in, waving their sticks. My fists clenched, and the power answered.

Dormant for too long, it came eagerly, singing in my head, seeking purpose. The dust around me stirred, lifting with a life of its own. My clothes crackled with static. I raised my head, looked into the eyes of the Splits. Saw fear.

"The Beacon," one of them said.

Too late.

I punched my fist into the air and the energy answered, spurting upward, flooding into the veins and conduits that fed the world, surging outward in a wave, an unstoppable torrent. I sent it to the darkness, and the Beacon exploded.

The power was beyond me now, racing onward, and my senses tumbled with it: a leaf in a maelstrom. The dark spot of another Beacon loomed, and the energy shredded it, quickening the land and awakening the Duals.

Around me, the Splits threw themselves to the ground and covered their heads, but they were wrong to be afraid.

This force wasn't destructive, it was life-bringing. The Duals felt it. They spun, arms outstretched, laughing. The earth cracked open and green shoots shot upward in a frenzy of growth, filling the compound, clothing the buildings. A profusion of color where only dun earth had existed.

The world changed.

Time slipped by. Seasons melted together. I had a new home and a world was unfolding where Duals were equals. We'd been wrong about the Splits: a name that was seldom used now. The Beacons used to influence them as well: fed their fear and distrust of us. Now three genders worked to become one people. Perhaps someday scholars would discover how it had all begun. Who had created the Beacons and why, but I couldn't care.

Kayla.

She was all I could think of.

The conception center's files had given me her details —but so much had changed. I searched but there was no sign of her. So now I wrote: emptying my pain onto the page and hoping there might be a clue in there to find her.

My room was silent. The pastries Rosen had left, uneaten. I'd lost myself in thoughts again. A sheet of paper lay crumpled in my hand, and I smoothed it flat. The official letter, apologizing that they had no further information relating to my inquiry. Perhaps I should visit one of the new administration buildings again. Other Duals were looking for their lost children, but they searched with hope and joy at their new lives. They held their pain close, but slowly it lessened.

Why was I different?

Had that moment of contact with Kayla forged a link? A link that left me floundering in a morass of pain and wouldn't let go.

I shuddered, got up, paced the room. There was no release.

The garden beckoned and I went outside, my fingers skimming lavender and thyme, releasing their fragrance. Lush moss, wreathed in tiny white star flowers, formed a carpet under my feet, and peacock-headed flowers bobbed among the waving grasses. I settled onto a bench wound about with honeysuckle, where green and purple jeweled hummingbirds flitted among the flowers.

I wanted to change. I did. There was sweet Rosen and a whole life beckoning. If only I could let go.

The ambient energy of the world whispered, and I opened myself to it, letting it slip into me and soothe the hurt. But it wouldn't last. It never did. Cold talons of pain would pierce my chest and clench around my heart.

Somewhere in the house, a sound echoed. Footsteps followed. The clunk of the front door. Voices.

More supplicants, bringing gifts, or maybe wanting a blessing. I closed my eyes and struggled to hold onto the golden feeling.

"River." Rosen calling my name.

Feet shushed against the moss and clothes rustled as shi came into the garden. "You have visitors."

I opened my eyes and shis face was radiant with smiles.

"Who...?"

Something flowered inside me. Something new.

Hope.

I stumbled from the garden to my room, and they were there.

309

Kayla, pale-skinned with a tangle of copper hair—Tobin, a tall nervous looking male at her shoulder. And leaning against Kayla's leg...

Our child.

Straight nosed like her father, copper-haired liked her mother, but her eyes, they were mine. Solemn for a moment, but something stirred in them. Recognition. I fell to my knees. She gurgled, clapped her hands together, and with a cry toddled into my arms.

The Longing

by MM Schreier

Where he fled, I was bound to follow. The gods played a cruel trick on our kind, splitting our souls in two. I didn't even know his name, but like a moth drawn to a flame, his half of our soul beckoned me. Oh, the longing to be whole! When he realized we were paired, destined to Unify, he took flight.

He sought sanctuary in Redmoor Wood amongst our half-brothers, the faekin. In the shadow-drenched forest, he loosed a flock of will-o'-wisps to lead me astray. The pinpricks of living light dazzled, flittering above my head in the crimson umbrage. They whispered in my ear, a bewildering cacophony of half-remembered dreams.

I shook my head, closed my eyes, and summoned a mask of tranquility that didn't touch my core. Tamping down my nerves, I breathed deep to catalog the lush perfumes of the forest—pine resin, shade roses, nightberries, iridescent toadstools. One by one, I discarded them, seeking that which did not belong to the mystic wood. There! His familiar scent of hoarfrost and stardust drew me onward.

Crossing into the Onyx Desert, he raised his arms and touched the Element of Air, reweaving the Universal Pattern. With dexterous fingers, he fashioned a new reality. Too far behind to stop him, I could only watch, unable to even taste the residue of his webwork. He conjured a sandstorm and hid within its wall of swirling grit. The wind swept away his tracks, smoothing the ebony sand, and a preternatural night descended as the tempest blocked out the sun.

I blinked my inner eyelids and engaged my second sight. In that barren wasteland, the light of his *élan vita*—his pulsing life force—flared like a single torch at midnight. Moved by the need to become whole, I hastened after the bright beacon of life-light. The distance between us closed.

Free from the desert, he disappeared into the dense, cloying haze of The Weeping Moor. The stench of sulfur infused with despair filled my nostrils and blotted out his scent. My second sight was blinded by a million life-lights— marsh serpents, twisted swamp oaks, and four-eyed quag 'gators. I wracked my brain, at a loss on how to track him.

A flash of insight hit me with the force of heat lightning. I needed only to know where he was going, not where he was. The only choice was the great trade port, Storm Harbor, beyond the sultry bog. Driven by purpose, I took a step forward and sank to the knee in sticky mud. The fog around me swirled with the hint of anguished faces, the suggestion of grasping hands. A haunted, ragged sobbing sent the tickle of millipede footsteps up my spine. The drowned shades of the mire begged for me to join them.

I wrenched my leg from the muck with a squelch. Surrounded by misty quagmire, it took naught but thought to lift ribbons of Water and change the Pattern. A novice's washing weave scoured the filth from my spider-silk trousers and sucked away the excess moisture. In the heat it took more of an effort to spin a latticework bridge of ice. The glistening span stretched above the morass, gaining me safe passage. As I raced across the frosty catwalk, the lost spirits of the moor wailed in disappointment.

Feet frozen and face flushed, I emerged from the bog with icy sweat trickling down my back. In the distance, the jewel-toned ocean reflected the knife-sharp rays of two red suns. Sprawling along the shoreline, Storm Harbor bustled with activity. A gentle salt breeze cleared the swamp's malodor, and I could once again detect him somewhere amidst the rambling buildings. I lengthened my stride, anxious that he'd slip away across the rolling sea.

Racing through the cobblestone streets of the port city, my heart pounded in my ears. I turned the corner and arrived at the wharf, out of breath and chest heaving. I skittered to a halt. A wall of blistering heat enveloped me, and I flung a protective arm across my face. My stomach clenched. The fleet burned; he'd set the hulls and sails ablaze like a funeral pyre. Across the bay, I watched him escape in a tiny skiff. I couldn't see his expression, but the mirthful, silver glint of his aura mocked me as he turned the bow into the waves.

Determined not to lose him, I studied the Pattern, then added strength to the Elements of Fire and Spirit. Smoky air seared my nose and ash tickled my throat as I summoned a phoenix. Like all of her kind, she was headstrong, and I layered the fabric with a second twist of Spirit. Still, it took a lifetime to plait the spell-harness and compel her to carry me across the sea. The delay rankled. Every league he gained weakened our connection.

I clambered between the phoenix's feathered wings and my stomach dropped as she took flight. We soared between cotton candy clouds, the wind snarling my hair.

Below, his skiff shrank to a flyspeck, then vanished. Limbs trembling, palms slick with sweat, I tightened my grip on the spell-harness and prodded the reluctant firebird to increase her speed. My energy reserves dwindled.

Ten thousand heartbeats later, my feathered conveyance and I made landfall on the far shore. Her clawed footprints left smoldering scorch marks in the grass. She screamed once and tested her will against my growing exhaustion. I clutched at the empyreal fibers of her leash, but they slipped loose, and the Pattern reclaimed its true form. The enchantment unraveled. Vast wings flapped, and the phoenix wheeled and disappeared in a puff of smoke.

I could feel the pull of my soul-twin behind me, and I turned to study Eventide Valley. I frowned in the light of perpetual sunset. Dozens of hot air balloons speckled the sky. I could barely discern his presence, perched in one of the far-flung baskets. Which one? A breeze laden with a flowery fragrance concealed his scent. At a distance, the passengers blinked like stars, and I was unable to differentiate between the varying *élan vita* signatures.

The balloons floated on a fragmented wind, drifting in every direction. To pursue one would be to lose all others. The magnetic tug on my soul-half dimmed as he drew further away. I whimpered. How could he resist the need to Unify? The weight of it squeezed my chest and I gasped, struggling to fill my lungs.

Desperate, I scanned the landscape. The province hovered eternally on the cusp of twilight. A ground-hugging rainbow of daybells turned their faces to drink in the rays of violet gloaming. Their spicy-sweet bouquet drifted across the valley, sensuous and potent. A swarm of stinging dragonflies buzzed amid the blossoms, their needle-sharp proboscises sipping on the nectar.

I grinned.

Once again, I reached for the Pattern. This time I twisted in filaments of Air along with the threads of Spirit. It was apprentice work to bend the insects' tiny minds, but it was master crafting to replicate the new Pattern, over and over, to control the entire swarm. Brow furrowed, beads of moisture streamed down my face as I scattered the dragonflies. Dozens of small bodies hurtled across the sky, each homing in on one of the balloons.

I shifted between them, borrowing their sight to peer into the baskets. Fighting to focus, I clenched my fists. Nails dug into my palms. Blink, shift. Not him. Blink, shift. Too old. Blink, shift. Female. Blink, shift, blink, shift. No. No.

Yes!

I watched through the dragonfly's eyes as he maneuvered the yellow and red striped balloon. My stomach roiled. At this distance he was approaching the edge of our connection. Shared soul or not, if he slipped beyond my ability to sense him, I feared I'd never find him again. I wasn't strong enough to survive the gnawing hunger to be whole.

There was only one way to reach him—Pattern jump. I swallowed. It was dangerous and would leave me spent, too weak to weave even the simplest spell for hours afterward. Helpless. Defenseless. The thought weakened my knees. I swallowed against a lump in my throat and stiffened my spine. It wouldn't matter once we Unified; I could rest when we were whole.

I reached into the Pattern. Instead of redesigning the existing world motif, I burrowed into the fabric of the universe. Slow and methodical, I created a gap in space-time. A wave of nausea rushed over me. I fought against the feeling that what I did was unnatural and forced the rift to widen. Taking a deep breath, I jumped through the breach.

In the airless between, the seconds stretched to millennia. Atoms ripped apart, I floated—an ocean of dust motes in starlight. Bodiless thought. This was what it meant to be immortal. Divine. Then time snapped forward and I was slammed back into myself. My own mortality bore down on me with the unbearable weight of reality.

I collapsed against the side of the basket, wheezing. Spots floated in my vision and my ears rang. My body ached, torn asunder and reassembled between one blink and the next. I shook my head then raised my chin to meet his gaze.

Arms folded across his chest, he watched me with eyes narrowed and lips curled down. The siren song of his soul—our soul—consumed me. It begged to Unify, to join our halves as one. I reached a hand toward him.

"Don't touch me." He jerked back. "I won't do it."

"Please. We're incomplete apart." I took a step forward.

He retreated. "No. Unity kills the individual."

"Yes. But when our soul-halves fuse, we'll be reborn."

Orange-flecked brown eyes flickered over the landscape, far below, then refocused on me. "I'd rather die on my terms."

He smiled, and my blood ran cold. Before I could move, he turned and launched himself over the edge. I fumbled forward. Grasping fingers clutched air, the Pattern out of reach. My well of power had run dry. I screamed, certain that the longing would destroy me. There was no choice. I closed my eyes and leaped.

Where he fled, I was bound to follow.

The Prince of Murk and Rot
by Erica Ciko Campbell

"This is the story of how I defeated society and my adversaries, and how I reached the stars. If it reaches you even now across these starless aeons, sleep soundly and with a blood-drenched, broken smile: for the worst is yet to come." – Viricula, Black Centuries III

Before the Blood Spines tore through the clouds and the Alnilam infiltrated the halls of the first Grim Kings, when Stargrave was young and the Lords of Silvenmyr were but a whisper of a ghost in the Empyrean Halls, I wandered the Mountains of Myr.

"But Vorn," they always ask, "Why have you wandered the Raizalarian countryside as a humble vagabond exorcist for all these years if you dreamed of the dissolution of reality itself since before the stars were young?"

Well, my friend, the answer is simple: because being a vagabond exorcist is fun—and all I've ever known.

The gift first awakened inside me when I was as young and desperate as the countless demons I've driven out: as vulnerable to possession, corruption, and other evils as the innumerable people I've liberated.

I was seven years old, and my dearest mother had come down with a particularly gruesome affliction. Her eyes had warped from the crystalline yellow of the moon to the bloodshot, blackened pits that only true desperation can bring. Her crimson hair, once as thick and lush as my own, had gone brittle and begun to fall out in clumps.

The local healer was convinced she'd contracted a particularly ugly case of rotbrain from eating bad meat, but he was as blind as my father, who had no idea he'd been sleeping next to one of Viricula's own fragments every night for an entire cycle of the moon.

Now, like any Syndragorean boy of seven, I'd heard so many stories about the Prince of Murk and Rot that his whispers reached me even in dreams. I knew that Viricula's spawn had been driven from the Halls of Time forever, to the darkest corners of our own world—but I struggled to accept that my mother's heart was a feast black enough to satisfy the vilest scoundrel of Raizalarian legend.

How could my own mother, the one who kissed my forehead and gave me sweets every single night, have been twisted and vile enough to draw one of Viricula's own spawn? Possession was something that happened to other families in nightmares and campfire legends—how could it happen to ours?

But this is the very line of thinking which allowed the fragment to slip past my father and the village healer for so long, unaccounted for. This is the very line of thinking that has led to there being a shortage of Raizalarian exorcists since the first bones of Stargrave were laid upon the Nightmoor when the world was young.

My seven-year-old brain nearly boiled itself to mush trying to drink it all in, I assure you. But my mother had been screaming that the townsfolk were breathing too loudly and needed to be suffocated under an ocean of their own blood for thirty-three nights straight, and finally I'd had enough.

In truth, I'd recognized she'd been possessed by a fragment of Viricula after the second night—but there are far worse virtues than curiosity that a young man could have chosen to explore, wouldn't you agree?

No one in the village suspected even for a second that a child could keep his composure through truths so jarring and black—which meant that I had the unique opportunity to study a fragment of Murk and Rot in the safety of my own home. I have not even the faintest shred of a doubt that my time with that shadowside fiend who pretended to be my mother made me into the man I am today.

But all sweet dreams come to an end, and all friendships must eventually be consummated in separation or final death: so on the thirty-third day, I knew it was time to set my mother free.

I woke up starving that morning, as I always did. My mother was sputtering curses and wishing for me to choke on my stew, as she had every morning after falling under the influence of Viricula's fragment. I still remember the pure, unrestrained loathing in her eyes as she shrieked of how I was a waste of perfectly good meat that didn't deserve to breathe—how she promised to chop me up and cure my meat and store what was left in the wooden chest with the giblets and summer sausage.

Something about the strings of spit flying from her lips that morning made me even hungrier than usual as she wished me dead. So I did what any adoring, admiring son would do, and I gave her a kiss.

319

To this day, I can't fully recall what nebulous delights consumed me. All I know is that I took something from her: something that is still with me to this very day—and from the moment I drew that sour, sacred cosmic essence out from her lips and past my own, my services were in-demand from my forgotten hometown in the Myrothian Foothills to the gates of Stargrave.

Word of my mother's miraculous return to health spread quickly in such a small town, and soon, the truth got out. Our local Priestess of Hermestra insisted that it was only a matter of time until the demon took hold of my own form, if it hadn't already—but to everyone's surprise, I remained completely and utterly unchanged. I was seemingly invulnerable to demonic influence, even though my father and the townsfolk were far too simple to ever deduce why.

No one ever noticed that I soon developed a violent, nearly-insatiable craving for cured meats that has stuck with me even to this day.

From the moment I passed beneath the ivy-licked gates of Lightsmourn, I was reminded of the still, quiet town in which my gift had awakened. Off in the distance, I glimpsed the ramparts of Castle Exfyre, like broken fangs screaming toward the lurid magenta sky. The towers were crowned with worn golden spires that seemed to twist their way past the bounds of the atmosphere and Syndragorean imagination.

Before the raven arrived with Duchess Exfyre's urgent plea, I had been planning on a long weekend lost deep within the Mountains of Myr to contemplate the glory days of rot and ruin—but few things could lure me more quickly away from the blackened freedom of midnight than the pleas of a desperate noble.

The Duchess was there to greet me at the castle gates with no small legion of guards and attendants ensorcelling her. Her ruffled blue gown was the color of tears, and her sublime golden hair made the ruby-encrusted crown she wore atop her head seem dull.

It had been many months since I'd drank in such sorrowful eyes, ripe with the hopeless, raw abandonment of true betrayal. It was as if her very soul was screaming for reprieve, for a consolation that could only be found in a mother's arms or the realm of childhood dreams.

"Thank you for coming," she muttered in an idle, distant tone, reaching for my hand in a gesture of trust that did little to quell my suspicion that I was not what she expected.

But with the sweeping finesse of a polished gentleman, I fell to one knee and kissed her warm mahogany hand and purred, "The pleasure is mine alone."

My entire body shivered as her carmine claws, embedded with garnets, brushed against my cheek as she implored me to stand. The smell of my own blood was thick and raw against the frigid night.

I felt the collective gaze of her entire gaggle of guards dissecting my every move as we swept across the castle, past banners of long-forgotten armies and suits of armor far too large for any living man. A sour disdain crept up at the bottom of my throat as we passed through the shadow of a vertebrae six times larger than my own form: it pained me to know these splendors of old Raizalarian legend would forever be locked away within the halls of Exfyre, far from the unworthy eyes of the masses.

We passed through libraries filled with books whose age-worn black spines held a wicked and limitless energy that whispered to me even from across the room. We passed by a door marked 'laboratory,' and I caught the scent of a cornucopia of tonics and poisons that even I'd never tangled with before.

The Duchess was silent until we'd reached the foot of the staircase that led up to the young Lady Exfyre's quarters.

"I... must admit, I never thought it could happen here." The urgency in her voice was more sublime than bathing in a pile of rose petals in a court of glass beneath the summer moon. Countless peasants and wayward travelers had been in debt to me for decades, but the desperation of royalty was something I'd never grown tired of.

"It can happen in any timeline and any generation, Duchess," My reassuring tone was betrayed only by the curious glimmer of my golden eyes. "It has an equal chance of happening to emperors and the ones who scrub out their chamber pots: to kings and the beggars who loiter outside their castle gates, trading their dignity for a single morsel of bread."

"Yet still, I never thought it would happen to my own daughter. Meadowlark is the gentlest girl I've known in all my life. She's always embraced the light and the new ways and turned her back on the dark. Her empathy for all living creatures is so boundless that I've seen her weep for the death of a mouse."

"Then it's no small wonder that a fragment of Viricula has preyed upon her," I mused, earning a scowl from half the guards in one fell swoop.

"Mind your tongue, conjurer," gnashed the guard closest to the Duchess, tightening his grip on his spear.

"Ah, the truth often awakens such rage in the minds of the frail," I smiled, raising both hands harmlessly to show I was armed with knowledge and nothing more. "Do I deserve to be condemned for revealing the uncomfortable truth that demons aren't drawn to good or evil, but *weakness* above all else? If so, then drag me down to the dungeons and let me rot: meanwhile, the Lady Exfyre can live a rich and fulfilling existence walled off in this tower as an echo in the forgotten corners of some demon's brain."

And so we began the trek up the winding staircase, past the chartreuse-and-violet stained glass windows, to the room where the fragment lurked. The turbulent silence in the wake of my insult, far louder than any scream, signified that all of them knew I was untouchable for as long as the Duchess's daughter needed my help. The posse began to thin out as we continued our ascent.

"Whenever the guards slip food through the slot in the door, she sends the tray out only a moment later, covered in excrement and chunks of hair," the Duchess muttered, as if that was the worst thing she could possibly conceive in a thousand lifetimes. "It took six guards to drag her up to the tower, and only four walked out."

A small red door smothered in chains awaited us on the platform at the top of the stairs. Aside from the Duchess and myself, only two of the most loyal guards remained. A lone black candle exhaled its dying plumes, and a sick crimson light crept out from beneath the door.

"Vorn of the Nightside Grove," she began, reaching for my hand once more and gently stroking it in the shadows. "Before it begins, there's something I must tell you."

Her ruby claws shredded the flesh of my hand, drawing blood. She lifted my fingers to her lips and lapped up the blood slowly, carefully, from between the crevices. I said nothing: the starless, night-black pits of my narrowed eyes spoke for themselves.

"I called you here today because of the unquestionable fact that you're the best at what you do in all of Raizalar. This is no ordinary demon that's taken root inside of Meadowlark's heart, and you are the only one I trust with my daughter's life."

"Is any demon 'ordinary,' Duchess Exfyre? It's hard to think of anything stranger than being injected with the nebulous sparks of eternal life, only to spend eternity riding the coattails of mortal dreams."

"Pardon my insolence," the Duchess conceded with a hint of sarcasm, relinquishing her grip on me with both her hand and her tongue. "All I can say is what I've already told you in the letter: heal my daughter, Vorn of the Nightside Grove, and any relic of your choosing from the halls of my castle will be yours forever."

My mind flashed back to the massive vertebrae, a portal to some forgotten time-before-time immortalized in bone. Then I remembered the spell books, the crumbling sentinels of all the forbidden secrets of the ages. My smile must have repulsed her, for she crinkled her nose and turned away.

"Go, now. And remember, I've entrusted the future of the entire Exfyre bloodline and all of Lightsmourn onto you."

Now, I have no doubt that this shard of Viricula was the most loathsome horror Duchess Exfyre had faced in this life or any other. But from the moment I stepped past the gates of these time-lost halls, I knew my soon-to-be-adversary was little more than a pathetic slave to a pathetic slave like all the rest.

But of course, it was crucial for the duchess to believe that her daughter's tormentor was the essence of agony itself. For if such a frail and spineless fragment could upheave her entire life, how would she ever sleep again if she knew what horrors lurked just beyond the somber refuge of night?

As I entered that chained-off room and heard the lock click behind me from the outside, I was still so lost in thought that it took me a moment to notice the Lady Exfyre hunched on all fours in the pulsing red light. All the curtains of the canopy bed where she rested were torn and crusted. The thick, ripe stench of rot dominated the entire chamber, and I knew the bodies of the fallen guards hadn't been removed long before I drank in their clean-picked faces.

I smiled at the Lady Exfyre, and she grinned back, her fangs adorned with strips of rotten meat and caked with corpse blood. Her red eyes flickered in the light of a hundred black candles burning low.

I drew closer to the bed, and her expression soon melted into the flat and anxious frown of uncertainty. She cringed back from me, feigning a sudden interest in the severed nipple of one of the guards that she'd nailed to the bedpost with a shard of bone. Knowing how common it was for these fragments to be shy in their hour of judgment, I gave her space and allowed her to contemplate her final moments in the realms of men in this silent, suspended kingdom of Murk and Rot.

I soon fell victim to the amorphous stirrings of empathy, as I often did before harnessing my gift: in truth, I knew the pain of the demon wearing the Lady Exfyre's face. For I too have chosen a path of isolation wreathed in pure cosmic blackness—but still, every cell in my body longs for the warmth of the moonlight of summer's end. I too have sold my soul to never know sadness, or hunger, or a twinge of pain, but every bone in my withered, impossibly battered form aches to know them again. I too have severed all ties from the world from which I came—but still, all the quiet spaces between my brain have been flooded with a wild and fervent longing to return.

325

"Are you going to send me back?" she gurgled, her pale lips encrusted with vomit and worse.

"What do you think?" I asked, reaching for her throat and gently stroking her lymph nodes, focusing.

"It's not how I thought it would be," the demon conceded, her eyes softening at last and brimming over with all the sorrows of the final twilight of a life wasted. "Mortal life, I mean."

"You can imagine something a million times, and it's still worth less than truly tasting it even once," I purred, licking my lips. She was a near-spitting image of the Duchess Exfyre with those cheekbones sharper than knives, but her hair was far darker. I could only imagine how sublime, how supple her chestnut locks had been before the corruption took hold and forced them to dry up and fall out.

"I know." When she sighed, her breath was so sour and thick that it momentarily choked out the stench of the corpses. "I miss unreality: it was a lot less complicated than here. Really, I'm kind of glad it's over."

"Oh, but it's only just begun," I hissed, reaching out to stroke the side of her face and redirect her resigned gaze into my own eyes.

She cringed back as our flesh boiled together, as if she expected me to change my mind and smite her at any moment. A hundred candles flickered in unison as I dragged her into the shadowside.

Outside time, the sky and all the forgotten secrets of the past were one, blanketed by the stars themselves. I urged her to gaze down into the abyss, to drink in what was ours once and would be ours again at the end of the universe: the collective dreams of entire civilizations compressed into bite-sized spheres of energy, waiting to be plucked from the gardens of eternity. The empty thrones of not only the kings of Raizalar, but of every planet and every galaxy yet unnamed. The silence of the grave and the cosmic sea between reality and dreams—all devoured and rolled into nothingness, forever.

"This is but a taste of what we lost when the Lords of Silvenmyr took hold," I told her. "And this is what I offer you in exchange for your cooperation."

"R-really?" she rasped, carefully, childishly. I expected no less: the brain she now wore had belonged to a girl who couldn't have yet reached her twentieth birthday. But still, the glimmer of wonder baptized in pure black atrocity soon came to life in her eyes, telling me all I needed to know.

"Yes," I declared, sweeping my arm grandly toward the eternal twilight kingdom, and the stars themselves flickered. "As long as you can promise to do one thing for me."

"W-what is it?" she whimpered, her tears reflecting the timeless essence of ethereal mysticism as the swirling red nebulae flickered back to life below.

"You have to trust me. You have to believe that I'll come back for you when I've freed the rest of your brothers and sisters."

"I... That's all?" She tilted her head, and finally her sobbing stopped.

"No: you also have to do a much better job at pretending to be Meadowlark Exfyre. After I exorcise her soul for all eternity, you'll be free to explore her brain without intrusion. You'll have full access to all her memories, and cravings, and woes. I need you to put on such a convincing performance that not even her own mother will ever realize she died, and I need you to always remember that the Lord of Murk and Rot gave you a second chance at life when the ones in power summoned him to swallow you down."

"Y-yes," she stammered, now staring directly into my own eyes for the very first time. "I think I can do it. I... feel better already, somehow."

"Your faith in me will sedate your soul and guide you to eternal freedom," I reassured her. "And no one will suspect a thing. After your precarious brush with Black Eternity, the ones outside will understand you need time to recover and return to your original self: I'll make sure of it."

She nodded, and I flexed my fingers in perfect unison as time wound itself back together again. We were back at Castle Exfyre, now, and the candles were burning far brighter than before. I leaned in to kiss her, and I closed my eyes and drank Meadowlark Exfyre's soul.

On the way out, I reached down and peeled away a strip of the guard's neck for later: I could never turn my back on cured meat, no matter how crude the preparation.

The Duchess took her place at the head of the table, presiding over rich and exotic offerings such as stuffed mare's head and spiced stew of dragon entrails. I was offered the position of honor at her left side, which I accepted with a gracious bow. The guards who once cowered in fear at the mere mention of Meadowlark Exfyre's name were now scattered across the banquet hall, guzzling mead and howling victory ballads to celebrate her return.

When one of the servants attempted to place a slice of meat onto my plate, I politely refused. I would not indulge in even a single bite of their food, but I drank the wine. Across from me, young Meadowlark Exfyre was fervently studying a bowl of wolfskin porridge with grapes and berries floating in it. The contents of her wine goblet soon joined the slurry.

"Meadowlark! What did I tell you about repulsing our guests?" scolded the Duchess, crinkling her nose at her daughter's unusual dining choices.

"If I may be so bold, Duchess Exfyre," I interrupted, placing my hand on her gilded knee plate beneath the table where no one would ever know. "Although Meadowlark's habits may be... unusual for the time being, please try to remember what we talked about. It could take weeks or even months for her to return to her true self, and any new cravings acquired on the shadowside may very well haunt her forever."

With a sigh, the Duchess smiled. "I suppose you're right. I should be glad to have her by my side at all, yes?"

"Indeed," I rasped, exchanging a dark and forlorn smile with Meadowlark across the table. After all, what kind of father would I be if I didn't show my own fragment a shred of approval now and again, after all she'd been through?

Guests were continuing to pour into the hall, and soon it seemed that half of Lightsmourn had shown up to celebrate Meadowlark's liberation. The feast carried on into the early hours of the night until the black torches lining the walls burned low. The ladies danced, the children shrieked, and even the Duchess herself drank until her cheeks were flushed red.

They sang for normalcy, and gluttony, and willing numbness to all the evils of the world. They drank to the return of a girl they claimed to love but couldn't tell from a demon. And without knowing it, they celebrated yet another glorious victory for Murk and Rot.

As the revelries continued into the early hours of the morning, the townsfolk were slowly beginning to drain from the banquet hall. Many of the guards had retreated back to their quarters as well. At long last, I was alone at the end of the table with the Duchess and Meadowlark.

"It's hard to believe that this nightmare has finally drawn to an end," the Duchess Exfyre said, dissecting me with her gaze while stroking her daughter's hand. "But you held true to your word, Vorn of the Nightside Grove. And now, my daughter and I are in your debt. So as promised, I invite you to walk through our castle and choose one single relic to keep for all eternity."

I considered allowing her to lead me back through her ancestral halls so I could snatch one of the forsaken tomes or one of the potions from the laboratory, but even I'm not that much of a snake: for I'd already taken the most pleasing, scrumptious souvenir that the Exfyre bloodline could ever offer me.

"I have no need for wealth or abundance, Duchess. I can't imagine a greater reward in this life or any other than your satisfaction."

"I can see why all of Raizalar trusts you with their lives and futures, Vorn of the Nightside Grove." The duchess smiled, stroking my hand without cutting me for the very first time. "You will always be welcome in the kingdom of Lightsmourn and the halls of Exfyre. And I'm certain Meadowlark will always remember you as the one who saved her soul and set her free, from now until the streams of time run dry."

Gentle Deserter
by Anna Ziegelhof

A vehicle landed on the island. Its three metal paws sunk in, first through the wind-swept grass then a small way into the soil. There was no tearing or bouncing. Mammals and in-ground-dwellers registered only the slightest vibration. A female organism emerged from the vehicle and added her own two feet to the three feet of her vehicle. There they stood, on the meadow, woman and vehicle. She had brought something new with her, an energy to be explored, probed, befriended, maybe.

For now, they had arrived: a vehicle, thinking as computers do, and an organism, thinking as organisms do. There was nobody else who thought just like they did on the floating island in space, no other computer and no other organism quite as self-aware as she was. The woman sat down on the ground. Her tension dribbled from her, into the soil, and the in-ground-dwellers sniffed and scurried.

The woman drew atmosphere into her lungs. She blew out CO_2. The plants got to work on it. The wind acknowledged her shape.

The woman's rough hands stroked the vegetation. Salty liquid travelled down skinny blades of grass. Some of the woman's tears seeped into the ground, some evaporated.

The woman left her vehicle in the meadow and began to walk around. Her steps slowed reverently when she got close to the edge. When she walked through the forest, her palms occasionally rested on the bark of a tree. Her touch sent a shudder of awe into the ground. Her presence had never been unwanted, but it had become more wanted already.

When the woman came to the river that gurgled across smooth rocks, she shed her clothes. Without them, she was lighter. She stepped across the stones, the warm soles of her feet feeling their way so as not to slip, so as not to step into anything spiky or sharp. She waded into the shallow water and found a deeper pool where she submerged herself fully.

The cold water surrounded her and read her entirely.

Why can't I store the memory of water for times of torturous thirst? Back in the desert, I could not even have imagined a place this beautiful, refreshing, peaceful. How can both even exist...?

Their torn bodies, their blood, sizzling in the sand— the face. No.

I'm still alive. I'm alive with every cell in my body.

It's so clear here. It's so bright. Maybe I'll camp close to here. It's uninhabited. The shelter of the forest, or maybe closer to the lander, in case they... and I need to get... No.

She emerged and water dribbled back into the pool from her hair and skin. She drew her hands through the water. She put some into her hollow palm and from there into her mouth and it trickled into her body and into her tissue.

Oh...

She rested on a rock by the river. The river water evaporated from her body. It might rain later, some other time, not tonight, not if she wanted to sleep outside. The river ran on and on through the forest until it reached the edge and floated out into space.

The woman picked up her heavy clothes. Her footsteps crossed the forest as gently as before. She closed the loop she had walked. She climbed into her vehicle—her lander—and fetched things from it.

A sheet flattened the grass. The in-ground-dwellers scuttled out of the way of the pegs. She shifted the island a little by carrying rocks, by carrying dead wood, by clearing some grass.

The heat of her fire when night fell was a delicious pain.

The woman lay her body down on the ground. Between her and the ground there were her tent's base sheet, a cushioning mat, her clothes, her skin, her skull.

Marieke, can I call you starlight?

No, silly.

That was laughter. It felt good.

Marieke...

Those were a man's eyes, starry and brown, the skin around them wrinkled a little from where the cells were aging, so frail, so fascinating.

What an inconvenient time to meet someone so precious.

I can't cry right now, I have a job to do, I have to do my job.

Quickened breathing. Stress hormones began rushing through the woman. It was time for the woman, Marieke, to wake up. Her body was just using its nervous system to replay bygone sensations and perceptions, didn't she know that? There was no threat here, didn't she know that? No threat.

When the war is over.

But, Lieven, what if the war is never over?

The war is bullshit.

You didn't just say that! My father and my father's father died in the war, Lieven! It can't be bullshit. They didn't die for no reason. Don't say their deaths were bullshit!

The face. The face was half-visible. Half of it was bloody, with bone shards and glass shards where the man's helmet visor had shattered. The one remaining eye was brown and the skin around it somewhat wrinkled.

The woman, Marieke, shifted and sat up from her lying position. Her breathing was heavy. She needed more oxygen after her experience.

Oh...

Some fructose would help her now, certainly, but the fruit trees had their own pace, otherwise she would have been showered in the island's sweetest fruits by morning.

Marieke crawled out of her tent. Outside, she sat up for a while, then she lay down directly on the meadow's flattened grass. The wind made her skin respond with little bumps, so the wind ceased, inconspicuously.

One, two, three, four, five... I've never seen those constellations, I should name them. There, that one looks like Fergle, doggy-doggy-doggy, Fergle. Tufts for ears. Over there, that's a snake.

Why don't you count to infinity, Marieke? Try it.

I actually tried for an afternoon, didn't I? Silly girl. Nerd, always, never had a choice but to travel among the stars. Why do people destroy everything that's nice? I wonder... to touch the stars.

Can I call you starlight?

People die, what's the big deal, I knew this from the start. People die in the war. It's a bullshit war.

Gosh, he was right, wasn't he...?

This is what it's like to be cold. This is what it's like to be alone. The grass is so soft.

Maybe if I got bitten by a scorpion or whatever this place has for scorpions? Then the war would stop. At least for me it would stop.

I'm still alive. Isn't the purpose of life to be alive?

Fucking dreams, though.

The woman, Marieke, didn't have any more dreams that night. She crawled back into her shelter and became warmer, her breathing steadier; her muscles relaxed, a fragile little organism. At least she had her tent to shelter her.

The next morning, she heated up water as hot as no water had ever been on the island. She mixed in a substance she had brought. She drank it, and when she emptied out the last few drops on the meadow, the caffeine was an amusing sensation. Then she began to run. She re-used the path her boots had made the previous day. She ran until her breathing was heavy again—so many different reasons for her breathing to become heavy. She stopped close to the edge. She hesitated.

No...

She distributed her body's weight onto her feet and knees and hands and she began to crawl, very slowly, closer to the edge. Her heart beat heavily. From physical exertion or from fear? A fear of death? Or an urge toward it, like in her thoughts during the night?

Before she reached the edge, the very edge, she lowered her weight onto her belly and continued moving forward, leaving belly tracks in the dirt. Her head stuck out over the edge now, but the mass of her body held her. She stayed still. Some of her saliva dropped and moistened the raw edge where island met space. She laughed.

She giggled again when she got to the river and submerged herself in the water.

I spit off a floating island. Others get an urge to jump from high places. I just get an urge to spit. Humans are weird! We're so weird! How are we even a thing?

She emerged from the water and her laughter reverberated through the forest. The birds heard it and responded in their language.

Marieke spent the rest of the day lying on the grass. The back of her skull was on the ground, her fascinating synapses were separated from the island by some skin, some bone. Her hands had picked up a thing made of paper and all day her brain hallucinated a story about adventure and love and creatures that were native to no place. Sometimes her laughter caressed the air.

Ah...

One of the mammals of the forest visited Marieke. It had been very shy since her arrival but it was compelled to check on her to ensure the safety of its offspring.

"Hey there," Marieke said. "What are you?"

Even though her heart beat heavily, Marieke stayed very still and allowed the mammal to observe and to sniff. The mammal didn't have the same language as Marieke, so it didn't explain its presence to her. It didn't judge her a threat and she didn't have much in common with its preferred foods. So it left.

Every night, Marieke rested her head on the island and projected her synaptic energy into it. It was hard, at first, to tell apart her day thoughts and her night thoughts. Marieke lay and slept and saw different things. She dreamed of an arched sky and a dramatic rainbow; she dreamed of sensing the island's meadow, its forest. In her dream she saw the forest mammal that had visited her. In her dream she submerged herself in the river and sometimes another human appeared, the one called Lieven, when his face was still whole. One time, in her dream, Lieven lived on the island with her and they submerged themselves in the river together. Their bodies clung to each other and Marieke awoke from sleep with a pleasurable sigh and heavy breathing, once again.

Ah...

After that one time she had crawled close to the edge, she had not done it again. Sometimes her tears still mixed with the island's soil, but she had stopped thinking about the end of her life so much.

But then, one night, came one of those dreams during which she sweated and whimpered and her jaw muscles worked to press her teeth together. The grass would have grown around her, to envelop her, to hold her gently, to make her feel utterly safe, but she was on her tent's sheet and the grass had its own pace.

They found me.

A black shadow descended from the clear blue sky.

I have to hide the lander. I have to run... it's too late...

Run, run, run, faster, I know the forest so well, I can hide in the forest. I can lure them off the edge. I can't... go... forward! The meadow is dragging me back. Shit. They've seen me.

"Deserter! Halt! There she is! There's the lander she stole!"

Their shouts, their shouts, their thrashing through the peaceful meadow.

Why can't I run? This isn't a swamp! There isn't a swamp on this island!

It hurts. They got me. That's it. They're taking me to prison, or worse: back to the war. I signed myself over. I promised myself to the war. They have every right. Bullshit war.

Marieke awoke. She breathed hard. Then she cried. Then she struck the ground with her fists.

Oh no...

The next day, she skipped submerging herself in the river. She barely moved from her tent. She was hard to discern, she exuded so little energy. It was almost as if she were choosing to die, to donate her organism to the island, but she wasn't part of this island. She was foreign. She was welcome to die here, but she was not supposed to.

Oh no...

Her day thoughts dwelled on her night thoughts. She observed the terrifying vision from her dream again and again. She had tried to run helplessly in her dream. She had remembered that she was a deserter. She had run away from something. She had taken her vehicle, the lander, without permission.

The furry mammals went to nudge her and to amuse her with their play. She stroked their fur. Eventually, she moved again, submerged herself again. But she also observed the sky a lot.

And one day, the grass of the meadow turned cold where a growing shadow struck it.

Oh no...

Marieke was in the forest, studying a flower, breathing its scent, caressing its velvety softness, when she, too, perceived the disturbance in the air. Her heart muscle moved faster. Sweat dropped onto the ground. Seeped in. Not good. Stress. And fear. Such fear. She didn't want to go back to where her Lieven had been turned into a human with only half a face, where her Lieven had donated his organism to the desert.

She backed away from the meadow, deeper into the forest, toward the river. She jumped from rock to rock to cross the river. A small distance away from the riverbank she cowered, leaning half of her weight against a large rock. She rested her head against the rock. The lichens reported back.

I would rather die here. I would rather die on this island. I would rather be gone than go back. I will kill myself before they get me. If they get too close, I will go into the river. I will float in the river and go over the edge and die in space, soaring, and I will not even notice, there won't even be any pain, no violence. I'm so tired. I just can't fight anymore. I can't run anymore.

The new lander crashed down on the meadow. No gentle, skillful landing: a hard thumping that disturbed the grass and the poor in-ground-dwellers.

No.

Two people emerged from it. Not like she had done, soft and steady and kneeling, dripping her tears into the ground for a first vulnerable greeting. Those people dropped and pounded. Their shouts perturbed the air; they didn't caress it like her laughter had.

This way!
That way!
Perimeter!
The deserter!

That's the lander! The stolen lander!

No.

A quick survey. Here and there the rocks at the edge had come loose over the years. Some plants could be coaxed to shed a large branch to make the forest less passable. The lichens were too slow. They could do nothing but comfort Marieke, who was slumped against them, her hot breath tickling them.

A little foreboding breeze to upset the mammal. *What was that shaking of my island?* the mammal thought, or an approximation thereof.

Go check, mammal. Be upset, mammal. You have teeth and claws and fast movement, mammal.

The new arrivals stomped across the meadow. One went this way, toward the closest edge. Another went that way, toward the forest, toward the river, stomping, crushing, angering the in-ground-dwellers.

No.

One of the hunters hunted along the edge.

The other hunter was headed toward where Marieke's weight was making an impression on the forest floor and her breath amused the lichens.

Maybe I'll die. Should I die? Lieven, are you there? Did you go to the same place I'd go to? I don't know. Lieven. I never told you. I loved you so much.

No.

The one on the edge first. The rocks were loose close to the edge. There had been lesser reasons to discard pieces of dirt into space. Those steps were so heavy, so unkind, so assuming.

How about if the soil were to loosen a little here and a little there?

The new arrival put his heavy weight on too tender a place. Relax even more, shiver a little, until suddenly the new arrival let out a shrill shriek. A piece of rock was shed into space. It crumbled off the edge. It took the new arrival with it.

Ha.

The other new arrival's heavy steps were directed toward Marieke, though she didn't know it yet. She sat there, slumped against the rock, speaking to the lichens, projecting her thoughts through her skin, her skull.

Oh Marieke...

It's fine. At least the last thing I will have seen was a place like this...

Oh sweet Marieke...

The steps approached. They had yet to cross the river. It would take too much coaxing and teasing to make a flash flood. The river had its own pace, like the fruit trees, like the grass.

The new arrival stalked closer and closer. He snapped twigs off trees. He trampled the forest's flowers. He scared some of the mammals into the underbrush. But others were already baring their teeth.

The new arrival approached the water. Hard, heavy, painful boots stomped down on one of the polished rocks by the river's shore.

Mammal, now. Now, mammal.

The mammal pushed off the ground with his soft paws. He landed behind the new arrival and growled. The new arrival spun around.

"What the..." he moved the air. The mammal approached him, growling, also moving the air with his anger.

"It's okay, kitty, kitty," said the new arrival and shifted the heavy weight of his weapon. Marieke's dreams had shown the danger of the weapon, but the mammal didn't know about it. The mammal pounced, fast and fearless. The new arrival took a startled step back before his weapon could have done its damage. There was algae growth on the smooth rock. So smooth. The new arrival toppled. His skin, then his skull, connected with the smooth rock. He displaced a lot of river water. The rocks were slick. So slick. The water danced. There he went, the new arrival. Water entered him, but not as nourishment as it had entered Marieke when she was thirsty, making all its molecules sing out with delight and love. This time, the water found cells that did not want to be submerged. In the wrong places, water can cause death.

Ha.

The river's pull increased closer to the edge. The new arrival's strength decreased the longer he had to fight the water and the more his skull was bleeding. There. He was swept off the edge. He soared. He donated his organism to space.

And it was quiet again. Marieke's soft pressure. There were two landers now on the meadow, both empty, but Marieke cowered until nightfall. She didn't know yet that she had been left alone again. Her last thought before she left her rocky hiding place was: *Why the fuck hasn't anything happened?*

She took slow steps through the dark forest. She stayed very still at the edge of the forest. There was no movement in the meadow that she would have been able to perceive. She crouched down. Quiet as a mammal, she moved through the grass until she got to her tent. She relieved the ground of the weight of her weapon. With it, she climbed the new lander and stayed inside for a while. The new lander transferred information to Marieke when she coaxed it. It reported that it had been searching in vain for life signs of the two organisms that had steered it here. Marieke hopped back down onto the surface with her sweet pressure, her dear feet.

She moved the air with her laughter. Then her tears dropped into the meadow.

When her head touched the ground that night and her thoughts and her sensations were shared with the ground, it was clear that she couldn't stay. Her urge to survive was stronger than her urge toward death.

I've loved it here. I've loved it here so much. Bathing in the river, my little tiger-raccoon friend, knowing of the edge. Oh, sweet island, I'll be back. But they know where I am now. I was ready to die earlier, but now I'm not. I was tired, but after one more night of rest, I will be able to run for another little while. I'll mark this island on my map. Maybe I'll come back when the war is over. Maybe I'll come back with a lover. With a child. The war is bullshit.

I love you, island.

I love you too, Marieke. Safe travels, Marieke. I'll be here, Marieke.

About the Authors

Catherine J. Cole

Catherine J. Cole won 1st prize in the *Metamorphose Vol. 2 Science Fiction Short Story Contest*, and an Honorable Mention in the 2020 Writers of the Future Contest. Some of her short fiction can be found in the magazines and anthologies *Candlesticks and Daggers: An Anthology of Mixed-Genre Mysteries, Distressing Damsels, One Hundred Voices Vol. 3, Broadswords and Blasters Issue 6, Chronos: An Anthology of Time Drabbles, Galactic Goddesses*, and *Breaking Bizarro*. Ms. Cole has lived in the United States, France, and Colombia. When not writing fiction, she may be engaged in SEO writing, transcribing podcasts, translating English-Spanish documents, or working toward her Master's degree in English/Creative Writing. Follow her on Twitter (@CJCole2U) and check out her website (www.catherinejcole.com).

Stephen McQuiggan

Stephen McQuiggan was the original author of the bible; he vowed never to write again after the publishers removed the dinosaurs and the spectacular alien abduction ending from the final edit. His other, lesser known, novels are *A Pig's View Of Heaven* and *Trip A Dwarf*.

Matthew Gomez

Matthew Gomez believes that stories connect us, and these insights grow empathy and help us understand our place in a world that sometimes feels full of others. He serves as the podcast editor for *Metaphorosis Magazine* where he produces weekly episodes featuring original science fiction and fantasy stories. Matthew is the recipient of the University of New Mexico's Lina M. Todd award for poetry, and his fiction has been published in *Conceptions Southwest*, *Flash Fiction Magazine*, and *All Worlds Wayfarer*. Find him online at his website (www.gomezwrites.com) or on Twitter (@golongria).

Frances Pauli

Frances Pauli writes speculative and anthropomorphic fiction. She has been the recipient of two Leo awards and one Coyotl award, and her complete works can be found on her website at francespauli.com.

Chrissie Rohrman

Chrissie Rohrman is a training supervisor who lives in Indianapolis, Indiana with her husband and five four-legged kiddos. She enjoys white wine and writing competitions, and is currently drafting her first novel, the kick-off of a fantasy trilogy. Find her on Twitter (@ChrissieRawrman).

Garrett Rowlan

Garrett Rowlan is a retired LA sub teacher and the author of some 70 published stories. He's the author of *To Die, To Sleep* (James Ward Kirk publishing) and *Too Solid Flesh Melts* (Alban Lake). His website is garrettrowlan.com.

Carson Winter
Carson Winter has acceptances he can't talk about, a novella coming out in Fall, and a story published with beautiful artwork at *Signal Horizon*. He likes rain, monsters, and coffee.

Joel Donato Ching Jacob
Joel Donato Ching Jacob is called Cupkeyk by his friends. He was the 2018 Scholastic Asian Book Award winner for *Wing of the Locust*. He was an Editor's Choice awardee for The Best Asian Short Stories 2019 for *Artifact from the Parent*. He lives in Bay, Laguna in the Philippines with his mother and dogs. He enjoys fitness and the outdoors. Follow him on Twitter and Instagram (both @chimeracupkeyk).

Jessa Forest
Jessa Forest writes poetry and dark fiction. Her work can be found at her website (jessaforest.com).

Britt Foster
Britt Foster writes speculative fiction with a focus in sci-fi. She has a passion for other worlds, extraterrestrials, and the more mystical aspects of existence. You can find her on Facebook and Instagram (both @brittfosterauthor).

E. Seneca

E. Seneca is a freelance speculative fiction author with a strong affinity for horror and dark fantasy. Her short story "Harvesters" was published in Grimmer & Grimmer Books' anthology *DeadSteam*, "Light in the Dark" was published in the second issue of *Aether/Ichor* online magazine, and "It Lives in the Mineshaft" and "A Specific Sort of Shared Madness" were published by Soteira Press in *The Monsters We Forgot* and *What Monsters Do For Love* anthologies, respectively. She has written original fiction since 2008, and she has a Twitter account (@esenecaauthor).

Steve Haywood

Steve Haywood lives in a small historic city in England. He has a distinctly uncreative day job, so likes to write to exercise his creativity. He enjoys writing short stories in multiple genres, with short stories published recently in various magazines including *Cabinet of Heed*, *All Worlds Wayfarer* and *Door is a Jar*. As well as writing short fiction, he blogs about short stories, novels and assorted topics at his website (http://www.inkypages.co.uk). He can also be found on Twitter (@Lancaster_Steve) where he regularly tweets to share stories he likes with anyone who will listen.

Roni Stinger

Roni Stinger lives in Vancouver, Washington. When she's not writing strange dark stories, she's wandering the forests, beaches, and streets in search of shiny objects and creative sparks. Her work has been published in Fantasia Divinity's *Isolation* anthology, *The Molotov Cocktail*, and *Nailed Magazine*. You can find her online at her website (www.roniraestinger.com) and on Twitter (@raestinger).

Dave D'Alessio

Dave D'Alessio is an ex-industrial chemist, ex-TV engineer, and ex-award-winning animator currently masquerading as a practicing social scientist. His short stories have appeared in venues including *Daily Science Fiction*, *Heroic Fantasy Quarterly*, and *Mad Scientist Journal* along with numerous anthologies. He blogs on writing and animation in his blog Overage Otaku (davedalessiowrites.wordpress.com).

AE Stueve

AE Stueve teaches at Bellevue West High and the University of Nebraska. His novels, short stories, poems, and essays can be found online and in print. To learn more about him, check out his website (aestueve.com) and follow him on Twitter or Instagram (both @aestueve).

Lisa Short

Lisa Short is Texas-born, Kansas-bred writer of speculative fiction. She has an honorable discharge from the United States Army, a degree in chemical engineering, and twenty years' experience as a professional engineer. She currently lives in Maryland with her husband, two youngest children, father-in-law and cats. Her previous publication credits include a fantasy short story in the October 2019 issue of *Metaphorosis Magazine*.

Aviel McDermott

Aviel McDermott is a queer transmasculine author of science fiction, fantasy, and poetry. He is a writer still at the beginning of his journey and a soon to be graduate of UC Berkeley. He has one poem published in *X Marks the Spot: A Nonbinary Anthology* and more of his writing can be found on his blog (transcendragons.wordpress.com) or his Twitter (@a_the_orange). He uses he/him and they/them pronouns.

Simon Brown

Simon Brown has written over 50 short stories which have been published in Australia, the US, the UK, Poland and Japan. A handful of stories have been picked up for *Year's Best* anthologies in Australia and the US. He has also written eight novels, all published in Australia; the last six were also published in the US and Russia. He is an Australian, but currently lives in Johannesburg, South Africa, where his wife teaches at an international school. Find out more at his website (https://simonbrown.co).

Carol Holland March

Carol Holland March lives in Albuquerque, New Mexico, where the veil between the worlds wavers erratically. She writes about the intersection of dreams, reality, and time and the entanglements that ensue when the lines among them are crossed. She teaches writing and creative expression at the University of New Mexico and enjoys bike riding with a demanding dog who gives her ideas for stories in exchange for treats. Her stories have appeared in numerous online and print publications. Her fantasy trilogy, *The Dreamwalkers of Larreta*, explores how love overcomes the barriers of both time and space. You can reach her at her website (CarolHollandMarch.com).

349

Nicola Kapron

Nicola Kapron has previously been published by *Portal Magazine* and in anthologies from Nocturnal Sirens Publishing, Rebel Mountain Press, Soteira Press, and Mannison Press. Nicola lives in Nanaimo, British Columbia, with a hoard of books—mostly fantasy and horror—and an extremely fluffy cat. Find her on Facebook (www.facebook.com/profile.php?id=100009529479337).

Julie Cohen

Julie is a library assistant living in New Jersey and is currently working on her Masters in Library and Information Science. She lives with her partner, their four cats, and an ever growing treasure hoard of books.

Coleman McClung

Coleman McClung lives in Dallas, Texas with his wife and soon to be born daughter. His short stories and other written works have been published on East of the Web and Dread Central collectively, while films produced from his screenplays have played in festivals all over the US. He also enjoys podcasting about middle-grade book series and playing overly complicated board games.

Carla Durbach

Carla writes a few things and reads a great deal more. She has been weaving tales since the age of 7, when she was unduly fascinated by robots and aliens. Speculative fiction has remained a favorite genre. Carla's fiction has appeared in *Heart of Flesh* and *Lost Pen*. Her poetry has been published in Little Rose, Bonnie's Crew, Royal Rose, Crepe and Penn and in a TL;DR press anthology (*Beneath Strange Stars*). She is a returning prodigal to the world of writing after a long hiatus.

Spencer Mann

Spencer Mann (he/him/his) is a queer author originally from Minnesota, though he has traded those cold winters for the endless dusty heat of central California. He is currently a graduate student and instructor in Native American studies at the University of California, Davis. In addition to his legal and historical research, he writes fiction aiming for queer literary fantasy, but occasionally landing elsewhere. His work has previously appeared in the Queer Sci Fi flash fiction anthology *Migrations*.

Kathrine Machon

Kathrine Machon is a lover of all things magical. She lives on the island of Jersey and spends her spare time scribbling stories about fantastical characters and places. She has had a number of short stories published and hopes one day to have her name on the front of a novel. You can find out more and follow her on Twitter (@KateMachon).

MM Schreier

MM Schreier is a classically trained vocalist who took up writing as therapy for a mid-life crisis. Whether contemporary or speculative fiction, favorite stories are rich in sensory details and weird twists. A firm believer that people are not always exclusively right- or left-brained, in addition to creative pursuits Schreier manages a robotics company and tutors maths and science to at-risk youth. Recent publications can be found in *The Corona Book of Science Fiction*, *Orca Literary Journal*, *Page and Spine*, and *Youth Imagination* magazine. Additional listings can be found at Schreier's website (mmschreier.com/publications).

Erica Ciko Campbell

Erica Ciko Campbell made her writing debut on backwater internet forums in the early 2000's. Since then, she's been published in the *Aggregate* anthology by Writerly, *The Fifth Di...*, and *The Kyanite Press*. She's currently working on a Gothic Space Opera novel series called *Tales of a Starless Aeon*. She holds a Bachelor's in Biology from Utica College and works as a freelance writer. If you're still craving the whispers of war-torn, dead galaxies, check out her website (http://starless-imperium.com/). You can also find her on Twitter (@ECikoCampbell).

Anna Ziegelhof

Anna Ziegelhof is originally from Germany but now lives in Northern California where she works as a linguist by day and writes fiction by night. On social media she is @annawithaz.

About the Editors

Rowan Rook

Rowan Rook is an agender, asexual, and aromantic speculative fiction author, editor, poet, and game designer/writer. They see the world through a lens of plot ideas and armatures, and storytelling is their passion. They are also an introvert, night owl, music lover, anxiety sufferer, and cat guardian. An indie soul, they prefer the strange and provocative to the familiar and safe. Rowan lives for stories that inspire wonder, evoke deep thought, offer exhilarating experiences, and leave lingering emotions. They live in a rural lakeside house while dreaming of the city. You can read their work at their website (www.rowanrook.com) or follow them on Twitter (@xRowanRookx).

Geri Meyers

Geri Meyers is an LGBTQIA+ fantasy fiction writer. Growing up in New Hampshire, Geri wandered the woods fighting off enemies and rescuing princesses, crafting homemade bows and arrows from downed tree branches and absorbing the magic of the mysterious lady slipper flower. Geri has carried that need for wondrous adventure into adulthood and strives to share it with others through writing and storytelling. Currently living in New Jersey, Geri works full time as a library assistant preparing books for circulation while dreaming of one day opening a fantasy-themed book store. Geri has a passion for writing stories full of vibrant characters, magic, sparkling things and intelligent dragons. You can follow Geri on Twitter (@Siobwen), support Geri on Patreon (www.patreon.com/GeriMeyers), or read Geri's work on Wattpad (www.wattpad.com/user/GeriMeyers).

All Worlds Wayfarer: Through Other Eyes

An Online Literary Magazine
www.allworldswayfarer.com

All Worlds Wayfarer is a quarterly literary magazine specializing in character-and-theme-driven speculative fiction. We celebrate stories that take readers on tours through wonderful and terrifying realms, evocative visions, and eye-opening new lives. When our readers come home, they should return ever so slightly changed for having made the journey. After all, the most powerful stories transcend, enlighten, and entertain at once.

"Books give a soul to the universe, wings to the mind, flight to the imagination, and life to everything." -Plato

If you enjoyed this anthology, look for our upcoming anthologies:

Prismatic Dreams (Release TBA)
Each Our Own (Release TBA)
Into the Dark (Release TBA)

Thank you for reading!

We hope you enjoyed the journey. All Worlds Wayfarer publishes issues every equinox and solstice. Please consider submitting your own speculative fiction stories or embarking on further adventures with us in upcoming issues and anthologies.

www.allworldswayfarer.com

CPSIA information can be obtained
at www.ICGtesting.com
Printed in the USA
LVHW011159151220
674215LV00006B/423